Kristina Lloyd writes erotic fiction about sexually submissive women who like it on the dark, dirty and dangerous side. Her novels are published by *Black Lace* and her short stories appear in a range of anthologies, including several 'best of' collections, in both the UK and US.

Kristina lives in Brighton.

Also by Kristina Lloyd:

Asking For Trouble
Darker Than Love
Split

Thrill Seeker

Kristina Lloyd

BLACK
LACE

1 3 5 7 9 10 8 6 4 2

Published in 2013 by Black Lace, an imprint of Ebury Publishing
A Random House Group Company

Copyright © Kristina Lloyd 2013
Copyright for 'Forbidden' © S. M. Taylor

Kristina Lloyd has asserted her right to be identified as the author of this
Work in accordance with the Copyright, Designs and Patents Act 1988

S. M. Taylor has asserted her right to be identified as the author of
'Forbidden' in accordance with the Copyright, Designs and
Patents Act 1988

The Random House Group Limited Reg. No. 954009

Addresses for companies within the Random House Group can
be found at: www.randomhouse.co.uk

A CIP catalogue record for this book is available from the British Library

The Random House Group Limited supports the Forest Stewardship
Council® (FSC®), the leading international forest-certification
organisation. Our books carrying the FSC label are printed on FSC®-
certified paper. FSC is the only forest-certification scheme supported by
the leading environmental organisations, including Greenpeace.
Our paper procurement policy can be found at:
www.randomhouse.co.uk/environment

MIX
Paper from
responsible sources
FSC® C016897

Printed and bound in Great Britain by Clays Ltd, St Ives Plc

ISBN 9780352347183

To buy books by your favourite authors and register for offers visit
www.randomhouse.co.uk
www.blacklace.co.uk

For Ewan, for coming back

One

Liam doesn't usually come when I'm sucking him, but on the night it started he was different. His groans were threaded with a darker note, and my throat was more open than it had ever been with him because I was thinking of someone else.

Outside, thunder edged closer, snarling above the sea. In my mind, I saw this strange, broken town, summer rain slicking its pink and gold domes, the black sky ripped by a storm. 'Trouble's coming,' I might have thought. Except I didn't. I didn't see anything coming. Well, apart from Liam.

'Don't stop,' he gasped, voice bordering on panic. I was kneeling on my futon and he grabbed my hair, not too hard because that's not his style. He drew me onto him. I spluttered, tapped his thigh and he eased back a fraction like a gent. Then he was there again, cock nudging at my throat, and I was trying to match his urgency, wet, firm, fast. His noises, half-pained and incredulous, made desire thump in my cunt. I wanted to tip him over the edge and hear his ecstatic cries but we were going too fast for me.

I clutched his thighs, thinking, if this were Baxter Logan, I'd take him and hold him till I ran out of breath.

Liam's groans thinned. 'Don't stop, don't . . .'

Why think about Baxter? Was it the rowdy weather? Or was I always thinking about Baxter? Of course I was. Don't try and kid yourself it's any different, Nats. Most days, my memories were a low-frequency hum but on occasion, Baxter Logan returned in all his glory, dominating my thoughts.

Where are you now, you bastard? Do you ever think of me?

My hands on Liam's hips, I steadied myself, relaxed, then eased my mouth forward, straight down the hatch. I was rewarded with a twisted cry of disbelief, as if the pleasure of being lodged in my throat were too much for him to bear. I stayed deep, relishing the calm intimacy of the act. Thunder rumbled closer. I pulled back, then bobbed to and fro, my lips tight, saliva spilling along his length.

'Oh, don't st . . . oh, yes.'

For a brilliant instant, lightning filled the room. In the corner of my eye, the tall mirror propped against the wall cracked with reflected sky. A woman on her knees was sucking a lanky guy standing on a futon. Liam likes to watch; I don't. I prefer close-ups and the focus on sensation. The sight of my own body distracts me. Still sucking, I gazed up at Liam even though my eyeballs ached. I cupped his balls, fondling their warm, slipping weight.

Liam looked down, mouth slack, face crumpling, his eyes blurred with delirium as if he weren't quite there. His muscular torso was milk white, his pubes a tangle of dark copper filaments, his thickly-freckled arms covered with sandy hair. I focused my lips on his end, pulling hard then down again. I saw him glance at our reflection. He gripped my hair and began to thrust, using me, fucking my mouth so I was no longer the giver but the recipient.

Baxter Logan liked using my mouth that way.

Seconds later, Liam came, his body jerking, his hands scattering touches on my shoulders. I drank every drop of him and cupped his buttocks, holding him close as his shudders faded. I listened to his post-bliss moans, keeping him in my mouth until he grew twitchy. He withdrew – ah, ah – laughing at his sensitivity, then dropped to the mattress, slender limbs collapsing like a house of cards.

'Oh man.' He rolled backwards, flinging out an arm. 'Sheesh. You got a world exclusive!'

I laughed and fell alongside him, nestling in the crook of his arm. His fingers strummed my back.

'I never come like that,' he said. 'Fuck. Awesome. I can't feel my knees. What are you on?'

'Form,' I said, proud of my achievement.

'I'll say. Oh, fuck. Seriously, Nats . . .'

He mussed my hair, lazily affectionate. We weren't done, not by a long shot. We'd have a breather then he'd make me come or squirt or both. Then we'd fuck again, maybe come again. We'd put on a CD, have another drink, roll a joint, chat, fuck, and on we'd go until we were sated.

'Man, oh man,' said Liam, more to himself than to me. I reached across his body for my tumbler of red on the floor by the bed. Tumblers, never stemmed glasses for sex, especially on a futon. Puffs of colour from the fairy lights around my mirror glowed in the wine and shone in the depths of the dark, hardwood floor. As I moved, my stomach squeaked against Liam's, both of us wet with sweat. I kissed his shoulder. It's a good relationship. We're friends and we fuck, and neither of us wants anything more than that. Or at least, not from each other.

We lay in silence as our breathing returned to normal.

Thunder grumbled then cracked. A car alarm started pulsing in the street on the far side of the house. Rain hit the bedroom window in squally bursts. After several hot, oppressive days, the cooler air was a relief.

'Can't move,' murmured Liam. 'I think you've broken me.'

I laughed. 'Do you need to move?'

Before he could answer, a huge crash punctured our mellow mood. I jumped, confused. Not thunder, not coming from the sky like the rest of the racket. A crash in the house from two floors below, kitchen by the sounds of it. Crockery? Glass? A lot of something smashed to smithereens. The window?

I scrambled off the bed, pulled a silk slip over my head then hurtled down the stairs two at a time. I heard Liam call, 'Nats? What is it?'

I didn't answer. My mind hopped through possibilities: a tree in the garden had been brought down, smashing the kitchen window. Or, I was being burgled. All I could think was, 'Cat, laptop, cat, laptop.' Desperate to protect these two most precious things, I didn't give a thought for my safety. One glass of wine and suddenly I'm a hero.

Would Rory be scared? Would she scarper, never to be seen again? Would they steal my laptop? All my photos, emails, documents, software? My clammy hand squeaked on the wooden banister. Oh God, some of those photos. For years, I'd been meaning to password protect the dodgy stuff. I needed to back up my files too. And leave instructions for my hard drive to be wiped in the event of my untimely demise. I wasn't ready to be murdered, wasn't ready to be burgled. I needed to get organised first. Just give me a couple of days then do your worst.

Instead of my life, jpegs of Baxter flashed before my eyes. So many beautiful, filthy images – his thighs, his cock, his chest, his arms, his cock by my mouth, his cock in my cunt – but rarely any pictures of his face. I should have known, shouldn't I? 'Not my face, hen. You know how shy I am.' This from a man who didn't have a shy bone in his body.

Mine is a tall, skinny townhouse built in the slope of Old Saltbourne. People say I'm lucky to own such a lovely house but if they knew the down payment came from money left to me by my father, they might not be so envious. I hoped I wasn't about to add a second early death to the family tree. I rounded the first flight of stairs and hurried across the living room where our discarded clothes were dotted like stepping stones. Rory was curled on Liam's jeans, a black and white ball of fluff raising her head in mild concern. She rarely moves except for food. I scuttled past her and braced myself against the lumpy stone wall as I turned onto the stairs leading to the lower floor.

'Liam!' I called, letting the world and its mad axemen know I wasn't alone. At the top of the stairs, I felt fresh air blasting inwards, cooling my shins. Halfway down, I saw curtains at the kitchen window flapping softly, gingham dancing and twisting. I stalled, suddenly rational. Someone might be there, waiting for me. Foolish to come charging down like this, a small, slightly drunk woman, unarmed, half-dressed.

I took the steps slowly, a pulse throbbing in my neck. How would Liam shape up if I were attacked? He certainly had the muscle and knuckle to land someone a hefty blow. Plus, out in the woods, he killed rabbits with his bare hands and never went anywhere without a penknife. He might be able to save me, assuming he wasn't too stoned and blowjobbed to stand.

I took another step down. Penknife? What good's a
penknife against a burglar, a rapist, a homicidal maniac?

Until then, I'd always felt safe in my own home, the
biggest threat to my peace an over-active imagination, easily
roused by Saltbourne's history of smugglers, secret tunnels
and fishermen lost at sea. Real danger didn't seem part of my
life except, sometimes, when I walked through New Town
late at night, the pedestrianised streets, garish red brick,
modern murals and glass-fronted shops of Castlegate Plaza
conspiring to create an unease rooted in the hollowness of
urban planning. Old Town, with its picturesque alleys, worn
steps, salmon pink domes, and haphazard streets overlooked
by cliff-top castle ruins, was a world apart.

My fingers inched over the wall's rough stone as I
descended to the kitchen. I heard nothing, saw no shadows
shifting. I crept down the final few steps then switched on
the light. Scanning the room, I tried to make sense of the
mess. Shards of glass sparkled on the drainer of the sink.
The windows were intact. No one was here. One window
was open, its drooping metal handle scraping against the
outside wall, hinges banging in the clattering rain. The
damp gingham curtains fluttered in the breeze, ditsy flags
of surrender. A vase. My glass vase on the windowsill had
smashed. A wine glass too, by the looks of it. The back door
was ajar. My heart was thumping, my throat parched.

Liam's feet banged on first flight of stairs. 'I'm coming,
you OK?'

On the kitchen table, as if waiting to be filed, was a sheet
of A4 paper in a clear, plastic polypocket. It wasn't mine.
I snatched it up. Across the page, in glued lettering cut
from newspapers, were the words: CLOSER THAN YOU
KNOW.

My hands shook. My legs seemed to vanish from under me. Coldness slid down my face while sweat pinched under my arms. I was dizzy, weak, yet somehow, I was still upright.

I remembered why Baxter Logan had been on my mind. Because I could see I was chasing sex and danger, taking stupid risks to try and heal the past.

I glanced at the back door, fearing the man would burst back in. Or was he in the spare room, behind the closed door? I swung around. No, not in there. Dirty, wet footprints reached the table and no further.

I tried to moisten my lips but my tongue had no power.

'Nats?' Liam was at the top of the kitchen stairs. I tugged open the cutlery drawer, stuffed the note inside, and slammed it shut. I didn't want to worry him, and anyway, he wouldn't understand.

'What happened?' Liam was at the foot of the stairs, looking as if he'd just run half a marathon. He was naked, no pocket for a penknife.

I took four wobbly steps to the back door and opened it fully. Rain sluiced down, a hard, glittery fall against the backdrop of dark shrubbery and overhanging trees. Light from the house glinted on plant pots, wet stone and on my cast iron chairs, huddled around the barbecue. Cool droplets tickled my toes and night air curled around my ankles.

'I think someone's in the garden,' I said.

Kagami says: *Hey Natalie, good to hear from you again. Phew, that was one hot email! Great to find a woman so sexually self-aware. I admire people able to stand against a puritanical, sexually-repressed culture and find their own truth.*

We appear to share common ground in our relationship

to D/s. Sensation play is fine but it's the psychological aspect I'm most drawn to. I want to be able to get inside her mind, to know what she likes and hates. I want to discover her darkest places. Nothing shocks me. I want to slowly overwhelm her until she can't help but give in and become a thing for me to use. Damn, I'm getting hard just writing this!

But as you say, chemistry's key. Just because I like to dominate and you like to submit, it doesn't mean we're going to make sweet music together (although, based on these messages, I think we have the potential to create the world's most mind-blowing opera!) Sex isn't a mathematical formula (yeah, I know; I'm mixing my metaphors). A burning fire starts with a spark. So we'd need our spark. And to that, I'd add mutual respect. I strongly believe that to play at being unequal, you must operate from a bedrock of equality.

I'm in New York right now, at a conference over five thousand kilometres away from you. I hope video-conferencing never takes over from RL conferences. I love travel and NYC is one of my favourite cities. I find hotels fascinating too, full of strangers passing through. No one belongs here. Liminal spaces bring out the beast in me. Boundaries are blurred, the usual rules don't apply and new rules haven't yet been formed. Here, it feels you could do something wild, decadent and twisted. Explore a dark fantasy with a stranger then walk away, leaving it behind along with the damp towels and messy room. Someone else tidies up and it's over, folded away. You return to your regular life, nothing to deal with, no consequences, not a ripple to betray the madness you shared. It's as if it never happened. And once again, life's as smooth and neat as a freshly made hotel bed.

I've never been to Madrid but your descriptions make me want to go there. Well, your descriptions of many things make me want to go there! ;) I'd love to hear more about the kidnap fantasy you mentioned. Sounds incredibly hot. Right up my alley!

This was just meant to be a brief note to say thanks for such a great reply, Natalie. I appreciate your openness. I have to head down to dinner soon so no time to list all the cruel, debasing things I'd like to do to you. Oh, fuck it, I just found time! Here goes: I'd like to make you mine. I'd like to see you on your knees, tied up roughly, your clothes torn from my eagerness to get at you.

You're powerless but you're also desperate and horny because you can't help yourself. I'm fingering you, making you wetter and wetter. You're moaning. You want to get fucked so badly but I make you suffer, make you wait for it. I tease, caress and twist. I stroke from your neck down to your nipples. You're vibrating under my touch, shivering, breathless, pleading for more. I want you in my control, want to make you bend and sway to my tune. You're increasingly turned on, lost in what I'm doing to you. I take you to the point of insanity, obsession, and then you're there, mine. You'll do anything for satisfaction. You're begging me to fuck you, begging and pleading so much it makes me laugh.

But I'm not done with you yet. I like to see you humiliated and suffering. So I carry you outside into the street. I set up a stall. I'm your owner. There's a sign saying 'Free Whore'. I make you lean across a big wooden crate. It's the crate I put you back in when I'm done with you. I lift your skirt so your buttocks are on show to all the passersby, so pale and innocent-looking. Your wrists are chained to the railings. A stranger comes along and asks how much to fuck you. I tell him you're free because you're so greedy. He fucks you hard. People walk past. A few stop to look. When he's finished, somebody else is in line waiting to take his place.

OK, I really must go down to dinner now. Christ, how the Hell I'll be able to sit down with my dick in this state is beyond me! Let me know if I've gone too far. Sharing fantasy is always a risk but I really think we're on the same wavelength here. I hope so.

Can't wait to hear from you again. I noticed you didn't respond to my 'shallow' questions from my previous email. Don't feel obliged, they're not that important. But I'd LOVE to know more! You've really piqued my interest. Take care.

Den xx

Natajack32 says: *You're making my head spin! That fantasy is so dirty! Makes me nervous. Excited, but nervous too. Maybe that's to be expected. I'm finding it strange being so open with a man I've never met. I have to confess, I've only explored this aspect of my sexuality with one other man, B, and that was a couple of years ago. I've dabbled with a few other people but nothing major.*

I don't have enough experience to know how well my fantasies might translate to real life. It worked with B, but I don't know if it can work again. Submission seems to mean different things to different people. I know I don't want to be an obedient slave to a strict master. That's not my cup of tea. I want him to be driven, slightly out of control, loving his power over me and relishing how he makes me suffer. Or maybe that's all I know and I'm trying to recreate the past.

Anyway, those questions! I'm 5'6" (I think it says this in my profile.) Dress size 10 and 34C bust (So shallow of you, yes!). I run three or four times a week so I'm in pretty good shape. The photos on my profile are a little out of date (taken last summer). My hair's longer and darker now but still wavy. And no, you can't have an undressed photo of me! I haven't even seen your face yet. Besides, you've had an awful lot from me already. I'm far too honest. I need to retain some mystery!

I'm envious of you being in New York, although not if the heat's anything like it's been here. So hot and muggy. I'm having to sleep with the windows open and just a single sheet as my bed cover. If it weren't for the sea, I think people would be fighting in the streets in Saltbourne. The sea's like a pressure valve, takes the heat off. Even so, everything requires so much effort right now. It's like wading through treacle. Or molasses, since you're in The Big Apple. We need a thunderstorm to clear the air and give the plants a good watering.

Anyway, you asked about my abduction fantasies. Like I said, I'm not usually so open with people I've recently 'met' but I feel comfortable with you. We seem to have complementary kinks, yes, and I feel as if you understand where I'm coming from. You don't think I'm weird or damaged, and you seem to recognise I'm not submissive as a person. This is a sex thing not a personality trait.

I appreciate your point about us starting from an equal base. Trouble is, we don't live in an equal culture, do we? Sometimes I struggle with that. I worry I'm a bad feminist for saying I want to be dominated by a man. But then I remind myself, this is how I get my rocks off and so do lots of women. It doesn't mean we're stepping back in time or we don't want equal rights. If anything, it's a step forward. Because what I'm saying, really, is 'Hey, this is how I like to get fucked so could you please take note, mister?' Historically, women haven't been able to say that, have they? Lie back and think of England. That's what we've had. And the fear of pregnancy or being called a slut puts a downer on things. But times change, thank God. And for whatever reason, this is me. It's how I've turned out. I'm sexually submissive. Who can say whether that's innate or acquired? And does answering that even matter? The result's the same, isn't it? I want to be tied up and taken over. I want to be hurt and used. I want him to do bad, wicked things to me so I'll have gazillions of orgasms and feel whole as a person. I have a strong submissive streak, sure. But I'm not a Stepford wife. I'm horny. Big difference!

Anyway, I think you get what I'm saying. I hope so. I liked your thoughts on hotel rooms. In that spirit, I'm putting a 'Do Not Disturb' sign on our door so I can share this fantasy with you. Be gentle with it, please!

How it starts doesn't matter too much.

It's being his that counts, being his prisoner, having choice removed from me.

I might be in a forest, running scared, aware he's on my tail. I might be bundled into the back of a car, two men keeping me quiet while he drives to a secret location. (I like that idea the most. He's driving, glancing in the rear-view mirror. He says something along the lines of 'What's she like? Is she wet? Test her for me.')

I might be in the Australian outback. I might be walking home from work, from the supermarket, the pub, the moon. But somehow, I'm captured. Strong arms, harsh words, a struggle, a threat. Then I'm taken to a place far away from my life. It's like your hotel room, I guess. The usual rules don't apply. (I work in admin for the local council – maybe I just hate my job and want an escape!) Anyway, he has me, he wants me. It's mainly him but he has allies. No one knows where I am.

Sorry. I wish I could turn my fantasy into a proper story for you but I can't. In my mind, it's just a jumble of bondage, blindfolds and gags; of being held captive and used by a stranger or, if I'm being honest, by several strangers.

I like the idea of being afraid and not knowing what will happen next. Someone else is running the show, a man who enjoys my fear and distress. It's impossible to truly fantasise that part because I'm creating it in my head so I know what's about to happen. But I suppose that's the emotion I'm chasing here. With sex in real life, not just in fantasy, the more authentic the danger feels, the hotter it is for me.

Sorry, I'm rambling. Where was I? Oh yes.

The place I'm held prisoner is off the map. It's derelict, hidden. No one can find us. I have to co-operate or things will get worse. Usually, my captors are a gang working together with one guy at the helm. He calls the shots, he's the manager, the ring-leader. He decides what I need or, more likely, what he needs.

Sometimes, he wants to see me get fucked by half a dozen men while he watches. Sometimes, he wants to fuck me himself then pass me around when I'm used and exhausted. Sometimes, he brings me food, slaps my face, and tells me I'll get cock tomorrow. Sometimes, he chains me to his bed so I'm there for him in the morning. He calls me his 'little bitch'.

Yikes. I should probably stop there or I might regret this in the morning!

I hope my fantasy doesn't sound too pervy. There's other stuff as well. More detailed scenarios. Stuff I masturbate to or think about when I'm with someone and close to coming.

But to go back to B, the guy I mentioned at the head of this message. Since we split about two years ago, I've been looking for a man who could satisfy my darker side as he could. A man who wouldn't be freaked out by my fantasies, a man who'd understand that even though I like to be overpowered in bed, it doesn't mean I'm a soft touch or a doormat.

Sometimes I wonder if B and I had a sexual connection I'll never find again. I hope not. I loved where he could take me. I want to go there again, to hand over control to someone who knows what to do with it.

I haven't seen a proper photo of you so this is kinda unfair (Send me a photo! You keep promising!) and I might be getting ahead of myself. But it does feel, sexually at least, that you're close to the kind of man I'm looking for. A pity you live 70+ miles away. How about we talk on the phone when you're back in the UK? You have my number.

N xox

Kagami says: *Natalie, I'm closer than you know.*

'There's no one here, Nats,' said Liam. 'Maybe the window got blown open and it knocked the vase over. Come on, let's go inside.'

We were in the garden, soaked, Liam starkers and me in my flimsy slip, the pair of us like some latterday Adam and Eve. The noise of rain on foliage surrounded us, and on the other side of the end wall, water gushed down the steep stone gutter of Tanner's Passage. A lantern bracketed to the brick of the passage cast patches of white light over the highest leaves, rainfall shimmering in the glow. I'd found the wooden door leading from my garden to Tanner's Passage unbolted. I'd eased the bolt back, saying nothing to Liam.

I figured he must have climbed in over the passage wall then exited by my gate. Either that, or he'd scaled the wall I shared with my neighbours, Benjamin and Steve, who were away celebrating a wedding anniversary in Berlin. But the latter route seemed unnecessarily difficult. My house was the last in the street, adjacent to Tanner's Passage. The wall between was easy enough to climb if you were fit and the coast was clear. And who on earth would be out on a night like this?

All my windows were open because of the heat. What had I said? *So hot and muggy. I'm having to sleep with the windows open and just a single sheet as my bed cover.*

The kitchen window's invariably open because I don't have a catflap and Rory needs to come and go. Kagami must have climbed in that way. He must be back from New York. Had he listened to us fucking? Would the sound carry from my bedroom down to the garden or kitchen? Would he have heard us above the storm? Or had he been deeper inside my house? Closer than I knew? No, the footprints stopped at the table. He was here to deliver his warning.

'Hold me,' I said to Liam.

From behind, Liam embraced me, strong arms tucked beneath my breasts. My heart was still banging at a rate of knots. I felt drained of strength. Liam's arms reassured me. Cool rivulets trickled between our bodies and when he pressed his lips to my neck, it felt as if his mouth were melting over my skin. Water dripped from my hair and streamed down my spine. My silk slip clung to me. Beneath my feet, the slate steps were cold and wet.

A fork of lightning split the sky, a silent, jagged bolt

illuminating the world. A few seconds later, thunder crashed so hard it felt as if the ground were being torn in two.

'It's moving inland,' said Liam. 'Getting closer.'

I clasped his arms, making him squeeze me tighter. His grip crushed my ribs but there was nothing he could do to quell the thrill of my fear.

Two

In my twenties, my father died, and shortly after that I embarked on a low-sex relationship that lasted for six years. Six sodding years! I wonder now if I was craving security after my bereavement and after what had happened with my piano tutor, Alistair Fitch.

Impossible to say. But crazy to think how long Jim and I stayed together in Dullsville. We met as students in Manchester, moved south together after graduating, and both thought we'd found 'The One'. That's a hard dream to let go of so, who knows, I might have clung on, irrespective of my past. During our last two years, Jim and I forgot how to fuck. We were practically pandas. We didn't even kiss. I'd make a play for him in bed and he'd say, 'Not tonight, Natty. It's a bit much.'

I began to feel I was a bit much: demanding, over-sexed, irritating, and on top of that, unattractive. So I stopped trying. Difficult to see what Jim was getting from the relationship. He said he loved me but I think most of all, he loved an easy life.

When we broke up, I emerged blinking in the sunshine

with my desire and confidence in tatters. I was barely alive. For months I lived in a daze, too scared to rebuild myself in case I discovered I was made of nothing and had no foundations on which to build. My life was over. I was emptied out. Here lies Natalie Lovell, age twenty-seven, loving daughter, sister and medical curiosity, a woman made of meringues, cobwebs and shadows of the dead.

Then a woman brought me back to life. She was a gift from a friend. I lay on a massage table in a warm, dimly lit room, my face resting in the table's hole. I was staring into the abyss, wearing a pair of paper knickers, and trying not to fret about being alone with a stranger. From the speakers came the faint twitter of birds, and in the air hung a cloying scent of spicy oranges. I was stiff and reluctant until she touched me. Her firm, oiled hands moved across my back and I remembered I had a body. For too long, I'd been living in my head and heart, all choked up.

With slow expertise, my life-saver stroked and kneaded, rubbed this way and that, told me my shoulders were full of tension. My skin hummed under her fingers, my nerve-endings drawing in sensation, synapses firing. She pressed and pummeled, making me wince in pain, but I liked it. I grew loose and floppy. When she smoothed her hands down the sides of my body, she skimmed the bulge of my flattened breasts. For the first time in months, I felt that old stirring in my groin. I imagined her continuing, rolling me over and paying as much attention to my front as my back. I wanted her healing hands everywhere. I barely knew this woman but it wasn't her I wanted, just her touch. The touch of anyone who cared enough to give me pleasure.

I left the treatment rooms a different person. Nothing had happened, no funny business. But I'd re-established a connection with my own body. I'd remembered the simple joys of physicality, of skin on skin, of silencing the chattering mind and taking pleasure in touch. Maybe I started to give off a different vibe after that, I don't know. But a few weeks later, no major effort required, I was dating Grant, a guy who reminded me sex can be life-alteringly glorious and that getting off was no bad thing either.

On our first night, Grant blindfolded me, fixed my wrists and ankles to all corners of his bed, told me to relax and enjoy. I swear, I felt like paying him afterwards. He had massage oils, velvet gloves, warm breath, clever hands and, it seemed, all the time in the world.

'What's that? Ah, ah, what is it?' I kept saying, frustrated by my sightlessness.

'Doesn't matter, just enjoy,' he cooed.

'Tell me, oh God. I don't think I can cope.'

He laughed merrily.

At one point, I was pulling on the ropes, begging him to tell me what he'd done. He'd been kissing my shoulders, my breasts and then, from nowhere, one of my nipples was enveloped in a blanket of heat. It wasn't a fiery, intense heat but a deeply comforting heat. My nipple glowed, the warmth radiating into the tissue of my breast. Then it happened to my other nipple, and I was lost.

'Please tell me what that is.'

He chuckled.

'Please,' I cried. 'I have to know. What are you doing?'

He'd capitulated on that one, telling me there was a glass of hot water by the bed. He'd been filling his mouth with the liquid then sliding his lips around each nipple. 'And that's all I'm telling you,' he said. 'No more questions. You'll spoil it for yourself.'

I have to confess, after his explanation the sensation wasn't as wild. Grant was right, I shouldn't have asked. But gradually, I relaxed, allowing him to stimulate me inside and out. He didn't seem to care about his own pleasure – getting his kicks, instead, from mine. To be honest, that aspect did get weird after a few dates. Soon, I was aching for him to lose control, to be so overwhelmed with lust he'd grab my hair, pin me to the kitchen counter and bang me six ways till Sunday. But no, 'Just lie back, Natalie, enjoy.'

When he came, he barely made a sound. Sex was a polite, luxurious affair. I started to feel bad for wanting it badder. Harder, nastier, dirtier. Unfurling inside me was a craving for unfathomable, dark satisfactions. The nicer Grant was, the stronger my hunger for something other, for a sexual passion capable of dismantling me. Soon, I was wanting to re-live the lust that Alistair Fitch, with his sharp eye for vulnerability and his predatory guile, had drawn from me all those years ago in his cluttered, blue music studio. But this time, I wanted to seek my own pleasures, to taste them without dread, shame and confusion.

Was I kinkier than most people? Quite possibly. But ultimately I figured Grant had control issues and anyway, if I was kinkier than most, I simply needed to find others in my minority. A doddle, no?

Grant and I weren't meant to be but I'll be forever grateful to him for instilling in me the need to avoid that dead, sexless jail that had trapped me for so long. He made me take stock and, over time, I became deliberately bolder. I realised I had two choices. I could stick my neck out and start being honest about my desires, or I could suppress my feelings and remain in the closet, hoping someone would eventually find the door to let me out.

Basically, I could live or die; or at least, live a life not fully realised. Giving up on certain aspects of yourself, the parts others might find distasteful or threatening, is the easiest thing in the world. It's the safest route, the path of least resistance. But I was starting to feel if I followed that track of inertia, my lost and abandoned fragments would return to haunt me. I'd end up restless and frustrated, hunting for the flawed, shining jewels shame and doubt had made me bury.

After my father was diagnosed, he said, 'And I never got to see the Northern Lights.' Everyone in the family insisted he still had time. We'd book a cruise for him and Mum, and he could sit on the deck, a tartan blanket on his lap, gazing up at the dances of a shimmering green sky. Of course, there was no guarantee the lights would show but at least we'd have tried. But stage four stomach cancer had other ideas and Dad left us, age fifty-two, with too many dreams unseen.

I didn't want to be like that, ticking along and pinning my hopes to a future which fate could snatch away. I wanted my Northern Lights, damn it. If my candor scared some guys off, then clearly they weren't for me. And I would never have met Baxter Logan if I hadn't embarked on a policy of openness, although I'm not sure that constitutes a recommendation.

But now, after my home had been broken into, I feared I'd pushed it too far. Had I, in talking so freely about my fantasies and desires, become a bit much? Had I lost sight of what was appropriate? Safe?

Behind me in bed, Liam stirred. He rolled away from our spooning, his hand dragging sleepily across my breasts. My back was damp. I fought the urge to roll after him for comfort, instead sliding my leg towards his to maintain contact with his body. My safety anchor. Tomorrow night, I would be alone. And the night after that.

No, Monday evening I had a date. If it went well, maybe I wouldn't need to sleep alone. Oh, what an awful thought! I couldn't go on a date in the hope of snagging an unsuspecting bodyguard. Besides, dates rarely went well for me, my first date with Baxter being an enormous exception.

I should tell Liam. He'd stay over if I asked. He wouldn't want me to be scared.

But I didn't want to involve Liam. He knew my kinks, more or less, and while he didn't share them or feel able to cater to them, he was cool with what I wanted. But this was on a different scale altogether. We weren't talking bondage and roleplay. Some guy I'd never met had found my address and broken into my house.

I lay on my back, staring at the dark ceiling, trying to get a grip. Regret kept lurching in. I'd been seduced by the intimacy of the internet, hadn't I? I'd revealed too much with scant regard for who was on the other side of the screen. Without knowing who he was, I'd trusted him.

Too late now. You can't unsay what you've said.

Damage limitation, then.

I could call the cops. That would be the sensible option but I knew I wouldn't for two main reasons. One, nothing much had happened and if they were to take the threat seriously (and yeah, as if they would), I'd have to tell them about our emails and risk having my sordid, sexual fantasies used as evidence in an enquiry. Or worse, my words would get passed around the police station and they'd all be sniggering, thinking, 'The dozy mare, what did she expect, telling that kind of stuff to a stranger? And whoa, what a slapper!'

No, I needed to keep this to myself.

But there was a second reason why I didn't want to involve the law or mention anything to Liam: I liked this man being closer than I knew. I liked the threat. I'd told him I got off on the idea of being afraid and not knowing what lay ahead. And now it was happening, I liked the actuality of it too. Paradoxically, it made me trust him more. He'd tapped into the heart of my fantasies by making me vulnerable and afraid, by showing me he was capable of playing by uncertain rules. I remembered him saying, 'It's the psychological aspect I'm most drawn to.' I guessed he was trying to mess with my mind.

It was a good start and a bad one. He'd breached my privacy, had over-ridden the need for a conversations where you negotiate likes and limits. I mean, I'm not exactly immersed in the BDSM scene but, hello? Safeword, anyone? Oh, he'd overstepped the mark on so many levels. Warning lights should have flashed but, romantic fool that I am, I thought his intrusive actions meant he recognised the need for a corresponding leap of faith from me.

Yup, this guy was so smart, so in synch with my sexuality we were practically telepathic. I could trust him to do the right thing, went my dubious, over-eager logic, because he was doing the right thing already. Besides, he was taking a major risk too. I could have called the cops. FancyFree, the dating site we'd met on, would be ordered to hand over his details, his ISP, or whatever it took to trace him, then *bam*!

But I didn't call the cops, did I? I even hid the note from my friend and made out everything was fine.

Clever, crafty man. He knew I wouldn't tell a soul.

I had to wait until Liam had left mine the next morning before I could check the break-in wasn't a dream. I knew it wasn't. I hadn't slept so how could I dream? So maybe everything was a dream, even this part now where I was going down to the kitchen to check it was for real.

The air was fresher after the storm. In the watery, late morning sunlight, my fears eased. I was careful to wear shoes in case we'd missed clearing up some glass. I opened the back door. Rory roused herself from the adjoining spare room and padded into the garden, white-tipped tail swaying loftily. I watched her tiptoeing among the foliage, tentatively sniffing plants as if the world were new to her and she needed to be on her guard. A puddle of water on the round table was molten gold, the sun caught in its mirror. Edging the garden walls, trees and ivy gleamed a deep, forest-green. Everything was calm and ordinary.

Leaving the back door ajar, I dug out a pair of rubber gloves from under the sink and removed from the cutlery drawer his note, with its old school, ransom-letter aesthetic. A few water droplets beaded the plastic covering. Awkward in gloves, I removed the sheet of paper and held it up to the window, looking for clues.

CLOSER THAN YOU KNOW

I slipped off my right glove and picked at the edge of one of the glued, newspaper letters. I didn't want to add too many fingerprints of my own in case the cops ever needed to dust the document. Underneath the glued letter were words from an article. I sniffed the paper, trying to scent the adhesive or him. I examined at the underside. Nothing but fragments from newspapers showing faintly through the white paper. I returned the note to its plastic envelope and slipped it into the drawer where I keep foil, string, birthday candles, receipts, vouchers and other stuff I should bin.

I snapped open a tin of Felix so Rory would return and I scanned the garden. Empty. I locked the kitchen door and looked around me.

Window closed. Check.

Cat safe and sound. Check,

All alone in the house. Check.

I headed upstairs to the living room, switched on my laptop, sat on the sofa and logged on to FancyFree. Despite the warmth, my fingers were shivery on the keyboard. Would Kagami have contacted me?

Hey Natajack32, you have seven new messages!

Back_on_beard says: *Oh, man! You fucking nailed it, Natalie – now i know why i hated that film! Sentimental dross, yes. Pisses me off when people accuse me of being a coldhearted bastard because sunsets at [read more]*

Terry1234 says: *Hi . . . if you fancy a latte sometime say hello Terry.*

DJ_str8talk says: *Hey Natalie, it was cool to meet you last week but I agree, I don't think we're compatible and we want different things, lol!!! Good luck with your search!*

DownAsunder says: *Fucking awesome profile! Loved the beach comment. :p Other side of the world to you, alas! Have fun, laugh loudly and live largely. Cheers, Ian x*

Legsman101 says: *Hello Natajack32, how are you this fine day? I hope your having a nice weekend. You seem an interesting ladie and I think we would get on even though I don't meet your criterias. I am a fifty-seven-year-old divorcee [read more]*

Cloudthunk79 says: *Hi Gorgeous, just checking we're still on for tomorrow, 8.30pm in The Smugglers Arms. Looking forward to it. You have my number so any change of plan,*

let me know. I'll text you when I'm on my way. I'll also give
[read more]
StrictSensualSimon says: *'If you want to play, I'll be your*
Christian Grey.' I am a loving, sincere, financially solvent
dominant. I have researched bronze-age women and I know
this is natural. You are dressed in a black dress, stockings and
heels. You are told [read more]

There were no new messages from Kagami. I don't know
what I'd been expecting. I skimmed through our previous
conversations, reams and reams of words going back several
weeks. My fingertips clicked and tapped, page up, page down,
words flying on the screen. Dark, dirty, shameless words
that now seemed cheap and crass, made of worn-out, porno
language.

I winced to read them back but I had to check, even
though I knew, that of all the idiotic things I'd told him, my
address wasn't among them. No, I hadn't told him. He'd got
my surname, though, hadn't he? I'd given it to him when
he'd offered to email a photo because he didn't have one on
his profile. 'Cool, thanks, I'm on natslovell@ymail.com.'

Lovell. It's a fairly unusual surname. He knew the town
I lived so, assuming he had a modicum of internet savvy,
he'd easily be able to find my address. I was ex-directory so
I figured he must have paid money to get details from the
electoral roll. He'd acted with intent, then, rather than been
inspired to break into my home after stumbling across my
details on an idle cyberstalk. And I couldn't criticise anyone
for cyberstalking because I was equally guilty. If I was flirting
with a guy who'd given me his name, then sure, I'd Google
him. A little extra information always helps and it's reassuring
to know they are who they say they are.

I paused over one of Kagami's messages, scrolling slowly.

And I pin you down. Your face is streaked with tears. I can see fear in your eyes. It makes my cock so hard. That's what I want from you: tears, fear, and finally, obedience. I adore your strength of character, your intelligence. When I break you, I know it means something. You don't obey anyone, you don't submit easily. That's why I want you to myself. You've got something special. I want to mould you to my will, make you mine. My sweet submissive whore. It might look like I'm destroying you but I'm breaking you down to build you up, to transform you into the thing you need to be.

'What do you want, Natalie?' I say to you.

You shake your head and sob. Tears shimmer in your eyes. A darkness crouches in your shadows. I want you to give me that darkness but you're scared. You don't want to lose yourself. You won't give it to me, so once again I have to take it from you. I'll keep doing this until you're surrendered, until that darkness is so vast you're longing for me to take charge of it. You need me to help carry this beautiful burden we've created together.

In a way, I'm serving you. Can you see that?

I touch your cunt and you're soaked. So swollen and sensitive. My fingers make you whimper. You know I can make you come in an instant, proving to me how much you want this. But you can't admit you want it, your mouth won't say the words.

That's the problem. Your mouth. It's filtering out the truth. It needs to loosen up, relax. That's why I have to keep on fucking it.

I stopped reading, my heart going wild, the wetness between my thighs flowing as fast as the first time I'd read that, the second, the third.

Had he discovered where I lived when he'd written those words? Had he watched from a distance, knowing how his message had thrilled me? Because I'd told him it had. I'd even thanked him, telling him his dirty words had fuelled several solo sessions. Admitting to that hadn't felt dangerous. None of it had felt dangerous but I could see how my behaviour might appear reckless to an outsider.

In Kagami's fantasy, I was ashamed, shy, unable to claim what I wanted, meaning his role was to force me. In my fantasies the dynamic was much the same, whereas in reality I was perfectly able to claim my desire. I was glad Kagami – Den – understood the paradox. Once, a guy I was chatting to online had said I sounded more dom than sub, as if kinking for submission equated to being passive. That relationship didn't go far.

When I'd started online dating, doubt and inhibition made me cautious. But I soon realised the people out there were as ordinary as I was. This wasn't, as the myth would have it, a world of conmen, psychos, stalkers and adulterers. Nor were these people lonely, sad or desperate. Like me, they were simply looking for love, or maybe a couple of beers and a jump, and they were using modern communications to do so. It beat the olden days where your dating pool was the local village or your workplace.

So if someone had my surname, that was no great shakes.

The last time I'd Googled myself, curious as to what was out there, I'd found my employer's website with my contact details, my twitter account, a letter I'd once written to *The Independent*, a page where I'd sponsored a friend running in the London Marathon, some dubious genealogy links and far too many photos on Facebook of me and various friends engaged in drunken exploits. Mark Zuckerberg claims privacy's no longer the norm, but he would say that, wouldn't he? Nowadays, I'm always adjusting my Facebook settings to keep nosey parkers out. But if I worried about these issues too much, I'd never do anything online. Nor would I walk down the street for fear some deranged thug were lying in wait to show me that a miniscule percentage of humanity can make us question what it means to be human.

But privacy and safety aren't the same issue. While I might not be comfortable with my virtual self scattering inerasable traces across the ether, I'd never felt the exposure left me vulnerable to anyone but spammers. I wasn't a child. And when millions of people were equally exposed, who cared about my few, boring details?

Well, Kagami did, obviously. I had nothing concrete on him. He called himself Den but I'd no proof that was his real name. His email address was kagamikagami@rocketmail.com. He'd told me he lived north of London, that he worked in the Arts, had an interest in physical theatre and dance, liked to keep fit, age thirty-six, height 6'2", athletic build. I didn't know if any of that was true but with online dating, these details matter less than the sense you get of someone in their messages. And I liked his messages. He seemed intelligent, kinky, respectful, interesting, and had that all-important GSOH.

I didn't have a picture of his face, though. He'd dodged that one, sending instead a beautifully lit, arty, black and white shot where his torso was bared but his face was masked. And damn he had a great body, his head shaved as if hair might detract from the streamlined form on display. I rarely chat to people who won't show their face but, oh, I am evidently shallow and lecherous, too easily dazzled by a man captured in a twist of dance, his ripped body full of energy and masculine poise.

I was immediately suspicious. Where was the holiday snap, the wedding-guest photo he'd cropped to hide his ex, the lop-shouldered self-portrait from a phone camera? Was he trying to impress me with a portfolio photo? Keep his distance? Was it even him?

I'd scrutinised the picture for clues to the person depicted but found little. Against a grey backdrop, barefoot and dressed in black joggers, he was lunging sideways, one arm drawn back. I stared, loving what I saw. Elegant yet aggressive, he was a classical sculpture brought to life, a sheen of sweat suggesting a fluid quality as if alabaster were streaming over sub-structures of bone and muscle. Light and shadow played across his skin, joining in this monochrome dance. On his taut upper arm, a black tattoo of a circle sporting three horns or flames removed some of the image's implicit anonymity.

Most striking of all was his head, the shaved dome of his skull sweeping round into a beaked Venetian mask, brightly jewelled but ominous. He was a freakish bird from a malevolent carnival, the phallic threat of his hooked proboscis creating, in my mind, a cloaked creature who haunted alleyways at night, stalking his prey.

The mask affected me. Without it, he might have been too clean and wholesome. But that grotesque edge gave him a darker charm, appealing to the side of me that thrills to a hint of threat.

Of course, I kept this to myself. I wrote back, thanking him and hiding my attraction with a cheeky dismissal. 'What is this? *Eyes Wide Shut*?'

Later, I wrote: 'So do I get to see your face?'

'All in good time,' he replied.

Like I say, I was wary. I can understand why someone might not want their picture on their profile. They might be shy, uncomfortable with online dating, or have a need to protect their privacy. But once you start chatting to someone, they send their picture. Den could be married, ugly or scarred. Or it might not be him at all and I was messaging an ageing, pot-bellied pervert tossing off in a bedsit in Birmingham. But something told me it was him, and if he removed his mask, he'd have a face I wanted to look at, eyes I wanted to swim in, lips I wanted to kiss. So I gave him the benefit of the doubt and kept writing to him, caught up with the magic and the mystery.

I liked him, this man without a face.

But now he'd entered my home, uninvited, and liking him seemed a stupid move.

I needed more on him. I wanted to check his profile. I hadn't looked at it much since we'd started chatting. When you check someone's profile, they can see on their home page that you've visited. Check someone out too often, and you might look stalkerish. Plenty of times I'd resisted the urge to revisit Kagami's profile. I couldn't remember everything he'd written. How had he answered the questions everyone gets asked? What were his drinking habits, his star sign? I remembered he was 6'2" but his BMI? Did it matter?

I toyed with the idea of not visiting his page, thinking my wisest option would be to cut all contact, don't even hint at being interested or disturbed. Quit this nonsense before it's too late. But I didn't want to quit. I would rise to his challenge and show him I understood his game.

My cursor hovered over his avatar, a cartoonish shadow

of a man in a Stetson, the default for guys who don't upload a photo. I decided to check his profile one last time. I'd take a screen grab for future reference. I was edgy again. I felt as if I was being watched. I hadn't put the radio on, wanting instead to stay alert to unusual sounds.

His profile took ages to load. Was this the right thing to do? When the page finally filled my screen, my blood ran cold.

This user no longer has a profile.

What was once there was gone. He'd deleted himself.

The blankness appalled me. I stared at it, willing it to be untrue.

This user no longer has a profile.

Instead, a bland, blue corporate screen. He'd vanished without a trace.

Crazy, illogical, but I felt as if he'd escaped. He was a spirit now made flesh, a manifestation with weight and purpose. Who was he? Where was he? I didn't know. I just knew he was out there somewhere, released from the internet and on the loose.

Three

The derelict fishing quarter on the east beach at Saltbourne used to be my favourite place for late night, al fresco sex.

Once, Baxter and I fucked in the scoop of a broken boat, its wooden sides yellow and ravaged like an old banana. No, that's not right. Baxter fucked me. He always fucked me. Sex wasn't something we did together. He would act as if he were inflicting it on me and I'd let him because that's how we rolled.

That night with Baxter was our first time at the beach. The moon was low and large, silvering the sea, and the tide was high. Waves crashed on the shore, shingle clattering in the drag. You could make out the whirs and squeals of the funfair near the west beach, a jangle of music seeping into the dark, the rides' gaudy lights spinning, flashing and swooping by the disused pier. In contrast, the east beach around us was apocalyptically still, a halted world of rusting winches, mouldering shacks, abandoned lobster pots, rotting rope and scattered, dead boats. The old net houses, tall, gaunt sheds with steep roofs and tar-black, weatherboarded walls, loomed over the wreckage like a creepy, elongated town in a fairy tale.

The broken boat was resting on a slant. Baxter had me face-forward over the plank of a narrow seat, his fist wound in my hair. He made my spine dip, my arse lifting towards to him, and my neck ached. I gripped the edge of the boat, struggling to keep my cries down as he fucked me like a man possessed.

'See what you make me do,' he accused, his Dunfermline accent rolling through gritted teeth. 'Fucking you in this nasty place, like a whore. A greedy little whore. Why d'you do it, hen? Why d'you make me fuck you like this, eh?'

The boat creaked and I feared it might break, its wood too brittle and splintered to take us. Baxter slammed relentlessly, his cock thumping at my core. He released my hair and hooked me around the waist, holding me steady as he powered on, his breath fast, his grunts spittle-moist and urgent. He was a hefty man with crude hands, his broad chest tangled with dark hair, his thighs as big as a warrior's. He was a few pounds overweight but proportionate so the extra layer merely added to his bulk and strength. Besides, I like a man with padding.

To look at him, sturdy in a suit, hair rumpled, jaw unshaven, his tie permanently askew, you wouldn't believe he could move with such grace and ease; wouldn't believe how his pelvis could undulate when he lingered over a slow, cruel fuck; wouldn't believe how fast he could move in the sack. But then to look at him, you'd never guess he was as broken as the boats around us, a big, angry, soft-hearted Scot with a weakness for women and whisky.

I loved him for a year and now I wish I'd never met him.

That night on the beach is etched in my memory as one of our high points, later to became a low because it was laced with betrayal. At the time, drunk on romance, I'd seen the desolate beauty of the fishing quarter as an environmental echo of Baxter. He was all around me, his masculinity echoing in the remnants of this coastal industry, in the coils of thick rope, the heavy chains and dark, dangerous secrets of the sea.

'C'mere, you wee bitch,' he urged, snatching himself from me. 'Suck my dick. Come on, jump to it.'

He maneuvered me into place, dragging me by my hair. I complained, resisting him because it was too dark to see and the boat was grotty. I wanted to know where I was putting my hands, what I was kneeling on. Was it clean, safe? Would we break the boat and end up in a heap of matchwood? But Baxter didn't care about niceties and he knew, at heart, neither did I.

I stumbled towards him on all fours. I was wearing cute, blue, hold-up stockings with a daisy detail on the ankle. Not so cute now. Baxter's thighs were bound with a confusion of clothing and his cock was hard enough to cut diamonds. For a brief moment, moonlight glossed his tip, adding a pearly pink sheen to the flushed violet marbling. The veins on his shaft were thick like those ropes, flowing with blue mysteries like the sea. He gripped himself, holding steady as he aimed for my mouth, pulling me on to him.

Had anyone been watching they might have wondered if I were consenting to this. But I was, very much so. Baxter's bossiness turned me on like nothing else. I saw his cock as him condensed, full of rage but exposed and vulnerable too. At that moment, I couldn't differentiate between wanting the man and wanting the cock. I wanted him and it to overwhelm me. Then I could disappear into him, like disappearing into the vastness of the black, boundless night. That's what I craved: the oblivion of dissolution, the intoxicating peace I found in the white heat, white light of lust, sweat and surrender.

I sucked his end, lips tight over his encircling ridge, then slid wetly to his root. 'Tha-at's right,' he cooed. His tender, selfish approval made my cunt loosen. He tasted of latex so I blew him with a quick sloppy mouth until he tasted of himself. Then Baxter took over. He held my head firm and began fucking my throat with brutal, pornographic thrusts. He used me as if my pleasure and comfort meant nothing to him. But Baxter was good, always judging it so he never went too far.

'No teeth,' he snapped. 'I dinnae want to feel teeth.' He made me cough and splutter. I didn't know how much more I could take but I wanted to take it for him. I wanted to be the best I could be. I shielded my teeth with my lips. Tears spilled from my eyes.

He pulled out, hand pumping on his cock, blurrily fast. 'Show me your tits.'

'Bax! Supposing someone—'

'Show me your fucking tits. I want to come on them.'

I surveyed the dark beach and unbuttoned quickly. This was no time to quibble. With his free hand, Baxter shoved my top from my shoulders, greed making him clumsy. 'Hang on,' I said, struggling to unbutton. I shrugged back my top, lifted my flesh from my bra and offered myself, my nipples crinkling, so tight and hard. Baxter groaned in approval. I had to wait like that, complicit in my own submission and debasement. But I loved feeling objectified, loved being nothing but a pair of tits Baxter could claim with his territorialising jizz. There, I felt de-civilised and free.

The distant fairground music floated around us. I was remote from our surroundings, wrapped in intimacy with Baxter. Waves crashed on the shore, giving the beach its timeless heartbeat. In my peripheral vision, a cluster of ragged black flags poked from a corroded oil drum, fluttering in the breeze. Stacked crab pots to my left became the wall of a rough, ancient cage made from wood and blue rope. We might have been in an underworld at the bottom of the ocean, those torn flags waving a dark, eerie triumphalism. We belonged here, not there where people were having brash, bright, candy-flossed fun.

Baxter's eyes were fixed on me, hand working furiously, face twisting. A lock of dark, wavy hair fell across his forehead as he hunched his shoulders, grimacing. Then he threw back his head, gave three sharp, agonised cries and came, cursing as if he wished it weren't happening to him. His liquid splashed in soft, warm hits then his noises faded, stuttering and slowing like the pearls tumbling from his cock.

'Fuck,' he breathed, panting. He gave me his hand to lick clean. Then, because he's a nice guy, he clasped my wrist and urged me onto my back.

He pinned me at an angle, an arm held above my head, his fingers linked in mine. I felt stripped bare, his come cooling on my tits, the underside of my wrist delicate and thin-skinned beneath the strength of his grip, my armpit open to attack. He nudged my legs wider with a crude stab of his knee. The night breathed over my slippery cunt.

'Let's see what you've got to give, eh?' he said, his whisper harsh and mean.

Other than a little wriggling, I didn't move from the position he'd put me in. He reached under my skirt and crammed thick fingers inside me, making me gasp. He fucked me like that, fast and furious, as if taking revenge for his own climax. When my cries got too loud he clamped a hand to my mouth, his face lit with crazy delight. He propped himself on an elbow, fingers still slamming.

'This is what you like, isn't it?' His voice was a growl by my ear. 'You trapped. Helpless. Me fucking you with my fingers.'

He slowed, stroked my clit, spread my juices higher. His words echoed in my head, driving me to my tipping point. He knew what I liked, knew my fantasies. Best of all, he could give them right back to me, no judgment passed, my desires embellished with his fierce imagination. No one else had ever done that for me until Baxter. I saw it as a gift and was grateful to be known.

Above me, beyond the bedraggled flags, a drift of silver-grey clouds floated across the dark. I panted, getting closer. Baxter breathed more obscenities in my ear, his words slow and clear. No shame or shyness from Baxter. His fingers filled my cunt, his thumb rocking my clit with a precise, steady rhythm. On my mouth, his hand was humid. I gasped against it as my orgasm tightened. 'Beautiful,' he breathed, seeing I was close. 'Aye, there she goes, my beautiful wee bitch, there she goes.'

In my thighs, sensation brimmed over, higher, and I was coming hard, pulsations wringing me out, squeezing and dancing. I cried as quietly as I could, allowing ecstasy to erase me, beyond skin, beyond words. White heat. Flight. Gone. Baxter lifted his hand from my mouth, becoming gentle as the shivers left my body. He smoothed a strand of hair from my face, licked my juices from his fingers then kissed me.

I sat up, tasting myself on my lips and rubbing his come into my skin.

Baxter chuckled. 'What a mess you've made of yourself.'

I wrapped my arm beneath his loose shirt, kissing his damp neck. He was briny like the sea air. I kissed and licked some more, his stubble grating.

Later, we stumbled from the beach, me giddy and high, Baxter grumpy and regretful. The boating lake by the prom gleamed like a dark mirror, a flock of moored swan pedalos gazing out with sinister, unseeing eyes. Baxter dusted himself down, complaining about the smear of seaweed on the knee of his suit, the God-knows-what on his jacket, the dampness of his shirt.

'Look at the fucking state of me,' he said. 'I'm a tramp. You lead me astray, you know that?'

A joke although not quite. Baxter was good at deflecting responsibility but I never saw that at the time.

He never left my place without showering.

He never let me mark him, no love bites, no scratches.

He always stayed at my house; I only once went to his.

Occasionally, I would tease him about his secret wife and he would laugh in that big, hearty manner of his because no, he wasn't fucking married, course he wasn't, are you for fucking real? He was separated. Debra lived in Scotland but that could be Jupiter for all he cared, and they barely had anything to do with each other no more.

In your dreams, Baxter Logan. In your fucking dreams.

Since then, I've been trying and failing to get him out of my system. No, that's not good enough: to rip him from the marrow of my bones.

Another date, another dollar.

How many since I embarked on this matchmaking merry-go-round? Fifteen? Twenty? And how many messages, memos, winks and pokes had I exchanged? Too many. Enough to sink a digital ship.

In return for all this effort, apart from my disastrous success with Baxter, I'd met only two guys I liked. One, pre-

Baxter, had stopped returning my calls after we'd been seeing each other for two months, no further explanation. The second, post-Baxter, had wanted exclusivity from the get-go, and I think that's a big ask in the early stages of a relationship. Besides, after Baxter's betrayal, I was in no hurry to commit or fall in love. I knew I'd be quick to bruise so I swore off men for a while, determined to heal before going in for another bout. When I eventually returned to internet dating, I wasn't looking for love. I just wanted some fun and the chance to keep exploring my sexual self, to seek my Northern Lights.

With Baxter, submission was more than I'd dreamed it could be. In the thick of it, when he pushed me towards my limit, I could go under and reach a place of beautiful, bombed-out absence, a strange sensation of being saturated in an ongoing miracle. Just held there, floating and far off. Untouchable. I learned the name for this: subspace; the word so ugly and inadequate for the experience it described. In that zone where I was lost to myself, dissolving and drifting, I felt more at peace than at any point I'd known before. So far, only Baxter had been able to show me that clearing. After him, nothing else could get me as high, but the compulsion to yield still clawed at me.

I didn't want that to be the case. I wanted to be able to submit on a casual basis but feared I might not be cut out for darkness with lightness, might not be able to surrender myself to someone I didn't adore and fully believe in. Tonight's date had described himself as an aspiring dominant. He was handsome and friendly, so I figured he was worth a shot.

It was a Monday evening and Old Town was quiet. A late evening sun cast skinny shadows across stone and sparkled on the gilt embellishments of Saltbourne's pink, domed turrets. Once, this fishing village had been fashionable. Then it fell out of favour, its genteel Regency visitors deterred by two destructive storms and the whims of the in-crowd. Those incongruous, Persian domes remain, adding a touch of Arabian Nights and misplaced frivolity to this rugged, sloping, half-derelict town.

After a day at work, the weekend's events seemed unreal and distant. Sat at my desk and typing up minutes, the break-in was a dream. Alone, the reality lodged most keenly. I hadn't slept much the previous night, all the creaks in the house coming out to torment me. Now, with my footsteps ringing on old stone, I grew uneasy again. Could Den see me? Was he on my tail? Should I confide in Liam?

My phone honked as I descended a steep passageway of steps scooped to thinness by centuries of feet. I waited till I was at the bottom before retrieving the phone from my bag. Still wary, I checked around me before checking the screen.

Another text from my date: *'Really looking forward to meeting you, Natalie! If I get to the pub first, I'll text you so you know where I'm sitting. See you soon. Paul. xx'*

I locked my phone. Minor doubts I'd had about this guy were turning into significant reservations. Too keen, too needy, too anxious. I was already feeling suffocated and while I don't expect a dominant to be all grrr and roar in regular interactions, an air of confidence doesn't go amiss.

I had another concern. He'd said, due to cheese, red wine and the gym, he was slightly heavier than in his profile pictures. Well, that could be OK, I thought. I like big blokes. Besides, cheese, red wine and the gym was a sexy combination. In his pictures, he was extraordinarily good-looking, a tall, slender guy with piercing green eyes and bone structure as fine as china. I couldn't see a slight heaviness detracting from that.

In The Smugglers Arms, a soulless, mock Tudor pub

that's useful for first dates because I don't know anyone who drinks there, I wouldn't have recognised him except that he was waving from a deep, leather sofa. He stood, jeans tight on his thighs. I greeted him with a peck on the cheek.

'I was about to text you,' he said. He had that first-date mania, smile a little too tense, eyes staring intently as if wanting to absorb me in case I fled.

I smiled, searching for some vestiges of those elegant bones in his bloated face and bull-dog neck. Perhaps I looked manic too. I wanted to say, 'That's not red wine and cheese, mate! That's burgers and kebabs.' Instead, I chirped, 'No need, I'm here! Nice to meet you!' He wasn't obese. He was stocky and it didn't suit him. In his photos he'd looked cultured and intelligent. Now he seemed slow and stupid. Give him a chance, Natalie, I thought. Judge, book, cover and all that.

We sat opposite each other at a long, low table, at our side a grand fireplace with dried flowers in its hearth. The space was awkward; both of us perched on the edge of our sofas, unable to hear properly because of tinny music coming from a speaker above us. Dreadful place. Why did I keep going there?

We talked about our jobs, music and travel, and failed to laugh at each other's jokes. I tried to picture him ramming his cock into my mouth and calling me names. The hand on his pint glass was chubby and I wondered if his fingers would feel good inside me. None of it worked. I couldn't see how this uneasy, approval-seeking man might step into Baxter's shoes by becoming a big, beautiful beast in bed. But if he *were* able to do that, maybe I could overlook the fat neck and lacklustre conversation to get my fix of twisted sex. And if that panned out OK, maybe I could stop pinning my hopes on a some faceless psycho who'd broken into my house to leave his kinky calling card.

Kinky? No, Den's calling card was beyond kinky. Again, I wondered if I ought to fess up to Liam so he could keep an eye out for me. No need, I reassured myself. I was safe. Den had removed his profile from FancyFree so there was a good chance he'd stopped already. And if he hadn't stopped, well, that was fine too. I could handle myself. I was smart enough not to get embroiled in something seriously risky.

'So how are we doing?' Paul asked as we neared the end of our first drink.

I smiled, stifling a sigh as I fiddled with the stem of my glass, thinking, stay or go?

I often find it useful to narrow my choices down to two. Live or die? Live or live a lie? My instinct said this wasn't going to work. Say goodbye, go home. But another voice, that of my devil's advocate who lodges in my psyche in a room marked 'desperate', started telling me I was too damn picky. Dating was meant to be fun, an experiment to see if I could combine kink with friendship. This wasn't a quest to find Baxter Logan the Second so why keep rejecting guys who were less than ideal? Lighten up, make some compromises, Natalie.

'Another drink while you think about it?' suggested Paul.

I met his gaze. His brows were tipped high, his smile wide. Too puppyish, too eager. Not my type at all. I shook my head. 'Sorry. I need to go. It's been nice meeting you but . . . sorry. I think it's best we call it a day. We aren't . . . I don't think . . .' I shrugged, hating this part. 'I don't think I'm your type. We're not compatible.'

Paul nodded, lips tight, eyes downcast. Eventually, he said, 'Well, thanks for being honest.'

I knocked back the remainder of my wine. 'No worries. Any time.' In a hurry, I gathered my belongings and left the pub, thinking what a dumb thing to have said. Any time? What did that mean in the context?

Outside, Old Town was quiet, and my footsteps echoed in the dreary sterility of a Monday evening. Sometimes, if I'm in a masochistic mood, I go running in Old Town although I pay for it later with aching calf muscles. The seafront is my preferred spot. Most days after work, I jog down the narrow, sloping streets then, when I hit the expanse of Sea Road, I turn up the volume on my iPod and pound along the prom, inhaling sea-salt air and letting the horizon suck away the stresses of the day. On the way back, I often cheat, taking the funicular up to the cliff top, just a few streets from home.

That evening, because I'd wanted to spend time tarting myself up, I hadn't gone for my run. Almost without thinking, after leaving the pub in a mopey mood, I found myself heading downslope rather than in the direction of home, hungering to see the sea. Paul wasn't going to rescue me from the clutches of Den by becoming another Baxter. Nothing had changed.

The traffic was sparse on the seafront with the funfair to the west a pale imitation of its weekend, high-summer dazzle. By the pedalo lake, the plastic swans faced the blue-grey night with vicious beaks and haughty stares. I crossed to the main beach, casting a glance eastwards to the abandoned fishing beach. Sometimes, I want to revisit places I associate with Baxter and overwrite old memories with new. But mostly, I don't want to lose the memories because they're all I have. Stupid to want to keep the lie as if it were truth.

I crunched towards the frothing grey surf, the hillocky bands of shingle slipping beneath my feet. When I was in the middle of the empty beach, I dropped to the ground and sprawled on my back, gazing up at pinpricks of stars emerging in the ink-wash sky. I was safe there, surrounded by space. Probably safer than being at home. More relaxing too, given how my house no longer seemed wholly mine. On the beach, no one could hide and jump out or approach without me hearing them. No one knew I was here.

Above me, a gull soared past, its underside as white as a ghost. The waves crashed on the shore, their regularity lulling me towards peace. I felt so tiny and alone, a speck on the coast of a country in the world. A good place to take stock and mull over whether to pursue online dating or take a break for a while. The constant disappointments weren't doing much for my morale.

As if to prove my solitude wrong, my phone honked. I lay in silence, trying not to think about Baxter and love, until curiosity got the better of me. A message from Paul: *It was nice to meet you. I thought we had a lot in common so if you change your mind, let me know. Good night. xx*

With a sigh, I returned my phone to my bag. No, that man was not part of my Northern Lights.

Tears stung my eyes. I wasn't sure how much more I could take of my hopes being raised and dashed. The stars above me swam in a blur. I recalled Alistair Fitch's blue music studio, a mural of Van Gogh's *Starry Night* swirling on one wall. I smiled to recall how artistic I used to think that room was and how cool Alistair Fitch. In reality, he was an ordinary piano tutor working from a gussied-up suburban dining room. I remembered how his Venetian window blinds obscured the daylight, cocooning him in a weird, other space, away from the everyday. Potted palms and ferns were dotted high and low amid the clutter of pianos, keyboards and stacks of sheet music, giving the studio the gloomy, oppressive air of a Victorian parlour.

Those royal blue walls used to make me feel I was trapped inside a box of night and eerie dreams. One wall featured the Van Gogh mural, its wonky church rising like black flames, the heavens made of splodgy brushstrokes, while the other walls were scattered with yellow stars spinning like crazy suns.

Trapped with Alistair Fitch, just as he would have wanted it. I was nineteen, I'd had boyfriends and some sex; I didn't think I was naïve. My father's diagnosis meant I'd stayed living with my parents while my friends left town for adventures at university. I got a brain-achingly dull job in a shoe shop and started piano lessons to give myself a focus and a goal. I liked the discipline of practising and the weekly tuition. Alistair Fitch was cute too, steel-rimmed glasses, short blond spikes, but in his mid-thirties so too old and sophisticated for me.

Or so I thought. I was sitting at the baby grand, struggling with the legato in a piece from Brahms. Alistair approached me from one side and gently closed the lid over my hopeless hands. My heart pumped. This wasn't right. Somehow, I knew Alistair wanted me to keep my fingers on the keys so I was motionless, the polished rosewood jaw resting on my wrists. 'Legato,' he said. 'It means "tied together". You're lifting your fingers too soon, Natalie. The notes need to flow, no silences between.'

I giggled. He made me nervous and the lid on my hands was silly.

'It's not a joke,' he said. 'You need to practise more. You've got to suffer for your art. Blood, sweat and tears.'

I sniggered again, my defensiveness kicking in. This wasn't my art; this was grade-two piano class I was paying for with shoe-shop wages. As an implicit challenge to Alistair's pompousness, I began playing *Chopsticks*, fingers crawling awkwardly, the shiny lid bouncing to the terrible tune. The lyrics ran through my mind. 'Oh, will you wash your father's shirt . . .'

Alistair let me play for a few moments. I was laughing inside, recalling his declaration at my first lesson: 'We don't play *Chopsticks* in my classes.'

Calmly, Alistair lifted the lid. He took both my hands in his and raised them high above the keyboard. 'Did you do that on purpose?' he asked.

Woah, this was new. My blood pounded, my cheeks colouring fast. What was he doing? We were shifting into illicit, unfamiliar terrain, I knew that much, but I said nothing, anxious not to make a fool of myself by appearing ignorant of some unknown seduction protocol.

'Are you trying to rile me?' he prompted.

I giggled again. 'Might be,' I said like a belligerent adolescent.

He jerked my arms higher and my world started to slide. There, that tug on my limbs, the sharpness in his voice, the attitude. Such minor details and yet the combination caused an almighty great commotion in my groin and heart. Did he like me? Was suburbia's answer to Jools Holland hitting on me? And why did that tug and tone have such an impact?

'Anyone would think you wanted me to punish you,' Alistair continued.

Punish. Oh God, what a word. What a delicious, horrible, compelling word. I'd never known it to have such a charge. My senses span, heat thumped between my thighs. In the corner of my eye, the crazy Van Gogh suns twirled on the wall.

'Do you want that?' He released my hands and I let them drop to my lap. My hair was short then and his cool hand touched the back of my neck, thumb and fingers spanning its width. I stared at the black and white keys before me, my pulse refusing to steady itself.

'Well, do you?'

I gave a tiny, breathless giggle. What were you meant to do when a man said that? Was he being silly or was he getting the same rush from this as I was? Punish. Hurt. Need. Lust. How did these mismatched things fit together? I raised my upturned palms as if for a schoolroom reprimand. 'If you want,' I said.

'Naughty girl,' he replied, his tone warmer and gentler. He walked away, returning with a wooden ruler. I stayed facing the piano, hands out, and Alistair stood by my side. He landed a light, cheeky tap first on one palm then on the other.

I laughed. 'That was pathetic.'

He hit my palms again, harder, each time letting the ruler rest on my hand. The ruler listed all the kings and queens of England. William I, William II, Henry I. He kept hitting me, making my palms pink, the ruler bouncing faster and higher. I soon stopped laughing. My hands stung and at the juncture of my thighs, I was a flood.

'Stand up,' said Alistair, the crisp, bossy note back in his voice. My legs were jelly as I moved away from the piano, my face burning with shame at my secret arousal. Alistair stooped and smacked the ruler against my bare calf muscles. I yelped, jerking my legs, kneeing the air.

What we were doing? This was wrong, we should stop.

'Bend over,' said Alistair.

I hugged my arms to my chest. 'What do you mean?' I said, although I knew exactly what he meant.

'Tip forwards. Hands on your knees.'

'Why? What are you going to do?'

Alistair hit his own palm with the ruler. 'I'm going to spank you on the B-T-M,' he said, his manner unusually jolly.

And I let him because I wanted it. Then, when he told me to bend over the piano stool, I was on my knees with barely a word of complaint. I held still, listening, waiting, blood thundering in my veins. I was so needful of something bad and unexplored, there was no saying where I might have drawn the line in that starry, blue studio. But it was Alistair giving the orders and re-setting our boundaries. Part of me said this was seriously warped but a louder voice said if Alistair thought it was acceptable, then it must be. I would go along with his suggestions.

Carefully, he lifted my skirt. I could hardly breathe. Oh my God, Alistair Fitch was looking at my knickers and I didn't even know which ones I was wearing. Piano class *so* nothing special. I could never tell anyone about this, ever. My heart drummed against the stool's leather upholstery and my head boomed, on the verge of a headache. With the same slow precision, Alistair hooked his fingers into my knickers then slid them down to the creases of my bent knees. Oh God, oh no, this couldn't be happening. Alistair Fitch was looking at my bare bum.

An eternity passed. My breath ran so fast I was close to panting. Could he see my cooch? My pubes? Oh fuckity fuck. He was around thirty-five years old. He must have had loads of women, seen loads of bodies. This was probably normal for him, while for me this was so thrilling I was in danger of fainting with arousal.

Then still using the ruler, he hit me. A stripe of pain bit into my buttocks.

'Ouch!'

'Don't say "ouch". Say "one".'

'One. Ow!'

'How many?'

'Two.'

'Good girl. We're going for twelve per buttock. So hold still, brace yourself.'

The little thwacks detonated in the silence, my flesh warming to make each strike worse than the last. The final few of each dozen stung sharply. I knew my rear was glowing and that Alistair was looking at it.

He rubbed the sore patches. 'There,' he said. I could hear his quick breath as if he'd significantly exerted himself.

Between my thighs I was a throbbing mass of sensation, my body hollowed out with need. I was loose and open, craving penetration and half-scared of my own raging appetite. I ached for relief but instead, Alistair told me to straighten my clothes and try the *legato* again. I obeyed.

I wish I could say I played like a dream but my hands were trembling, my concentration shot, and my fumblings probably had Brahms spinning in his grave. But it didn't matter because I felt transformed, as if I'd tasted a new life of dangerous excitements and there was no returning. Even as I was screwing up the notes, I was telling myself I needed to practise till I was perfect so Alistair would approve.

And I did practise, and my playing did improve. But every week from then on, Alistair would punish me for some minor keyboard error, exactly as I wanted him too. During those weeks, he never touched me *there*, nor did he ever suggest I touch him, and he always used the ruler, never his hand. We rarely spoke about what we were doing, as if acknowledging our actions might bring us to our senses. And all the while, although I longed for our sessions and obsessed over Alistair, I was consumed with guilt for enjoying how he treated me. I thought I was a weirdo. I felt so desperately alone in my desires.

Years later, I would look back and realise Alistair took advantage of my emotional vulnerability and naivety. He knew my friends had left town and my father was starting to die. After a couple of warped months, I quit the lessons. My longings left me too troubled and confused. Later, I was able to recognise that part of what I felt was simply due to the self-loathing women are often made to feel for indulging in pleasures of the flesh, be they derived from food or sex. But in addition to that, our tacitly agreed refusal to discuss the spankings left me believing these desires were immoral and sick. Ours was a secret so shameful and appalling we couldn't even confront the reality ourselves.

When I tell men I meet online that I first explored my submissive side with Baxter, or B as I call him to strangers, I'm being economical with the truth. Alistair Fitch was my first, although explore is probably not the word to use. He saw something in me, or took a potshot that paid off, and I responded because I found it erotic. The role Alistair played in his studio helped me make sense of a range of desires I'd known prior to him. My experiences began to cohere. I could see how certain moments in books and films that had turned me on matched to an attitude I found sexy in men.

But Alistair left me feeling so shabby about myself and what I liked that I didn't go near those intoxicating hungers until years later. It was imperative to resist, to just say no. If I followed my urges and sought satisfaction, everything would get worse and I'd end up dead in a ditch. So I kept my lusts to myself, drawing on them as fantasy material during masturbation or sex with Jim, and never telling a soul. If the internet had been as widely available then as now, I'd have been able to explore and educate myself. Instead, I struggled alone and my secret sexuality turned sour on me.

Only after my relationship with Jim ended and nice-guy Grant frustrated me with his gentlemanly approach to sex did I understand I could embrace this hidden part of me and become the architect of my desires. If I were to live a fulfilled life, I needed to not be silent. Silence eats you up like a slow disease. My policy of honesty paid off, big style, when I met Baxter Logan. The great joy of Baxter was his lack of shame. He loved the sex we had and the dark paths we ventured down. He revelled in my appetite and encouraged me to explore my twisted imagination. Guilt and inhibition were not part of Baxter's world. Finally, I felt loved for who I was and free to be true to myself.

Baxter Logan. Oh, why did everything keep coming back to him? Why did he still have such a hold on me after two years of being apart?

I inhaled lungfuls of air and scrunched pebbles into my fists. The stones were cool and gritty in my fingers, their coating of tacky saltiness making my hands feel dirty. They clattered softly by my side while, somewhere beyond my feet, waves crashed and shushed, scraping pebbles into the water. Above me, the stars twinkled more brightly. They were light years away, many of them probably dead already. I was gazing at a snapshot of the past, the truth still travelling through space to be recorded by human eyes.

My phone honked, interrupting my reverie and bringing me back down to earth. I rummaged in my bag, thinking I ought to be going home anyhow. Navel-gazing while star-gazing could only lead to trouble. I'd text Liam to let him know how the date went then, once I was home, I'd check the doors and windows and go to bed with a book. If Rory was in the mood, maybe she'd curl up by my feet. Tomorrow was another day. Everything would be fine. I'd give dating another whirl. Maybe put a new photo on my profile. One more month then if I hadn't met anyone, I'd give it a rest.

I lifted the phone above my face, not bothering to sit up.

A text. Number unknown to me.

Friend or foe?

Saturday night's break-in came soaring back to me. He'd found my address, had entered my home and now he'd escaped the internet. For a while, I'd forgotten him but suddenly, I was a nervous wreck again. I clicked the message icon. I can't recall precisely what was running through my mind but I think even then I knew it was him. The text read: *'EVEN CLOSER NOW.'*

Oh fuck. I sat bolt upright, scanning the dark beach, twisting around. The emptiness, which had felt safe when I arrived, now seemed dangerous. I had nowhere to hide, was such an easy target to track. Where was he? Could he see me? Why the Hell had I given him my number?

I stuffed my phone into my bag as I scrambled to my feet, shingle slipping. Don't panic, Natalie, don't panic. Stumbling, I hurried across the beach towards the street lamps of Sea Road, the fairy lights strung between them promising the brightness of safety, traffic, people.

The pebbles were quicksand, the small slopes vanishing as I tried to climb them. Keep calm. Less haste, more speed. To the left, the sparkly fairground swirled and tipped. My breath galloped. I cast around me. No one about. To the east, I could make out the black shapes of the derelict fishing beach, rising from the ground like a ragged graveyard of love.

I tried not to look, tried not to think of Baxter and how safe I once felt with him.

He was gone. We were over. Safety couldn't be trusted.

Four

Run, Natalie, run.

But you're not meant to run, not meant to look afraid. I hurried across the wide road, away from the prom, inland towards streets and buildings. My pulse thundered in my ears and the warm night air thickened in my throat. So much pressure inside my head, as if my brain were expanding, throbbing against my skull. I needed to pee. Needed to breathe properly too. The air was a blanket and my lungs were full of fluff.

I passed a handful of people, wondering if they'd turn out to be witnesses, one of the last to see me. Was he following me? I heard no footsteps on my tail, saw no shadows in doorways. Supposing he'd predicted my move and was lying in wait? What to do? Take the fastest route home, that's what. Stupid not to have done that in the first place. Lunacy to lie on a dark, empty beach as if I hadn't a care in the world.

Damn, should have flagged a taxi down on Sea Road. Double back or keep going? An image popped into my head. I'd get into a taxi, slam the door shut. As we moved off, the driver would turn to me, his face a beaked Venetian mask.

The thought made me pick up speed again. I'd watched too many films, that was the trouble. But this wasn't a film. He'd broken into my house. This was real. I might be in danger. Might not be. Same wavelength? Or psycho?

Whatever, just keep running, Natalie, run like the wind. Save the risk assessment for a later day.

Then another plan struck me, one so audacious compared to my original notion it might have sprung from a different mind. I would phone him back. Right there and then, I would call Kagami in the street. Forget running scared and being the victim in the dark. I would take charge of the situation whether he liked it or not.

I slowed, breathing hard, legs quivering. Don't think, just do. My hands shook. I pressed 'call', listening out for a ring tone starting up nearby.

I heard nothing except the tone in my ear, the pump of my blood surrounding the sound.

Voicemail. It would go to voicemail.

Third ring.

A robotic, female voice, that's what I would hear.

Fourth ring.

A man answered. I didn't think my heart could thump any faster but it did. There was life on the other end.

'Natalie,' he said. 'Glad you called. I hoped you might.' His voice was deep, his tone amused.

'Where are you?' I said, heaving for breath. 'Can you see me? How close is close?'

'I can't see you,' he said smoothly. 'But I'm close.'

It took me a moment. 'Psychologically?'

'Yes,' he said.

'But not physically?'

'Not yet.'

'You're scaring me.'

'That's the point.'

I paused, leaning against the cream wall at the side of a townhouse, trying to catch my breath. 'Which makes it less scary.' One up to Natalie.

He laughed crisply. 'Then I'll have to try harder.'

'Trust me. You're doing fine.'

'So . . .' he said, adding no further words.

'So,' I replied. Across the street, a lank-haired man in an oversized suit walked by, occasionally lurching in a drunken sidestep. I was in ruined, period-drama territory, tatty townhouses forming orderly rows and gentle crescents, the pavements lined with tall railings like regimented black spears. Sepia net curtains hung in the windows, despondent 'Vacancies' signs repeating along the streets as regularly as the lanterns and peeling stucco columns. I watched the drunk man fumble at an enormous door then stagger into a dim hallway of nicotine-stained light.

'So,' I resumed. 'You broke into my house.'

'I need you to know I'm a serious player.'

'Oh, I've got that message,' I said. 'Loud and clear.'

'Who were you fucking that night? It sounded sweet.'

I began to walk on, too much adrenaline to keep still. 'None of your business. You've intruded enough already.'

'I've barely started.'

I tried to conceal my choppy breath. I wondered if he could hear my footsteps on the flagstones. 'If you push it too far –'

'I won't,' he said.

'You might,' I replied. 'You don't know what's too far for me.'

'True. But I'm a good judge, I pay attention. And if I push it too far, I think you'll let me. I think you'll like it.'

I said nothing, afraid it might be true.

'I know you better than you realise,' he went on. 'I've seen you running on the seafront in the evenings. You're determined, disciplined, focused. But even when you run, you look as if you want to escape that drive and order.'

'Why do you watch me?' I asked. 'Where do you live? Don't you have better things to do with your time?'

'I'm not stalking you, don't worry,' he said. 'I just want to get a good sense of who you are, of what makes you tick. I take my responsibilities as a dominant very seriously. If we're going to take this further, I need to see you when you're off guard. Easy for anyone to present a version of themself to someone online. That's not enough for me, not if we're going to play dangerous games together.'

'Is that what we're going to do?'

'I think we're doing it already.'

'I'm not sure what you mean by dangerous.'

'No,' he replied. 'If you knew, you could opt in or out, and that would remove the feeling of danger. You have to trust me.'

'Why should I?'

'Because you want to.'

I gave a hollow laugh as if to imply his answer was inadequate. But at the same time, I recognised he spoke the truth. I wanted to risk trusting him because I believed he could help satisfy my hunger to submit in a situation charged with danger. He knew, as did I, the allure of danger lay in its promise to make me experience submission as being brutally imposed upon me, a prospect infinitely more thrilling than yielding to him willingly like a doe-eyed puppy.

'I've met other women like you,' he continued. 'Women

who delight in being used, treated like a slut. Worthless. Insignificant. Just a cunt for me to shove my cock in. Women who need a man to take them over so they're free to be who they really are.'

'I can't have this conversation right now,' I said. 'I'm walking home. It's not convenient.'

'No need to be ashamed.'

'I'm not. But I can't respond properly. Someone might hear.'

'Then stop and listen to me.'

I kept up my brisk pace, still not knowing what to do. Pursue this? Or play safe? 'Pursue,' said my lust. 'Play safe,' said my head.

'I don't know you from Adam,' I said.

'Not true. We've shared a lot, been incredibly intimate and open with each other.'

'I don't know what you look like, where you live, who you are.'

'Do you want to know who I am?'

'Course I do,' I said, my casual tone belying my eagerness to meet him and discover more. 'I wouldn't tolerate your intrusions otherwise.'

'So trust me.'

I passed the gated entrance to Saltbourne Community Crafts where Liam has his workshop. A security light clicked on, flooding the cobbled courtyard with brightness. Liam would be horrified by my recklessness. With distance, I'd probably be horrified too but I was buzzing with fear and excitement, aching to hand myself over to this confident, challenging stranger who promised so much.

'And if I do decide to trust you,' I said, 'and give you a chance to prove yourself, then what?'

'Then I'll take this up a notch. I intend to kidnap you and hold you prisoner. My prisoner.'

'Whoa, steady on!'

He didn't reply. I walked faster as if trying to escape him but carrying him by my ear all the time. The silence continued for so long I feared he might hang up and leave his threat lingering. I assumed he wanted me to say yes or no. But I didn't know what I wanted to say so I kept quiet.

Sure, I'd shared an abduction fantasy with him but it didn't follow I wanted him to act on it as literally as he'd just implied. He must mean a scene, something we'd roleplay when we finally hooked up.

Eventually, I stopped hurrying, although my heart and mind kept up their wild, crazy paces. In the quietness, my footsteps were loud and lonely. I turned a corner and walked up a steep street of terraced stone cottages, slivers of light peeping through curtains. The small front gardens were tired, hollyhocks on the brink of toppling, their faded flowers of late summer rendered colourless by the night. The row was narrow with cars half-parked where people walk. There was no traffic at this hour. With an instinct for personal safety, I took to the middle of the road.

'You still there?' he asked. 'Or have I scared you off?'

'I'm still here.'

'You don't scare easily, do you?'

'Depends,' I said. 'I'm just trying to be realistic here. You're toying with me, I can see that. I don't think I'm in genuine danger.'

'But you can't ever be sure,' he said. 'Does that scare you?'

'I'm pleasantly scared,' I said. 'I guess I'm starting to trust you. I might regret this.'

'You won't,' he said. 'I'll make sure you don't.'

Above the rooftops in the distance, the castle ruins on the cliff-top were a hunched black tumble against a charcoal sky.

'It would be good to talk about this kidnap thing some more,' I said.

'Yeah?' He sounded breezy and sarcastic. 'You want to talk now?'

My heartbeat faltered. I turned, scanning the quiet street, unnerved by the threatening edge in his voice. The curtains were open in one of the cottages and on an enormous, wall-mounted TV screen images played of a bomb-ravaged dirt road in the Middle East.

'Where are you?' I said. 'Are you nearby? Are you watching me?'

'What do you think?'

'Hey, this isn't fair.' I began striding quickly, my senses sharpening. 'I'm a woman walking home at night. Don't fuck with that. I need to know what's real danger and what's play.'

'Calm down,' he said. 'I'm miles away. You're safe from me.'

I slowed. 'OK, good, thanks.'

'For the meantime, at any rate,' he added.

'Ha ha,' I said dryly, trying to show I wasn't afraid.

'So this kidnap thing,' he said, echoing my choice of words and making them seem trite. 'You up for it?'

I swallowed, my throat dry as a bone. 'Maybe.' I sounded cheerful and unfazed, not at all how I felt. 'I need to know more though. Maybe we should meet for coffee and discuss.'

He laughed loudly. 'Coffee? I don't think so.'

'Why not?'

'Too easy, too pat. I want to give you the best experience I can and take you close to the reality of what you crave. No good if we've chatted nicely over a latte beforehand. The thrill is on the edge where fear and lust don't know which way to fall. Don't you agree?'

Jeez, he understood what I wanted so well.

'What's the plan, then?' I asked. 'How do we do this?'

'You want to hear what I have in mind?'

I was almost home but I didn't want his voice inside my house, didn't want him that close again. A short flight of stone steps cut into a low wall led to a tarmac path edged with straggly grass and a rusting, municipal handrail. Up there, an expanse of cloud-veiled darkness lay over a shabby football pitch, a hut selling tea and ices, and one of the designated routes to the ruined, cliff-top castle. I hunkered down in the steps, hidden and safe, protected by slumbering stone and by the silence of the centuries.

My voice was a whisper. 'Yes, tell me.'

'I intend to kidnap you and hold you prisoner,' he repeated. 'I'm going to snatch you when you least expect it and take you far away from your life. I'm going to take you over completely. I'm going to lead you down dark paths where you'll meet someone you don't know: yourself. This isn't about handcuffs or pain or roleplay. Those are just props I use to reduce you to a deep state of submission. And when you're there, you'll let me do anything I want. You're so gone you can barely even speak. You're not my prisoner at all. If I told you to walk away, you'd beg me to keep you safe. Not safe in my arms but safe in my sadism. That's where you want to be. That's where I want to keep you.'

I gulped nervously. He seemed to know what he was doing. His confidence alone excited me, not to mention the content of his words. For a moment, I forgot my strategy of honesty and self-assertion. I wanted him to take over entirely and give me no say in the matter. Then I remembered it was important to let him know we were matched in our desires, and that I agreed to this. 'I think I'd like that,' I said, speaking softly in my stone-step nook.

I strained to catch the sound of him breathing. Was he aroused on the other end of the line? Was he jerking off?

After a pause he said, 'Listen. And listen carefully because you need to understand this, Natalie. I don't give a single fuck what you like.'

With that, he ended the call.

Five

For days, his parting shot echoed through my mind. I told myself he did care, of course he did. He was merely role-playing the bad guy, assuming I'd find it horny. And oh boy, did I ever. I loved the idea he'd be rough and cruel, that he'd make out my desires were of no significance and he'd fuck me this way and that, using me to satisfy his own unrestrained hunger.

Den was a far cry from nice-guy Grant who would instruct me to lie back and enjoy. And that's what I was searching for, wasn't it? A dark, twisted dominant man who'd be part of my journey towards my Northern Lights. Those lights, my shimmering destination, didn't reside with an individual. They were the glow of me understanding and accepting my weird, kinky self. Den was a train ride on that journey. So at last, it appeared my luck was in.

Nonetheless, I longed for concrete details. I figured Den was withholding practicalities to add realism to our kidnap scenario. I simply had to do what I'd said and trust him. Or more accurately, take a chance on him.

Mostly I was prepared to take that risk. Just sometimes,

alone at night when the house was taunting me with its creaky, old bones, I feared he might break in, carry me off to an unknown place and I'd never be heard from again. In the clear light of day I dismissed the notion. I had a job to go to, a cat to feed, friends who would notice my absence.

One evening, watching a band play in a local beer garden as part of a mini festival, I grew convinced he was in the audience. Moths flickered in the halogen glow of floodlights while chatter burbled below the music. The air, warm and still, smelled of cigarettes, beer and a pungent, heady perfume, night-scented stocks or honeysuckle. From a tangle of foliage, a small, ornamental lion smiled up at me. In my veins, the Rioja to blood ratio was high.

I loved life. There and then, it was held and perfect. Everything around me glowed with a quality apparently greater than itself, as if the essence of the thing had leaked beyond its edges. Then I noticed a guy at the back of the beer garden, standing with a pint in his hand. Tall, built, shorn head. My heart flared even as I told myself that plenty of tall, muscular guys shaved their heads.

But the idea took hold and in the evening's wine-smudged enchantment, the thought of him watching me became conceivable and exciting. I kept glancing over my shoulder to try and catch him looking my way. To my disappointment, his focus stayed on the band.

When the song ended, applause clattered. I leaned across to Marsha, speaking loudly above the noise. 'Hey Marsh, I've got a new man on the go!'

I wasn't even sure why or what I was telling her. I'd no intention of fessing up to anyone about the kidnap fantasy, especially not Marsha, eight years married and safe as houses.

She'd think I was nuts and probably come up with a hundred and one reasons why I needed to stop.

'Yeah?' Marsha moved her glass to rest her arms on the table. Red-wine stains bracketed the corners of her mouth and her tongue was purple. 'Where d'ya find him? The internet again?'

I laughed. 'Where else? He's called Den, thirty-six years old.'

'Go on.'

I realised I didn't have much else to tell. 'I haven't actually met him yet but we're getting on great in email.'

Marsha grinned. 'Well, good luck with that, babes. Keep me posted, eh?' Then she sat back as the next song started, a haunting ambient warble bleeding into the night.

We're getting on great in email. I had to admit, it sounded lame.

Moments later, when I glanced over my shoulder, the man had vanished. I felt as if I'd conjured him up by enthusiasm alone and he'd dematerialised as a consequence of Marsha's disinterest.

I said nothing else to anyone for a couple more days. Heard nothing either. That was the worst of it. I kept wondering whether to text him. '*Hi, I enjoyed our chat the other night.*' Or '*So when do I get kidnapped?*' Or maybe something porny. '*I want to suck your big, hard cock like a dirty little slut.*'

But I didn't text. Sometimes I checked my phone history to look at the time of his initial text (23.53) and my return call (00.02). I wasn't looking for anything, just proof of a connection.

The following week, I went to see Liam. I'll tell him everything, I thought. Well, nearly everything. Since Liam and I had started seeing each other a few months previously, we'd always let each other know if someone else was on the scene, even if they were just a potential date. Our understanding was another relationship wouldn't necessarily affect what we had, unless a new lover wanted monogamy, but being open about these things was polite and decent. Besides, honesty kept complications at bay.

It was a Tuesday, and I'd worked till half six, finishing off an urgent report whose formatting had acquired a life of its own at the last minute. Everything is urgent in my job and yet nothing is. I work for Saltbourne Council's parking department. We're not performing open-heart surgery and yet my line manager acts as if we are. She's a woman who causes everyone's stress levels to rise merely by entering a room, half-running in a stiff-legged kind of way, hobbled by her pencil skirt.

When I left the office, I fancied a drink and some non-parking related conversation so I texted Liam to see if he was around. He was still at the workshop. '*Drop in*,' he replied. '*Am carving something I think you will like.*'

I bought four bottles of fancy cider, Liam's tipple of choice. He suits cider. His hair is russet like autumn apples, his skin creamy like their flesh, and he spends a lot of time hanging out with trees. Saltbourne Community Crafts, the location of Liam's workshop, is a council-supported, co-operative venture housed in former stables in the shabby Georgian part of Old Town. Centuries ago, when storms sent the fashionable set hurrying back to London, mud on their breeches, seaweed in their ringlets, the townhouses were left to rot.

Today, they're B&Bs and cheap hotels. Several are derelict, their windows boarded up, puny buddleia sprouting from their cracks. When I'd spoken to Den while leaning against one of these buildings, I hadn't thought it might be unwise to linger in a slightly dodgy part of town. Ah well, I'd survived, hadn't I?

Community Crafts is one of the areas small successes. The workshops edge the old stableyard and when the weather's good, some of the artisans set up stalls on the cobbles or open their doors, inviting the public to watch them work.

The place was quiet when I arrived, just a couple of guys across the yard from Liam's place smoking by a cluster of reconditioned furniture. At the security gate, Liam greeted me with a kiss, his copper curls flecked with sawdust, scruffy T-shirt hanging from broad, angular shoulders. He smelled of wood and sweat. I wanted to eat him. In the workshop, he opened two ciders. My groin gave a quick thump at the sight of his enormous, long hands, his thumb on his Swiss army knife, his wrist angling in a flick on the bottle tops.

He passed me a bottle and our fingers brushed together. He has such beautiful hands, big, knuckly, vigorous and clever. Even when they're at rest, those hands seem full of life, as if every action they ever performed simmers below the surface and every future action is on the brink of being realised. They are hands that can carve wood, slice leather, fashion rope from nettles, build fires in forests, break the necks of small mammals, roll joints, construct shelters and make me come and gush, time and again.

'Cheers!' We clinked bottles and I sank into a low chair of chrome and torn leather, feet on the cluttered worktop. A fluorescent strip light hummed faintly above us, its cold glare outshining mellow sunshine filtering in through high, dusty windows at the rear of the room. Scraps of leather, chunks of wood, sawdust and twists of metal littered the cobbled floor while all around us, tools poked from pots or dangled from racks like small, medieval torture implements. Liam stood, arse perched on the worktop's edge, and circled my bare ankle with his fingers, rubbing while I moaned about my boss.

'I'm glad you're here,' he said when I'd finished. 'I've been thinking about you a lot. Well, about your vagina, to be precise.'

I laughed, taken aback. Liam and I generally take a while to catch up and settle into each other's space before we start getting sexy. By now, Baxter Logan would have had my clothes off and his cock in my mouth, but not Liam. We don't share that lustful frenzy. The 'buddy' takes precedence over the 'fuck'.

'Oh? And what did you conclude about my vagina?' The word was amusingly clinical between us.

'I'm making you a dildo out of cherry wood.' Liam reached across the table and held up a thick, L-shaped dildo, curved in unusual ways. The wood was pale and unpolished, its surface channelled with rough, narrow grooves, its bulky length striated with a deep pink grain. Liam turned the object in his hands. I sat up for a closer look.

'See, it has an upright handle. Easy to manipulate if you're on your own. I'm thinking of drilling a hole in this ridge so a bullet vibe could go in.' Liam's slender fingers moved across the wood in synch with his explanation. The object seemed an expansion of him, a natural creation flowing from his body. The connectedness of his hands and the carving struck me as having a profound simplicity. This was a timeless craft being employed to enhance a timeless activity.

'This flared part should stimulate your G.' He ran his thumb over the lump. 'Designed with you in mind, the anatomy of your cunt.'

My body responded as if he'd stroked, not the dil, but me. 'Can I see?' I asked.

Liam handed me the piece. The intimacy of the exchange moved me, leaving me choked, but I hid it well. Liam's hands had been inside me so often and he'd combined this knowledge of my body with his talent and skill to design an item we could use together to make sex even more magical. I caressed the hard, rippled surface, fingertips running over a hundred tiny chisel-marks, each one chipped by Liam. Had he been thinking about us as he'd carved, flakes of wood falling around his feet, his cock lifting in his combats?

I suddenly didn't want to tell him about Den. Liam was so sensitive and earnest, so considerate and good, that my fantasies, relative to his world, seemed corrupt, black and ugly. Liam wasn't judgmental but, nonetheless, I feared introducing the concept of Den might sully what we shared. How, after Liam had spent hours carving a dil to give me pleasure, could I explain I'd been flicking my bean over a bloke I'd found on the internet who'd hung up on me after saying, 'I don't give a single fuck what you like'? Oh, and that this stranger had been stalking me, had threatened to kidnap me, and I hadn't called the cops?

'It's beautiful,' I said. 'Thank you.' I inhaled the wood, savouring its bright scent. 'And big! And hard. I'm worried it might hurt.'

Liam smiled. 'It's not finished yet. I could smooth it down if you want but I thought the texture might feel nice. It needs to dry for a few weeks then I'll seal it with—'

'Whoa, hang on! Are you saying I don't get to test drive this till autumn? Too cruel!'

Liam laughed. 'I'm never cruel.' He said it as if it were a bonus. 'Do you like it?'

'Adore it.'

Liam tipped back several gulps of cider then grinned at me. 'Last time . . .' he began. He thumbed the rim of his bottle. I recalled Liam coming in my mouth, the crash downstairs, and all that had happened since then.

'It was . . . I felt different,' Liam continued. 'Maybe it was the storm. I felt like I'd released something.'

'You did that all right.'

Liam laughed. 'Something primal, aggressive. Dunno. For some reason, I felt like I could give in to an urge. An urge I can't quite explain. I keep re-living that night in my mind.'

I felt guilty because I hadn't thought about it much. I'd been preoccupied with the mysteries of Den, distracted by a disappointing date, stressed at work. 'It was great,' I said. 'And you can always be primal and aggressive with me. As if you need telling.'

Liam moved towards me, grinning. 'Roar,' he said jokily. I tried to overlook his self-consciousness.

He knelt by my chair, stroked a hand along my jaw and leaned in for a kiss. His lips were cider-cooled and moist. I held him close, sliding my fingers into the red-brown curls at the nape of his neck.

He pulled away. 'Mmm,' he said, smiling. He stroked a hand down my chest, skimmed my breasts through my clothes then nudged my top higher so he could caress my bare waist. 'You make me massively horny,' he whispered.

His hands felt good. I gripped his hair again, tugging at his short curls, encouraging him to be more forceful. He groaned in pleasure, which wasn't the result I'd been aiming for. Slipping a hand under his faded T-shirt, I scraped his back with my short nails. He arched his spine, giving a hiss of enjoyment. I moved in for a kiss and pulled on his lower lip, sucking it between my teeth, nipping hard before he slipped away.

'Ah!' He dabbed a hand to his mouth, checking for blood.

I grinned and he stared back before it dawned on him I was offering a challenge. He laughed lightly and moved between my knees, reading my body language and responding to my tacit invitation he take control. He pushed my arms up against the leather chair, pinning me with one hand and signifying without pressure that my arms should stay raised. He wrinkled my skirt high and nuzzled at my clothes, scattering kisses where he found skin, his free hand swirling and massaging on my thighs and midriff.

The contrast between his slender, calloused hand and the plump wetness of his lips left my body tingling, the folds of my groin fattening with desire. I groaned quietly, basking in his indulgence until, fingers twitching, I slid free of his imprisoning gesture. When I tipped forward to cup his crotch, I found him big and stiff, his shaft trapped by his combats. My pulses raced as I explored, palming the angled heft of him through heavy cotton. A breath caught in Liam's throat, a noise like a sudden breeze rushing through brittle trees. He gazed down at me, eyes droopy with lust.

With a single, slender finger, he grazed my gusset. The silky fabric was as thin as molecules. My breath came faster and I felt like I was falling. I closed my eyes, blotches of mustard-yellow and violet swelling and dying in the dark behind my lids. My limbs turned syrupy and it was with some effort that I swivelled in the chair to grant Liam better access. He bent over me as we rubbed and kissed, moaning softly, breathing deeply. His body was smooth, sinewy and warm, hard muscle shifting as he moved. His work-roughened fingers scoured my skin, his touch sure and strong. Everyday life was swimming away and we were slipping towards that gauzy zone of mutual lust, no distinction between giving and receiving.

My touch inspired his touch; his lust fuelled my lust; my gasps met his groans.

I kissed his neck, bristles prickling my lips, and tugged impatiently at his top. When he leaned back to drag his tee over his head, his torso stretched to expose the corrugations of his ribs and the neat scoop of his pecs. Rust-tinged hair flamed in his armpits while his biceps and their pale undersides flexed athletically. He cast his tee onto a heap of lumber while I tried to ease his belt from his buckle. My fingers were all thumbs so Liam took over, stripping completely and dropping his remaining clothes onto sawdust-strewn cobbles. Muscle and sinew corded his arms, his summer-bronzed skin dappled with freckles, the hair lightened to a fuzz of strawberry blond. His cock was high against his belly, laced with veins, its stout head glossed to an obscenely ruddy hue. He stood tall and still, confident in his nudity and pausing with a thought.

'One sec,' he said. He padded away to turn the key in the rickety stable door, his arse flexing cutely as he walked. The sparseness of hair on his upper body, set against the thick, wiry growth on his legs, made him look like an escaped faun.

I was dressed for work and briefly at a loss as to where to put my clothes. I was about to unbutton my shirt to hang it on the lathe but Liam was returning already, cock bobbing stiffly. He dropped to his knees between my thighs. Hell, who cared about clothes? I sank deeper into the chair, raising my hips so Liam could remove my underwear. He tossed my knickers onto his clothes then held my thighs apart, gazing down. I squirmed under his attention, feeling more exposed than if I were naked. The blood in my groin pumped harder, leaving my lips so engorged I fancied Liam might have seen them bloom like a flower in fast-motion.

He dipped down to flick his tongue over my clit, an isolated, teasing touch. I whimpered, rubbing his shoulders, my hips tilting in search of more. He printed kisses on my inner thighs, nuzzling lightly before he covered my moistness with a wide, generous mouth. Oh, so hot, so wet. He waggled his tongue into my slit, sliding my flesh apart, and lapped at my crease, letting his fluids wash over me. I shut my eyes, mewing while his mouth danced to a languid beat, his tongue flicking and churning.

For the next few minutes I was gone, my mind blank, my clit throbbing, as I dissolved into Liam's slippery caress. I might have stayed in that lost space if my phone hadn't started ringing in my bag. Liam glanced up at me, his dark ginger curls askew, eyes unfocused, lips and chin glinting wetly. 'You need to get that?' he asked in a throaty voice.

'No,' I whispered. 'Don't stop.'

'Let me try the dil,' he said, reaching for it.

I was coasting on a high of arousal, amenable to pretty much anything. Only one thought threatened to draw me from the moment: was that Den calling? No reason why it should be but I hadn't heard from him for a while. And friends and family generally text rather than phone.

Liam rolled a condom over the dil, telling me the wood wasn't seasoned and needed protecting from moisture. Well, I was beyond moist so that made sense and the sheath stopped me worrying about splinters. He positioned the hard head of the phallus at my entrance. All my thoughts returned to where I was, to the pressure at the lips of my cunt. Slowly, Liam eased the wooden length into me. I gasped at its inflexibility, crying out when the thickness of the G-spot bump prised me further open. 'Gorgeous,' said Liam, his energies focused on my enjoyment.

I heard my phone honk. Text message, maybe voicemail. Fuck it. Forget it. Liam nudged the toy up and down, pressing against that tender spot inside me. Soon, I was mindless again, overtaken. My inner flesh thickened fast. I knew what was coming next. I would ejaculate. I wouldn't be able to help it. Liam would take the release from me, extracting pleasure as no one had ever done before.

He scissored his fingers either side of my clit and rubbed steadily. I grew breathless, dizzy. When I was close to something – I hardly knew what, to coming or gushing – Liam withdrew the dil and replaced it with his middle fingers. He hooked them on to my G, pressing back and forth, hard, ruthless and fast. Sensation crested, became urgent, and a hot cascade of bliss trickled inside me. I wailed, my pelvic muscles spreading to a loose, easy freedom as warm liquid poured onto Liam's wrist and splashed against my thighs.

'Yes,' hissed Liam. 'Fuck, yes.'

I flopped back against the chair, panting.

After a while, Liam asked, 'You OK?'

'Totally,' I said, grinning. 'I need a bit of a breather though.'

I drew Liam close to rest his head on my stomach. Ejaculation, still relatively new to me, often left me shocked and drained. For me, gushing wasn't climactic but it was damn close. When Liam had first made me squirt, I hadn't even noticed the tipping point when liquid rushed. Sure, his actions brought intense pleasure but squirting wasn't peaking. A lot of fuss about nothing, I'd thought. All that pressure on women to find their G-spot was due to squirting's popularity in porn where evidence of pleasure counts for more than her experience of it.

But the more Liam made me squirt, the better it became. My body responded quickly, and I learned to ride the rise and fall. Before long, without me even trying, I was gushing fast and hard, sensitised to its triggers and craving the release it brought. Sex with Liam was scattered with sopping-wet pleasure-bombs, an extravagant mess we made en route to the euphoric heights of orgasm.

'I think we need a towel,' I said as Liam sat back.

He fetched a clean cloth from a drawer and I mopped squeakily at the leather seat as Liam rolled a joint. 'Well, I heartily approve of the new dil,' I said.

'Me too.' Liam glanced up from sprinkling grass and grinned. 'Perfect fit. I'm thinking of making more. Not for you. To sell.'

'Where? Here? Bit risky, isn't it? Supposing the *Saltbourne Echo* got wind of it? You'd be all over the papers. The council might boot you out.'

'Online.' He lit the joint and inhaled deeply. 'I've made a prototype of some leather cuffs. I'll show you later.'

'Oh, wow. Cool.' I watched Liam release a slow trickle of smoke. I tried to let a decent interval pass before saying, 'Could you pass me my bag? Just want to check who called.'

Liam obliged, placing the bag at my feet. I rummaged for my phone. One missed call, number unknown. And a text. Oh boy, oh boy. It was Den! My silly heart went skippety-skip. I realised I was grinning and quickly stopped. Turning, I glanced at the high row of dust-clouded windows to the rear of Liam's workshop, half-fearing a beaked face might be peering in. I thumbed through to his message. It read '*FIVE*.'

I was unable to repress a confused, tetchy 'Huh?'

'Everything OK?' asked Liam.

'Oh, fine. Just family nonsense from my sister.' I returned the phone to my bag.

Liam passed me the joint.

Five? What did that mean? Had we ever had a conversation about numbers? Not that I could recall. I tried not to dwell on it, knowing full well he was trying to screw with my mind.

Five what, though?

Five other women in his life?

He wanted to fuck me five times fast?

His house number?

The most times he'd ever come in a single day?

I wondered if he was expecting me to reply. I considered doing so but ultimately opted to play cool and ignore him.

The next day, at a similar time, he sent another text: '*FOUR*.'

My world slowed as his meaning became clearer.

He was coming to get me. The countdown had begun. He was going to snatch me in the street or grab me in my house. Or maybe he was going to laugh when we reached zero and nothing happened.

The following day, he picked up speed, two messages within twelve hours:

'*THREE*.'

'*TWO*.'

Six

At Saltbourne Borough Council Parking Department, the staff attend so many meetings they barely have time to do their jobs. We hold meetings to decide whether to hold meetings. When someone phones for a colleague who's away from her desk, we say, 'Sorry, she's in a meeting,' and genuinely mean it.

Inevitably, when Den texted, I was in a meeting. I held my phone under the table, thumbing surreptitiously while someone quacked on about a topic I cared next to nothing about. His message appeared, a single, stark word: '*ONE.*'

I kept my head low, gazing at the screen, fear and excitement making my cheeks flame, my heart pound. Words from a world where parking restrictions mattered floated around me. Mundanity receded, became surreal. Double yellow what? I held reality in the palm of my hand, a text from this intimate stranger, finalising our deal without detail. We would hook up, and soon. This was happening.

With the moment closing in on me, my saner self urged caution. The cons marshalled to threaten the pros. We had no safeword. Supposing I got cold feet and cried, 'No!' when he jumped me? He'd think I was acting, creating the illusion of being a terrified abductee as part of a roleplay. I had visions of him bundling me into the back seat of his car, my protests falling on deaf ears. 'Shut it, bitch,' he'd snarl, silencing me by tying a stocking around my mouth.

The thought of him ignoring me, hurting me with his careless greed, made my cunt pulse with dark, treacherous longings. How quickly the cons had become pros.

Because the trouble was, I couldn't imagine not wanting this.

I knew that fantasising about danger and the reality of treading a thin line were different. But as far as I could see, the only significant problems were someone seeing us, getting the wrong idea and calling the cops. Or him shoving me in the boot of his car, a space as cold, dark and airless as a coffin. Should I mention my mild claustrophobia? I knew I could take control if I wished. I could refuse to be cowed by sneery comments about lattes and insist on discussing the kidnap scenario beforehand. I could state my limits, fix a safeword, arrange a time. We could draw up a contract so everything was crystal clear. And if he didn't like that approach, well, the deal was off. I would return to internet dating with renewed determination and find someone else to play with.

But, being honest, I wanted our arrangement to continue along its same uncertain track. I reckoned if I genuinely wanted us to stop at any point, I'd be able to communicate that. I would change my body language, address him directly and say something crisp and efficient, such as, 'I would very much like this to stop now. I am no longer enjoying it. Thank you.'

Only an idiot would misread that and be unable to distinguish it from me saying, 'No, stop!' when I was feigning resistance. And Den wasn't an idiot. I could trust him to set safe parameters and not put me in serious jeopardy. After all, Baxter and I didn't start with an agreed safeword. He learned to read me in bed and I worked to show him how I liked it, just as a couple might do during vanilla sex. And the limits of our play flexed and expanded as we got to know each other better.

Besides, I'd explored kink online and I knew safewords weren't compulsory. 'Edgeplay' was a concept I'd recently discovered and I'd added it to my mental BDSM dictionary along with other words which had once seemed peculiar in the context of sex, such as 'scene', 'submission' and 'play'.

Although the definition seemed hard to pin down, I understood edgeplay to mean scenes where kinky activity takes place on the threshold of the submissive's fear. Safewords aren't used since they remove the fear. I was pleased to learn about edgeplay, not least because its existence made me feel less alone in wanting to be taken to the edge of safety, to the zone where my lust could blossom in darkness.

I recalled a word Den had once used in email: *liminal*. I'd had to look it up. Liminal, I learned, referred to times and places which were neither one thing nor the other: the margins and boundaries; the in-between spaces; those unstable moments of change such as the hours of twilight, the greying, glittered suspension between day and night.

That's where I wanted to be, not secure in a walled fortress but blissing out on submission in the shifting magic of dusk.

Ultimately, my greatest concern was not my welfare but that, in clarifying an arrangement, Den and I might negotiate its heart out by stripping away risk and fear. What would be the point? I wanted to feel this in my veins, in my deepest shadows. I wanted lust spiked with terror. I wanted to be in his power, my desires ostensibly secondary to his. I wanted to know the truth of my fantasy of being abducted and taken to a place where I would be tested. How far could I go? What would happen to me on the margins of fear? Who would I become? That's what I wanted. I didn't want us to arrange to play a nice game by nicely discussed rules.

Potentially dangerous, I know, considering I barely knew him, but that potential thrilled me. I was drawn to the edges. I wanted an adventure with him, with this mysterious man whose face I hadn't seen. On paper, the risk seemed enormous. He could be anyone, some internet freak intent on hoodwinking me with false photos and lies. But in my gut, I felt he was sincere, experienced, and a key part of the journey I wanted to be on.

On reflection, I think I imported my trust in Baxter Logan – sexual trust, not emotional – into this burgeoning relationship. Baxter screwed me over, big time, but he never let me down in the sack. He would err on the side of excess rather than caution, and I appreciated that. He knew women weren't porcelain dolls. And although Baxter could take me to the edge of fear, especially when I was first getting to know him; although he could break me and leave me sobbing and lost, afterwards he'd always hold me tight, locking me in protection and comfort.

My phone vibrated again, a quiver in my hand as if it too had a nervous heart. I peered below the meeting table, angling my head, my eyes low. Den again. More words this time: '*WATCH YOUR BACK.*'

I almost swung around. Was he here, hiding behind the projection screen? Under the trolley of beverages? I was so flustered, I missed hearing the resolution to the saga of bollards being illicitly placed in reserved parking bays in Kelhawk Close.

Later, when I was leaving for the day, my colleague Sandra enquired after my weekend plans. On Sandra's desk was a diorama of soft toys so excessive you could barely make out the angles of her PC. I imagined all the floppy-eared rabbits, teddies in dresses, dangling monkeys and pink hippos clasping their mouths in shock if I told her the truth: 'Ah, you know, getting abducted by some pervert I met on the interwebz. Yourself?'

I walked across town, heading home without diversions because I didn't want to confuse him if he was tracking my usual route. Walking across town is like walking into the past. Modern office blocks, newly paved streets and Castlegate, our big, bland shopping plaza, lead to labyrinthine stone streets, pink and gold domes, and in the distance, the huddled, cliff-top ruins of the castle.

Den occupied my every thought. The beat of my feet on the pavement echoed the drumming in my heart and cunt. Ordinarily I'd listen to my iPod, but not today. I needed to stay vigilant. Summer was on the wane, the air carrying a slight drop in temperature and a whiff of damp, crumbly earth.

I figured if Den were going to abduct me in daylight, he'd choose Old Town where the streets are quiet and narrow. But a Friday when people were heading home from work, buying bottles of wine, bunches of flowers, bags of crack and so on, wasn't ideal.

I considered taking back routes to give him a better chance. I imagined his strong arms around me, one clamped to my mouth, the other hooked around my waist as he tugged me off the main drag. And for the next few hours, though I might struggle and protest, I'd be his captive, his sex slave, his whore. The prospect thrilled and horrified. I wanted it and I didn't.

For the first time, another danger presented itself to me: supposing I fell in love with him? I wasn't looking for love, not by a long shot, but I could accept these things happen when you're least expecting them. This might start as an exploratory, no-strings-attached encounter and develop into something else, just as my relationship with Baxter had done.

But I was older and wiser now, less permeable to another's attention. Well, I hoped I was. The trouble is, love and lust are capricious beasts. I couldn't be completely sure I was invulnerable to the former, and didn't want to be either. I didn't want to be hard, to reject love to protect myself from pain. Nor did I want to be soft. My need to stay guarded conflicted with my insistence I should try to be open. No one likes a cynic, apart from fellow cynics, of course.

I kept walking, feeling as if my feet were on a tightrope. Decisions and diversions happen in a moment. I could take a left here, then a right to walk that half-dead street parallel to my usual route. But it didn't happen. I tried again. Nats, go down that squashed, cabbagey alley behind the market place. But still nothing happened. My mind kept suggesting new routes but my feet were running the show, being practical and sticking to routine, keeping their distance from the fantasies of my head. I thought about Saltbourne's secret tunnels, dug hundreds of years ago by smugglers bringing in tobacco, sugar, alcohol and silks, and wondered if he might be lurking down there like an underground troll.

I passed a household store, dustpans, buckets and squeegees amassed outside, and heard my name being called. *Natalie, Natalie!*

My senses seized up. I turned. A blur of gaudy plastics swept past my eyes. Upside-down brooms and mops loomed like bouquets of huge, alien flowers. Pan scourers rushed past, clouds of pewter on a sky of pavement. Yellow sponges like honeycombs. Feet, trainers, sandals.

'Watch out!'

'Sorry, sorry.'

I kept walking, my heart going crazy. I was alone. I'd survived. I'd passed the buckets and brooms, the chemist's, the kebab shop and was crossing the road to more salubrious streets. It must have been the wind calling me – *Natalie!* – a trick of the air. *Natalie!* As if I were trapped in a murmuring seashell.

I was tempted to stop off at the little Sainsbury's, a familiar, ordinary place, then I pictured myself on CCTV, a grainy ghost on the TV news in the hunt for a missing woman. Jeez, Nats, such a drama queen! You're not about to go missing, OK? You're gearing up for some kinky sex, that's all. Lots of people do it. Well, maybe not lots. Some.

Either way, I didn't stop off at Sainsbury's.

I made it home unscathed. After the adrenaline pump of my journey, I was deflated. Yet, moments after I'd closed the door, kicked off my shoes and stroked Rory behind her silky, black ears, I was relieved to have avoided any drama. The evening ahead was mine. I was tired. I wanted to drink wine, eat good food and watch bad TV. I rarely went running on Friday nights. It was my time to kick back. I used to hang out on FancyFree, shooting the digital breeze, but not any more.

From the basement kitchen, I went into the high-walled garden where a diffuse September light glowed among deep green foliage. I checked the wooden gate to Tanner's Passage was bolted. In the kitchen, I locked the back door and drew the gingham curtains. As an extra precaution, I shoved the kitchen table against the back door. I refreshed Rory's litter tray. We would stay home, both of us safe and sound.

By that point, I was tired rather than excited. I was no longer in the mood for kidnap. I went to the top of the house and worked my way down, closing all curtains, shutting out the daylight and him. If he came snooping, it would look as if I were out for the evening. I would watch TV in the dark.

Downstairs in the kitchen again, I did a final check, turned off the light then tiptoed upstairs with my microwaved meal, ready to clock off and chill out. I felt pleased with myself for being cool and calm. I'd taken charge of the situation: hey, mister, you can abduct me when I'm good and ready, OK?

Only later, when an overly loud TV advert had me frantically turning down the volume, did I realise I hadn't shut him out at all. I'd shut myself in. I was cowering, hiding away to protect myself from what I craved. For all intents and purposes, he was here with me, a sinister, invisible companion. He was lurking outside the window, in the garden, behind the sofa and in every one of my Den-obsessed brain cells.

It was as if he'd kidnapped me before we'd even started. Or kidnapped my mind.

That night, it took me ages to get to sleep. I counted hundreds of sheep but the slightest noise startled me. When I relaxed, my imagination conjured up scenes of him making me surrender to his power and aggression, or of him seducing me with clever manipulations. He'd wrongfoot me, as Alistair Fitch had done, meaning I couldn't be held responsible for my actions. I'd be free to do anything I fancied, no matter how filthy, and no one could judge or blame me, least of all myself.

Fantasy, pure delicious fantasy.

I brought myself off thinking of Den toying with me. I was standing naked in a room, accepting his touches, a stroke here, a caress there. He kept his distance, watching me all the while, murmuring words that left me weak with desire. He smiled when I begged him to fuck me and he laughed, victorious, when I begged him to stop.

Afterwards, I thought about Stockholm syndrome and wondered again if I might fall in love with my faceless captor. No, impossible. Just some guy on the internet who'd caught my imagination. But as I grew sleepier and logic started to sway, I figured I'd already fallen.

Or at least, I'd fallen in love with a fantasy.

'Go to The Pepperpot Café on Sea Road between 11.30 and 12. Go via Belmont Gardens and Little Kent Road. Don't be scared.'

My heart pumped at triple speed. Way to make someone scared: tell them, 'Don't be scared.'

But at least I knew the score. No more waiting and wondering. We were on. Either I would meet him in The Pepperpot or he would accost me en route. Both options were grand, and beyond that, well, we'd see.

I had little over an hour to get my act together. Should I pack an overnight bag? No, too much. I flung underwear from drawers onto the futon, surveying my range of lycra and lace. Black boy-shorts with lilac rosettes? Sable and cream cami and knicks set? Or maybe the vampish leopard-print briefs with a mismatching bra to indicate I hadn't over-thought my lingerie.

I scoured the contents of my wardrobe. Too many clothes but never enough. What does one wear to an abduction? Not jeans or trousers. Too tricky to remove in a fight situation. But that could be a plus. I had to remind myself, I might not actually like him, nor him me. We might not have chemistry. It might be an awful date-cum-fantasy kidnap that we'd call time on after ten minutes.

In the end, I left the house as if I were heading in to town on an ordinary Saturday. Well, almost. My underwear was fancy and in my handbag were condoms, facial wipes, moisturiser, a travel toothbrush kit and make up. If we were going to have sex, I'd need to freshen up afterwards.

I gave the house a cursory tidy in case we returned to mine. I didn't know where he lived. Maybe he'd booked a hotel room. If so, I hoped it wasn't in one of those ghost-of-Jane-Austen B&Bs near Liam's workshop. Perhaps he had a garage. The thought of being held captive in a garage appealed: slightly squalid and concealed, masculine and implicitly dangerous. People kept dark secrets in garages. No one stumbles across what's inside unless they've actively gone looking for something.

My hands shook as I locked the front door.

I walked quickly, desire weighing in my cunt. The day was unseasonably cool and grey. It made me anxious, as if the weather disapproved and were advising me to stay home. I tried to imagine his face by matching it to his body and what I knew of his personality. Intelligent, confident, worked in the Arts. Either a dancer or a liar. Liked to cultivate an air of mystery. But he wasn't a jigsaw and all I could conjure up were hazy images of blandly handsome faces, the sort you'd see in magazines. Yet I felt sure I'd recognise him when I saw him.

We were on a journey together. I imagined he would take me to places in my psyche I didn't know existed, places even Baxter hadn't probed.

Cutting through Belmont Gardens, a small park of

winding paths and rose beds, my excitement began to race. I felt I had a life I myself might be envious of. Here I was, a young woman with a half-decent job, own home, plenty of friends, and I was striding through a twee little park, full of yearning. Not only that, unbeknown to all who passed by with their tiny dogs and bread for the ducks, I was acting on those longings, following my own paths. I wasn't going to stay home steeped in shameful, guilty dreams. I was claiming my desires, about to meet a man who would whisk me to a hidden world.

I smiled to myself, glancing around the park as I walked. Was he in the bushes? Behind that old oak? Under the ornamental bridge?

No, not in any of those places. Then I was out of the park, heading along George Street, a soft breeze bringing saltiness to my nostrils. Passing one of the steep roads leading to the front, I glimpsed the steely sea in the distance, strings of bunting above Swan Lake's pedalos providing a flutter of cheerless colour. Next stop Little Kent Road.

But I didn't make it that far.

I turned left. Coldness wound around my ankles, an odd sensation like being grabbed by nothing, cuffs of ice rather than leather.

Weird. But no, not for me. Just a refrigerator truck unloading plastic crates at the back of a shop, cold air seeping out in a cloud of frostiness. I kept walking, goosebumps prickling on my bare legs. I wondered if sandals had been the right choice of footwear. Always hard to know how to dress when the seasons are changing and you're heading off to a kidnap.

A flash of heat hit me. Darkness. I stumbled, flailed. Screamed but couldn't. I was squeezed tight, shoved into blackness. Crushed lungs. Heart attack. Having a, no, stop! For an instant, I was blank with fear. A terrible grip wanted to kill me. I couldn't breathe. Dying. Heart attack in the street. Face on fire, so hot, burning up, here. Loosen my collar. Too young. Loosen my ribs. Don't want to. Someone help me, please, dying, loosen me, too young to –

'Don't look at my face.' The voice was in my ear, coming from behind. His breath warmed my skin.

Him, the man from the internet. Natalie, you fucking idiot. What *were* you thinking?

Oof! I was slammed against a hard, flat surface. My head was bagged in dark fabric. I couldn't see a thing. The hood, or whatever it was, smelled faintly of sweat. His sweat. Even though we'd never met, I recognised his scent, his history, his body; could almost feel the prints of his fingers on my skin, inside me already.

'Stay still, act natural,' he said. I heard a car go past. 'Move it. Now. Fast!' I stumbled as he hurried me forward. My hearing sharpened, compensating for my blindness. To my right, a van door slid open with a low swoosh. Every breath I drew sucked the fabric against my mouth.

'Get in,' he said. 'Leg up, higher, that's right. Head down, this way. Hurry up. On the floor. Down! Chrissake, get down!'

The van door clanged shut, making the vehicle shudder. I fell in the direction he urged me, scrambling sideways onto softness, my protests muffled by the press of fabric on my face. Noises from the street went dull. At a guess, I was on a mattress, an old, thin thing without much bounce. I heard him panting, his breath almost as fast as my heart. I listened for other presences but heard nothing. Was someone in the driver's seat?

We were silent for several seconds, him clutching the fabric around my head, motionless. Perhaps he was as scared as me. Had we been spotted? Were we safe? My throat was thick and tight, my mouth dry.

'Turn on to your front.' His voice was level and insistent, expecting no challenge. 'Lie down properly. On your front. Slowly. Don't try to look at me. That's right. Don't look and you won't be harmed. Nice and slow, that's it, good girl. I don't want to hurt you.' He paused and gave a crisp laugh. 'Not yet.'

The hood made my breath dampen my face. The sound of my pumping blood merged with muffled noises outside the van, adding to my disorientation. As instructed, I turned slowly and lay face forward. The man straddled my buttocks, carefully tilting my head back by clasping the cloth to my eyes. The weight of him on my arse aroused me and I realised I was wet, a pulse between my thighs hammering as fast as that in my terrified heart.

The man. What was his name? Baxter Logan. No, not him, Nats. The other one. The new guy.

'Keep your eyes closed.' That same steady, authoritative tone.

Den. That was it. A mysterious monosyllable. I wished I could see his face.

He lifted the hood from my head and moulded a hand to my eyelids. I smelled tarnished metal, petrol and cardboard. 'I'm blindfolding you,' he said. On a blink I couldn't suppress, I caught a glimpse of an eye mask and the fat, faded roses of a mattress before I was plunged into darkness again. Den adjusted the mask over my nose then wrapped an extra binding of fabric around my eyes until I couldn't see a peep of light. Or a keek of light, as Baxter might have said.

'Stay there. Open your mouth.'

He pinched my cheeks and slotted a hard, rubber ball into my mouth. I protested, less at the object, more at Den's crude speed. I had to remind myself I wanted this. I'd asked for it, had tacitly agreed he could set up a kidnap scene for me. My teeth latched on to the ball as Den fastened the strap behind my head. My groin melted a little more. Ball gag. This was a familiar object from my time with Baxter. He hadn't been keen on, as he'd once called it, 'all that paraphiliacs' paraphernalia', claiming he preferred to make me scream using his charm alone.

I remembered him telling me that. I was naked on my knees, hands roped behind my back. 'Look up at me,' he'd said, standing there with his big, handsome cock jutting from his suit. I obeyed and he slapped me across the face. 'Charm, see? Like that!' I began sinking into my submission, face stinging, room spinning. 'Baxter Logan, he likes to charm the ladies, charm his wee bitches then make them choke on his dick.'

Baxter Baxter Baxter. What was he doing here? His words sounded so harsh now but at the time, they'd made me swoon. The idea I was one of many women Baxter could pick and choose from and use for his own gain, got me right in the groin. Were that scenario true, I'd have been devastated. But as a fantasy, because I was safe in the reality I was the only woman Baxter loved, it thrilled me. His faux-boastfulness made him, in my mind, all the more powerful and ruthless, a man ruled by his greedy cock. And I loved that. Loved that he could play with the concept of being a profligate, sexually voracious bastard while being a loyal, sexually voracious boyfriend.

Except he couldn't, as I discovered. That wasn't what he'd been doing.

I wished I could delete him. Nearly two years, and I still kept comparing new lovers to him. But remembering him in the midst of playing kidnap was a new low, a sign I needed to work harder on letting go. Oh, but if only he were the one doing this to me. Instead of a frightening faceless man, my abductor could be, in another dimension, Baxter Logan, his big hands on my body, his nasty words in my ears.

I rested my tongue against the wedged rubber ball, disliking the taste but finding that position more comfortable than trying to keep my tongue out of the way. Gagged and blindfolded, I grew calmer. I recognised the feeling, that slow process of unravelling, of handing myself over to someone ready to take me.

For a moment, that someone was Baxter. He was here, busying about my body, collar undone, his tie as crooked as his smile and his heart. In my mind, his face was clearer than it had been for ages. I saw the unkempt hair, the heavy brows and rough-hewn handsomeness. I saw eyes so brown their darkness was almost indistinguishable from the black of his pupils.

That's what I wanted to surrender to: the dark, wild chaos of Baxter's unchecked passion. But no, that ship had sailed. He'd betrayed me. So why wouldn't the longing fade?

I pulled my mind back to the present, trying to get a grip, stay focused.

I was alone in a van and my abductor had no face. Such a stupid risk to take.

Den edged down my legs and shoved up my skirt, rocking my thighs left and right to accommodate the material. There was a pause, physical and auditory, when he revealed my underwear. I sensed his eyes assessing me, sliding from ankles to arse. The backs of my knees itched as if his gaze were a ticklish caress. I bunched my fists, fighting the urge to bat my skirt down and restore a semblance of modesty.

With a masseuse's technique, Den spanned each calf muscle and ran a hand up either leg.

'Ve-ery nice,' he said. When he reached my buttocks, he nudged my knickers higher, crumpling the flimsy fabric into a band and wedging it to form a makeshift thong in the crack of my arse. Behind the ball gag, I groaned in frustration, hating his scrutiny and the small precise manner in which he'd rendered me vulnerable. But at the same time, I liked being forced to endure his inspection; liked his inevitable enjoyment of my discomfort.

I remained motionless as he caressed my rear cheeks, his hand gentle like a lover's. I didn't trust that hand one jot. I heard people walking past the van, a woman calling after her child. Den leaned forward, his breath on my neck, his lips touching the tip of my ear. He nibbled there, light as a feather, then traced his tongue along the edge of my lobe. With a gentle touch, he pushed my hair aside to lightly kiss my neck. I couldn't respond, couldn't move or kiss back. All I could do was lie in my own darkness, breathe through my nose and wait.

His voice was low and close in my ear. 'You know what I'm going to do?' he murmured. 'I'm going to strip you bare. Completely bare. Not your clothes. You.' His hand roamed over the naked swell of my buttocks. The pulse in my cunt beat harder. 'I'm going strip away your will, your personality, your self-respect. I'm going to break you, reduce you to a sobbing wreck.'

A fantasy, a game, much like Baxter's talk of getting fellated by a bunch of obliging, awestruck women.

Den wrapped his other hand in my hair, trapping my curls

in a fist and forcing my ear against his lips. Nearness made his voice fuzzy, his lips brushing the shell of my ear as he spoke, his breath almost as loud as his words. The touch of his lips made my desire leap.

'I'm going to get so far inside your head, you won't know who you are any more,' he said. 'And that's good, because you won't be anyone. You'll just be a thing for me to use.' His hand slipped between my legs to stroke the damp pouch of my briefs, the scrunched fabric only just containing me. A shiver chased along my spine, leaving prickles on my neck. My groin felt unfeasibly swollen, so responsive to his delicate, teasing touch.

'And from nothing, I'll make something,' he went on, tender voiced and darkly seductive. 'I'll rebuild you and make you mine. My little bitch.'

My heartrate quickened as my mind flashed back to a FancyFree exchange where I'd shared my fantasy of being kidnapped, chained to his bed and referred to as his 'little bitch'. At the time I was no doubt chanelling Baxter Logan who often called me his 'wee bitch'. Was Den speaking words I'd offered or using his own? I wondered if I might end up chained to his bed and began to regret saying that. I didn't think I'd like the reality of being cold, stiff and unable to sleep.

Increasingly anxious, I tried to recall what else I'd said. Rash fragments swam in my mind: '*I like the idea of being afraid because I don't know what will happen next . . . a man who enjoys my fear . . . a jumble of bondage, blindfolds and gags.*'

I wasn't sure what I most feared: this mysterious stranger or the capacity of my overwhelming lust to urge me along dumb, dangerous paths.

'Put your hands behind your back,' he said.

I did. He took one wrist and wrapped it in a soft cuff, presumably leather, then pulled the buckle tight. He did the same on my other wrist then, with a click, linked the two cuffs together by the small of my back. I tugged, testing the small amount of slack between my wrists. The resistance I encountered sent lust surging to my groin.

'So, let's take a proper look at you,' he said.

He hooked his hands either side of my knickers and unceremoniously dragged them down and off. His touch brisk and firm, he splayed my thighs, holding me open. I could feel him examining me, eyes locked on the place where I was bloated and slick. Instinctively, I jerked at my cuffs. The short link between them jolted my wrists, sparking another corresponding jolt of need in my groin. I heard myself groan and the sound, though muffled, was filthy, awash with desperation.

Den gave a victorious little laugh. He'd sussed me out, had seen how predictably easy I was and how much his unkindness aroused me. I couldn't hide it from him, even if I'd wanted to. He stroked between my legs, fingers paddling in my drenched split. I groaned heavily, thinking I might die if he didn't penetrate me. But he didn't, he just laughed again.

Kneeling between my legs, he raised one ankle, easing it towards my butt. He buckled a bond around it. I caught the creak of leather, the clink of metal and felt the tug as he tightened it. Another cuff. He slipped a finger between leather and leg, checking the fit, then repeated the action on my other ankle.

'You're very acquiescent,' he said. 'This bodes well for the things I plan to do to you.'

My entire body was shot through with lust, my cunt made

of hot, wet throbs. I squirmed against the mattress, unable to prevent my hips lifting in search of his hands.

Metal clanked again. A cheaper, tinnier sound this time. Another object. He fumbled with one ankle, then the next. Only when he drew back and I tried to move did I realise my legs were pinned apart, a rod between my ankles preventing me from closing them.

What did you call them? A spreader bar, that was it. I'd seen them online during one of my many fantasy-shopping sprees. A rod of hollow metal linked to ankle cuffs, forcing the wearer's legs apart.

I thrashed and sobbed. The position was excruciating, exposing me, splitting me, making me long to get fucked. I tugged my feet inwards. The bar rattled but the extra few inches I gained offered no more dignity, serving only to emphasise my powerlessness. What a cruel, clever device the spreader was, forcing me into a brazen display of pink-lipped greed, mocking me for my need while intensifying the very thing it created and offering no respite.

I gave a petulant double-kick at the mattress.

Den laughed, satisfied. I felt cheap, whorish and objectified, as if the point of my existence to him was my wet, eager cunt. Not my mind, my nice eyes, personality or infectious laugh. Cunt. That's what I was to him: cunt. And every nerve in my body sucked in the dark pleasure of that, cradling its delicious baseness.

'We're going for a little drive now,' said Den.

I writhed, tipping my arse to him and groaning in complaint. I didn't want to go for a drive. I wanted to get fucked.

'When I open this door again,' Den continued, 'I want to see you in exactly the same position.' He leaned close, his breath dusting my ear, his hand bunching my hair. 'If you try to do anything stupid, I'll make you pay. So don't bother. Just lie there, nice and still. OK?'

I nodded, huffing for breath through my nose and making a vaguely affirmative noise behind my gag.

The van door slid open and I squealed, afraid of being seen by passersby. Quickly, the door swooshed and banged into place, leaving the van rocking. In the ensuing silence, I felt horribly alone. If only I could see who this man was. I hoped he'd remove my blindfold when we got to wherever we were going. What if he didn't and I never got to see his face? Hell, I should have thought this through more.

I'd never set out to snag Mr Right but I'd veered so far off that track I was now at the mercy of Mr Dangerously Wrong. If the thrill of my fantasy weren't so addictive, I'd be coming to my senses about now. But clarity of thought counts for little when you're bound and gagged, intensely horny, and are being taken into the unknown by a man you've never seen.

The floor beneath me rumbled as the engine started. I noticed a ticking somewhere by my feet. Clock? Time-bomb? The mattress beneath me swayed as the van moved. A short while later, I sensed us turn a corner. Left or right, I couldn't say. A small wave of motion sickness lifted inside me. The ticking stopped. What was it? Where was he taking me?

Another fragment: '*the more authentic the danger feels, the hotter it is for me.*'

I lay there in the dark, thinking, 'What a dumb, reckless thing to say to a stranger on the internet.'

If only I'd said it to Baxter when I'd had the chance, I could have got this fantasy out of my head without fearing for my life.

Seven

Baxter used to say, 'What a mess you've got yourself into. Look at the state of you. How d'you end up up like that, eh, hen?'

I remembered being half-dressed and roughly bound, face forward over the back of my armchair, arse upturned, dainty dress bunched beneath the ropes. Baxter came upstairs from the kitchen carrying a bottle of beer. Just the sight of him acting all cocky and leisured after rendering me helpless made my groin flare. I loved how he was so masculine without being macho; loved how that was expressed in so many different ways: the suit, the beer, the easy swagger, the hard-on, the pace, the control.

He took the bottle-opener from the mantelpiece and flicked the lid off his beer, watching me all the time. My lust blazed to feel his eyes roaming over me. I tried to picture what might be running through his mind. I felt like a target he was plotting to destroy, his cunning hunger homing in on the weak spot of my desire, aiming to ruin me by taking me to ecstasy and back.

'What a fucking mess,' he said, shaking his head in despair.

He took a swig of beer then proceeded to stalk me, circling the chair while acting baffled and sympathetic. Occasionally he'd readjust a rope or stroke me with possessive tenderness, continuing to make out I was to blame for having ended up in such a humiliating position.

All I could do was wait for him to unleash himself on me. The more he made me wait, the wetter I became. And as ever, the wetter I grew, the more horny, triumphant and grateful Baxter was when he finally started to fuck me. 'Ah yessss,' he'd hiss, spinning out the 's' as he sank in deep. 'What a beauty.'

Another memory: Baxter making me confront myself in the full-length mirror in the bedroom. I was on my knees, hands cuffed behind my back, both of us naked. I'd just been sucking his cock, or rather he'd just been fucking my mouth. He once taught me a word: *irrumatio*. Not *fellatio*, where I suck his cock, but *irrumatio*, where he fucks my mouth. 'Learn to love it,' he'd growled, hands in my hair, cock driving hard enough to make me splutter.

When he withdrew, he stuffed my knickers into my mouth, feeding in the last of the fabric with two big fingers. My cheeks bulged, pink lace foaming from my lips as he turned me to meet my reflection. He held me by the hair, waggling my head in warning when I tried to look away. Black tears streaked my face, my eyes bloodshot, my skin hectic and blotched. Next to me, his cock was ramrod-stiff, gleaming with my saliva, his pubes curling damply.

'Look at the state of you,' he said brightly. 'How d'you end up like this, eh? Dirty little cocksucker. You know why your panties are in your mouth, eh? Do you?'

I shook my head, grunting into cotton.

'Because I dinnae want to hear you speak,' he said. 'All

that mouth's fit for is being used. Not got a dick in it? Then it's surplus to my requirements. Now come on, suck me again. Do it!'

I grunted to indicate he needed to first remove the underwear from my mouth. My hands were tied, see? Baxter was having none of it. 'Spit them out,' he said. 'Prove how much you want my dick.'

I did as told, glad to be rid of the knickers, gladder still to have Baxter gliding into my mouth again. I loved the strength in his shaft, loved to breathe in the intimacy of his pubes as he bunched my hair in his fists, pulling me close. And most of all, I loved it when he told me what to do. He knew I got off on that because I'd tried to explain it numerous times. I couldn't say why I liked being forced to submit, only that I did; that I longed to be overtaken and reduced in this way. I didn't so much get off on the act of submission but in being made to submit. I wanted to resist as if I hated it, the pleasure arising from the process of him doing what was necessary to push me to that place where I had either become greedy and willing or was too weak to fight back.

Does everything, I'd once wondered aloud to Baxter, have to be explained before it gets a pass? Does the nature-nurture debate need to be resolved before I'm allowed to fuck who and how I want? Didn't gay people get asked the same question – Are you born this way or made? – and discover the answer is: 'Accept us for who we are, don't pathologise and try to fix us'?

Baxter took it in his stride, not seeking justification but happy to be with someone he viewed as on a par. My kinky desires were as legitimate as his, and together we could celebrate what we relished, and make each other happy.

What a mess you've got yourself into.

I could almost hear him and wished he were with me. Alone in the back of the van, I was suddenly wretched, the pain of my loss spiking like it hadn't done in months. Oh, it was nothing compared to the immediate, soul-crushing loneliness I'd experienced when Baxter and I had split. But I felt it again, a loss too entangled with longing for me to come to terms with a Baxter-less future. Get over him. Move on. But that's easier said than done. I've never yet discovered how to speed up the process. All I've learned in life is to not act on the pain of heartbreak, to understand that grief doesn't grant you any rights. You've just got to sit it out like a hangover.

Tick, tick, tick.

The noise in the van kept coming and going. It sounded as if my time were running out, a countdown to the start or the end of something. Earlier in the journey I'd realised the ticking came from nothing more sinister than the van's indicator lights. Nonetheless, I couldn't disassociate the noise from that of a bomb about to explode.

Tick, tick, tick.

The van stopped, engine off. Moments later, the door rumbled open, bringing in a sweep of fresh air. Instinctively, I tried to close my legs. The spreader bar clanged its refusal, the leather cuffs jerking around my ankles. A slice of light peeped through a new chink in my blindfold. The floor of the van dropped as Den climbed in. He didn't close the door so I guessed we were in a place hidden from public view.

'You OK?' His tone was sharp, the question perfunctory.

I nodded although I wasn't sure.

He removed the spreader bar and ankle cuffs. Grateful, I drew my legs together.

'Kneel up, move back,' he said. 'This way. We're getting out. Come on. Trust me.'

But I couldn't see a thing. Like a nervous animal being led by a friendly vet, I shied away from whatever was in front of me.

'Come on, it's OK,' he cajoled, his voice gentler.

The blackness was behind my eyes and I was walking into the void, being taken to the edge of a precipice at midnight. Den got out first, feet thudding on the ground. He hooked his hands in my armpits to help me down. I let him take my weight as I climbed from the van in a terrified half-crouch.

My feet touched the ground. I stood alone. The van door banged shut. Traffic mumbled somewhere in the distance. Gulls shrieked. The sounds carried, suggesting we were close to the seafront, not hemmed in by buildings. I thought I heard far-off waves then decided the rhythmic slush was simply the pounding of blood in my ears.

'This way.' Den gripped my upper arms and we walked, his pace too fast for my tentative steps. Impossible not to believe the unseen ground was littered with dangers. I flinched, stalling, when an object flicked from my path with a wooden thunk. A little further on, glass crunched underfoot. I froze, shaking my head, protesting behind the ball gag, my shoulders hunching. Jeez, I was wearing sandals. Couldn't he pay a little more attention?

'Sorry, missed that,' he said. 'It's OK, I've got you. Clear ahead. Good girl. Left here. Nearly there. Nearly. Perfect, now stand still.'

I stood shivering, cool air under my skirt reminding me I was without underwear. I listened to keys jangling, heard a door creak open. Den led me forward. The door closed behind us with a dull thump. Even through my blindness, I could tell we were in a trapped, dark place, a bad place that stank of mouldering wood, dust and sadness. I heard bolts being shot. Ah, fuck. What was this? A castle? A dungeon?

'This part's tricky,' said Den, 'so I'm going to remove your wrist cuffs. Don't do anything stupid.'

Yeah right, like what? Try and beat you up while ripping off my blindfold and gag?

He removed the cuffs. I flexed my fingers, arching my back to stretch out the muscles.

'I'm going to pick you up,' he said. 'So work with me.'

Suddenly my feet were off the floor and my head was where my stomach had been. I squealed within my mouth and reached for him, accidentally clouting him on the jaw. I found his shoulder and clung on. I was in his arms, scooped up as if he were carrying me over the threshold like a new bride. Some bride. Some groom.

We moved forward, slow and effortful. I heard him kick away debris, sensed him edge around obstacles. Once, my feet brushed against a wall. I grew nervous of stuff touching my face, cobwebs and fallen things, so I nuzzled into his chest to shield myself. He was broad and solid, and I felt safe. He bumped a door open and took us through. I breathed him in, eager to have the smell of his body masking the smell of mildew and age. I strained for the sound of his slightly laboured breath. Jesus, who was he? Whose arms was I trusting? Where on earth had he brought me?

When he set me down, the sounds around us were different, the dankness less offensive to my nose. Our movements echoed in a cavernous space. High above, I heard pigeons cooing and I caught a drift of healthier air.

'We're going down some steps now,' he said. 'Take my hand.'

Blindly, I reached out. He hooked his arm in mine, linking

fingers and locking our forearms together in a supportive hold. Our hands were tacky as if we were equally nervous.

'Shallow steps,' he said, as I faltered on the first.

We took the steps one at a time, me shuffling like an old woman. He gave me tender rewards: That's right, good girl. Low in my body, every word turned to a voluptuous throb. After an eternity, we paused. Den released my hand. Without his touch, I felt isolated and unsteady, half-fearful I might fall over on my own two feet.

'You want to see your new home?' he asked.

I nodded, thinking, Actually, I want to see you.

He fiddled with my blindfold then swept it from my eyes. I blinked, my ball gag trapping a gasp, my visual cortex overwhelmed by a spectacle of crumbling decadence. We were in a dark, derelict fairytale, monsters lurking in the shadows. No, in a tilting, gothic amphitheatre of chipped gilt and torn velvet. I turned, scanning wildly. No, no, this was an old Victorian theatre, fallen into ruin.

We stood among a high tier of seats, curving rows of scruffy, crimson chairs sloping towards a balcony edge. What would you call it? The dress circle? In the drop below would have been the stalls but now it was a chairless arena, the flooring stripped back to scarred concrete. The stage, flanked by ornate gold columns and romping cherubs, was bisected by a scalloped, bottle-green canopy hanging at forty-five degrees. One green velvet curtain pooled on the bare boards, tassels of gold floating on its surface like strange, precious water lilies. Below the stage, the barrier of the orchestra pit echoed the richness elsewhere, invisible musicians penned in by a fence resembling decorative brocade.

Although the auditorium was empty, it seemed as if rows of skeletal ghosts were gazing at that stage, vintage programmes flaking in their laps, everyone frozen by a play without end.

I looked left, right and above. Curlicues of gold licked at elegant pillars, at balconies and boxes that might have been crafted from sugar-frosting. Bald patches of plaster gaped through the splendour. Higher still, in a domed ceiling swirling with reds and golds, hung an enormous chandelier, tiers of glass pendants grey with dust, supporting wires twisting like vines around its stems. Chunky lights in the dome cast a diffuse milky haze, rendering the theatre vaporous, on the verge of disappearance.

Ozymandias, I thought. *My name is Ozymandias, look on my works, ye mighty, and despair.*

'Impressive, isn't it?'

His voice startled me, so close and yet so small in the theatre's desolation. I swung around, shocked by his presence, shocked I'd been too stunned to give him my immediate attention.

As if my struggle to absorb my surroundings wasn't enough, there he was, my captor, my tormentor, standing on a step behind me. My heart leaped into my mouth. I recoiled, tottering dangerously, hands raised in defence. I screamed but the noise was locked in my throat.

I'd been cheated, betrayed.

He was there and yet he wasn't.

Once again, he was masked. He had no face, no eyes.

Athletic build: check.

6'2": check.

Face: no check; no fucking check!

Instead, I gazed at stark, white features too smooth to be human. At a scuffed, fibreglass mask patterned with grids of small black holes. I thought of Munch's *The Scream*, that elongated face melting into terror. But the mask was hard and nasty too, a warrior's mask. Two sharp red triangles slashed the cheekbones while between the eyes, a third red mark suggested a vicious frown. The marks sparkled with red glitter. He was a cyborg, an alien.

An old ice-hockey mask. Of course. *Friday the 13th* came to mind and I screamed again.

Deep inside the eyeholes, something flickered. Him.

I heard him laugh, the sound muffled by that mouthless false face. The light behind the eyeholes flared brighter, relishing my reaction.

I reached for my gag, wanting to tear it from my mouth, wanting to be ordinary and free and far, far away from him. Why had I trusted him? Who was he? Quick as a flash, Den grabbed my wrist, stilling me with harsh fingers.

I stared at the blankness, aghast.

'I knew you'd like it,' said the mask.

Eight

'You have a choice,' he said, his words dulled by his disguise. 'Either I'm masked or you're blindfolded.'

I made a noise of protest, shaking my head.

'What?' he said. 'You want a voice as well?'

I nodded, making more urgent noises.

'Are you hungry?' he asked.

I rolled my eyes and harrumphed as best I could. I was inches away from stamping my foot.

'OK, here's the deal,' he said. 'I'm going to remove your gag and I want you to tell me if you're hungry or not. I hear anything else and the gag goes back. Got that?'

I nodded again, more subdued this time.

He unfastened the strap and freed my mouth. I wiggled my jaw and licked my gums, glaring at him. The mask glared back, a dirty cream facade speckled with holes and twinkling with those three red, glittery slash marks.

'Well,' he said. 'Are you hungry?'

'Absolutely ravenous,' I said. 'I haven't thought about anything else since you shoved me into the back of that van. Why? Is there a café in here?'

With deliberate exaggeration, I surveyed the decrepit glory. Obviously, I was being sarcastic. My stomach was in knots. Food was the last thing on my mind.

'OK, then. Are you horny?'

Truth to tell, I wasn't. Fear and anxiety had obliterated my earlier excitement. Everything was unreal. This masked man in this spectacular ruin might have been a creature in a dream I was having; or he was an actor who'd slipped from an on-stage drama to confront me, the sole member of his audience.

'No,' I said. 'I can't do horny right now. This is too freaky, too fast.'

'Then we'll eat.'

'But I'm not hungry.'

'Tough,' he said. 'If you don't eat when I feed you, there's no second chance. I'm not here to wait on you hand and foot.'

'Yeah, and I'm not here for a sodding lunch date.'

He laughed from behind the mask. The grille of holes covering his mouth distorted the sound, making his amusement seem further away than his body. 'No, you're right. You're here to be turned into a pitiful creature I can mould to my own will. Here to be beaten and broken, used and abused until you're entirely mine, no desire but to do my bidding.'

'I've changed my mind,' I said. 'I'm starving.'

Another muffled laugh. 'I need to fetch some stuff from the van.'

'Where are we?' I asked.

The mask turned left and right, red glitter sparkling in the theatre's murky light. 'Den's den,' he replied.

I heard the implication he was always dragging women here, trapping them in his ravaged, abundant lair. 'You sound like a psychopath,' I said.

He reached to position my hands behind my back. 'Maybe I am.' He buckled the cuffs around my wrists again, linking them together with a snap and oh, the smell of him when he was close. My knees softened and my groin did likewise, softening, pulsing and swelling. Ah, Hell. Such a small thing, the tug and click of being bound. Yet it got me right there, so hard and swift my arousal felt like an assault rather than something originating within me.

I heard the cold rattle of a chain and felt him attach its length to my restraints. 'This way.' He tugged the chain as if it were a leash.

'I brought a bag with me,' I said. 'It's in the van. Could you –'

'I know,' he said. 'I'll bring it, don't worry.'

He led me down more of the steps that formed an aisle between the dusty chairs, some seats flipped up, others flat as if a theatre-goer were sitting there. I trooped obediently after him, the chain sagging between us. I began to feel smaller and sub-human, already turning into his little thing, his obedient, ever-ready fucktoy. Near the balcony edge, he had me stand by a slender black column that rose to the tier above us, its flared tip merging into rococo edging sculpted like beribboned curtsies.

I peered over my shoulder to watch as Den looped the chain around the column, fixing one link to another with a small padlock. His ears were neat and well-proportioned, his hair close-cropped, his neck strong and shadowed with stubble. His shoulders were wide under a black hoodie, his torso tapering to narrow hips. The hockey mask fastened around the back of his head, three brown leather straps meeting in a T-shape. The straps looked to be joined by nothing but a couple of studs. Easy to pop open, I thought.

Then, no. Don't even consider it, Nats. Besides, you're not exactly in a position to launch an attack.

When Den released the chain, the loop slid down the pillar, hitting the ground with a clank. I was tethered like an animal, room to roam but no means of escape.

With ostentatious precision, Den placed the padlock key on the balcony's crimson lip. It glinted on the dusty velvet, out of reach but not out of sight. I read his gesture as a signifier of how precarious my freedom was.

'I won't be long,' he said.

'Don't go!' Panic gripped me. 'Don't! Don't leave me. Please . . .'

The white mask looked at me, hollow-eyed and impassive. I struggled to articulate my fear. It was no longer of him but of something else, something irrational and gloomy. 'I don't want to be left alone,' I said. 'Please. I'm scared. This place . . .'

'I won't be long,' he repeated, stern and formidable. And with that he departed, taking the shallow steps two at a time, the sound of him receding as he disappeared from view.

'Think of nice things,' my mother used to say when I was restless in bed, nightmares on the periphery of my consciousness. 'Think of holidays, of playing in the sea at Devon. Think of Aunty Marjory's new kittens and all the balloons at Gregory Markham's party last week.'

But this nightmare was too real and no amount of remembered balloons, kittens and Devonshire surf could counter the dark thoughts corrupting my reason. The ossified theatre held the strange reality of a play being enacted, but it was a sick, twisted play, teasing my imagination while showing nothing of itself. Alone, I performed the drama in my mind, conjuring up ghouls, squatters and litters of feral cats nesting in squalid corners. I half-fancied a phantom cast was waiting in the wings below; that the lights would dim, the silence would hush itself; and unseen stagehands would winch those slumped, green curtains high, revealing Hamlet in breeches, Yorrick's skull in his hand.

Stupid, stupid thoughts.

Then more thoughts came, worse ones. Supposing Den didn't return and I was left to rot among the architecture? Which would decay faster, it or me? Time moved so slowly here. My friends. When would they notice I was gone? If I failed to turn up for work on Monday, would they call the cops? This time next week, would I be registered as a missing person?

A clatter in the domed rooftop made me shriek. My voice sounded tiny. Above, a pigeon flapped across cloudy shafts of light, the beat of its wings lingering in the silence, dust stirring.

I drew deep breaths, willing my heart to calm. After an age, I heard the thump of a distant door followed by approaching footsteps. He was back. At least, I hoped it was him.

'You OK?' he called, his voice devoid of concern.

'Yes.' My voice was hoarse, my throat tense.

Den jogged down the steps, depositing my bag and a holdall across the arms of a seat. He moved with a springy athleticism, decision in every action. The red glitter on his hockey mask winked in the half-light.

Hell, I needed to get a grip, think clearer. Something was wrong here. Why the mask? Was he scarred? Burned? Deformed like the Phantom of the Opera?

All I knew about this man were the elements that mattered to me: his preference for sex on the dark side; his guilt-free ownership of that; his personality as expressed via email; and his commitment to the two of us making sweet music together. He'd used that phrase himself then taken it up a notch to a 'mind-blowing opera'.

But scratch the sweet. Fuck the opera. I'd invested a great deal of trust in this guy and he wasn't giving much in return. Again, I thought how easy it would be to pop apart the straps of his mask, once I'd regained the use of my hands, that was. But unethical to do so if he were disfigured in some way. Then again, unethical not to let me know if he was.

He faced me, if 'face' is the word. Instinctively, I retreated, chains rattling until I bumped against the column. I pressed my hands to its cold, gritty curve, its solidity providing a security of sorts. My breathing quickened, my throat twisting in on itself.

Den followed me. 'Your fear is so delectable.' He reached for my shirt and briskly undid the top two buttons.

'Hey!' I backed harder against the pillar.

'Your eyes,' he said. 'I wish you could see them.' He continued to unbutton my shirt, his pale fingers moving efficiently between my breasts. There was no seduction, no tease. I might have been undressing myself before getting into bed on a regular midweek night. He fumbled with a button at the mid-point, gave up, and rammed the loosened garment over my shoulders. The stitching gave with a tiny rip.

'Oi, my top!' I shook my head, wriggling. My arms were trapped by my side, my bra thrust out in a flagrant display of delicate, lacy intimacy. I tugged at my cuffs, wanting to cover myself. This was too direct.

'The more you struggle, the harder my cock gets,' said Den. 'And the harder I get, the more I want to see you struggle.'

He pushed my bra straps aside and lifted my breasts from their cups. No one was here but I blushed as if we had an audience.

'Please,' I whimpered.

He massaged with moist, crushing hands. Every nerve in my body sparked up, lust zinging in my veins. The mask looked at me, dead except for the brightness of his eyes behind the holes and the crust of glitter on those red slash marks. The heels of his hands rippled over my ribs as he pummelled, the underwire of my bra digging uncomfortably.

'Do you like nipple torture?' he asked matter-of-factly. He pinched my nipples between thumb and forefinger then pulled, stretching my breasts to points.

Oh jeez. I tipped back my head, gasping, not knowing the right answer.

He held me like that, squeezing harder. 'Well?'

I could feel my flesh tenderising in his grip. He released me fractionally, twisting my nipples this way and that until I was yelping in pain.

'A bit,' I gasped.

'What?' he said, continuing to hurt me. 'You like it a bit or you only like a bit of it?'

'I don't know,' I said. 'Please. Don't know what you have in mind. I don't . . . ouch!'

He yanked my bra further down, creating an awkward belt below my ribs. I flinched as he raised a hand, fearing he was going to slap my face. He laughed, paused, hand still in the air. 'You think I'm going to hit you?' He feigned a slap, his hand stopping short of my cheek. Instinctively, I shrank back and he laughed again. 'Look at me,' he ordered.

I faced the mask. He tapped me on the cheek. It wasn't a slap, it was worse, a patronising, humiliating tap. He did it again, gently knocking my face off-centre. 'Look at me,' he repeated.

When I did, he tapped me again. A strand of hair got caught in my mouth. I blew it away. He swiped my cheek again, harder this time. 'Look at me,' he said. 'You like that?'

Every time, I looked at him, he hit me, forcing me to turn aside and fail his instruction. 'Look at me!' My face began to glow and my senses grew fogged, the theatre jumping in my vision.

'You like this, huh?'

I nodded.

'Tell me what else you like.' He followed his request with another slap.

I shrugged, feeling shy before the anonymous mask. 'Cock,' I murmured.

'Louder.'

'Cock!' I barked.

'That's better. What else?' With a milder touch, as if he were trying to chase the answer from me, he gave my face a quick succession of taps, my cheek making silly popping noises beneath his fingers.

'Cock and fucking,' I said.

He struck me hard, leaving a sting on my cheek. I gasped, anger jabbing inside me.

'Stop being coy,' he said. 'Stop acting as if you're an ordinary fuck. You think I'd be interested if you wanted nothing more sophisticated than cock? And fucking? I can get that anywhere.' He landed another cruel, reprimanding slap on my cheek. 'I didn't bring you here for a fuck. Arranging this has cost me time and effort. Now show some appreciation for that. Show some gratitude.'

I winced, struggling for the right words. This had been so

much easier to express when he was a man on the other side of the computer screen. But communication wasn't the point here. The point was to humiliate me, to bring my defences down until I was weak and horny.

I waited for him to slap me again, wanting the excuse of being forced to speak, but he held off. 'Well?' he urged. 'Tell me what you get off on.'

I drew a deep breath, my eyes cast low to dodge the blank gaze of the mask. 'Being used,' I said. 'I like feeling sluttish, nasty. I like being forced to do things I shouldn't really do.'

I stopped but he pinched my chin, forcing me to face him. 'Keep going,' he said.

I breathed deeply again, trying to summon up courage. I stared into the eye holes of the mask, trying to find the man behind it and create a connection. 'I like being made to take it,' I said with a hint of defiance. 'To take cock. And shame and pain and whatever he wants to inflict. I like feeling powerless. Overwhelmed. Stripped of control and responsibility. I like being afraid because I don't know how far he'll go. I get off on the thrill of that. On fear because it feels as if my life is in his hands. I like . . .' I scoured my brain for something to encapsulate my desire. 'I like to feel subsumed in a man.'

Subsumed. I'd been searching for that word for too long. I resisted the urge to supply further clarification, to tell him being subsumed wasn't a smallness because I could only be subsumed when he was vast and powerful. Kind of like giving it up to God.

'Whore,' said Den, demonstrating a flagrant lack of interest in my attempts at articulation. He brought a hand swooping across to swipe at my breast, making my flesh jiggle and snapping my attention back to my body. I yelped and he repeated the action with his other hand on my other breast.

The dreadful blankness of the mask enhanced the sense he was an emotionless torturer, no facial expression to betray his feelings. His aloofness compared to my reactive state heightened his power and my subjugation. The imbalance excited me, as did the ever-present fear that I didn't know who he was and, for whatever reason, he intended to keep me in the dark about that.

He kept slapping my breasts, right and left, his right hand providing the sharper hit while I squealed and flinched. My flesh bounced, ligaments pulling, skin tingling with the heat of his stings. I was breathless with shock and arousal, my nipples now lurid, pink tips advertising his effect on me.

He stepped closer still and dug his hand between my thighs, bunching my skirt into my naked crotch. 'Where do you feel it?' he asked. 'Here, like a cheap whore?' He jammed his hand higher, his gesture aggressive and crude. 'Or here, like a clever whore?' He withdrew his touch and tapped my temple. He sounded so posh when he said 'whore'.

He paused to let me reply. High above us, the emptiness of the domed ceiling quivered with the coo of pigeons.

'Both,' I whispered. My body's reaction challenged my answer. The thudding in my cunt filled my tissues as swiftly as if I were being pumped up, the sensation so fierce it threatened to overwhelm my mental faculties. A woolly question flitted across my brain. How can I be psychologically affected when I'm turning into an animal?

'Thought so.' His voice was soft with something bordering on compassion. Lightly, he stroked my jaw, his touch kind. His tenderness made me nervous. I felt sure it was a trick.

'Have you ever been fucked in the arse?' he asked.

I cleared my throat. 'I'm thirty-two years old. Of course I have.'

The fingers continued, tracing a line down my neck to the dip between my collarbones. 'Do you like it?'

I shrugged. 'Yes, sometimes. But I've got to be seriously in the mood.'

'No worries,' he said. 'I can get you seriously in the mood.'

I swallowed and looked aside. His fingers drifted downwards, tracing swirls over the upper swell of my breasts. 'Good nipples.' He toyed lightly with the stiffened nubs. Pleasure shivered under his touch and my breath grew shallow.

I inhaled slowly, trying to steady myself. 'Take your mask off,' I said.

He laughed, scoffing at the idea. 'Maybe later. Once we've taken off yours.'

I shook my head. 'There's no mask. This is me.'

'There's always a mask,' he replied coolly, still playing with my nipples. 'Many masks. Concealing, projecting, transforming.'

He dropped his hand to lift my skirt, baring me. Without pre-amble, as if he were testing for wetness rather than intending to stimulate me, he pressed a finger into my swollen crease. He sawed to and fro, making me groan.

'You're soaked,' he said. 'No mask there.'

I ached for him to continue, to shove his harsh, cruel fingers inside me, but he stopped and grabbed my upper arm. He jerked me away from the column. The chain rattled behind me like a stupid tail.

'This way.' He shoved me towards the balcony, fingers stabbing my flesh. 'I'm going to annihilate the clever whore.'

I stumbled, scared but too randy to care overmuch. Briefly, he released me, stepping aside to pocket the key that lay on the crimson velvet edge. When he returned, he clasped the back of my neck. 'Bend over.'

'No!' He pushed me forward, tipping me towards the balcony edge. My fear exploded like a bright, white light. The patchy, concrete floor of the decimated stalls below lurched at me.

'Bend. Fucking. Over.'

My knees crumpled. The gilt-edged boxes reeled and the stage slid sideways. I fell to the ground as if worshipping at an altar.

'Up!' he snapped. He hooked his fingers into the waistband at the back of my skirt, trying to lift me. I let him move me out of sheer dread, my feet scrabbling for purchase, my hands battling against the cuffs. My body was as heavy and cumbersome as a sack of wet sand. With some difficulty, Den manoeuvred me until I was leaning over the balcony, screaming into the drop below. I felt vertiginous, the concrete floor presenting me with the horror of its hard, merciless expanse.

'I'm going to fall,' I cried.

'No you're not.' The mask made his voice boom weirdly. 'Keep still.'

He pushed my skirt up over my arse, shoving it under my bound wrists.

'No, please!' I was motionless, petrified except for the tremors racking my body and the pulse booming in my cunt. I heard him unzip and rubber up. He pressed a hand to the small of my back, pinning me to the edge. Again and again, I cried out, begging him to stop but knowing I didn't mean it, not quite, not yet. The head of his cock butted between my thighs. I feared his penetration might shunt me over the edge and send me tumbling toward my death. I'd asked for this, hadn't I? I'd just told him I got off on feeling my life was in his hands. He waggled his end at my entrance.

'Please,' I begged.

With a solid, swift lunge, he entered me, grabbing my hips as he did so. He filled me inside, his vast girth prising me apart, immense and terrifying. Keeping a firm hold on me, he began fucking with fast, furious strokes, every thrust making the concrete pit leap closer. His cock, the point where we were most connected, felt as if it were both my safety anchor and my potential destroyer.

His hands gripped harder as he picked up speed, his groans of pleasure punctuating my desperate howls, our cries trailing across the dusty space. Despite or because of my panic, my body responded to him, my pulpy walls sucking on his cock, my blood pressure rising to flood my face with heat. Adrenaline exacerbated my lust. He clawed a fistful of curls, making my neck angle backwards as he pounded into me. His cock banged deep, his body brushing against my trapped fingers.

'Not so clever now, are we?' he gasped.

He was right. I was reduced to the barest part of me, mindless with terror and near-ecstasy.

He clasped my hips again. 'I'm going to fuck it all out of you,' he said. 'Fuck your thoughts to dust. Erase you.'

He had my life in his hands as I'd wanted, and it broke me. I stopped fighting. I gave up. I let him have me, placing everything I had and I was with him. He wouldn't let me fall, I was sure of it. He had taken me over and I would trust him absolutely. I had no choice. At that moment, I was nothing without him holding me on the edge, ensuring I was safe. And with him, fucking me so dangerously, I was nothing too. Nothing but high-octane bliss.

I had surrendered, I had submitted to this hidden man. I was etherised, zoning out in a place beyond my body. I filled the theatre, lost to myself. My awareness of him fucking me became nebulous, remote. A memory of Baxter floated into my mind, a recollection more emotional than visual. I'd experienced this with him, had touched this place of pure self-abandonment. I was back. It had happened.

Den's distorted groans twisted like smoke, winding tracks through my scattered consciousness. At my core, I was awash with heat, his slamming cock holding me below the surface, keeping me in oblivion.

'Fuck you,' he said. 'Till you're gone. Till you're mine. Free for me to use.'

The words echoed dully behind the mask. I had enough presence to register he was close to coming. His noises intensified and he clutched my hips with punishing hands.

'Ah God.' His words sounded as if they were being dragged through rubber. 'Yes. Ah!'

He came with a deep, dark groan, his body shuddering, his hands biting as he emptied himself.

Then silence, just his breath and mine, shaking like the coos of those distant pigeons.

For a while we didn't move. I was still out there. I couldn't come back to myself. He withdrew, cast his condom to the floor and helped me off the balcony edge, zipping himself up before pulling me to him.

'You OK?'

I couldn't speak. Could barely walk. The deadness of the mask was worse than ever, a shield on his self, conflicting with the big reveal of his orgasm. He guided me towards the steps and unbuckled my cuffs. We sat close in the aisle between the rows of tatty velvet seats. He clasped my head to his chest, stroking my hair.

I began to tremble.

'There, there,' he said, his tone almost gentle.

Feeling feeble, I wrapped an arm across his torso, nuzzling into his clothes. I wanted to disappear into him, to melt into his body, safe and held. I remembered when I'd first got my cat, Aurora, aka Rory, and the time I'd accidentally stood on a paw. She'd yelped and jumped away. Seconds later she was back, butting at my ankle for comfort, trusting me despite the fact I'd just hurt her. It was like that with him.

'Sshh,' he said. 'It's all OK now. Everything's fine.'

A sob swelled in my chest but wouldn't rise. It pulsed there, a caged thing snagging on my breath.

'Let it all go,' he said. 'I'm here. Just let it all go.'

After a time, the damn broke and I wept without restraint. He hushed me, rocking back and forth, murmuring it was all OK. And it was, it was fine. I didn't cry from pain or anguish. I just needed to release something to break the intensity of where I'd been. I craved this, being flung out and pulled back. Craved it more than I craved coming. Baxter had shown me how it could be and until Den, I hadn't fully remembered the profound sense of completion I found in being both broken and mended by someone.

Maybe my previous knowledge of this state caught Den unawares. He thought I needed more aftercare than I did. He was a good, responsible dom who would go through the motions of comforting me for as long as it took. And yes, I did want to stay in his arms for longer, but I wanted something else too. I couldn't run the risk of him slowly releasing me, easing us apart to dry my tears.

So I spun out the clingy phase of the process, lulling him into a false sense of security while my mind grew sharper and nastier. I reached around, making out I was idly rubbing his back, relaxed and lazy. He accepted the touch. My hand edged higher towards the straps of that loathsome mask.

'You OK?' he asked.

I sniffed and hooked a leg across his lap, embracing him. 'Don't go,' I pleaded.

'I won't,' he said. 'I'm here for you.'

'Hold me.'

He hugged me, squeezing hard. 'I'm holding you,' he said, his words clipped and empty as if he'd trotted them out before. 'I'll hold you till you come back down to earth.'

But I was already there, rooted, focused.

My hand darted up to the back of his head. His shorn hair rasped beneath my fingers. I found the poppers on the mask straps. Tugged. He jumped but it was too late. The studs popped apart. He swung around, crying out. His hand flew to his face. A pigeon flapped high in the rooftop. The mask clattered to the steps at our feet, inert and hollow, straps trailing limply.

Nine

Don't let him get to you, Nats. Don't fall in love. Sure, he's just fucked you like an animal but that's not reason enough. And in addition to that? It's just a face. What does that even mean? Some good genes. He got lucky, or you did. No biggie.

Oh, but what an intoxicating face, broad and strong, sloping and slanting. Stubble peppered his jaw and a pair of beetle-black brows pulled in a frown over eyes that were narrow and small-lidded. Blue eyes. A startling mint-blue. His nose was neat and wide, sweeping gently towards pronounced cheekbones, and his skin was lightly pitted with the scars of teenage acne. He looked thuggish and mean, his mouth fixed in an angry line, his fury a sharp contrast to the deadness of that menacing mask.

'What the fuck do you think you're playing at?' He touched his cheek again as if to double-check he was maskless.

I tucked my breasts in my bra and shrugged my shirt back on. 'I want to know who I'm fucking,' I replied, fastening my buttons.

'I'll let you know when I'm ready.' He stood abruptly, glowering down at me, hands thrust in his pockets. I wondered at his racial heritage. He had that rugged, Mediterranean darkness with a suggestion of Asia in the slender elegance of his eyes. Such unusual coloured eyes.

I shook my head. 'No, not fair.'

'Who's calling the shots here, me or you?'

I stood, not wanting to be lower than him. 'At base level, neither of us,' I spat. 'I think we already said this. We meet as equals and we agree to play a game of being unequal.'

He sighed and sat on the step again, knees wide apart. He ran a hand over his head. 'Correct me if I'm wrong, we agreed to that game, no? Where we make out we're unequal.'

'You never mentioned a mask.'

'I didn't mention a lot of things I intend doing.' His body language was flinty although his movements were contained, shoulders twitching as if he were trying to stop himself from lashing out. 'But that's what you get off on, isn't it? Fear. Uncertainty. Being in someone else's power and dancing on the edge of danger.'

'Well, yes but . . . but this other person, he doesn't have absolute power.'

'I don't have that,' he said, 'or we wouldn't be having this discussion.'

'A discussion you're trying to close down!'

He locked his fingers together and tugged. 'So. Do you want out?'

I was astounded. 'What?'

'Easy question,' he said. 'Do you want out?'

'That is seriously unfair,' I said. 'It's tantamount to blackmail. I want to talk and you threaten to bail. Way to shut me up, no?'

'OK, what do you want?' He swiped invisible dust from his knees. 'Tell me, I'm all ears.'

I sat next to him on the step again, becoming fearful I might regret trusting him, might regret discovering the concept of 'edgeplay' and thinking I could run with that. At length, I said, 'I want a safeword.'

'The safeword is "safeword",' he replied.

'And it's a pretty useless one if I don't even know it.'

'It's obvious,' he said. 'It's practically universal.' He leaned back against the shallow step, propping himself on his elbows. 'Anyway, you know it now. And since we're on the subject, tap three times, foot or hand, if you're unable to speak because I'm shoving my cock in your throat, trying to fuck those vocal chords into submission.'

I breathed hard and slow. 'Sometimes,' I said, 'it's hard to know whether you're playing the nasty dom or being genuinely contemptuous.'

'I am playing. The nasty. Dom.' He spoke with exaggerated clarity, patronising me.

I pulled a false, tight smile. 'Funny that. You transition in and out of role so easily.'

'And presumably that's why you're here.' He sat forward and rubbed the heel of his hand into his frown, pensive and frustrated. 'You like it because it's unsafe,' he said, turning to me. 'And you're hoping it *is* safe. Safe like a ride at the funfair. But the truth is, you don't really know. And you don't want to know either. But you can't have it both ways.'

I looked away without replying, fearing he was right. My thoughts returned to our emails when the distinction between roleplaying and regular life had been clearer. I remembered his analogy of sexual fantasy as a hotel room where the usual rules don't apply. He'd described hotel rooms as liminal. What had he said? 'Liminal spaces bring out the beast in me,' that was it.

But hotel rooms have walls and doors. You can see the limits and you can leave. Now, in playing out a sexual fantasy, it felt as if our hotel room might be as big as the world, the boundaries too distant to have meaning, making the game indistinguishable from non-game.

Yes, in the beginning, it was clearer. We had an implicit start and stop button. Clearer. More manageable, more mutual. And less dangerous. Less exciting.

'So,' he said, 'you happy now you've got your safeword?'

I sighed heavily. 'Yes. And I safeword your mask.'

'Evidently,' he replied. 'But the problem is, I might not have agreed to that. Might have chosen to walk away instead. But you gave me no option. You unmasked me without my consent.' His frown grew hard again and I held his gaze, determined not to appear intimidated. 'And so you've seen my face. It's too late. We can't put the mask back on.' His eyes flared to the bright blue of a gas flame. 'Which means,' he said, 'as I'm sure you realise, that now I'm going to have to kill you.'

I blanched.

He gave me a long look but his expression was as empty as the mask I'd torn off. Was he waiting for me to react? One false move and I'd be dead? Then his face crinkled with quick amusement. He laughed, flashing strong, white teeth. 'Hey,' he said. 'It's fine.' He reached out to ruffle my hair. 'I'm joking. The mask was just to freak you out. Make you vulnerable. I need to own your mind before I can own your body. I'm fucking with your head again. Can't you see that?'

I nudged my hair into place, refusing to be mussed by him. 'Yes,' I said. 'I'm virtually blinded by it.'

'I like you,' he said. 'You've got sass.' His smile faded and he leaned closer. 'But you pulled off my mask and later I'm going to seriously punish you for that.' He paused, his eyes flicking because he was too close to see the whole of my face. 'I'm going to make you regret your silly little rebellion, going to make sure you don't ever pull a stunt like that again. Ever. Because that's what you want, isn't it? My punishment.'

I shrugged even though his words made my heart pound with a crazy mix of dread and excitement. I wasn't sure I even liked this man although I liked what he offered. I felt weak for wanting him, ashamed and afraid that in pursuing this, I might be making too many compromises, taking too many risks. My concern was that I, rather than he, might not know where to draw the line.

'Now, then,' he said, sitting straighter. 'Lunch.'

I raised my hand in a slow, sarcastic salute. 'Yes, sir.'

He laughed again, standing and moving a couple of steps down. Then, with a sudden shift of mood, he lunged forward, his foot landing with a thump on the step-edge by my shoulder. He grabbed a clump of my hair, his expression turning cold as he leaned towards my ear, tipping my head. I could smell the tang of sweat on his body. The closeness of his revealed face had me yearning for the moist contact of a kiss, for the scratch of stubble against my skin, for something human and reassuring. And yet, even while I wanted that comfort, the resolute withholding of it thrilled me. A lust for danger made my blood pump hard, made my cunt twitch and swell.

Through gritted teeth, Den said, 'The more you challenge me, the more I want to take you down. So consider this your warning, Ms Natalie Lovell: Push it too far and I will break you into tiny little pieces. Got that?'

I wanted to maintain my irony but instead my voice came out thin and pleasure-soaked. 'Sir.'

*

The word 'Sir' had never sat easily with me. When I'd explained this to Baxter a few months into our relationship, he'd said, 'Aye, well, that can be your safeword.'

We'd laughed at the perverse irreverence of his joke. We didn't have a safeword, didn't feel we needed one because we'd built up such a strong connection. I felt Baxter could read me like a book. Although he would act as if he were laying waste to my body, he was always observant, always measuring me and checking in, reacting to my cues and responses to take things up or down a notch. I felt so safe with him.

And yet during an atypical moment, 'sir' did become my safeword. We seldom played with hardcore pain or engaged in formalised discipline sessions and roleplays, preferring to incorporate ouches, shaming and threats into our lovemaking as smoothly as we did kisses and caresses.

When I safeworded him, I hadn't passed my pain or fear threshold; I'd simply hit my limit of what I could tolerate that night. I'd had enough, *e-fucking-nuff*, but Baxter, rabidly horny and eager to continue, wasn't listening to my weary pleas for mercy. Or rather, he couldn't hear the sincerity in them.

'Bax,' I gasped. 'I'm getting close to my limit.'

'Yeah?' he growled. 'Then you're not there yet.'

For almost three hours, he'd subjected me to what he later proudly termed his 'reign of terror'. I'd been bound and brutalised, had had wax dripped on me, been thwacked with a skanky piece of MDF he'd found in the street on his way to mine. I'd been fucked every which way, had come three times, had been blindfolded, spun around then ordered to crawl in search of cock. The best and the worst of it was when Baxter paused to examine the silicone dildo he'd just been forcing me to suck.

'You got a broom?' he asked.

I drew my hand across my wet mouth. 'Why?' I managed to gasp.

'Just answer the fucking question.'

I directed him to the kitchen downstairs, glad of a few minutes' respite. He returned with the broom's wooden pole, the brush head removed, and promptly rammed the dil on one end. He huffed and cussed as he skewered the toy onto the stick. I'd never even noticed my dil contained a hole at the base but Baxter, whose imagination seemed capable of corrupting everything in his path, had spotted it.

Satisfied with the fit, he gave his new tool a shake. 'Open your legs,' he said. When I did, flat on my back, he proceeded to fuck me from several feet away, turning me to a grunting, gibbering wreck while he looked down at me, gleefully cruel as he shoved the customised pole back and forth.

After too much of that, he tried to make me deep-throat the obscene object. I couldn't manage it. The dil was too resilient and big. I gagged and spluttered, pleading for a break. As punishment for my failure, Baxter slapped my bruised, tender arse, his beefy hand cracking hard onto my cheeks. Then he popped the dil off the pole, slammed its thick shaft inside me and eased his hard cock into my arsehole. On all fours, I widened around him, gasping, his girth in my rear making the dil press in my cunt, everything squashing up within me to accommodate the double insertion.

Then, ordering me to hold the dil in place, Baxter banged away at my butt. He was building up to his third orgasm and I knew he'd be hammering at my arse until he got there, which likely wouldn't be anytime soon. I felt on the brink of collapse, my body scorched and exhausted,

my mind reeling from the depths to which we could sink.
I feared I didn't have the mental or physical stamina to
hold out for much longer. Sure, I wanted Baxter to have his
orgasmic hat-trick, not least because I loved the desperate,
agonised noises he made when eeking out the last of his
ecstasy, but I wanted him to get there fast. And to be honest,
I was also getting bored.

I begged him to hurry but to no avail. And when I told
him I was close to my limit, that only seemed to invigorate
his desire to make me suffer. He thought I was play-acting.
He began squeezing my nipples, really squeezing them as
he rode, and my discomfort outweighed my pleasure. Most
times, when I'm close to maximum endurance, I take pride in
not safewording, so I couldn't blame Baxter for not spotting
a difference between those times and this.

But for some reason, something gave up inside me that
night. Additionally, I guess I'd become confident enough
with Baxter that I felt safewording would be OK, not an
indicator of failure on my part or his.

I heard myself crying out, 'Sir, sir, sir!'

'What?' he snapped, still fucking and squeezing.

He'd forgotten my safeword.

'Stop,' I wailed. 'Stop, sir. Sir! Stop!'

He froze. 'Ach, your safeword.' He snatched himself free
of me, full of concern. 'You OK, hen? Did I hurt you?'

He tried to embrace me but I gently pushed him away,
needing a moment's space. I flopped onto my back. 'I'm fine.
Not hurt.'

'You traumatised?' He knelt up on the futon, frowning at
me, his hand moving gently on his cock.

I shook my head. 'I just needed you to ease up and you
weren't listening.'

'Ah, fuck. Sorry. I'm such a cunt. Can't believe I missed that. Not like me at all.' He raked fingers through his tousled hair. 'You sure you're OK? You want a wee cuddle?'

I shook my head again. I didn't want a cuddle. I wasn't being a hero in rejecting the offer. I genuinely wanted my space and a moment's distance from him. 'Just need to lie still and catch my breath.'

'You sure? Fuck, I'm sorry, hen. I feel awful.'

'Honestly, Bax. It's not a big deal. You didn't screw up. Don't go all guilty on me.'

'I'll take it easier next time, I promise.' Still kneeling over me where I lay sprawled on my back, he waggled his fingertips against mine.

'No, I said. 'I'd rather you took risks than didn't. Don't make me feel bad for safewording.'

'But I *do* feel bad,' he replied.

'Then please bottle it,' I said. 'Let's not make this into a drama about you.'

'Ay, you're right, sorry. So you're OK, then?'

I nodded. 'Yes. Fine.'

His hand returned to his cock, still hard. His fist shunted slowly. 'Then do you mind if I risk asking if I can wank on your tits?'

I laughed hard. God, but he was adorable. When he came, he released a volley of dark, twisted cries, peaking on a rattle of raw bliss as his heat spattered down on me. Later, as we lay in each other's arm, we agreed 'sir' was too confusing to be an effective safeword. Baxter said, 'My trusty perverts' manual recommends the word "amber" for go slow and either "red" for stop. Or a long, distinctive word.'

'Seems sensible,' I said.

'So from now on,' said Baxter. He leaned on one elbow

alongside me, nudging a coil of hair from my face, getting stern and serious. 'I want you to remember that your safeword is "supercalifragilistic . . ."'

I laughed and flung my arm around his neck, planting a smacker of a kiss on his lips. 'You're funny,' I said, sinking back into the pillows and pleased that using a safeword hadn't caused a major angst.

Baxter beamed down at me, his dark, dishevelled hair backlit by my bedside lamp and outlined with an unlikely halo. He traced a finger across my smile and after a while said, 'I have a wee confession to make.'

I raised my brows.

He looked at me for too long, making me nervous. What had he done? What was wrong? At length, he said, 'I think I'm falling in love with you.'

I kept smiling, afraid and delighted because for a while I'd been trying not to say a similar thing myself. When we'd started out, Baxter had expressed reservations about getting involved after the collapse of his marriage. He'd said he needed to play the field, needed to rediscover himself before committing to someone new. I'd accepted that, warning myself to keep my distance and not fall in love.

But the magic was happening, despite my attempts to resist it. The excitement of physical lust was swelling to become something far greater and deeper. I was walking on clouds, always longing to see him, and my life seemed to glow with possibilities. Everything I discovered about Baxter made me want to discover more. I wanted to do everything and nothing with him, and wished we could spend more time on the latter, just hanging out at mine. But Baxter was always so busy with work, so full of energy, that mellow times were rare. Perhaps that would change now Baxter had fessed up to his feelings. I was about to return the compliment and celebrate our moment with a kiss when he cut in.

'And that wasnae meant to happen,' he said.

It never crossed my mind it wasn't meant to happen because his marriage was still intact.

After a spartan lunch of bread, cheddar and water, Den showed me to the dressing rooms in the basement below the stage. He carried a Maglite, its beam swooping left and right across a corridor made sickly by the greenish hue of fluorescent lights. Glossy, beetroot-red paint on the walls had shattered into crackle-glaze fragments so the corridor appeared to be tiled in mosaics. Den's torchlight swept into dark rooms and over scrawls of angular, illegible graffiti. The fear of other trespassers made sweat prickle on my back.

I followed Den, my wrists fixed in front of me, a length of chain running from my leather handcuffs to a belt loop in his jeans. I watched his feet, trying to put mine where his had been, scooping up the slack chain when I got too close to him. He wore black Converse All Stars, the soles worn at the heel. I bet he's from London, I thought. Hardly anyone wears Converse in Saltbourne.

As we passed along the corridor, Den shone his torch into the dressing rooms, revealing a range of interiors as garish as children's building blocks: pea green, daffodil yellow, electric blue. Other than that, the rooms were similar: small, windowless spaces, their walls lined with broken mirrors framed by blank bulbs and empty sockets.

Damp and mustiness permeated the air. What stories these walls could tell, I thought.

'When did this place become empty?' I asked.

'Late eighties. It's an absolute tragedy. Ours is an era of advanced philistinism.'

'So where are we? How did you get in? Is it safe?'

'It's safe enough,' he said. 'And we have electricity in some areas and running water so more civilised than it looks.'

'But where are we?'

'No more questions,' he said. 'Or I'll gag you again.'

He showed me a shower we could use in a large, fuchsia-pink dressing room which also contained a sturdy toilet cubicle. A harsh, chemical scent of cleaning fluids spiked the stale air. 'I've spruced this room up for us,' he said. 'It's not the Ritz but it's good enough for a couple of days.'

'A couple of days,' I echoed in shock. 'Come on, get serious!'

'I've kidnapped you, remember?' He raised the Maglite and shone its beam into my face. I flinched, the chain rattling as my cuffed hands jumped to shield my eyes from the glare.

'Yeah but . . . a couple of days is a long time.' I wasn't sure if his was a genuine plan or another attempt to mess with my mind. I squinted at the light, trying to read the face behind it, but was too dazzled to make anything out. After weeks of him being my faceless fantasy, I wanted to gawp at him until every feature was etched on my mind. Whether by accident or design, Den seemed determined to deny me the chance.

'What are you afraid of?' he asked.

'Um, rats,' I said. 'The police. Getting sacked if I don't turn up for work on Monday.' My temptation to add 'you' was silenced by my stubborn reluctance to give him the pleasure.

Den lowered the torch and grinned. In the weak, green-tinged light of the wrecked corridor, he looked monstrous;

a monster made more dangerous by his beguiling beauty. 'Trust me,' he said. 'Those are the least of your worries. Come on. I'll show you where you're going to be chained.'

Ten

We returned to the arena of the former stalls in the shabby auditorium. After the gloomy, below-stage corridors, the expanse was exhilarating, the hazy pearl light and richness of colour a welcome relief. My sandals rang on the concrete as we crossed the empty space while Den's trainers barely made a sound. The chain sagged between us, occasionally scraping on the ground.

'There,' said Den, signalling to the far corner of the room.

By one of the pillars supporting the dress circle, a cluster of furniture and belongings made a strange, homely room, albeit one without walls. A stage set appeared to have escaped and regrouped. The surreal sight bordered on the supernatural, the half-room's existence suggesting unlikely beings dwelled here, unseen by human eyes.

I guessed we were the unlikely, unseen beings, cooped up in this forgotten theatre while the world outside went about its business.

'Did you set this up?' I asked.

'Of course.'

The bed was the most prominent feature, a duvet-covered

double mattress on a low platform of wooden pallets, the sort used for moving goods on forklift trucks. An armchair draped in a red throw was angled towards nothing, and at a polished, pine dining table, two high-backed chairs awaited their guests.

'I'm flattered,' I said sincerely. 'All this effort.'

As we drew closer, I noticed other objects at odds with the suggestion of familiar comforts. Objects which stirred feelings of unease and excitement. A length of chain dangled from a hook fixed to the balcony above. Each curvaceous leg of that nice pine table was looped with chains. Although they made me nervous, I understood those chains. I knew what they would be used for.

What I didn't understand was a peculiar piece of furniture resembling a medieval stool, although not one you'd choose to sit on for comfort. It was made of deeply polished oak, the seat a bowed, narrow plank with a sturdy, carved ring at either side. The back of the chair was painfully narrow too, sloping away from the seat, and topped with another carved ring. I could imagine it once being used for tying people up in the market square so they could be pelted with rotten tomatoes.

'What's that?' I asked, pointing with both hands. My voice surprised me with its quietness.

'A birthing stool.'

Ah, of course. Legs spread, something to grip, lean back and push.

'Hey,' I said. 'I like you but there's no way I'm having your baby.'

Den laughed as we crossed to the object. 'Don't worry. I don't plan on keeping you here that long.'

'It's a gorgeous piece.' I twisted in my cuffs to run my

fingers over the chair back, the chain clanking against varnished oak.

'Isn't it?' he said. 'It's Victorian Gothic revival. I got it from Community Crafts in Saltbourne. As soon as I spotted it, I saw its potential to be used for nefarious purposes.'

Liam's workshop was at Community Crafts. The thought of that made my head spin. Everything seemed wrong all of a sudden, too out of synch with reality. Weird to think that Den had visited Community Crafts but no reason why he shouldn't or wouldn't if he were in the area. The venture Liam was part of had a good reputation. But the reminder of everyday reality threw me. What was I doing here? Where was the rest of the world? Was it daylight outside? My phone was in my bag. I had no idea of the time.

'We'll sleep here tonight, OK?' Den gestured towards the raised mattress.

'Sure,' I said. 'You didn't put little chocolates on the pillows, though.'

Den smiled, unclipping the chain from his belt loop. In silence, he unbuckled my cuffs, briskly checked my wrists for marks, then walked away to deposit the cuffs on the large table. I stood, small and uncertain in the midst of so much space. Den took a seat in the red-draped armchair and rested one ankle on his opposite knee, hands on the chair arms, grand yet casual. 'Take off your clothes,' he said. 'Let me look at you.'

Oh Hell. These shifts of direction were unsettling.

'Now?' I said, stalling for time.

'Now,' he said.

My heart thumped. I wished I could ask the same of him then I could feast my eyes on that honed, muscular body I'd only so far seen in an arty photograph. Stupid

D/S dynamic! I also wished he would undress me himself, hands instead of eyes on my body. Physical intimacy was much easier than being on display. Taking a deep breath, I kicked off my sandals and quickly unbuttoned my shirt. I placed my top on the birthing stool and unfastened my bra with my back turned him. Silly to feel awkward about being naked when he'd already shagged me stupid. But I did feel awkward.

'Slower, slower,' he said. 'It's not a race. Turn around. Show me your tits.'

I swallowed my nerves. Still in my skirt, I turned, shoulders back to give myself some oomph. He gaze dropped brazenly from my face to my breasts. Had he been expecting me to do a coquettish strip-tease? I hoped not. *Cosmo* would recommend a move like that, and everyone knows theirs are the daftest sex tips in the world. Besides, I was too shy to be coquettish, and my role in this was not the seductress.

'That's better,' he said. 'Now touch yourself.'

I repressed a sigh and cupped my breasts. I massaged and thumbed my nipples, making them erect. I felt porny and false. Ordinarily, I wouldn't touch myself this way to get off. Someone else touching my breasts, awesome. Me touching them myself, not much doing, I'm afraid.

'OK,' he said. 'Now keep undressing.'

All that remained was my skirt. My knickers were in his van. I unzipped, stepped out of the skirt and draped it on the stool. I faced him, half-raised my arms in a self-conscious flappy way then tapped my hands against my thighs.

'Step forward,' he said.

I did, feeling brutally naked.

'Stop there.' From a few feet away in his chair, he examined me, pale blue eyes moving with deliberate assessment. I swear, the tracks of his gaze practically had my skin colouring where they roamed.

He nodded as if satisfied then gave a bossy flick of one finger. 'Turn around.'

I might have been up for sale in a cattle market. His cool evaluation appalled and aroused. I turned for him, cringing. The concrete floor was cold and scruffy underfoot. I stared at a panel of flock wallpaper several yards ahead while he, presumably, stared at my arse. Perhaps the absence of people in the theatre affected me, as did an awareness this place had once buzzed with excitement, the corridors thronging with men and women in furs and monocles. Eyes other than Den's seemed to leer at my naked body, hundreds of hidden eyes running over breasts, thighs, buttocks and pubes, drinking me in. I felt humiliated, objectified and diminished. And I loved every awful minute of that.

The armchair creaked. Den's trainers snagged on the floor's crumbled surface. I kept perfectly still, focusing on the flock fleur-de-lys as he approached. My breath gave a hitch as his hand trailed across my buttocks, the flimsiest of touches. He circled me, his hand continuing to drift across my belly. His fingertips painted goosebumps, sending messages of arousal deeper into my flesh. I barely breathed, let alone groaned. A pulse fluttered in my neck, while in my groin a heavy beat boomed in fat, liquid throbs.

Den kept his head low as if following the path of his hands. His head was beautifully shaped, a perfect dome shaded by stubble, curving inwards to meet a sun-kissed neck scattered with tiny hairs the razor blade had missed. I longed to lick him there. His hand scooted lower, fingers gliding into the neat fluff of my pubes. He stood before me, rubbing gently at my mound.

An exhalation left me, a soft whistle like that from a coffee bag being punctured. My legs almost buckled. I willed his fingers to move lower, but no. They kept on stroking through my hair, teasing the skin beneath. My mind grew dumb, fixed on nothing but the need for his fingers where I wanted them.

When he finally touched me, I groaned but it was a cheat's touch. His fingers skimmed the frill of my labia, denying me the firm penetration I craved. He brought his sloping, scar-roughened face close to mine. 'Are you ready for some pain?' he asked.

My heart skipped a beat but I nodded, my horniness convincing me I was ready for anything he cared to dole out.

'Good girl.'

I watched him hoik a holdall onto the table and unzip. The jaws of the bag gaped, revealing an assortment of kit, too jumbled for me to identify anything much. Jeez, did I want this? I glimpsed leather, metal, rope, cables, fabric and who knew what else; a pervert's paradise, packed away in an innocuous travel bag.

My heart wouldn't stop racing. I'd never done anything so hardcore before. Baxter would overpower me without all this rigmarole. Nonetheless, the dark secrets in Den's bag fascinated, the allure of their mystery and taboo urging on my desire. I was keen to know if I might enjoy being hurt and disciplined but I was scared too in case I hated it or got injured. Jumping in at the deep end might not be the ideal way to experiment but then when had I ever been cautious in this? I hoped Den knew what he was doing.

He took the leather cuffs from the table. 'Hands in front,' he said.

I gave him my wrists, fists bunched together. 'Don't hurt me too much.' My voice was throaty and frail.

Without a word, Den buckled the cuffs then joined them together with clips and a short length of chain. Again, the sensation of bonds being fixed around my wrists took me closer to the place I like to be; a place not simply of arousal but of submission.

'I'm not used to heavy pain,' I added.

'This way,' he replied, acting as if he hadn't heard.

He led me towards the spot where the chain dangled from the balcony. He raised my coupled wrists, holding the chain above us with his other hand.

Despite my desire, I panicked. 'No, wait!'

My body did its own thing, cowering, crunching, trying to withdraw. The edge of the cuffs dug into my hands as I retreated. Den held firm, refusing to let me go. His determination to hold on made me even more afraid. My arms kept trying to pull back from him. My feet did a stupid little dance as if I were standing on hot sand.

'No, please! I can't, I can't.' My voice echoed across the space.

Den released the hanging chain and gave a reprimanding tug on the links between my wrists. 'You're going to take it,' he spat. 'You're going to shut the fuck up and take it.'

Beneath his hunched black brows, his eyes were slits of blue ice, the tendons in his neck as taut as wires. I looked down, ashamed of my fear, wanting to accept this despite my instinct to recoil. A hefty knot in the crotch of Den's jeans did nothing to placate me. Supposing he got carried away on a crazy rush of lust? Supposing he didn't know when to stop?

'It's too much,' I whispered. 'Please.'

He took a step closer and this time I didn't draw back. The chain slackened and I tried to relax my arms. Resisting him hurt my shoulders.

'What do you want, Natalie? What's the problem?' His voice was soft and charming, a parody of seduction. 'Are you afraid of enjoying this too much? Of having to face yourself afterwards, knowing what you like?'

I shook my head. I didn't know what I was afraid of.

Den took another step closer, drawing me to him, his hand warm on my naked buttocks. We stood like that, pressing lightly against each other. His erection bulged against the back of my chained hands. I rubbed then wriggled inside my cuffs to find him more fully with my fingers. Seeking cock was familiar territory. I stroked his shaft, my thumb and forefinger spanning the ridge behind the denim. His hardness thrilled, tempting me to go along with his plan so I could get a piece of that inside me.

He nuzzled at my ear, his breath warm on my skin. 'Greedy little whore,' he said.

I whimpered because he made me feel that was true. I wanted him in my hand, wanted the naked weight of his cock in my fist, and most of all, I wanted that solidity driving inside me. He caressed my arse cheeks and we stayed like that a while. I grew calmer, hornier, more pliant.

Eventually, he said, 'Now let's try that again, shall we?'

I nodded, all meek and accepting. He led me back towards the dangling chain, and this time I followed without protest. My thighs were smeared with my wetness. I was so obvious. I stayed silent, allowing him to lift my arms above my head. He fiddled with the clips, connecting me, then stepped back. My limbs sagged, jerking on the resistance of the chain. I was strung up, exposed and vulnerable, completely at his mercy. At anyone's mercy. I wished I could shield myself or at least lower my hands. The baring of my underarms was worse than that of my breasts.

Den walked towards the table. He tugged off his hoodie, slinging it onto the armchair as if he really meant business. My stomach fluttered at the revelation of more flesh. His T-shirt was a faded khaki green, hanging in a way that revealed, without clinging, his broad shoulders, toned, muscular chest and flat stomach. His forearms were hairy and his biceps hard, their veins snaking under a coffee-pale tan. High on his left arm, peeping below the sleeve of his tee, a faded black tattoo of a ring topped with three curly flames stretched over the bump of his muscle.

Finally, I had confirmation this man was the same as that in the photograph I'd received. In the flesh he was bigger, more pumped up. I wondered how old the photo was.

Den rummaged in his holdall then walked towards me, slipping something into his jeans pocket. Damn, he was beautiful, his wide, sloping face a haunting mix of composed and ferocious. He stood in front of me, lips curling in a smug smile. The vastness of the theatre seemed to shrink, becoming this one small space he and I occupied. Even though our bodies didn't touch, my skin felt receptive to the fabric of his fully-clothed body. Placing his hands on my waist, Den ran them up and down, watching my expression. I bit back a groan, trying to conceal my lust. I wanted his hands to go both higher and lower but I asked for nothing, accepting his modest caress.

Eventually, his thumbs rose to nudge the underside of my breasts and I couldn't help but moan. He traced lines to and fro along their uplifted swells then bobbed down to suck on one of my nipples. I moaned again, reeling at the intensity of his wetness and the flick of his tongue where he held me in the warm cavern of his mouth.

So gentle, not at all what I was braced for. Sensation

shivered to my groin. He moved to tongue my other nipple, his hand massaging my other breast. I swayed, arousal making me unsteady. My raised arms were hot and crampy. The chain creaked above us. I hoped that thing was safe, hoped the balcony circle wouldn't come crashing down on top of us.

KINKY COUPLE KILLED IN THEATRE GAME

Oh, what was I doing? Why these risks? Why did I like them so much? But why did anyone like or hate anything? Why did I like running or red wine or certain types of music? No answer to that, or no reason need underpin a preference for anything. The reason was the result, was in the negative or positive outcome created by the thing itself. May as well ask a person why they like pleasure. I shouldn't doubt myself by wondering about my strange desires. Best instead to accept their validity and focus on enjoying them.

Den stood straight again, his lips shining with wetness. He tucked his hand in his front pocket and removed a small, silver object. He held it in front of my face, grinning. A nipple clamp. He pumped its jaws, making them go chomp-chomp-chomp. The clamp's tips were covered in stippled, cream rubber, a dozen tiny teeth to latch on to me. Still smiling, Den took a nipple between thumb and forefinger, creating a sharper point for the clamp. His watchful eyes flicked from my tits to my face as he brought the pincers closer to the nub of flesh he was positioning.

'I don't know,' I gasped. 'Don't know if I can take it.'

'Don't know till you try,' he said smoothly.

Slowly, he closed the clamp on my nipple. The bite grew harder and I wailed as the pressure rose, my tip crushed between the rubber-toothed jaws. Finally, I was at my limit, unable to take more pain.

'Enough,' I breathed.

'It's OK,' he said. 'Nearly there.'

'No! No more.'

He allowed the clamp to take its final, deep bite. I howled as he withdrew his hand, the weight of the dangling clip adding to the pain, the chain clanking above me as I thrashed.

I kicked against my own shin. 'Get it off, no!'

'Count to five,' he said.

'I can't.'

'You can!'

The pain was abating before I'd even reached three, and believe me, I was counting fast. I drew deep breaths. 'It's OK, it's fine, I'm there.'

He pressed a hand to my cheek. 'Well done. Brave girl.'

His approval made me determined not to be such a wuss for the second clamp. But what can I say? Mice and men. I squealed as Den slowly closed the clamp on my other nipple, bracing myself for the impending spike of pain. Again, the rubber teeth gripped until I was convinced I'd reached the limit of my tolerance. I couldn't imagine a worse pain but I knew it was about to pounce; and I knew I could take it because I'd already done so.

Den knew that too. At the last moment, he released the spring with an open-handed flourish. I cried, cursed and writhed, the chain jangling above me like a dungeon's rattle. I tried to roll with the pain, not fight it; tried to rise with the bruising heat. Bastard, bastard, bastard! Then again, the pain subsided and I settled into a woozy ease. Den watched me all the time, coolly observant, a trace of irony lifting his lip and glinting in his eyes.

I loved that knowing control and how it contrasted with my freak out. Motionless and silent, he waited. When I'd calmed, accommodating the pain as best I could, Den smiled.

Then, blithely sadistic, he flicked one of the clamps.

'Aieee!' The pain exploded, tugging where I was tender, an internal burn fusing with the outer bite. When my gasps had quietened, Den did the same to my other nipple, making me howl again. Then he went back and forth, playing me like an instrument, smiling all the while and clearly relishing my pain.

'That good, huh?' he asked sweetly, as if he were spoon-feeding a baby.

It was and it wasn't. The pain blazed. As an isolated, physical sensation, I wouldn't have cared for it. But the pain was inseparable from the delirium it provoked, seducing me into a liberating madness.

'Yes, good,' I said, my voice cracked.

Den's fingers stole a path through my pubes. He cupped my swollen vulva, his warm fingers paddling at my wetness. My nipples throbbed, their heightened sensitivity charging my cunt. With his other hand, Den pulled gently on one clamp, a reminder of my soreness and the power he had over me.

His fingers slid along my slit and he reached around to wind his other fist in my hair. He held my head firm, stepping closer so his clothes brushed my skin. I looked up at those flat blue eyes, at the low, sweeping plane of his nose and his scar-speckled cheekbones. I became disconnected, dreamy.

'You,' he said kindly, 'are a nasty little fuckslut. I can feel you dripping all over my fingers.' He eased two fingers inside me, moving them up and down with leisurely control. My wetness clicked, a tiny sound in the surrounding silence.

I gave a low groan, aching for more. For a long time, he refused me. Cruel and steady, he fucked me with two fingers but it was the slowest fuck in the world. After a time, he released my hair and inserted a third finger, stretching me wide and tight. Again, I begged for it harder and faster. All he did was smile and continue with his unhurried fingerfuck, his knuckles bulky within my slippery, wet flesh.

When he pulled out of me, I was so crazed with need I could barely breathe, never mind speak. I tried some words but even I didn't understand them.

I watched, dazed, as Den walked away to rummage in the kinky chaos of his holdall. He removed a thick, leather tube, flipped off its cap and tipped out an object I recognised as a flogger. It was a beast of a thing, its hefty, polished handle striped with a dark rainbow of colours, red leather fronds streaming like a flaccid fountain. Den twirled the baton in one hand, his wrist churning with a practised rotation so the streamers span in a quickening blur. He held out his other hand, then brought the lashes down onto his palm with a satisfying thwack. Then another and another.

Fear and hunger chased each other around my body, hunger taking the lead by a margin. Den returned to me, smirking. I tensed, ready for an onslaught, my senses sharpening, goosebumps of anticipation lifting on my skin. Still grinning, Den stood before me and raised the flogger high, allowing the tips of the dangling strands to rest above my breasts. He swished the implement left and right, its soft ends tickling my skin. Occasionally, the gentle movement caught one of the clamps, knocking an edge of pain into my nipple. But the sensation was slight compared to earlier, and the flogger as soft as a kiss.

Den trailed the lengths of leather over one shoulder and lightly swished. His gentleness brought me down a notch but at the same time made me wary. I had to remind myself to breathe, relax. He moved behind me, broad leather tips still brushing here and there, skimming the swell of my buttocks, my shoulder blades, my back.

Eventually, he began tapping my upper back with a sway of the strands that grew into a series of firmer touches. I murmured in pleasure, my skin tingling as the hits striped across the canvas of my flesh, painting heat on top of heat.

'So biddable,' he said.

Moments later, a fiercer hit fanned out. The weight of it shoved me forward, leaving a warm, stinging patch in its wake. He hit me again. Then again but to the left. Each blow slammed, a thud streaked with intensity, knocking me off balance. Before long, I was gasping with the impact of the blows. Den moved lower, the leather thumping across me, licking my waist. I began to feel zonked, calmed by the pain. Den hit my butt, left cheek, right cheek, harder and harder. I hissed as the straps lashed my flesh, those vicious streamers whipping around my curves, biting nastily.

'Open your legs.' His request was quite casual.

Oh fuck. This was too scary. I hesitated, reluctant to give him access.

Again, in a stronger command, 'Open your legs, whore.'

I complied.

'Wider,' he said. 'I want full access to your cunt.'

I shuffled my feet apart, staring at the domed, red and gold ceiling as I braced myself. When I looked down, Den was swinging the flogger between my legs, the red straps arcing back and forth. The leather ends caught my inner thighs. After a few more swings, the lengths curled onto my cunt with a light tap. Again and again, he hit me there. It didn't hurt. It was worse. The caress of the straps toyed with my sensitised flesh until I was mad with lust. I wanted to tug down the balcony above us, anything for some let-up. I hardly cared if I brought a ton of rubble on our heads.

'Please,' I gasped, 'please do something to me.'

'Like what,' he said smoothly. 'Make you come?'

'Yes, I need to. Please, please.'

'Let's see how badly you need it, shall we?' He stood in front of me, brandishing the flogger as if the stripy handle were a cosh. 'You have to hold this in your cunt, grip it with every muscle.' He stooped a fraction, matched the smooth, carved tip of the handle to my entrance and began feeding it into me, inch by inch. 'If you let go of it, you lose your chance to come.'

I bleated as he inserted the handle, squeezing as hard as I could with my muscles. I was so wet and open I feared the flogger would slip from me the instant he let go. But it didn't, and I focused all my energy on keeping the handle within me, no mean feat, especially with the weight of the hanging straps trying to thwart my attempt.

Then Den touched my clit, rolling it expertly beneath his fingertip. I cursed, my body clinging to the flogger, unable to indulge in the sensation in case I relaxed too much. With his free hand, Den tapped one of the nipple clamps.

'Remember,' he said. 'Hold on tight or you don't get to come.' He opened the clamp, releasing my nipple. Pain sky-rocketed as the bloodflow returned to my crushed tip. I wailed, trying to process the feeling, to hold on to my sanity: it's just pain, it'll pass! But Den released the other clip and my mind went into meltdown, so overwhelmed by the physical it couldn't hold a single thought.

His voice drifted into my agony. 'There we go. All over.'

He brushed my nipples as if that would soothe them but his fingers were made of fire. My nipples throbbed while my groin dissolved. Den clasped the lodged handle of the flogger, drew it down then up. I cried with gratitude, glad not to be gripping the damn thing. My body softened around the wooden shaft as Den fucked it in and out of me, harder, faster, his biceps flexing in the blur of my peripheral vision. My wetness ran freely and when Den touched my clit, I was so fat and sensitive I began to come. I thrashed, pulling on the chain as my orgasm tore through me, shivering and squeezing. Tremors of pleasure darted up to my face and down to my toes, leaving me flushed, weak-kneed and panting for breath.

Den withdrew the flogger, smiling. He crossed to the table, set down the flogger, and from his bag, selected a long, thin cane of rattan or bamboo. A slim, corded handle made the implement resemble a rapier. Den took the cane in two hands and flexed its bendy length.

'Do you know why I brought you to this place?' he asked.

I shook my head. He walked towards me, painting the air with the cane as if testing his technique. With a smart whip of his forearm, he slashed at the emptiness. A blood-chilling whistle rushed from the cane. Den gave a contented smile, admiring the implement.

He looked at me, searching my face for a reaction. Through a fog of submission, I gazed back. In the theatre's pale, hazy light, it seemed no one existed but me and this strange, savagely beautiful man. And me, I wasn't even sure I existed. I was becoming remote, fading from myself as if I might be turning into one of the ruined building's many ghosts.

'Because in here,' said Den, 'no one can hear you scream.'

Eleven

I dreamed I was trapped in the theatre. Alone below-stage, I wandered down crumbling corridors like a videogame avatar, unable to find an exit. I reached dead ends, climbed stairs that led to nothing, opened doors to reveal barricades of brick. Over and over I tried to escape, my attempts thwarted at every turn.

When I woke, I remembered I was trapped. I was alone too, lying on the low, makeshift bed in the theatre's chairless stalls, my wrists and ankles loosely bound. Where was he? Earlier, he'd sat in the red-draped armchair in the strange half-room he'd built, ignoring me by ostentatiously reading a book in the emptiness. I'd lain on the mattress, trussed in a hog-tie, my body bending back like a bow to meet the bundled connection of my wrists and ankles. My mouth had been fixed open with a claw gag. I was there purely for him, Den told me. I was a body whose greedy holes he could avail himself of at any given moment. The claw gag, a pair of two-pronged hooks on a strap around my head, pulled on the insides of my cheeks, making it impossible for me to swallow.

The loss of dignity and agency was darkly, deliciously

liberating. The bondage and the claw gag which, let's face it, wasn't a pretty object, allowed me to cast off my respectable, social veneer. In submission and humiliation, I could put inhibition aside and revel in my enjoyment of gloriously filthy sex with this man whose imagination could spin scenarios I hadn't yet dreamed of.

Den had fucked my mouth while I was gagged but he hadn't climaxed. I think the point was to prove he could treat me like his sex slave. I'd loved being made to take it but then he'd re-tied the ropes, removed the gag and told me to get some rest. Somehow, I'd slept. On waking I had no clue of the time or whether Den was still here. He would be, I told myself. You don't leave a woman in an empty building, tied up from kinky sex-games. Was he watching me from a hidden vantage point, trying to see something new in me by catching me off guard as he claimed he liked to do?

I kept still, not wanting to be a monkey in his cage. I was beginning to feel uncomfortable with our game. Though the sex thrilled me, an emotional coldness was setting in which I didn't much care for. I wanted the comfort of aftercare but Den was less than generous with himself. Through Baxter I'd learned the importance of aftercare, of checking your submissive partner is OK, then giving them what they need to come back to themselves and relocate. Sometimes I needed space and the knowledge Baxter was beside me, waiting. Sometimes, I needed to be held against his strong chest, enveloped in gentle arms, rocked and hushed. *There, there, it's all OK, the nasty brute has gone.*

Den kept checking I was physically OK but emotionally, he kept me at a distance. Perhaps I'd brought that on myself by unmasking him the first time he'd offered kindness and comfort. Had I made him wary, reluctant to step out of character in case I used his vulnerability against him? Or maybe this apparent performance *was* his character. Or at least, the cruel, aloof role was the only side he would show to me in here. He'd seemed easy-going and nice enough in our emails. Was his humanity an act he couldn't sustain? Or did he refuse to access his sensitivity and decency once engaged in a D/S relationship?

My mind began to drift, revisiting all that had happened since our arrival in the theatre. I tried to organise the pleasure into a coherent narrative but my memories were too tangled, individual events inseparable from a general excess of flesh, sensation and climaxes, of gloomy corridors and the desolate, palatial beauty of the half-lit auditorium that held us. Because, yes, that's how it felt: as if Den and I were held here. Like theatre-goers, we'd been transported to an unreal world and now we were captives in that magical space, transfixed and unable to flee.

I flexed my shoulders and stretched my neck. The chandelier and dome of the ornate ceiling loomed over me, an unchanging sky, home to roosting pigeons and no other birds. I wondered how long Den been planning this. I was seriously impressed by the effort. When we returned to our ordinary selves, I would ask how he'd managed it, ask to see the smoke and mirrors.

And that's when I remembered Rory, the thought springing from nowhere. I hadn't left any food out for her, poor puss. She'd be starving by now, wandering round the house, whining and clawing at the carpet. Jeez, Nats, how could you?

Guilt and self-loathing swamped me, the intensity of the feelings disproportionate to the consequences of my momentary, unintentional neglect. In a panic, I processed the implications of an empty bowl. If we were going to stay overnight, that would mean at least twenty four hours without food. She had water and a probably a few biscuits lingering from the morning but even so. What time was it now? My heart twisted to think of Rory hungry and distressed, no one coming to her aid.

I was ashamed to acknowledge how easily I'd forgotten her in my excitement of leaving the house for my assignation. I'd never seen myself as one of those women who's quick to sacrifice her lifestyle and priorities as soon as some cute guy with a big dick lands on her doorstep. That wasn't me. My sense of self was stronger than that. I liked to believe I didn't bend and sway to male attention; I didn't go off the rails when lust got the better of me. But lying there, tied up and horny in an abandoned theatre with my cat's needs all but forgotten, I glimpsed an image of an idiotic, man-obsessed woman who looked remarkably like me. Oh, Aurora, I'm sorry!

Something else bothered me too, a profound discomfort that didn't fully make sense. Was that part of the comedown I seemed to be experiencing or was something else troubling me, something I couldn't identify? But no, come on, Nats. The key issue was not self-analysis but how to rectify the situation. Was it too late to call Liam and ask him to pop round and feed her? But what would I say? I still hadn't revealed anything to him about Den or what I was up to. If I had a better sense of the time, I could maybe work out what to do.

I heaved myself into a sitting position, awkward in ropes. 'Den!' I called out. 'Den, where are you?' A faint echo blurred my words.

'Here.'

I turned to where Den was crouched on his haunches

by the orchestra pit, bare-chested and apparently examining the ornate barrier of the pit. He stood, tugging free a piece of wood, then cast it to the ground after a cursory inspection.

'You OK?' he called.

'No!'

He strode towards me through the pearlised half-light. He was naked from the waist up, the wedge of his torso sloping to narrow hips. He seemed mythic, like an unearthly creature of the gloaming. His skin gleamed with a silvery film and my restless gaze skated over his body, taking in the black-ink tattoo, the dustings of dark hair and his chiselled physique. I felt weak to think of what the heft in those muscles had done to me.

'What is it?'

'I want to go home.' I said the words before I'd consciously thought them. Immediately, I realised how desperately true they were. I wanted to click my heels three times and be whisked away. I wanted to hop into the funicular as I did after running on the seafront. I wanted home and Rory and comfort. 'I forgot to feed my cat,' I said.

Den stood by the mattress and gazed down at me, half-puzzled, those blue, almond-shaped eyes striving to read my face. Maybe my reason sounded lame, but it was partly true and the best I could come up with at the time. It was too late for us to use my usual dating opt-out: I don't think we're compatible. Besides, I wasn't sure that was accurate. I needed to take stock and reflect on what Den and I were doing. With hindsight, I could see we'd been hugely ambitious in planning this kidnap game for our first meet up. Maybe we needed to slow things down a fraction and discuss what we both wanted from this sort of relationship.

'Your cat?' he said disparagingly.

'Yes,' I replied, my tone defensive. 'My cat.'

Den shrugged as if he didn't believe me or didn't care. He knelt on the mattress and everything in his manner seemed to say 'whatever'. The scent of his sweat tormented me, and I had to resist the urge to lean closer for more of him.

He began fiddling with my bondage, the rope whistling coldly against itself as he unthreaded. He eased the tangles from me, working in silence. Concerned I might be sabotaging our prospects, I tried again with a better explanation and more gratitude.

'Today's been wonderful,' I said. 'You organised everything so perfectly. Really, it's been great, thank you. But I have to confess, this place does weird me out.'

'That was part of the plan.' Den looked up from the snarled rope he was working on. 'But if you don't want to go through with it, that's acceptable. We'll wrap things up here.'

I wanted him to sound more disappointed. 'I just wasn't organised for this,' I said. 'I didn't think I'd be out all night. I have other commitments, stuff to do tomorrow as well. And I should have thought about the cat. Stupid of me to forget to leave food out. Embarrassing, really. But I've had a brilliant time. Seriously, it's been wild. And again, thanks for setting this up. So impressive. No idea how you did it. I can't wait for the next time. I think we've only just scratched the surface here. We've got so much more to explore.'

Den shook his head, pinning me with those serious blue eyes. 'No,' he said. 'We haven't. When we leave here, it's over between us.'

I felt my face pale with shock. 'Are you roleplaying?'

Den straightened out the last tangle in the rope and stood briskly. 'No. This is all I wanted. One chance, one meeting.'

He shook the rope, matched the ends together and ran the smooth lengths through one fist.

I stared at him, struggling to absorb his meaning. 'But what about me? What about what I want?'

Den made a loop with the rope then began weaving it into a fat chain, preparing it for storage, for next time. 'I told you once,' he said, casting me a casual glance. 'I warned you. Don't you remember? I made it quite clear from the start.' He gave me a direct look. 'I don't give a single fuck what you want.'

On the day that would have been my father's sixtieth birthday, Baxter turned up at my house with a black and white cat in a lilac cat-carrier.

'I thought it might help with any sadness,' he said.

Behind the grille was a beautiful, green-eyed creature with fluffy white boots and a face that looked as if it had been dipped in a pot of white paint. She was, explained Baxter, the pet of a work colleague and needed re-homing. Her owners were due to have a baby and feared the cat-baby combo might prove problematic.

When this tiny panda-like creature tiptoed out of her carrier and nuzzled against my ankle, all practical concerns as to the wisdom of me being a cat owner vanished.

'She's called Minx,' said Baxter, smiling proudly.

'Minx?' I said softly, not wanting to startle her. 'You *are* joking, aren't you?'

'Fraid not. Why, you got a problem with standing at your door shouting "Minx"?'

'Yes,' I said, laughing. 'But you know, ugh. Too cute and girlish. All kinds of wrong.'

'Well, I doubt she knows she's called Minx.' Baxter stroked

the cat, his hand enormous against her slender, bony body. 'Wee thing's only a year old. Aren't you, eh?'

And so Minx became Aurora in honour of my father and the dreams he never had time to claim, especially his dream to see the Northern Lights. Over time, Aurora got shortened to Rory but in her green eyes I still saw my reminder of the need to live life to its full potential, and to not neglect dreams, desires and important aspects of myself.

When Den dropped me back home, I began to suspect that's why I'd wanted to leave the theatre so suddenly. I needed to feed Rory but I also wanted to return to what she represented in my subconscious. I'd had an urgent longing to get back to me, my priorities, and the space where love and kindness had once been. At the time, I hadn't been able to put my finger on the impulse, but it didn't matter. I wouldn't have tried explaining that to Den anyway.

I overfed Rory then curled up in bed, sore, aching and confused. Did Den really not give a fuck? Had he viewed this as a one-off encounter from the start or had he decided he didn't want to pursue a sexual relationship with me because I'd turned out to be a disappointment? One chance, one meeting. Did I fail the chance? Was I not up to scratch as a lover? Was I doing something wrong? Was it obvious I wasn't hugely experienced when it came to kinky sex? But I'd never professed to be an expert so why should that matter?

We'd had little opportunity to talk on the way home. Den had insisted on blindfolding me before leading me to the van where, again, I'd had to clamber blindly into the back and endure the journey from the discomfort of the mattress. His justification was he didn't want me to know where we'd just passed the last several hours. He'd spent a long time setting up our roleplay. He'd taken risks. He didn't want to chance

me running to the police and accusing him of breaking and
entering

'I won't,' I said. 'That's a ridiculous notion.'

'So do me the courtesy of respecting my request.'

I'd gone along with wearing the blindfold primarily
because I was eager to get home and didn't want to waste
time negotiating how we could achieve that. As soon as he'd
slid the van door shut I removed the eyemask, but I was in
pitch darkness, no windows to see out of. We were home in
about ten minutes. It had felt much longer the first time. I
wished I had a better knowledge of Saltbourne's abandoned
buildings but there were so many of them, boarded up and
derelict, that they didn't register as individual structures, just
part of our broken townscape.

Den had stopped at the bottom of my narrow road and
slid open the van door. He made no comment on my lack of
blindfold. There was no need to keep me sightless any more,
and the D/S dynamic we'd been playing with was evidently
in the past. He wasn't going to chastise me for disobeying
him as he might have done in a different situation. We were
in our civvies, back to normal. Game over.

'So you're really saying that's it?' I asked. It was around
two in the morning and the streets were dark and quiet, the
moon a high crescent behind thin, smoky clouds.

Den handed me my bag. 'Let's give it a few days, see how
we feel.' He bent forward and pressed a kiss to my forehead.
'Go and feed your cat. It's late.'

I turned on my heels, feeling patronised and messed about.
Nonetheless, I was glad he seemed to have had a change of
heart about quitting.

Despite the hour, I couldn't sleep that night. I was no
longer fearful of Den breaking in again. Instead, my mind

wouldn't rest, hopping over all that had happened and trying to understand Den and his intentions. I didn't know what to make of him. Him professing not to care about me didn't synch with the brief, parting kiss and more tender suggestion we contact each other in a few days. I struggled to work out what I wanted from him because I was struggling to work out who he was. Which aspects of him were sincere and which a roleplay?

Baxter's expression of sexual dominance was more integrated into who he was. I thought back to one of the times Baxter had spanked me. He'd done it briefly a couple of times prior to that but I wasn't over keen on scenes of discipline and corporal punishment. Alistair Fitch, with his wooden ruler at the piano, had possibly put me off but I think my desires had simply developed. Maybe the spankings and shame inflicted by my piano tutor had been my gateway kink. Over time, my fantasies had got darker, tending towards rough play, verbal abuse, debasement and being forced. Sexual submission, I'd grown to appreciate, can take many forms.

We were in the living room at mine, chatting, Baxter in the armchair, me kneeling on the floor close by. I was trying to explain why I didn't go a bundle on spanking.

'It's just a bit too nice,' I said. 'I know lots of women are into it and, yeah, the sensation of being hit on the bum is pleasurable. But the set-up surrounding spanking just . . .' I shrugged. 'All the "naughty girl" talk, the teacher-pupil roleplays. That side of it. I find that infantilising rather than erotic. Makes me feel like a spoilt little princess being rebuked. I guess it's not my thing, that's all.'

Baxter was listening to me talk, nodding contemplatively. When I paused, he said, 'You think too much. You ever been told that?' There was a warning edge to his voice, playful rather than sincere.

I shot him a look. 'Only by people who don't think enough.'

He raised his brows. I could see he was trying not to smile. 'Did you just call me stupid?' he asked. He edged forward in his seat, hands on the chair arms, poised.

For a moment or two, we froze, trying to hide our amusement, wondering who would jump first. Then Baxter pounced. I yelped and lunged away but, despite being a big bloke, Baxter was always fast. 'You cheeky wee bitch!' He grabbed me around the waist, dragging me back across the floor. 'You know what's coming to you now, don't you, eh?'

I laughed and squealed, helpless against his strength as he pulled me towards the chair and upended me over his lap. He flipped up my skirt and yanked my knickers as far down as he could manage while I wiggled and laughed. The position alone was enough to humiliate me and start my lust churning.

His broad hand cracked onto one cheek. Again and again he hit me, raining blows down on my flesh, and my laughter soon faded. 'That nice, princess?' he bellowed, panting and still thrashing me. Every whack landed with perfect resounding force, making my buttocks wobble as he turned them to flame. He had such an excellent, effortless wallop, and his arm took a long time to tire.

When he was done, he set me on my knees by his feet. My arse was raw and my groin throbbed, so plump and wet.

'Now what are you thinking?' he said, pinching my chin. 'Anything at all except how you love getting spanked?'

I shook my head because it was true. I had nothing else on my mind. 'Yeah but only by you,' I said.

'Ay well,' he replied. 'Plenty more where that came from.'

And it was true. I did love how Baxter doled out a spanking, rough and ruthless without a hint of headmaster in his demeanour. Discovering that new pleasure was a delight to us both and spanking became one of our many available options. But I loved the man, too, loved him with passion and tenderness.

By contrast, Den was some guy I'd recently met online who'd managed to get under my skin. I should perhaps try to accept emotional distance was an inevitable consequence of casual kink. Probably a healthy thing too. Helps keeps everything simple. But the other issue was I didn't know the ground rules of the game Den and I had embarked upon. He seemed loath to set any, and I'd been trusting him to know what he was doing. Then, just when I thought I was getting to grips with his style, he would pull the rug from under my feet. Should I resolve to forget him because his lack of clarity confused me? Or should we try to work things out?

When I finally slept, I was still no closer to an answer.

The following day it rained non-stop, grey rain like a forerunner to November. I paced up and down the house, overfed Rory again, checked the weals on my bruised arse in the mirror and obsessed over what had happened. Was this my fault? Was I, half-blinded by an enormous need to submit, missing the warning signs that ordinarily would highlight that this guy or that guy was bad news? Should I start mistrusting my desire? Could I be happy and whole without fully expressing my sexuality?

Ordinarily, when I want to clear my head to focus on an issue, I go running. But my body was too bruised for exercise. Instead, I played loud music, drank wine straight from the bottle, and, increasingly angry, had imaginary conversations with Den in which, with my perspicacity and scalpel-sharp wit, I reduced him to a remorseful, apologetic wreck begging for forgiveness and the chance to pick up where we'd left off.

The gentle goodbye peck on my forehead now mattered less. I decided he'd been nasty and callous, and trying to revoke that with a kiss didn't win him any points. Conversely, it made his erratic behaviour even more unacceptable, and seemed to be a furthering of his attempts to mess with my head. I didn't know if he had a grand plan or if he just enjoyed playing with his partner's emotions as part of his D/S fun. If that were the case, I told myself, I should have nothing further to do with him.

In our fantasy arguments, I said as much to Den. And when he wheedled and whined, I stuck to my guns, refusing to take him back because I had no interest in a man on his knees. He was a pitiful specimen, and I told him so. And then my dreams would warp because I didn't like to imagine Den taking 'no' for an answer. His lust was too strong for that. So I made him fuck me instead, made him pin me to a bed and pound into me with uncontrolled need, grabbing my hair and spitting, 'Shut up! I don't give a single fuck what you want.'

Anger galvanises. It gets you to the other side, to a better place. And boy, was I getting angry at his apparent mistreatment. But then I continued drinking, pouring out actual glasses rather than slugging wine directly from the bottle, and my anger ran out of steam. Instead, I became melancholy and tearful. The pain resulting from Den's seeming disregard for me opened wounds I preferred to believe were healed.

But maybe we don't heal. We simply become more adept

at walking around with our injuries. I wondered how Baxter Logan was faring with his share of scars? The last time I'd seen him was about a fortnight after our bust-up when he'd persuaded me to meet for coffee after work. I was all for shutting him out of my life once I'd discovered he was married but I'd relented when he'd begged for a chance to explain. A scrap of hope convinced me that meeting up was worthwhile. I was still in shock, unable to believe that, for a whole year, I'd been in a relationship with this man, oblivious to his other existence. I couldn't believe he didn't love me. I wanted to hear his side of the story.

When Baxter suggested coffee, he meant whisky. We met near the train station in The Railway Bell, a bleak, seedy pub frequented by alcoholics, commuters and dealers; a place where no one gives a damn about anyone else's business and the yellowing decor hasn't changed in decades. I'd never been before but Baxter, who worked in Saltbourne but lived in suburbia, was evidently a regular. He was waiting for me at a table in a booth of dark oak and stained glass, being burly and tragic while cradling his usual, a large Islay malt with three teardrops of water. Wanting to signify my distance and avoid joining him in a maudlin, Scotch-addled descent, I ordered black coffee at the bar.

I slid onto the bench opposite his in the booth, willing my heart to freeze. I wanted him to be a monster or an imposter then I could hate him, but he wasn't. He was Baxter Logan through and through, as big, beautiful and chaotic as he had been two weeks previously.

'My Natalie. I'm –' He reached for my hand across the table. I snatched it back as if bitten. He squeezed his bloodshot eyes, tipping his head to the ceiling before addressing me again, his face puffy with recent tears.

'Thanks for coming.' He laced his fingers together as if to stop his hands straying and the effect was an uncharacteristic primness. 'I didn't think you would and I know I don't deserve it.'

'Bax, I don't want to hear your self-pity. Just tell me why you lied for thirteen months. Thirteen fucking months!' Already I was raising my voice, my words thinned by the clenching of my throat, sobs threatening to sabotage communication. I inhaled deeply, aiming to speak calmly. 'You lied to your wife too. Everything we had, every good time we shared, it's dust. Dust and ashes and dead things. You've poisoned every memory I have of us. I don't know who you are any more. You're a fraud, a complete and utter fraud.'

I drew another steadying breath. I could see Baxter was itching to reach across the table to take my hand. He opened his mouth to speak but I shook my head. I hadn't finished. 'I used to think you were the . . . the warmest, the most sincere and honest man I'd ever met. You've made a fool of me, Bax, and a mockery of our relationship. I can't even preserve the good times. It's like . . . like the past has gone. Like someone stole the colours from all my photographs.'

Baxter combed his fingers through his mop of dark hair. His entire body seemed to tilt, the shoulders of his suit listing, his tie seeming to swing. It was an aspect of him I adored, the impression he gave of being about to fall apart at the seams, his enormous heart thrumming with the potential to disrupt cold order and regularity. I could almost believe him to be unwittingly capable of causing earthquakes, snowstorms, flash floods and hurricanes.

'You have to believe me,' he said, 'when I tell you I don't love her. Her existence makes no difference to my feelings for you. Our good times, they're still true.'

I sipped my coffee and grimaced.

'That not so nice?' asked Baxter, gesturing to my cup.

'It tastes of greasy metal. And it's barely even warm.'

'I'm sorry.'

'For what?' I said. 'The coffee or all your lies?'

'For everything,' said Baxter. 'For every idiotic, fuck-headed thing I ever did, and God's strewth, I've done a few. For the coffee, for getting married and staying married. For hurting you so badly. For letting you down. For being a selfish, thoughtless, irresponsible cunt. I'm sorry. I'm so desperately fucking sorry and I dinnae ken what I can do to make this better.'

Emotion strengthened his Scottish accent as it often did.

'Does your wife know about us?' I asked

He shook his head vigorously, eyes pinched shut.

'Not so fucking sorry, then,' I said.

He reached across the table for my hand again. This time, I didn't recoil and he took my fingertips in his. 'I love you, Nats. You're my beautiful wee bitch.' With his other hand, he gripped my wrist, a possessive, kinky gesture that had me wanting to abnegate all responsibility, to erase the pain by sinking into the self-obliteration of surrender. 'I love you so fucking madly,' he went on, 'and it's tearing me to pieces to think –'

'Not the point.'

'And Debra, my wife, she loathes the air I breathe because it allows me to keep living.'

I withdrew my hand from his grip. 'And you're still together because?'

He shrugged, put his elbows on the table and clawed both hands into his hair. He massaged his scalp then sat back with a sigh. 'Mortgage. Habit. Cowardice. Guilt.' He folded his arms and looked aside before leaning forward to speak. 'We wanted kids but discovered a while back we couldn't. Ach, well, we kind of gave up trying. It was too painful, hopes all over the shop. And Debra, she hit a low after that and we've just been ticking along ever since. We're stuck.'

'And I was your bit on the side,' I said. 'Your chance to grab some fun without confronting the issues.'

'Aye. I admit I'm not unusual in that respect and I'm not proud of my behaviour.' He swirled his whisky around the glass. 'But it became more than that. Remember the time you sucked my dick in the old boat down on the beach? I treasure that night, Nats. And it was actually my wedding anniversary.'

I gave a long, bitter laugh. 'And that's meant to make me feel special?'

He winced. 'I'm just trying . . . What I'm saying . . . Nats, you mean more to me than my wife does.'

I shook my head in despair. 'Jeez, Baxter, what planet are you from? Do the words "cake" and "eat it" ring any bells?'

He knocked back his drink, returning his empty glass to the table with a slam. 'All I wanted was some sex, a laugh and a few highs. Then I went and fell in love with you, didn't I? I never meant for that to happen but it did then it was too fucking late and now look at us.' He glowered at me but I knew he was angry with himself, not me. Trouble was, I doubted he even recognised that himself. 'I'm getting another drink,' he said. 'What'll you have?'

I sighed. I knew I should leave. We could talk endlessly about what had happened, what we meant to each other and where we might go from here. But I could never trust him again so it was futile. I needed to stand up, walk away and forget I'd ever met him.

'I'll have whatever you're having,' I said because I wasn't yet strong enough to stop loving him.

Twelve

'You sure you don't mind doing this?' asked Liam.

I laughed. 'Come on, Liam! It's me you're talking to. Course I don't mind.'

'OK, cool. Just checking,' he said. 'Could you open your mouth for me, please?'

'You're very polite.'

'This *is* a bit strange,' he said. 'Would you prefer it if I were impolite?'

'Ooo, maybe,' I teased. 'But I might get all hot and bothered. And then where would we be?'

Liam put on a gruff voice and wagged a finger at me. 'Open your mouth, you naughty, naughty girl!'

I laughed. 'Yeah, OK. You're right. Stick with polite.'

He put his hands on his hips, puffing out his chest. 'Are you saying I cannot be a master you would wish to obey?'

I began to feel uncomfortable. 'Liam,' I said. 'Don't take the piss.'

'Hey, didn't mean to.' He returned to his normal self, a sinewy, copper-haired guy with a laidback attitude. Cupping the back of my head, he drew me close to print a kiss on my forehead. I pushed aside the memory of Den doing similar.

'Just having a laugh,' said Liam. 'Didn't mean any offence.'

'Sure, none taken,' I replied. 'And anyway, that was a terrible impression of what I'm into.'

'It was meant to be.'

'Fair enough,' I replied. 'But . . . Well, I don't want to make this into an issue but, you know, plenty of people out there think that what I'm into is ridiculous or wrong. And it just felt . . .'

'Yeah, I get it,' said Liam. 'Most effective way to negate the power of something. Laugh at it. But I wasn't laughing, I swear. I have a lot of respect for you. You know that. I didn't mean – '

'It's fine, honestly,' I said. 'Doesn't matter. I'm over-reacting. Just been feeling slightly conflicted about kink recently. I'll get over myself soon enough. Now stick that . . . that contraption over my head.'

'You sure?'

'Liam,' I warned. 'Just get on with it, please. Your model is getting bored. She doesn't usually get out of bed for less than a tenner.'

Liam grinned and lifted his creation, stepping behind me as he lowered it over my face. The 'contraption' was a work in progress, a strappy, leather head-cage reminiscent of a scold's bridle from medieval times. We were in Liam's cobble-floored workshop, and I held still, feeling slightly awkward, as he adjusted various straps. The air was steeped in scents of sawdust, leather and tobacco. The pragmatics of Liam's craft combined with his workmanlike attitude stirred contradictory responses. On the one hand, being fitted with the harness felt reassuringly prosaic yet, opposing that, was my attraction to the world of secrets and submission where the leather half-mask belonged. The latter felt furtive, my desire concealed and disavowed by our necessary pretence of ordinariness.

Liam's long fingers fluttered around my head, fixing and adjusting. The bridle was a prototype in thin black leather. A broad band across my forehead connected to the main structure of the piece, all neatly fastened at the back of my head. From the band, two straps ran either side of my nose to meet silver rings fitted to cheek straps.

'Say "ahh",' said Liam.

A strap ending in a stainless steel claw ran from each ring towards my mouth. With gentle fingers, Liam pulled my mouth into a rictus by hooking a cold, round-tipped claw inside each cheek. His careful touch reminded me of a dentist's. 'You OK?' He checked the hooks, ensuring I was comfortable.

I nodded, feeling foolish. Memories of Den stretching my smile wide with a similar gag were impossible to repress. But then I'd been thinking about him more or less constantly since he'd released me from the theatre, kidnapping me in reverse by bundling me in the van and taking me home.

In the last ten days, I'd re-read the messages we'd exchanged on FancyFree dozens of times, looking for clues to suggest he was only seeking a single, elaborately constructed encounter at the end of a unnecessarily complex, protracted courtship. Nope. He hadn't made that clear at all. The only hint I found was in his hotel-room analogy when he'd talked of fantasy roleplay having different rules; and afterwards there's nothing to deal with, no consequences, life's as smooth and neat as a freshly made hotel bed.

I'd texted three times and had emailed once but no replies.

I'd stopped short of calling him, not wanting to make a fool of myself if he wasn't interested. Time and again I recalled our first phone conversation in the streets of Saltbourne at night. I'd sat on those old, stone steps and he'd ended our conversation by saying 'I don't give a single fuck what you like.'

But he did, I'd told myself. Of course he did. This was part of the game, the roleplay. He was going to use me and that was neat because I liked to feel used, liked to have a man so horny and aggressive he'd fuck me however he wanted. He wasn't really using me because I got off on that.

But now with this apparent sudden ending, had he genuinely used me? It certainly felt that way. The kiss on my forehead presumably meant nothing, given that he wasn't returning my messages. What I'd initially believed to be a mutually beneficial relationship had turned out to be distinctly one-sided. Den was calling the shots, and I was potentially responding to him much as I'd done with Alistair Fitch in his starry, blue music studio all those years ago. And hadn't I vowed, after splitting with Jim, I was going to seek what I wanted? You couldn't say I hadn't tried or that hooking up with Den wasn't a consequence of my efforts. But Den's attempt to take the reins and deny me a say in the matter seemed an unjust reward.

'That OK?' asked Liam.

I nodded, unable to speak.

'Like I said,' continued Liam, 'these photos are just for the client. I'll blur out your eyes and photoshop your hair. You won't be recognisable. He just wants to see what the mock-up looks like.'

I nodded again. I'd already agreed to this. I wanted to help Liam's craft business grow and if some merry pervert with money to burn was asking for photos of a work in progress, then I would gladly offer my head, so to speak.

The only problem so far was that modelling the headgear generated a horribly frustrating horniness, one Liam couldn't satisfy because D/S simply wasn't his thing. I could probably ask him to kink it up and act bossy in bed but I wouldn't ask because it wasn't him. And even if he were willing, anything we did together could only operate at the level of mild bedroom fun, a roleplay where Liam would need to be a character far removed from who he was. Unlike Baxter and Den, he didn't have an unshakeable sexual hunger to crush women underfoot, nor did he get off on seeing pretty faces streaked with tears. But he did have one major advantage over the pair of them: he wasn't a bastard.

I still couldn't quite believe what had happened. Recollections of the theatre ghosted my thoughts like a dream. Every morning, I woke thinking this would be the day Den would contact me and consolidate those memories. And every night I went to sleep knowing it wasn't. The more days that passed, the more concrete our ending became and the more surreal and remote our encounter. I began to wonder if the kiss in the moonlit street near my house was a fiction I'd invented.

I considered phoning him rather than sticking to more distancing texts and emails. Something, call it blind hope or a gut response, told me this wasn't over, not by a long shot. If Den had hurt me with his cruel dismissal it was only because he'd trusted me too much, trusted me to understand he didn't genuinely mean what he'd said. I'd known from an early point he wanted to mess with my mind so it was feasible he was now doing so by pretending to vanish from my life.

But, no. I couldn't give him the benefit of the doubt. His attempts to psychologically destabilise and dominate me were compelling and effective, but this ending was beyond the pale. I wasn't prepared to get hurt as part of the process of getting my rocks off. I'd been hurt enough in recent years, thanks very much. I wanted a lover, not a manipulative, sexual bully. I wouldn't get in touch again. I would resist, stay strong.

Liam pulled on a strap, tightening the bonds encasing my head and stretching my gagged smile a fraction wider. The extra tug made me crave Den and Baxter with a rawness that scooped me out and left me despairing of ever meeting my match. Den and Baxter were the only men who'd touched my submissive heart. And they'd both turned out to be self-centred, short-sighted swines who cared next to nothing for me.

Oh, Baxter had claimed to love me. But words without actions are meaningless and he wouldn't leave his wife for me. They never do, do they? That's what my friend Amy had said: they never leave their wives. A mistress is forever a mistress. Accept what you were and forget him. Move on. Start afresh.

If it were that easy, I'd have cleared him from my head a long time ago. I'd have erased Den too. I wished I knew more about him. I still didn't know his surname so couldn't even seek the dubious solace of Googling him. What I had done, though, was Google derelict theatres, reaching the conclusion I'd been held captive in Saltbourne's abandoned Hippodrome, just off Bath Road on the seafront. Photos of the theatre's interior in its heyday confirmed my suspicions. I wanted to take a closer look at the place but, at the same time, I was too nervous to even walk past it. Supposing he was there? Supposing he played kidnap every weekend with women he found online?

Liam aimed his digital camera at the side of my head. 'Say cheese!'

Unable to speak, I flung out my hand to cuff him playfully across his chest. He laughed and moved behind me, the camera whirring as he captured images of my trussed up head.

'I think I need to have better adjustments on this strap. And the final version won't be riveted so no rubbing or snagging for the wearer.' He touched the cheek piece. 'Not too tight, is it?' he asked.

I shook my head.

'You OK for me to take some shots of your face? Like I said, I'll blur you out.'

I nodded, thinking, please do it fast before I start drooling and embarrassing the pair of us. I closed my eyes as he worked, unable to meet his gaze. In the darkness of my mind, I was elsewhere, in silent alliance with strangers who shared my taste for unusual sex.

'It looks great,' said Liam. 'The plan is for this to connect to a thick belt, almost a corset, and that'll have points for wrist and leg cuffs to be attached to it. The client sees it as a piece of kit that has the potential to grow organically. The idea of the harness is that different kinds of gags can be attached to these cheek-rings. And he wants it all in brown leather and brass. It's the best commission I've had in ages. Brass carabiners are seriously hard to source, though. Still haven't found any I can afford. And I'll have to get the hooks made by a metal worker. It'll need to be food-grade brass, obviously. I just got these stainless steel hooks from a cheapo bit of bondage gear I bought online.'

After what felt like an eternity, my ordeal was over. Liam loosened the cage and eased it from my head. 'Thanks for that,' he said. 'I really appreciate it. Do you want to see the photos?'

'No, thanks. I think they'd give me nightmares.' I fluffed my hair back into shape. 'So business is booming, then? Word's getting out that you're our local, kink-friendly craftsman?'

Liam grinned and pulled a pouch of tobacco from his combats. 'Seems to be. Not sure how this guy found out about me. Said he'd heard a rumour someone at Community Crafts was making fetish gear on the side. I was the first he approached. A lucky guess.'

'Nice one.' I poked around the detritus on Liam's workbench while he rolled a joint and told me about a machete blade he'd been re-profiling. We smoked, sitting in the tatty leather and chrome armchairs, chatting lightly.

'What do you know about the old Hippodrome in town?' I asked, passing the joint back to Liam.

'Not much. Been empty for years, hasn't it?' Liam drew on the joint. He held the inhalation in his lungs then let smoke curl from his lips. 'Probably a listed building they can't knock down. So the owners will let it rot then go, uh, sorry everyone, it's knackered. Beyond repair. Then they'll raze it to the ground and sell the plot to property developers.' He swivelled in the chair so he was reclining sideways, long legs hooked over the chair arm, languid and relaxed.

'Yeah. I've heard it's stunning on the inside.'

'I'll bet it is,' said Liam. 'Wouldn't surprise me if it's been squatted and trashed, though.'

'I don't think it has been,' I said.

'No?'

'Well, I'm not sure. I think I must have read about it

somewhere. Do you think these places are easy to break into?'

Liam flicked ash onto the cobbles. 'Depends on the security they've got installed.' He took a deep, thoughtful drag. 'Can't imagine they'll have spent much on it, though. So yeah, if you know the tricks of breaking and entering, it'd be easy enough.' Smoke drifted from his lips. 'Why, wanna try it?'

I laughed. 'You serious?'

'Sure, why not?'

'You know about this stuff?'

Liam wriggled in his armchair, reaching out to pass me the joint. 'I've lived in squats. I've broken into buildings. I have a crowbar.'

I laughed uncertainly, looking at him, not quite able to process what he'd proposed. I'd only asked about breaking in to try and get a handle on how Den had managed it. Liam's suggestion took my curiosity in a whole new direction.

'Come on,' he said. 'Let's do it. It'll be a laugh.'

One of the great things about Liam was his competence when it came to manly activities such as fixing stuff, making things with tools and now, breaking into abandoned buildings with a crowbar. I could trust him to lead the way and do it right.

The question was, did I want to return?

'Be good to take some photos of the place before it gets demolished,' said Liam.

'Makes me nervous,' I said. 'Will it be dangerous?'

Liam shrugged. 'Only a bit,' he said.

I laughed and dragged on the joint, thinking over the idea. I could barely hold the smoke in my lungs. 'OK, then. You're on.'

*

It's hard to believe Saltbourne was once a coastal resort people actively wanted to visit rather than a town where they accidentally ended up living. Decades ago, Brits would have holidayed here, eating fish and chips on the prom, feeding coins into slot machines and sunning themselves in deckchairs on the shingle beach.

Amusement arcades still line the seafront opposite the fairground but their glitter is dulled, their magic tarnished by the shadowy presence of adult-only establishments where gambling is a grimmer, more serious affair. Our pier fell into disrepair years ago and the once-gaudy displays in souvenir shop windows are leached to pastels by the sun's rays. The pubs are chain-owned; large, soulless places with identikit chalkboards whose cartoonish fonts advertise Sky Sports and Stella Artois.

I don't often visit that part of town but when I do I always think it looks like someone else's memories. Turn off the main drag, and the picture's even bleaker with boarded up shops and To Let signs reminding anyone tempted to regard Saltbourne as a fun place that it's a dog-eared seaside town whose glory days are gone.

The Hippodrome on Bath Street serves as one of those reminders. Trying to act casual one midweek evening, Liam and I scanned the domed building from the other side of the street, checking out its security. The road was wide, capable of accommodating far more traffic than was currently gliding along it. At the bottom, the fairy lights of Sea Road gleamed like strings of pearls above the darkness of the beach beyond. The shift of traffic lights through red, amber, green, seemed a waste of colour in the emptiness.

A cheerless expanse of boards sprayed with graffiti blotted out The Hippodrome's front, a sharp contrast to the dilapidated curves of lavish architecture I knew to be inside. Dirt streaked the peeling pink and gold dome, and the letters P and M were missing from the fascia, making the theatre's grand name a stark, gap-toothed mouth.

'Looks quiet enough from here,' said Liam. 'Nothing to protect so they're hardly going to splash out on state-of-the-art security. Theatre's probably been ransacked, all the wire and lead stripped from it. Probably riddled with asbestos as well. Come on. Let's go round the back. Find a way in.'

Liam set off towards the road. I grabbed his hand. 'Liam, I'm not sure about this any more.'

He turned to me, grinning. In the orange hue of a streetlight, the curls peeking out from below his knitted beanie cap were redder than ever, and his eyes shone with boyish excitement. 'It'll be amazing, I promise,' he said, giving my hand a squeeze.

Standing on Bath Road, both of us in dark clothes and thick-soled shoes, me with my hair tied back and a baseball cap in my pocket, made me worry everyone knew what we were plotting. We could have been dressed in stripy tops and carrying swag bags for all the subtlety we lacked.

'I'm nervous again,' I said.

'That's part of the fun! Come on. Where's your sense of adventure?'

'She's in hiding,' I said. 'Scared we might get arrested for trespass or vandalism.'

'I'm not going to take any stupid risks.' Liam set off towards the road again, tugging on my hand. 'We might not be able to get in. Might be alarmed. Let's just take a look, eh? No pressure.'

I relented, infected by his enthusiasm. We hurried across the deserted road, towards the back of the theatre. On a street running parallel to Bath Road, a tall, redbrick wall and a tatty barrier of corrugated steel blocked access to the rear of the building. Liam tapped gently on the metal sheeting, searching high and low for weak spots. I thought back to how I'd arrived with Den. I'd been blindfolded but I'd imagined him parking the van in a private area before guiding me towards an entrance. I remembered how I'd heard gulls and felt a sense of space, correctly surmising we were near the seafront.

Now I'd seen Den's face, it was impossible to remember that moment as it had been. In recollection, I couldn't help but see the face behind the mask. But seeing his face and spending time with him still hadn't given me an insight into who he truly was. And now I couldn't tell whether he pre-occupied me because I found him intriguing or because I wanted him. And if I wanted him, was it because he was a relative blank onto which I could project my own, other desires? Desires that were, perhaps, for Baxter Logan?

'We don't want to hang about too much,' said Liam. 'Come on, keep walking. I think part of it might extend onto Ship Lane.'

I scurried after him, struggling to keep pace with his long-legged stride as he headed eagerly towards the next step in his plan. Ship Lane was a rickety alleyway and sure enough, part of the theatre's pale, stucco walls, marred by rust stains and crumbling masonry, were visible at the end of a gap running between a couple of nondescript buildings. A wheelie bin at the foot of the narrow, weed-thick passage suggested a deliberate dead-end, but it was evident this split between buildings was nothing more than an accident arising from urban unplanning. This sliver of an alley was off the map.

We slunk towards the wheelie bin, the passage so narrow

we had to go single-file. At ground level, the theatre's windows were boarded up while those above were a mixture of boards and glassless frames, twiggy shrubs poking through gaps, ivy crawling across the patchy stucco. A fire escape led to a black door, and I could see Liam eyeing it up as a possible entry point. After taking a glance beyond the big bin, I moved several feet away, keeping guard by casting over my shoulder for passersby on Ship Lane.

The trouble was, the fire escape didn't quite reach the ground. Its lower steps were strangled by ivy, heaped with rubbish and, quite possibly, weren't even there at all. Watching Liam assess the situation reminded me of why I'd first lusted after him. That resourcefulness and easy, physical confidence got me right in the groin. I loved that he was orchestrating this while I, his partner in crime, stood watch.

My motivations for wanting to break into the theatre were becoming less clear. I couldn't convince myself there'd be anything new to discover about Den if we did manage to gain entry. But it was thrilling and fun. And on top of that, I liked the idea I could reclaim the space of the theatre if I broke in with Liam, make it an arena over which I had some control. Doing so wouldn't register on Den's psyche but could have a positive impact on mine.

'Psst!'

Liam hissed for my attention, beckoning me towards the wheelie bin. After checking over my shoulder, I went to join him, resting my hand on the small of his back as I listened to his whispers.

'I reckon we can get in there.' He indicated a tall slab of corrugated steel blocking a gap between buildings. 'Looks like it leads to a yard or something. But once we're in that part, I think there'll be more entry points.'

I cupped his arse and gave his neck an appreciative kiss. 'You're the burglar-boss. If you reckon that's good, I'm with you.'

'Yeah?' said Liam. 'You're not thinking of bailing any more?' He turned more fully to me, hooking an arm around my waist and looking down with a cheeky grin.

'Nope. All for one and one for all!' I reached up to kiss him and pulled our groins close, stalling when a stiff length of metal dug against my thigh. I fondled it, momentarily perplexed, then laughed. 'Liam Hamilton, is that a crowbar in your trousers or are you just pleased to see me?'

'Pleased to see you,' he replied, grinning. Playfully, he rolled his pelvis in a slow grind, clutching my buttocks. I responded with a similar action, tipping my lips in search of a kiss while feeling his cock stiffen against my belly.

'Mmm,' said Liam. 'And when we're done here, we can go back to yours and fuck each other's brains out.'

'Deal,' I murmured, and I half-wished we were already in bed, safe, warm, naked and horny.

'OK, wait here. Let me give it a shot.' Liam withdrew the crowbar from his combats, flicked on a red-filtered torch and sidled behind the back of the bin. The beam of rosy light danced erratically across brickwork and chinks of grey sky. I stood there like a spare part, glancing anxiously back to Ship Lane then ahead to Liam's progress. Metal scraped against concrete, a sound so loud in the alley's silence that I braced myself for the screech of sirens and thud of law-enforcement boots. Nothing happened.

'We're in!' Liam's voice was a jubilant whisper. 'Follow me!'

I hurried after him, the crunch of twigs and glass underfoot popping like explosions. Liam held open a gap in the corrugated, makeshift gate and I squeezed in to join him on the other side. He bounced red torchlight over a weedy, rubble-strewn piece of land edging the walls of the theatre; the lower windows again blanked out by boards, the higher ones accessible if you were thirty foot tall.

'Wow,' I whispered. The sense we'd arrived in an unexplored zone made me light-headed and giddy. A small, uneasy part of me said we should return to safety but my adrenaline was pumping and I wanted to explore. Liam shone his torch over a tumble of old fridges in a far corner then higher to a window above.

The dancing beam reminded me of all the tedious parking presentations I'd sat through at work with someone aiming a red laser pointer at a projected map. This was infinitely more exciting. As I followed the track of the beam I could guess at Liam's thoughts. He was wondering if the fridge hillock was high and stable enough to be climbed. Then down to the lower windows. Were any of those boards loose? What was on the ground? Which part of the theatre was this? What was beyond that second barrier of corrugated steel at the end of this passageway? Let's take a closer look at this window.

Liam touched my hand, encouraging me to move forward with him. I trod softly, feeling we were walking across landmines. Liam's stride was bolder but he was a bloke, he had a crowbar and could probably run twice as fast as me.

We stood by a boarded-up window, Liam flashing his torch over the edges. The red beam caught a small scrawl of graffiti and Liam allowed the light to hover so we could read it.

Our love will never die.

I stifled a laugh. 'Oh, jeez. This is creepy.'

Liam spoke in a hoarse whisper. 'I'm going to try and jemmy these boards off but it'll be noisy. Ideally, I want to time it so we get covered by other noise. Need the pubs to empty or a massive lorry to go past.'

We stood and listened, hearing only the faint purr of traffic, of gulls calling out, and then a distant shriek of female laughter.

'We could be here all night,' I said in a low voice.

Liam switched off his torch, set down his crowbar and leaned against the wall. 'Yeah, but let's just wait a bit. If we attracted anyone's attention on the way in, best to keep still a while before making another racket.'

'I could go and kick a car,' I said. 'Set off an alarm. In fact, I could go along the street and kick loads of them.'

Liam grinned. 'Half an hour ago you were scared.'

'Yeah, but now I'm unstoppable. I hope we manage to get inside.'

'Did you bring your camera?'

I patted the pocket of my gilet. 'Yup.'

We fell silent, listening. Liam removed a packet of tobacco from his pocket and rolled a cigarette.

'How long should we wait?' I asked.

Liam lit his roll-up. 'Let's give it ten minutes,' he murmured.

'Oh, crikey, that's ages,' I complained. 'Not sure I've got the patience for this.'

'Well, try.'

'Should I suck your cock?'

Liam laughed, smoke spilling from his lips. 'Nats!'

I shrugged, grinning, and reached for his crotch. 'It'll pass the time.'

Liam glanced about but I could tell he was interested. He

dragged on his cigarette, the tip an amber glow in the dark. I rubbed, feeling him harden. 'Well?' I asked.

'Yeah, OK,' said Liam. 'But on the proviso we stop if there's a useful noise.'

'What? Like the sound of you coming?'

'You know what I mean.'

'OK, promise.' I unzipped him, scuffing the ground by his feet in an attempt to clear away debris. 'This is sexy,' I breathed. 'Outside, in the dark. Not meant to be here.' I popped open the button on his waistband and reached into the warmth of his open fly, feeling his shaft flex and swell behind the soft jersey cotton of his underwear.

'Yeah, it's good.' A catch of lust roughened his whisper. He drew on his cigarette as I lowered myself to my knees. I lifted the tenting fabric of his boxers away from his erection, allowing his cock to spring up from his nest of ginger-brown curls. I licked the velvety, vein-snarled underside, tracing his bone-hard ridge with my tongue. Above me, Liam exhaled smoke.

I sucked the smooth knob of his tip, nudging slowly down to mould my lips to the circlet of his foreskin. Liam pulled on his cigarette, its burn crackling faintly.

It wasn't intentional on his part, but Liam smoking in silence and without touching me suggested he was indifferent to the fact I was on my knees giving head. In reality, his attitude was circumstantial. He was keeping quiet because we were trespassing and he wasn't touching me perhaps because he held a cigarette or was too on edge to be fully engaged with the situation. But the reasons didn't matter. The implication of arrogance, ingratitude and disdain got me right in the groin.

I was just a cocksucker, an obliging pair of lips, as

insignificant as the cigarette he would toss to the floor and grind out beneath his boots. Lust thumped between my thighs. Being dehumanised and turned into a thing made me a creature suited only to sex. I grew wetter and wetter, picturing myself as an object Liam would discard, just like that cigarette.

In the fog of my desire, I had a flash of appreciating the fantasy I conjured up mapped neatly on to Den's termination of our relationship. Had he thought I'd find it hot to be genuinely cast aside? Couldn't he understand my fantasies weren't an appropriate template for a relationship? I wished I could put him from my mind but it was damn difficult. Even now, in the middle of a scary adventure with another man's cock in my mouth, my thoughts returned to him. Still, at least I wasn't obsessing about Baxter for a change.

Above me, Liam groaned quietly, resting a hand on my head. His body jerked as he flicked his cigarette end to the ground. I came back to the moment, sucking hard on his shaft, remembering who he was and being grateful for his integrity and decency. He placed the fingertips of his other hand on my head. Slowly, I slid my lips as close to the root of him as I could manage. Liam groaned again and held my head steady, trying to keep me impaled on his length. I stayed deep then pulled back, gasping. In the pitch-black yard, my noises were worryingly loud.

I teased his tip, slid halfway down, worked him a little with my hand then eased forward again to take the entirety of him. Tears pricked my eyes but the bulk of him nudging at the lock of my throat felt good. Just a little further. Liam gave a wheeze of bliss, winding his fingers in my curls.

Then he tensed, he flinched, movements too fast for pleasure. 'Nats!'

The ground crunched to our right. And again. Footsteps approaching.

Liam pushed at my head, shoving me off him. I turned to the sound, then screamed. My vision was filled with the white flash of a torch. The cops. We'd been rumbled.

'Please,' said a man's voice from several yards away, 'don't stop on my account.'

I squinted at the dazzle of the torch, shielding my eyes and panting in shock. No, the cops didn't say stuff like that.

'I'm enjoying the show,' said the man. 'Just wanted a better look.' His footsteps crunched closer. 'Go on, keep sucking. I want to see him come all over your face.'

Thirteen

I moved to stand while Liam battled to tuck away his fast-shrinking boner.

'I said don't get up,' the voice warned, taking another step closer. 'Don't stop. Keep sucking that dick and I won't turn you in to the authorities.'

'Who the Hell are you?' Liam asked softly.

The voice flashed the light at Liam's face. I could make out a stocky figure in army boots and a bulky jacket. 'Security,' he replied. 'And yourself?'

Still on my knees, I drew long quivering breaths, searching for my voice. I placed a hand on Liam's thigh, wanting to remind him we were in this together.

'Come on, mate,' said Liam. 'Give it a rest. We were just mucking about. No harm done.'

'You broke into private property,' said the man, 'then you gave me a hard-on. So that's two problems that need fixing. I'll overlook the first if we can sort out the second.'

I found my voice. 'You are not touching me.'

Liam placed a protective hand on my shoulder.

'No intention of touching you.' The voice dropped the

torchlight back to my face. 'But I don't usually see something this interesting when I'm doing my rounds. So if you could just wrap your lips round that dick and keep at it till the money shot, I'll forget this ever happened.'

'Hey, listen,' said Liam. 'This is bang out of order, mate. We only –'

'No, you listen to me, kid.' The voice was distinctly nasty now. 'Do what I fucking tell you. Stick your dick in her mouth, fuck it till she chokes then shoot your load over her face.'

Liam's body tensed. I pressed harder against his thigh, clutched his hip with my other hand. 'Liam. Don't. It's OK.'

'It is not fucking OK,' said Liam through clenched teeth.

Liam's no fighter but I could imagine him making an angry lunge at the guy to protect me, and my honour. This arrogant little thug probably wouldn't hesitate to knock Liam's teeth out. We needed to tread carefully to avoid violence.

I glanced around on the dark, messy ground by my knees. The crowbar lay at an angle, inches out of reach. Liam had the torch in his pocket. If only we had a couple of minutes together we could probably co-ordinate an escape plan. Without that we were divided, uncertain, and while we both wanted out, we had different priorities to consider. More than anything, I didn't want to see Liam and the thug in a fist fight because Liam was bound to come off worse.

Violence horrifies me. I feared our adversary wouldn't punch a man once or twice and leave it there. He'd keep going. I could picture it already, Liam curled up on the ground being booted in the guts, the back, the head, his sweet, serene face turning to a pulp. Oh God, what to do? I was terrified Liam might attempt something foolish.

'Liam,' I said. 'It's no big deal. Let's just do what he wants and leave.'

'No way.'

'Listen to your girl,' said the man. 'Go on. The little slut's begging for it.'

Liam lunged forward to attack. I slammed his hips against the wall. 'Liam,' I hissed. 'Don't be the fucking hero.' I dropped my voice further. 'Play along. I've got a plan.'

After a few moments, Liam's body relaxed. He looked down at me, frowning and doubtful. His copper curls gleamed in the beam of the torch, eerie shadows fluttering on his face as our thug examined us. Liam had every right to look doubtful. I didn't have a plan. Or at least not one he'd approve of.

I rubbed my palm against his half-open flies. 'Trust me,' I said, gazing up at him.

The thug took a heavy step closer, lowering the aim of his torch to a less intrusive angle.

Liam looked down at me, brows knitted. 'If you're trying to get me hard,' he said quietly, 'you've got a serious amount of work to do.'

'Please, Liam,' I said. 'For me. Just relax. Go with it. Forget who's watching.'

'Not possible,' muttered Liam but when I searched past his zipper, he twitched under my fingers, already lengthening in his underwear. I rubbed and fondled, not wanting to release him until he was fully hard. My hand was shaking with nerves, and I had to press and pummel to keep the quivers at bay. When Liam's cock was straining against the jersey cotton, I freed him. His shaft sprang out, bold and bouncy. He cursed himself under his breath. I licked around his end and he made a noise closer to one I would make, an anguished moan of wanting and rejecting.

In the corner of my eye, I saw our observer readjust his crotch. 'That's the way, kids,' he said. 'Glad you appreciate the favour. A cocksucking demo for your freedom.' His footsteps crunched closer.

I edged my mouth down Liam's length, knowing he wasn't likely to come because he rarely does from BJs. My mind was blank. All I could do was keep sucking, playing for time in the hope an answer would present itself or something would put a stop to this. But I didn't like those encroaching footsteps. I hadn't anticipated that.

''Cause, you know, it's not a lot to ask, is it?' the man continued. 'Especially when she's already on her knees. And is clearly a greedy, cocksucking cumslut.'

Liam groaned, a sound that shocked me. I fought the impulse to jump up and thump the thug. I knew he was trying to antagonise us for kicks. But oh, that noise! Liam had groaned as if he couldn't help but take pleasure from the man's nasty, pornographic vocabulary. It wasn't a noise intended to communicate as groans sometimes are. It wasn't encouragement or affirmation. It was a noise of someone giving in, despite himself. I imagined Liam was already wishing he could suck the groan back.

Glancing sideways, I saw our man casually rub his groin. I hated him and I imagined Liam would do likewise if he didn't have my lips wrapped around his cock. Scary how your standards can slip when you're lost to lust. But I wasn't lost, not by a long shot. I was doing my damndest to think on my feet. Well, on my knees, to be precise. But I had no thoughts to act on, nothing that would help us. My mind was blocked by terror.

Then to my horror, I heard and saw the security guard unzip. I cupped Liam's balls, pulling harder and faster with my lips, wanting this to be over before our observer got carried away with ideas of joining in.

'Ah, yes.' Shamelessly, the man gripped his erection and began jerking off. He seemed as lost as Liam. No, much further gone. Too excited. 'A double load of come on her face,' he said, panting. 'How about that?' He shuffled quickly closer, hand pumping faster. 'Show me your tits, sweetheart. Come on. Look what I've got for you. Another dick. Look at me.'

Panic squeezed tighter, my heart banging behind my ribs. I kept sucking Liam, fighting my instinct to react. Think, think, think. Come on, Nats. Find a way out. Think!

'I said look at me,' the man repeated, his tone laced with threat. 'And show me those fucking tits.'

Another footstep.

I withdrew from Liam and looked at the thug, glancing up from his cock to his face, an idea rapidly forming. In the dimness, I could make out a heavy-browed man with short, bristly hair, his mouth slack, his eyes locked on me. He appeared caught up in his own pleasure, fascinated by the scenario, watching us as if this were XTube, not life. I stole the advantage and began groaning heavily, rubbing my tits through my clothes while gasping in the direction of the guy's cock. Liam grabbed his own cock but kept his hand motionless. He would, I hoped, sharpen up, recognise my act as porny insincerity and brace himself for action.

To my relief, the thug seemed to believe in me. 'That's right. Come and get it,' he taunted, waggling his erection.

I groaned, lurching for him as if desperate for cock. I faked a clumsy tumble, dropped forward, swept my hand across the ground. When my fingers found the crowbar, I grabbed. Swinging with all my might, I brought the bar smashing onto the side of the guy's knee. He yelped, legs buckling. Quick as a flash, Liam landed a swift right hook across his jaw, fist meeting face with a clean hard crack. The guy's big, black boot came hurtling towards my shoulder, light glinting on his toecap. Still on the ground, I reeled then swung the crowbar at his leg, once, twice. I tried to stand, felt a rough hand in my armpit, heaving me to my feet. I rammed the crowbar upwards as I stood, not knowing where it would land. Our thug roared in pain and doubled over, clutching his groin. Lucky strike.

Liam stooped to grab the guy's fallen torch.

'Leg it!' he said.

But I was already ahead of him, hurtling towards the corrugated gate, vowing never to return to the derelict theatre again.

I first met Baxter Logan online. Not at FancyFree. On another site whose name I can no longer recall. As with Den, he had an articulate profile write-up but no accompanying photograph. He described himself as having a hardwired dominant streak and a high-pressure job. He was separated from his wife and currently not looking for anything more than friendship and sex.

I had no photograph on my profile either. I was new to internet dating and still shy about revealing myself. And since the site was explicitly for kinky people, I was even more reluctant to be recognised. As part of my new policy of directing my sexuality, I'd stated I was interested in exploring my submissive side then had sat back, nervous and excited, unsure where this might lead.

After getting over the guilt of enjoying spanking at the hands – or rather the ruler – of my piano tutor, Alistair Fitch, I'd realised the craving to taste submission wasn't going away. I'd kept a lid on it during my time with Jim in Dullsville, sticking to secret fantasies and later to occasional explorations of kink online. To my surprise, during these explorations, I'd discovered there was more to BDSM than the image regularly projected of whip-wielding women in PVC catsuits and men wearing strange straps on their chest. Of course, people into fetishwear are part of the subculture but I soon realised the community, if you could even call it that, also included plenty of other people who declare themselves 'non-scene'. So when I started kinky dating online, I'd followed their example and defined myself similarly.

I spent a few weeks fending off the wrong sort, then, just as I was despairing of the whole enterprise, Baxter Logan got in touch, sending a down-to-earth, warm, amusing memo with a link to a photograph. I clicked his link and bam! Lust at first sight. I stared at this blokeishly handsome man with unruly dark hair, heavy cheekbones and skew-whiff tie, and he stared right back, his gaze so direct I felt he could see behind my eyes.

It's fascinating how sometimes a single photo can capture someone's personality so effectively. My immediate impression was of a tender tough guy; a man passionate, warm and, most attractive of all, dangerously ungovernable. And though his unsmiling expression appeared full of mean intent, the laughter lines radiating from his eyes suggested this was a man who knew how to enjoy himself.

When I'd first met him, under the clock in the train station at Saltbourne, I said, 'What do you want to do?' Meaning, shall we go for a drink, a walk, some food? He grinned and in that sexy-as-Hell, Scottish accent, quietly said, 'I want to fuck the lights out of you.'

Half an hour later, he was doing precisely that. I swear, no one had ever fucked me that way until Baxter. He took me over, forcing me to take it however he damn well wanted, ramming his cock high and hard, slapping my face, arse and tits, and sprinkling the session with verbal humiliation that tripped so naturally from his tongue. Without any kinky kit or formalised domming, he made me come time and again, making me feel gorgeously sluttish and base for doing so. I welcomed the erotic charge of shame. I adored his enthusiasm, his wild nastiness and all the victories he claimed from my suffering.

Less than two hours after meeting him, I was reduced to a deliriously blank and broken creature. Next to me in bed was this magnificent, exhausted, grateful champion. He held me lightly as I sobbed, told me it was all OK, just let yourself go, I'm here for you, hen, I'm here, and fuck me, that was fucking amazing, you're a beautiful wee lass, you know that?

After a while, I resurfaced, sniffing and smiling, Baxter's chest hair wet with my tears. I felt cleansed and exhilarated, my entire body buzzing with some crazy chemicals I'd never experienced before. While I hadn't anticipated the high I'd get from this new kind of sex, Baxter was everything I'd hoped him to be, and more. Oh, so much more. Already, our relationship felt precarious, as if our connection was potentially too profound to be confined within the limits of friendship and kink.

I'm going to get hurt, I thought. And I was right, although I'd expected the hurt to come from me wanting more and him skedaddling when he got wind of that. But we fell in love, both of us equally scared and astonished at the speed with which it happened. Before long, we were a couple, albeit a rather odd one because we had different lifestyles and interests, and he had such an erratic, hectic work pattern that we never quite settled into a routine. Or at least, he used to claim his random unavailability was due to his job. He met my friends a few times, and I once met some old friends of his at a party we attended in London. We spent practically all our time at my place. I went to his only once. He lived in a suburban house he allegedly loathed because it contained too much of his wife's stuff. The area was poorly served by public transport and since I don't have a car, it wasn't easy for me to travel to his place.

I later learned that the time I'd slept at the marital home was when his wife was away on business. Baxter had gone to great lengths to hide many of her belongings, stack removal boxes in corners, and generally create an impression he was still living uncomfortably with his ex-wife's possessions since she was determined not to fully leave until their divorce settlement was finalised.

In the living room, on the mantelpiece, was a framed photo of the newly-wed Logans. She was a petite, red-haired woman in an empire-line dress while next to her, grinning broadly, his feet planted wide, was Baxter in a blue-green kilt and thick, cream socks. Damn, he looked good, so solidly sexy.

'So what are you wearing under the kilt?' I'd asked, picking up the picture.

'Ach, that shouldn't be there.' Baxter hurried to take the picture from my hand then dropped it in a drawer as if the object meant nothing to him. 'Sorry. You know how it is. Sometimes you see things so often, you stop actually seeing them. Hadn't noticed it was still there. Must sort this place out.'

I'd swallowed his excuse hook, line and sinker. I had no reason to distrust him. As Baxter did in his professional life, I believed in the presumption of innocence in my personal life. But with hindsight, I can see our time together was littered with big, flashing warning signs I would have noticed if I hadn't been so utterly besotted. And he kept promising it would get better once they'd sold the house and he'd got the promotion he was aiming for. Promises can carry you a long way if you believe in them.

In most other respects, as far as I knew, he was who he said he was: Baxter Logan, a criminal defence solicitor working for a law firm in Saltbourne. Mainly legal aid cases, he said. Low level stuff. Anti-social behaviour offences. I could Google him, as I had done before we met, and find a picture of him on the firm's website and, elsewhere, his name on Saltbourne's magistrates' court duty solicitor rotas.

With Den, I had no starting point. And clearly I was becoming desperate, clutching at straws in a bid to find some route towards him and unravel the mystery. Going to the theatre with Liam made no practical sense but I'd taken that option because I had so little else to go on. Sometimes, my blood ran cold to think how much worse our confrontation with the thug might have been. We'd got off lightly. But most appallingly, though the encounter had been vile and terrifying, and memories of it made my blood boil, the incident wasn't enough to deter me from trying to discover more about Den.

I wondered how low I might go to find him. I worried, too, that my sexual hunger for submission and suffering might be seeping out to infect my day-to-day life. I'd wanted to temporarily surrender my dignity and autonomy to Den but now that opportunity had been denied me, was I subconsciously sacrificing valuable parts of myself in my pursuit of him? Was I trying to re-channel my needs in an unhealthy, dangerous manner? Was wounded pride making me want to challenge his rude exit from my life?

But amidst these worries about the wisdom or otherwise of choices I'd made, and might continue to make, was my stupid, stubborn obsession with Den. I couldn't dislodge him. He'd taken root in my brain. Den. Was that even his name? Was it short for Dennis or Denham? Or could he actually be called, say, Darren or Gavin? Again, I wished I could erase him but that would entail erasing my memories of him in the theatre. I loved what I'd experienced there, and what I'd learned about my sexuality. I liked the pain and strictness more than I'd thought, although I missed the rough spontaneity of Baxter. I still wanted Den. I wasn't proud of myself for that but, while my reason recognised I ought to forget him, my dark desires craved satisfaction. And that longing refused to be hushed by logic.

One night, drowning my sorrows with a bottle of Malbec, I emailed him again. This time, I told him he was a bastard, told him he was an emotionally stunted, arrogant, deceitful cunt. I dithered over delete or 'send'. This could change everything. He might respond and explain himself, perhaps apologise. Or he would do nothing and my suspicions he was gone for good would be confirmed. If I hit 'send' I would be taking charge of the situation, expressing my feelings rather than nursing them alone. Would I regret it in the morning? Was my tone too aggressive? Should I save it in my 'drafts' folder and send when sober? On an impulse, I hit 'send'.

I sat back, triumphant and relieved. Seconds later

postmaster returned my message as undeliverable, informing me there was no such address as kagamikagami@rocketmail. com. Defeated, frustrated and angry, not to mention drunk, I couldn't let it drop. Minutes later, I got the idea to Google the meaning of 'kagami'. I'd never thought to do that before, but then I hadn't been quite so determined to flush him out until now. I put the term into the search box, clicked Wikianswers in my results, then felt distinctly unsettled when the site starkly informed me: It means mirror.

I wanted to ask, and what the Hell does that mean?

But search engines don't know everything. Eventually, I went to bed feeling I was succeeding only in generating mysteries rather than solving them.

In the morning, slightly hungover, I checked the message I'd attempted to send and was relieved I'd been thwarted. I didn't want to give him the satisfaction of knowing how upset I was. Once again, I decided to put more effort into forgetting him. I resolved to stop trying to track him down, to put the ugly episode with the thug behind me, and parcel it all up as belonging to a short period of my life where I was conned and I made mistakes. I hadn't been running quite as regularly. I needed to get back into the habit. I always feel better about life when I'm running.

And all that might have happened if Liam hadn't emailed me a link to a short news item in our local paper about The Hippodrome. 'Thought you might be interested in this,' he wrote. 'Looks like good news.'

ENCORE FOR SALTBOURNE'S HIPPODROME
A new partnership between Save Our Old Theatres (SOOT) and the University of South East Arts (U-SEA) looks set to raise the curtain on Saltbourne's Hippodrome

after winning a bid to forge community links through restoration of the derelict theatre.

The 120-year-old Hippodrome, once host to luminaries of the stage and music hall, has fallen into disrepair since closing its doors in 1987. The collaboration between SOOT and U-SEA will transform the theatre into a cultural, learning and community hub, bringing the arts to a wider audience and generating research activity in the university's Department of Contemporary Arts.

Dr Dennis Jackson of U-SEA said, 'We're delighted to be working with SOOT and are looking forward to seeing this important building rise from its metaphorical ashes.'

SOOT and U-SEA are leasing the Grade-II-listed building from its current owners, Glender Mayfield, for a nominal rent and estimate the cost of repair to be at fifteen million pounds. Businesses and individuals wishing to contribute to the project are advised to contact project manager Eleanor Riley via SOOT's website.

Dr Dennis Jackson.

I turned the name over in my head. Den Jackson. Dr Jackson. Was this him?

My fingers were trembling as I hurriedly tapped in 'U-SEA' and 'Dennis Jackson'. I clicked the first link on the returned results. And oh boy, I'd hit paydirt. Gotcha Dr Dennis, snared by the internet!

A small recent photograph on his staff profile page accompanied text I could barely comprehend in my urgency to scan for the gist. Dr Dennis Jackson, senior lecturer, former dancer and performance artist. Now choreographer, writer and director. A particular interest in the drama of masks, Noh theatre, and community arts.

I clapped my hands and gave such a loud, gleeful laugh that I startled Rory from her sleep. I was back in business, already on a high and craving more details.

I Googled again and again, testing a range of permutations: Den, Dennis, SOOT, Noh, dance, Saltbourne, masks and so on. Information about him kept on tumbling and repeating. I pieced together the sort of haphazard half-history you get when you play Google detective, discovering nothing about his personal life but plenty about his career and the subscription charges I'd need to pay if I were to access journal articles he'd had published. I read about dance tours he'd been on several years ago, theatre companies he'd worked with, papers he'd given and performers he'd directed. On YouTube I watched clips of his work, hoping he might make a Hitchcockian cameo appearance, but he never did. He stayed behind the scenes, the man pulling the strings of performers creating strange, leaping contortions in productions described as 'darkly humorous' and 'visually stunning' but which looked solemn and pompous to me.

I didn't know what I could do with this wealth of new information. Nonetheless I was delighted to have unmasked him again. He appeared to be a big fish in his small pond, relatively famous although not famous enough to get stopped in the street. I could see why he might not want his profile picture on a dating website. Then again, it could simply be that he was married. I mustn't ever forget that as a possibility. Not that I was likely to.

After about forty minutes of Googling, I struck gold – a gold so precious it terrified me. In two days' time, Dr Dennis Jackson was presenting at 'Intercultural Theatre: bridges, borders and blurrings', a one-day conference held at Falchester University. My heart quickened. Falchester was thirty or forty miles away, relatively close. He was gaining materiality again. Would he get in touch? Where did he live anyway?

Those might have been the only questions I'd asked myself if I hadn't continued to explore the conference website. My thirst for info was unquenchable so I checked the schedule for the day. When I saw the title of the paper he was giving, my heart beat faster while a sick sense of dread stole over me. '"One chance, one meeting": trance, transformation and transience in Japanese Noh theatre.'

One chance, one meeting.

That was the exact phrase he'd used when terminating our time in the theatre. What did it mean? Had I been an unwitting participant in a piece of private performance art? Was this man incapable of separating fantasy from reality? Was he insane?

I felt as if I'd been the victim of a scam, although I didn't have a clue what the scam could be. The emotions I'd been trying to escape, the anger, frustration and pain, came hurtling back. I didn't think too long about my next step. Fired up with passion and determined not to be Den's victim, I clicked on the tab marked 'Register Now'.

Minutes later and forty pounds poorer, I was a conference delegate and, without having borrowed one single library book, an independent scholar.

Fourteen

Deliberately, I turned up late for registration. A young woman with a silvery-peach bob and a welcoming smile sat behind a long table dotted with oblong name tags. I was relieved to have found the conference venue after several nervous minutes of wandering down broad, clean paths set in clipped green lawns, praying I wouldn't bump into Den. Here and there, taped to walls and trees, A4 signs in polypockets advertised the conference, corners of the pages fluttering in the October breeze. The words on the signs were printed in large black font while arrows giving directions were added in thin blue biro.

The campus, with its new buildings, architectural experiments, miniature bank and forking paths, felt like a toy village, a sanitised Utopia peopled by youthful creatures in layers of colourful clothing. What was the name of that town in *The Truman Show*? Seahaven, that was it. Except here, optimistic blue skies and sunshine were in short supply. Dark, bulky clouds crouched over distant hills, and the paths I walked along were scattered with autumn leaves. Did I look out of place? Everyone seemed to be carrying too much stuff: books, laptops, bags. Should I have brought more stuff? When I'd read English Lit and History a decade or so ago in Manchester, had I looked as fresh-faced as some of these students?

Feigning confidence, I gave my name to the peachy-haired woman at the table, got ticked off her list and was handed my badge, a programme and a voucher for lunch. I briefly regretted signing up under my real name and hoped Den hadn't spotted my badge when he'd collected his.

'They're about halfway through the first session,' said the woman. 'Some seats by the door if you want to sneak in.'

'I'll wait till the break, thanks.'

The conference suite, set back from the bland landscaping of the campus, was housed in the original college, an imposing nineteenth-century building whose air of gravitas contrasted starkly with the Fisher Price chumminess I'd just walked through. I went for coffee in a gaudily-furnished bar with pointy, leaded windows overlooking a cloistered courtyard flanked by a small chapel. I pretended to read a book, unable to concentrate on words but doing my best to look like an independent scholar rather than a stalker.

Should I have done this? Spending forty pounds on the event had been a spur of the moment decision. I could forgive myself for acting on a whim. But I'd followed up on that action by arranging a day off work then taking a train and a taxi to this remote campus set in rolling countryside. My actions were no longer quite so casual.

Was I losing perspective? Hunting someone down like this had to be the mark of a deranged person. But he'd hunted me down, hadn't he? This had started with Den finding my address and breaking into my house. I was merely giving him a taste of his own medicine, although I conceded he might not be quite so excited by my attentions as I'd been by his.

I wished my lust for him weren't so strong, wished he hadn't been so adept at catering to the drive I have to surrender and suffer. I remembered his parting kiss in the late-night street. 'Let's give it a few days,' he'd said, 'see how we feel.' Why had he said that if he had no intention of getting in touch? Was he trying to get shot of me without a fuss? Had he meant it at the time and had since grown uncertain as to the wisdom of us continuing?

I set down my book and gazed out at the sombre cloisters, wondering if my sexuality was a blessing or a burden. A blessing, surely, if it gave me such deep pleasure. But a burden too if the specificity of my tastes meant my needs couldn't easily be met. I only wanted to submit to a man who would regard me as his equal, even when I was on my knees, spattered with his come. I was starting to feel these men were as rare as hen's teeth. I'd thought Den might be such a person, and in many ways I still did. He'd never treated me with kid gloves. He'd never doubted my lust or underestimated my hunger for submission. We were like sexual sparring partners. But he'd since blocked me out, his action implying my needs mattered less than his. Perhaps he'd underestimated my hunger, after all. Or perhaps he thought being sexually dominant gave him the right to call the shots beyond the bedroom.

One chance, one meeting.

Not if I have it my way, Dr Jackson.

When it was time for the delegates to break for coffee, I returned to the foyer, staying at a safe distance in the hope I would see before I was seen. My heart thumped when the double doors of the lecture hall opened and people began drifting towards a table where jugs and urns were stationed. The delegates were bright, theatrical and lively, a far cry from the desk-bound, monochrome-suited world I was accustomed to in my job.

For a while, I lurked by a corner, watching at an angle while pretending to text so I could keep my head low. People swarmed around the long table, chatting eagerly and reaching apologetically across each other for sugar sachets, milk and so on. Cups and teaspoons clinked, the chatter of conversation rising to the vaulted stone ceiling.

Where was he? I feared I might be drawing attention to myself by loitering and fake-texting. Would it be better to mill among the crowds? Well, even if it was, reaching them by crossing what seemed like an acre of corporate, pale burgundy carpet would leave me too exposed, so no point wondering.

I'd decided to take a few steps back when I spotted him, instantly recognising that smooth, shaved head and those wide shoulders. My heart flared. How strange everything felt. In this focused bustle of people, half of them resembling carnival escapees, he seemed both improbable and hyper-ordinary. With my pulse racing hard, I couldn't help but gawp, knowing I ran the risk of him turning my way. He wore a black velvet suit jacket over a checked, deep-blue shirt, jeans and those black Converse trainers. Even without my knowledge of his physique, it was easy to see that under his clothes this man was powerfully athletic.

He was talking intently to a short, floppy-haired guy in leggings and silver Doc Martens. He held his cup and saucer with a peculiar delicacy, energy trapped in every tiny movement he made. His narrow eyes and neatly sloping nose were strikingly familiar. I felt as if I could walk over there, claim him as my own and return him to my life and my dreams where he belonged. And yet in another way, I didn't feel like that at all. I felt as if needed to hide in the Ladies till the coast was clear then skulk off home, acknowledging the foolish indignity of pursuing him.

Then, oh Hell, heading for the Ladies is precisely what I was doing, face burning, heart pumping, as Den set down his drink and began walking towards me. I span around and fled, barging into the toilets, the door handle thumping against the tiles. Damn, damn, damn! Forgot my need to stay alert there. Had he spotted me? I caught a glimpse of him as the door swung shut behind me. No, the neutral expression on his face suggested I'd got away with it. He appeared to be doing nothing more dramatic than heading for the Gents.

In a tizz, I checked my reflection in the mirror. I looked hectic and alarmed, my cheeks flushed, my eyes too wide, my curls too curly. Easy, Nats. Get a grip. Nobody's forcing you to do this. I drew a deep breath. If I were going to go through with this, I had to seize my opportunity. A now or never moment. I counted one, two, three then *now*. I left the Ladies, striding confidently across the dark pink football pitch and towards the doors of the lecture theatre. Chin high, I bypassed the coffee drinkers, chanting a silent mantra of 'independent scholar, independent scholar'.

Even though I'd paid my money and had every right to be there, I feared I was about to get busted. But I made it across the foyer unchallenged, and found myself standing on shaky legs in a large, brightly lit auditorium, gazing up at near-empty rows of tiered plastic seats. A low, false ceiling obscured most of the chamber's high gothic arches while enormous grey roller blinds hung in front of slim, pointed windows, the conference suite once again veiling the venue's history in an apparent bid to be as featureless as a contemporary hotel chain.

Feeling shifty, I took my place halfway up the rows, sitting to the right in the hope I wouldn't be seen too quickly from the low stage on which stood a long table, four chairs behind it, a glossy white podium and projection screen.

My breath was pumping so fast I might have sprinted to my seat. I inhaled slowly, trying to steel my nerves. I no longer knew how to achieve what I wanted. My plan had always been to play it by ear but that no longer seemed sufficient. I wasn't sure what I wanted either. I could see I was becoming increasingly foolhardy. 'Act now, think later' is fine if you're in danger but as a motto to live by, it sucks.

Then I remembered what I wanted: to be acknowledged. I wanted to take some control of the situation. I wasn't going to play meek victim to a guy who thought it was acceptable to embark on a relationship then vanish without a trace.

I kept my head down as delegates returned to the room. When I saw Den, I ducked below the narrow shelf of a row of mini-desks in front of me, pretending to fiddle with the contents of my bag. When I bobbed back up, he was talking to a woman behind the lectern, the two of them setting up a laptop. After a time, a guy joined them, and Den took his seat behind the long table on the dais.

To my horror, he began confidently scanning his audience, smiling slightly as he gazed out. I ducked down again, mentally apologising to my heart for all the shocks I was inflicting upon it. This time I remembered something useful in my bag, a notebook I'd brought as part of my lame disguise. I set the pad on my desk-cum-shelf, pretending to write so I could hunker down and hide.

I only stopped when the first speaker took to the lectern. For the next thirty minutes, I watched a woman draped in plastic jewellery talk about the choreographer as artist. I say 'watched' because her words, steeped in academic jargon, were largely impenetrable to me. I watched Den too, slyly peeking around the shoulders of a tall, frizzy-haired woman who'd helpfully sat in front of me, screening me from Den's view if I stayed slumped in my seat. Realising that of all the people in the audience, I was the one who'd seen him climax, gave me a sense of mild advantage. I was the one who'd turned him on, who'd felt his cock and fingers inside me, who knew his dark, twisted secrets.

After an interminable length of time and much clanking of bangles, the Chair introduced Dr Dennis Jackson as our next speaker, confusing me momentarily when she described him as a researcher at You See. Then I clicked she meant U-SEA, The University of South East Arts. When Den took to the podium I became nervous for him having to speak in this grand, intimidating arena. But he was confident and relaxed, scanning his papers and loading his PowerPoint presentation onto the big screen before clearing his throat and addressing us.

I slithered down to hide behind the bush of hair in front of me. My heart went pitter-patter, the simple familiarity of Den's clear, commanding voice enough to excite me. Weird to think that this voice, now rising in the hall and using words such as 'metaphysical' and 'methodological', was the same one I'd heard say, 'Suck it, whore,' and 'I don't give a single fuck what you want.' I tried to focus on his paper, hoping for an insight into his character, but while most words were individually intelligible, when assembled into sentences, their overall meaning eluded me. I experienced moments of comprehension, occasional paragraphs rising like islands from a murky sea of gobbledegook.

The proposal Den appeared to be making was that Noh theatre couldn't be understood from the perspective of Western traditions. Most fascinating to me, in elucidating this point, he informed us his mother was part Japanese, part Dutch. Such an unexpected, personal snippet was a joy. I listened hard, doing my best to concentrate. I learned only one rehearsal takes place prior to a Noh performance. One chance, one meeting, and in this was transience, a key aspect of Noh, and Zen Buddhism. But why had he said that phrase to me in The Hippodrome? Did he mean something by it? Something I was too ill-informed to appreciate? Or was he just pulling esoteric-sounding phrases from his brainy life to mess with my mind?

I drifted off as he went into tedious detail about a particular Noh character. My ears pricked up again at the phrase 'roleplay'. From what I could glean, characters in Noh are abstractions of emotions rather than representations of people with biographies. And the actor's role is an imitation of this inner essence rather than a mimicry of outward mannerisms. And true masters of the art, in nullifying personality, identify so deeply with the abstracted state that they become this. They have gone beyond roleplaying.

I grew so interested in what Den was saying that I relaxed too much. The clever words leaving his mouth made him strange to me. I wondered if his roleplay theories could be related to BDSM. The zonked state he described reminded me of the floatiness of subspace, of self-annihilation through bliss, a condition reached by powerplay but existing far beyond a role.

One day, I thought, I'd like to ask him; I'd like to sit down and have a drink with this erudite man who commanded audiences from the stage. He seemed a different being to the one who'd kidnapped me and behaved too cruelly. The hard masculinity of his shorn head was less menacing when teamed with a black velvet jacket and brushed cotton shirt. He still looked good, though, seriously sexy.

And then he saw me. No, no, no! Oh, I'd wanted him to spot me eventually, of course I had. I'd wanted to wrong-foot him by turning our power dynamic on its head. Not our sexual power dynamic; I was comfortable with that. But the real imbalance where he had me running around after him; confused, thwarted, desirous, hurt and hopeful.

My half-baked fantasy plan had been to stay unobserved then ask a question at the end of his paper. I'd imagined myself raising a hand, bold as brass, making him sweat, suffer and stutter as he responded, unable to do anything but reply in this formal, crowded space. He'd be in no position to say, 'I don't give a single fuck about your question.' But, in the catching of an eye, my grand plan collapsed.

He faltered, briefly losing his thread before checking his script and regaining composure. All the moisture disappeared from the inside of my mouth. His eyes kept darting back to me as he continued speaking. I sat up straighter, edging sideways and clear of the fuzzy-haired woman. I'd unsettled him. I allowed myself to smile at my minor victory. Den clicked through to another slide on his PowerPoint presentation. From the screen a wild, crimson mask with fanged teeth, furrowed brow and a ferocious scowl glared at the audience.

Den turned from screen to audience. 'The red Shikami mask,' he said, projecting his voice across the auditorium, 'is the demon, a representation of masculine rage'. Deliberately, he focused on me as he spoke, clearly less flustered than moments ago. Was this his way of covertly communicating his displeasure? My smile broadened, my satisfaction increasing. I'd definitely disturbed him. I'd pissed him off in front of his peers and there was nothing he could do.

My glow of triumph remained throughout his presentation and the content of the third paper passed me by, all my thoughts fixed on Den. I watched him throughout the delivery of the final paper and he didn't once look in my direction. The session was wrapped up with questions from the audience, one of which went on for so long it was tantamount to filibustering. People fidgeted, whispered, checked their phones and watches.

Finally, we were done. Lunch. We would reconvene at two. I didn't have a clue what might happen next. My biggest fear was Den might ignore me, as was his wont. I took my time gathering my belongings, pacing myself so I could leave the lecture theatre when he did. The big-haired woman turned around to ask if I could recall the name of the Italian choreographer mentioned at the end of the first paper. I couldn't but managed to spin out a short conversation enabling me to linger less suspiciously.

Den was taking forever, engaging in conversations as he made his way from the stage. Unable to stall any longer, I collected my bag and jacket, and walked down the shallow steps of the aisle. When Den glanced in my direction, my pulse skipped a beat, anxiety replacing my earlier smugness. He touched a colleague on the elbow, a gesture signifying he was making his excuses to leave. In a daze of uncertainty, I kept on walking towards the exit then out into the foyer where people talked in clusters.

Seconds later, Den was looming up behind me. He grabbed my arm above the elbow, fingers stabbing. My heart was going like the clappers. I turned to him, afraid of the anger clouding his face. 'Down here,' he said. He steered me along an airy, burgundy-carpeted corridor. 'You insane bitch. What the Hell are you playing at?' His grip tightened and he gave my arm a furious shake. 'This is my career. It is not your territory. You have no right.'

I winced in pain from his fingers, trying to wrench myself free, but he only squeezed tighter. In silence, he marched me along the quiet corridor, flung open a door and jostled me into an empty classroom. Grey, plastic desks were arranged in a rectangle framing an empty space and he shoved me towards the back, making me stumble down an aisle between the wall and the tables. Metal chair legs clanged against each other.

Fearing I'd pushed it too far, I stood petrified, clutching my bag and jacket to my chest. Den grabbed the nearest desk, and half-dragged, half-swung it towards the door, blocking us in. He shrugged off his velvet jacket, slung it on to the desk and began rolling up his shirt sleeves as he stalked to the other side of the room. With snappy movements, he tugged on thin chains to bring blinds clattering down over diamond-paned windows.

He turned to me. 'You have seriously fucked up this time,' he said.

I gulped, my throat dry as dust. I had a horrible feeling he was right.

Fifteen

Den glared at me, his chest rising and falling.

'Well?' he snapped. 'What is it? What do you want?'

Summoning up the remnants of my bravery, I set down my belongings and met his glare, hands on my hips. 'Why are you acting like a prick?' I said. 'Why didn't you get in touch?'

Den gave a harsh laugh. 'Wow, stalker alert.' He swiped the heel of his hand across his forehead. 'Seriously, you travel all this way to ask if we can talk?' He began moving around the back of the classroom, approaching with an intimidating swagger. 'I'm not sure whether to be scared or flattered.'

My nerves got the better of me and I retreated, edging back towards the blocked door, trailing my fingers along the row of chairs. 'Well,' I said. 'Now you know how it feels.'

When I reached the gap in the oblong of desks, I moved into the central space, putting a row of tables between us. Den leaned forwards, hands on the table-top, the dark hair on his bared forearms making me ache for his body. He fixed me with a fierce stare, his black brows furrowing over his shallow-lidded eyes, the wings of those scar-raddled cheekbones somehow underscoring his fury. At times, I'd seen a peaceful quality in his wide, angular face but when he glowered, all the sloping planes became slash marks of rage.

'I didn't fucking stalk you,' he said, 'I observed from a distance a couple of times. And I broke into your house once to give you a quick thrill. It was practically an arrangement we'd agreed upon. This. Fucking. Isn't.'

He gave a small lurch forward as if attempting to peck me. I darted back, fearing he were about to vault over the desks. Straightening, he continued his leisurely pursuit until he was standing squarely in the gap he'd made, trapping me in the frame of desks. Even while he was doing his best to unnerve me, and succeeding very well, I couldn't help but take pleasure in the sight of his lean hips, his low-slung leather belt with its big, macho buckle, and the muscular thighs beneath his jeans. He was hard too, the bar of his cock visible among the folds of worn denim. Anger and desire. Not a great combination. But then I was feeling much the same so who could blame him?

'Why did you do that and vanish?' My voice shook with emotion. 'Is that what you do? Meet women and discard them? Is that how you get your rocks off?'

Den's eyes flickered around the room then landed on a nearby clutter of equipment. He didn't move but I could tell he'd registered something of significance.

'Shall we play another game, Natalie?'

I drew a deep breath, trying to steel myself. 'Dunno. What's this one called? Acting like a cunt, part two?'

Den crossed to the stack of equipment and rummaged among a tangle of wires. 'It's called "Tying you up and fucking you",' he said. A beep sounded as he unplugged a couple of sockets. My heart galloped, heat flushing my cheeks. He wouldn't attempt to do that here, would he? Was he testing to see if I was hypothetically up for it?

He faced me again, standing in the gap of the square of desks into which I'd backed myself. He was a human gate, blocking the exit of my pen, a length of telephone wire in his hands, its black plug dangling. He gave the wire a deliberate tug.

A surge of lust nearly knocked me off my feet. His threatening bondage and the evident pleasure he took in tormenting me inspired a clawing, maddening hunger. Memories of our time in the theatre flooded my mind and my groin. I wanted him. Here, elsewhere, anywhere. I didn't care about the risks or consequences. We were so good together, so hot. My heart thundered and I was swamped by a flurry of desperate urges. I wanted him to fuck me till I could barely breathe, wanted him to use and abuse me, to claim me by hurting me.

Right then, nothing else mattered. I knew I'd been right to seek him out. Neither of us had been expecting this: mouse had turned cat, the hunted was now the hunter. My heart kept racing and my cunt throbbed as he strode into the pen of desks. I backed away, arousal and fear battling for precedence in my roaring blood. Between my thighs, I was wet and bloated, the ferocity of my desire rendering me muddled and weak. Was he pursuing me or was I luring him into my trap so I could get what I wanted?

When I reached the line of desks, I rested my arse against the edge, waiting, my breath shivering in and out of me. As he drew nearer, the scent of sharp, clean sweat sparked a fierce longing for the familiarity of his body, skin against skin, cock in my cunt.

'Tell me what you want,' he said again. 'Tell me why

you're really here. What drives you to these extremes? Why does this matter so much?'

The air was charged, as if an electricity we exuded completed a circuit.

'Doesn't it matter to you?' I replied.

He took a step closer. I half-expected the space between us to crackle. He grabbed my hair at the nape, phone wire in his other hand. 'Yes,' he said. 'It matters. We're probably more alike than you know.'

The closeness of his face sent my arousal several degrees higher. Lust urged me to lean forward and kiss him, to forget words and fighting so we could simply melt into each other's mouths. But the edge of pain from his fist in my hair was a cruel reminder that in this game, my desires were portrayed as secondary to his. And therein lay the irresistible paradox. Being at the apparent mercy of his desire was, effectively, my own desire. My instinct to embrace and taste him was subdued by my yearning to submit, by my pleasure being bound up in delayed gratification, sacrifice and suffering.

'But I'm asking the questions right now,' he continued, 'so tell me what you want. Then maybe we can discuss where we go next.'

He tugged on my hair, making me wince. My heart was going crazy and, in a rush, I told him, my voice quivering. 'You scare me,' I said. 'I like it, I liked being your prisoner. I like how you make me feel. Cheap, greedy and ashamed.' I looked him dead in the eye, drawing on my ebbing strength. 'But I don't like how you vanished. You started something and now you have to finish it. Because I need this too. I need it just as bad as you.'

For a couple of seconds he stared back at me, his eyes livid blue slits. Then he zoomed in, his lips hitting mine, and we were kissing with mad, angry excitement, trying to devour each other in a mess of wetness, lips, tongues and teeth, our vast hunger attempting to squeeze itself into the confines of a kiss. It felt less like a kiss, and more like we were trying to fuck each other with our mouths. In the cotton of my knickers I grew as messy as our mouths, my flesh wet, wide and pounding with desire. Den kept his grip on my hair, pulling with increasing pressure until my head was tipped so far back I couldn't respond. Instead, I became the recipient of his kiss, my head held tight, hair nipping at the base of my skull.

Slowing, Den took my bottom lip between his teeth, stretching it out until he bit so hard I yelped. We sprang apart.

It was the nastiest, most violent kiss I'd ever known.

'How badly?' said Den.

I was shocked to taste the coppery tang of blood in my mouth. I sucked on my lower lip, running my tongue over lumpy tenderness, assessing the damage. Before I could speak, Den spun me around by the shoulders, grabbing my hands and jerking them behind my back. Using the phone wire, he began binding my wrists, looping the squeaky, plastic length in a figure of eight around my wrists. The cool grip of the wire and the process of being bound made me weak with the need to be overtaken. It was all I could do stop myself from falling to my knees in a gesture of instant submission. People walked past the door, footsteps and chatter. I didn't care.

'How bad?' Den repeated.

'Bad,' I croaked. 'Bad enough for me to come here and let you do this to me. Even though you've been a prick. And I want it the way you want it, the way you dole it out. Hard, nasty, debasing. That's how I want it. That's how bad.'

220 Kristina Lloyd

'You like being used?' he asked.

'Yes.' My answer was an impatient syllable.

'You like getting tied up?'

'Yes.'

He continued threading the phone wire into awkward manacles. 'You like getting fucked in the mouth?'

'Yes.'

'Arse? Cunt?'

'Yes, yes.'

He finished off his tie, allowing the heavy plug to dangle behind my knees. Its weight added to the security of the bondage, reinforcing the pull I felt to sink into the blissful stupor of submission.

'You like the idea of getting fucked by a bunch of guys?' Den continued. 'A gang of them using you, passing you around.' Briskly, he began unbuttoning my shirt. 'A slut. Party favour. Whore. All of them treating you like meat. Ramming their cocks into your holes, fucking you senseless. You like that?'

He shoved my top and bra straps past my shoulders then crudely scooped my breasts from my bra. I was wired with arousal, lust shooting and simmering.

I felt woozy. 'Yes,' I breathed, wondering how many times I'd fantasised about me and three or more men in a bed.

Den reached past me to grab one of the long, plastic tables and tugged it towards the centre. Chairs clattered behind it, metal legs entangling. One chair fell to the ground, feet in the air.

'Lie on the table,' he said. 'On your back.'

I glanced at the door. If anyone tried to open it and push at the table behind it, we were done for. But if they merely peered in through the narrow glass panel, then we wouldn't be seen. How badly did I want it? Badly enough to chance getting caught? Oh yes. Besides, given that Den was here in a professional capacity, the risk he took far outweighed mine.

I hopped on the central table and swivelled into position, my cunt thick and wet for him. At last we seemed to be reconnecting, lust glowing white-hot between us. After this we couldn't possibly go our separate ways again. Clearly, we shared something special. We were wild for each other. Den simply needed to admit that to himself and we'd be fine. I wouldn't need to return to online dating and, with Den's help, Baxter Logan would soon be a distant memory. I lay down, my bound wrists bulky in the small of my back, the sway of the hanging plug pulling on my bonds.

'More this way.' Den tucked his hands into my armpits and slid my body higher up the table so my head had nothing to rest on. I allowed my neck to arch back, my upside down head perfectly positioned for him to drive his cock into my mouth. 'I'm going to make your dreams come true,' he said.

Confused, I gazed at the inverted classroom, table legs, window blinds and up to the cream, tiled ceiling. Which dreams? Should I check or trust him? Den moved around me with jerky aggression. I listened to him stride to the other end of the table where he shoved my skirt up to my hips. He removed my knickers in a couple of tugs. The plastic table was cool and hard beneath my buttocks. Grabbing each inner thigh, Den opened me up, forcing me apart until one leg was crooked over the table's edge, the other angled back, my swollen wet folds on brazen display. My breathing quickened as, without complaint, I allowed him to arrange me.

I tracked him as best I could, watching his legs stride over to a flipchart by the whiteboard. I missed what he was doing and before I knew it, he was at my side again. I caught a tiny pop then a sharp, chemical scent. He leaned over me, an uncapped marker pen in his hand. 'You just need a couple of labels then we're done,' he said.

He pressed the pen tip to one inner thigh. The soft nib tickled my skin as he wrote. I counted out four letters. He moved up my body and wrote across my chest. Again, four letters. I thought ahead, realising these words would show above my top once I was dressed. Tissues and spit. I'd be fine. Then, appallingly, Den cupped my head in one hand, supporting it as he touched the pen to my forehead.

I cringed, pressing into his hand. 'No,' I whispered. 'Not my face.' I didn't dare move any more in case that caused him to accidentally mark me.

'Yes,' he said calmly. 'Your face. Keep still.'

The marker pen moved on my skin. I forced myself to accept the touch, again telling myself tissues and spit would fix me up. Den marked my forehead with four letters. This was so much worse than him writing words on my body. I felt branded, as if he were imposing a new identity on me by changing my face.

'What have you written?' I asked, lifting my head and craning forward.

Den stood back, smiling. On my inner thigh, in upper-case lettering, was the word 'cunt'. Across my chest ,the word 'tits'. I raised my eyes to indicate my forehead. 'What's here?'

'Lie back,' said Den. 'It says "hole". That's all you are. Cunt, tits, hole. It's not even a mouth. It's a hole. Nothing to do with words, your voice. Nothing to do with you. It's all for me. Just another hole to be filled by my cock.'

Oh, jeez, he was crude and vile. And yet I still didn't regret pursuing him one iota. Quite the opposite. I was glad. I felt debased, humiliated and deliriously cheap. But most rare and precious of all, I felt understood and accepted. I was becoming more convinced that, with a connection such as this, maybe a relationship with Den, even a sex-based one, could help me lay to rest the ghost of Baxter. Den's committed domination could show me Baxter wasn't the only man capable of fulfilling my dark desires.

Den stood by my shoulder, towering above me, his legs at the periphery of my vision if I kept my head upside down. Blood filled my face as I waited for him. What was he doing? I twisted to see him. He had his mobile phone in his hand. He raised it to his ear.

'Ty,' he said cheerfully. 'My good man! Remember Walthamstow?' Den laughed. 'Yeah. Anyway, I got us another one.' A dark, smug laugh. 'Thought so. Room 114. Yep. See you in five.'

I sat bolt upright, appalled and afraid. 'Who's that?' I snapped. 'What are you doing?'

Den pushed me flat on the table.

'Giving you what you want.'

My mind raced, rushing forwards and backwards. Was this more of Den's headfuck stuff? It had to be. He couldn't have someone else here within five minutes, could he? Did he want to test me? See how I'd react?

'I don't believe you,' I said. 'You're trying to mess with my head again. You just faked that call.'

'You think so?' Den asked.

'Yes,' I whispered, my panic abating. I was becoming wise to his ways. He thought I was so naive he could spin me this way and that, but he couldn't. I was starting to see through him. 'You're full of crap,' I said. 'You act like you have a grand plan and you're in control but you're making it up as you go along. Same as everybody.'

'Of course I'm making it up,' he said. 'That's why I phoned Ty. Wasn't expecting to see you here but now you are, I'm running with it.'

'I still don't believe you.'

'Well you ought,' he said. 'Because Ty'll be here in a few minutes.'

I wasn't convinced. 'Yeah? So who is he?' I asked, playing along.

'A colleague,' he replied. 'And a dom. You said you want to get fucked by a bunch of guys. Short notice, so I'm afraid the best I can do right now is two.'

I began to fear he might be speaking the truth. 'No,' I said. 'Not good. I don't know him.'

'Trust me, you soon will do. At least, the back of your throat will.'

Again, I tried to sit up but Den pushed me down. He held me to the table, a hand on my chest. 'Two guys, Natalie, and it's all for you. Aren't I kind and generous?'

'I don't know him,' I said again. 'You haven't checked if it's OK with me.'

Den trailed his hand from my chest, across my belly, through my pubes and down between my thighs. Lust made me dizzy, all the blood in my body pumping into my engorged folds. In my groin, arousal thudded so hard I felt faint. His fingers parted my flesh and plunged into me. I groaned deeply, feeling I might expire.

'It's pouring from you, Natalie,' said Den. 'Don't pretend you disapprove.'

I fought for my voice. 'Not fair,' I gasped. 'You haven't asked if it's OK.'

Den withdrew his fingers from me. 'I just asked your cunt,' he replied. 'And it said "yes".'

'No.' I hardly knew what I meant. I squirmed and panted, desperate to have his fingers inside me again. The prospect of having another guy join us thrilled me from my head to my toes. Excitement made my veins swell and simmer, my entire body strung out on lust. I just wished Den had asked me before calling someone. Wished he hadn't assumed I'd agree. Wished he hadn't presumed to know my desire.

'Yes,' said Den. 'Because your cunt is where we get the truth from. You can protest. You can act offended, act like you want me to respect you, but your cunt's always going to tell a different story. It's always going to betray you.'

He understood me too well. He was playing along with my fantasies, knowing I would protest if I truly wasn't keen; knowing that this game would lose its edge for us if I were to say, 'Yes, please! Bring it on, daddio!'

I heard a tap at the door. A pulse in my head boomed so heavily I felt my brain was expanding beyond my skull. Was this Den's friend, or someone wanting access to the classroom?

'Don't move,' said Den.

I could have moved. I could have sat up and said 'enough'. I could have wriggled my wrists free from the phone wire. I could have done many things to make it clear I didn't want a stranger in the room. And ultimately, so there was no mistaking my wishes, I could have said, 'safeword'. But I did none of these things because I desperately wanted him, whoever he was, wanted him with every nerve in my body. Right there and then, although I was scared of where this might lead, I wanted a second guy more than anything. I didn't care who the newcomer might be. I wanted Den to act as if he were forcing me to take cock from someone of his choosing.

In future, I told myself, if we repeated this sort of scene, I'd insist we negotiate first. But for now, what the Hell? Never look a gift horse in the mouth. I just hoped we wouldn't get rumbled. Supposing this room was booked for a lecture? Oh God, I pictured being trussed up like this as bemused students drifted into their class.

I lay stock still on the table, face flaming at the thought of being publically displayed, my body marked in ink, my acquiescence a declaration of my desire for humiliation. I listened to Den moving furniture away from the door, heard male voices and laughter.

'Ohhh yes!' came a new voice as soft footsteps fast approached me. 'Fresh pussy.'

I saw his lower half first, desert boots and skinny black jeans. I twisted to see more of him and when I did, I knew I was lost. I knew I would let these two guys do whatever they wanted to me. Ty was a lanky black guy with smiling eyes and long dreadlocks fastened in a fat tail. And he was a fast mover, already unzipping as he strode towards me, while Den put the table back to block the door.

'Don't mind if I do.' Ty positioned himself by my head, his erect, purplish-black length bobbing above my eyes.

'Yes, yes,' I said, my voice hoarse with greedy urgency. I gaped for him.

'And she's keen,' said Ty, voice singing with enthusiasm. He cupped my head, supporting me as he angled himself to the right height. His blunt tip nudged at my lips then, with a low noise of satisfaction, he drove into my mouth.

After a few slow strokes, he grew rough and careless, slender hips pumping as he slammed. I tried to grip him with my lips but his aggressive rhythm made me cough and splutter. I couldn't keep my legs still and within seconds my eyes were streaming.

I remembered the word Baxter had taught me: *irrumatio*. The Latin sounded far more acceptable than 'throat-fucking' but whatever you called it, the action invariably got me hot, made me feel gloriously wanton and sluttish. Ty's pounding felt like an attempt to break down my resistance, not that I had much apart from an under-active gag reflex. But I fancied that, in forcing me to submit by shattering my defences, Ty was aiming to make me game for anything. Well, I pretty much was already. I'm sure both men could see that but I wasn't going to stop our fun by declaring that he didn't need to be quite so rough.

Ty popped out of me, giving me a short breather. 'Oh man,' he asked, 'where d'you find her?'

Den approached, upside down in my vision and blurred by my tears.

'A street corner,' said Den. 'Plying her trade.'

Ty held my head in both hands then, taking his time, eased his cock past my lips, gliding to the back of my mouth. 'Take it, take it, take it,' he urged as he pushed gently against the barrier of my throat. 'That's it. Make it disappear. Hold it there.'

I kept him lodged in my throat until I couldn't stand it any more. When I writhed and thrashed, he snatched his cock free, spilling saliva onto my face. As I gulped for breath, Ty used his cock to slap my face, bashing himself against one cheek then the other, smearing wetness over me.

'How's she doing?' asked Den.

'She's good, man,' said Ty. He sank his length back into my mouth, slowly this time. 'Hold her legs still.'

Den grabbed my thighs, pushing my legs open and flat to the table. 'Better?'

Ty nudged fractionally to and fro, allowing me to recover my breath and steady myself. Then for the second time, he eased himself deep into my throat, ordering me to take him. His balls rested against my nose, their velvety warmth half-smothering me while he uttered cries of 'oh man' and warnings of, 'Not yet, hold it, girl.'

When he pulled back, leaving me gasping and gulping, Den said, 'I'm going to make her come. Make her prove to us how much she loves this.'

'Good plan,' Ty enthused. He used his cock to slap my face again. 'You hear that, girl? We're gonna make you come. And you're gonna show us how much you love getting your face fucked.'

Again, he began thrusting into my mouth. I groaned awkwardly as Den slid a bunch of fingers into my wetness, twisting and turning them. The two men drove at me, filling me at either end. The intensity rising in my cunt had me whimpering around Ty's cock. I could hardly keep open for him, could hardly grip, but he didn't seem to care. He just used my mouth like it meant nothing to him, as if any cocksucking skills I had were worthless.

When Den started paying attention to my clit, I knew I was moments away from coming. Ripples shivered along my thighs, reaching in deeper. I wailed around Ty's length, gasping for breath, my nearness clutching and tightening.

Den kept up a deliberate, consistent rocking on my clit. 'She's nearly there,' he said.

'Come on, girl,' said Ty. 'Show us how much you love this.' He grabbed my breasts, a hand on each, squeezed and slapped my flesh. 'These tits,' he said. 'Oh yes, look at these tits.'

Calm and workmanlike, Den kept rubbing – his fingers inside me, his thumb on my clit. 'Nearly . . . nearly.'

'Oh man, yes,' said Ty. 'Gonna get my cock so deep in your throat when you come, girl. You won't make a sound. Gonna fuck your cries right back inside you.'

My tightness squeezed faster, higher.

'Here we go,' said Den. 'She's nearly there. You ready, Ty?'

Ty took my head in his hands, holding me steady. I fought to regulate my breathing, on the verge of coming. Den circled my clit, his thumb rocking the tiny bud, keeping me on a plateau of nearness. I was desperate, delirious, consumed by the need to climax. Then Ty's end was pushing at my throat and I started to come, my throat muscles softening for him.

'There she goes,' said Den. Ty lodged himself in the depths of my throat, blocking my cries as I tumbled into my rapturous finale. I couldn't gasp and thrash, needing to follow a focused stillness to accommodate Ty's cock. Every ripple, clench and shimmer of my orgasm lifted me higher. Ecstasy and my body were separate entities. I was scattering like a million stars pouring from a champagne bottle and filling up the skies.

'Oh, wow,' said Ty. 'This chick's loving my cock, ain't she?'

Waves of bliss clutched. I had no breath left. Sensation shivered in and out, parts of me sinking, parts of me rising. Den pulled out of me, laughing softly.

'Way to go, man!' said Ty, snatching himself free. The two men high-fived each other over my body.

My orgasm faded, leaving me with a sudden headache and weakened legs. I gasped for air as Ty began wanking. 'Let's wash that nasty word off your face,' he said.

Den laughed again. 'Never let it be said Ty's not a gentleman. Say "thank you", Natalie.'

I said nothing, too stupefied to speak. Ty pumped on his cock, making rich, deep noises of pleasure, his hand a blur. He aimed himself at my face, his violet-dark tip inches away. Seconds later, with a series of groans, he unloaded his release. His come jetted onto my chin and cheek, chaotic splashes of warmth. I squeezed my lids shut, not wanting him dribbling into my eyes because experience had taught me that it stings.

With a heavy sigh, Ty stepped back. So physical, so crude. Had he seen stars as well when he'd come on my face? He smeared his fluid onto my forehead, rubbing at the inked word.

'Say "thank you",' repeated Den.

I stayed silent, refusing this tiny additional humiliation. A few moments passed, nothing but the sound of our breath in the classroom.

'If you don't say "thank you",' said Den, 'I'm going to walk out of your life once again, Natalie. All I'm asking for is a little politeness, a little bit of respect for my friend.'

My mind swam with confusion. Was he saying we were potentially back together? I was assuming that would be the case after this unexpectedly horny reunion. And yet already he was threatening to deny me that prospect.

'Just two little words,' continued Den, 'to show me how badly you want this. And then maybe we can talk.'

I breathed as steadily as I could, wishing my hands were free so I could wipe the come from my face. I opened my eyes, blinking against the sting and the blob of pearly liquid resting on the lashes of my left eye. I half-wondered if the droplet were full of champagne bubbles and stars.

'Well?' said Den. 'Cat got your tongue?'

I shook my head. Though my voice emerged croaky and weak, the meaning of my words rang out as clear as a bell. 'Thank you,' I rasped. Then, hoping to grab back my dignity by injecting a note of sarcasm, I added, 'Thank you ever so much.'

Sixteen

And so it seemed we were back on track.

The two men waited till I'd tidied myself up, and they had to wait a while because the ink was seriously hard to remove from my skin. Den put the tables back in their correct place. In those minutes, the mood lightened to a friendly atmosphere where the three of us, on a post-sex high, were able to banter lightly. The guys, Ty in particular, were careful to check I was OK while maintaining physical distance.

'That was great,' I said. 'A bit of a surprise but . . .' I checked my reflection in my compact mirror. 'Ty, don't ever think of selling your come as ink remover. Doesn't work.'

Ty laughed. 'Noted. But hey, worth a shot.' He laughed at his inadvertent pun, adding, 'So to speak.'

I wondered if he were single, my contingency if things went nowhere with Den.

'I'll call you,' said Den.

I almost laughed. It sounded like the sort of polite lie you'd give to someone at the end of a dreary date rather than a promise you'd make to a woman covered in come and ink after twenty minutes of rough, humiliating sex.

'If you don't,' I said, 'I'll call you.'

'New phone, new number, so no you won't. But I'll call, I promise.' Den lifted my chin with one finger, inviting me to look him in the eye. 'You've taken this up a notch and I respect that.'

We left the classroom and went our separate ways, me with a raw, pink forehead. I headed straight for the Ladies to do further repair work on my face. When I was presentable, I found a small cafe-bar away from the main dining area where the delegates were finishing lunch. I drank Earl Grey tea and ate a huge, restorative slice of sticky chocolate fudge cake. Replete, I sat back in my chair, steeped in the afterglow of sexual and sweet-toothed indulgence. I felt elated and untouched by guilt, feelings I wouldn't have allowed myself to experience several years ago.

I had no further interest in the conference and would have gone home except for one thing: I didn't want Den or Ty to think I'd run away in shame or embarrassment. So I returned to the lecture hall for the post-lunch session and made a deliberate effort to talk to a couple of people, hoping to appear relaxed and content. I left at the mid-afternoon break, overwhelmed by long words. But I didn't merely slope off. I politely interrupted a conversation Den was having to say my goodbyes then I sought out Ty, saying, 'Lovely to meet you' before returning to the train station. I walked on air, proud of myself for refusing to stay home waiting for the phone to ring as if this were courtship in the 1950s.

A short while later, as the train sped towards the coast, I was gazing out at louring grey skies and velvety fields of undulating downland, cocooned by a new sense of peace. I told myself only time would tell if Den would make good on

his promise to call but ironically, it no longer seemed quite
so important. Rain started to fall, spattering the window. I
tried to work out if I liked Den for his personality or his
sexuality. But the two elements were inseparable so I had no
answer. Either way, I was pleased I'd been in the driving seat
for a while, obliging him to be the one reacting rather than
steering. If we were to make a go of it, we had a lot to sort
out first. I was still unhappy with the way he'd gone cold
on me after declaring 'one chance, one meeting'. I never did
establish what that line was about. I'd ask next time, if we had
a next time.

Back to everyday life in Saltbourne, I braced myself for
no phone call. He might vanish on me again. Well, OK, if
that happened, I would quit. No point chasing someone who
either wasn't interested or couldn't communicate except via
mixed messages. The evenings were dark, the clocks would
change soon. Spring forward, fall back. It was the time of
year for settling, for quietening. Maybe I'd just had a late
summer of lust, no more.

As it happened, Den contacted me within a few days. I
was at Liam's workshop doing more makeshift modelling for
the leather head-harness he'd been commissioned to make.
The harness was turning out to be a gorgeous piece, its ruddy
brown leather, hand stitching, burnished edges and brass
attachments giving it a faux-Victorian aesthetic, an object for
a steampunk torture chamber, if such a thing existed.

Even though it was Liam tightening the buckles, adjusting
the straps and hooking the claw gag inside my cheeks, I felt
aroused as I stood on the sawdust-strewn cobbles for what
felt like the umpteenth time in recent weeks. The sensation
of having my head half-encased, and the objectifying thrill
of the hooks denying me ownership of my mouth, got me

in the groin. I could tell, too, that Liam's relationship to me wearing the kit was changing.

Previously, his enthusiasm for seeing me in the bridle had been about an admiration for the structure he was building and a satisfaction with his own craftsmanship. He'd kept his distance from the D/S implications of the piece, treating it as something I was into while he wasn't. I wondered if he were growing more comfortable with kink or if an unexplored aspect of his sexuality was emerging. Would it work if I tried encouraging him to be more dom? Ever since our confrontation with the security guard in the grounds of the theatre, something had shifted between us. There was a new edge, a deeper connection arising from us having shared such a dark, scary encounter. We'd seen how the other had reacted to the threat. I could still hear Liam's groan in response to the thug calling me a greedy, cocksucking cumslut.

At the time, I imagined him regretting his expression of pleasure. He probably did even now, and I'd be the same. The words used against me weren't our choice but sudden lust tends to short-circuit the intellect. Liam knew I'd heard him, and we both knew the other hadn't been as fazed at being forced to perform as many others might be. That night had drawn us together in a way that couldn't yet articulate itself.

I wondered idly if Liam could get off on games of humiliation, power play and verbal abuse. Could that work between us?

'You know, you look strangely beautiful,' said Liam, adjusting the final buckle. 'Almost wish I didn't have to sell it. And I tell you, I've really earned my money on this. Seriously, one of the most demanding customers I've ever had the misfortune to work with. Always coming up with minor changes, wanting everything done yesterday. And then all these sodding pictures we've had to keep sending him. Total nightmare. I'll be glad when I'm rid of him.'

Liam stood in front of me and touched a hand to my jaw, smiling. I gazed back, struggling with the discomfort of my enforced silence, gaping wet mouth and facial immobility.

'Weird,' said Liam. 'Makes me want to kiss you even though you can't kiss back.'

Oh God, he *was* changing, he was definitely changing. He bent to my mouth. As he moved, I caught the scent of his copper curls, an appley hint of shampoo mixed with the freshness of new wood and an undertone of tobacco smoke, a smell so suited to his autumnal colouring it might have originated from his actual body. Gently, he nibbled on my lower lip. I closed my eyes, deeply uncomfortable and trying to slurp back saliva. Gags always embarrass me and this one was worse than usual. It made me look ugly, undignified and dumb, a borderline animal. I loathed it as much as I loved it.

With a hand on the small of my back, Liam held me, bending his knees a fraction to roll his groin against mine. The press of his erection made lust hammer between my thighs. I took him in a loose embrace, letting my hands rove over the sweep of his back before I dipped under his sweatshirt to find skin. He was cool and smooth beneath my fingers. The disparity between our mutual, tender caress and my leather-strapped head frustrated more than it excited. In the context of gentle touches, the bridle humiliated in all the wrong ways. If Liam hadn't been quite so taken by the piece, I would have gladly removed it.

My phone beeped with a text message, momentarily snatching me from the here and now. Was it Den? Gah, I was supposed to be no longer bothered whether he called. I needed to get in the habit of putting my phone on silent when things were likely to get sexy. Little interruptions could potentially kill the mood.

I swirled my hand under Liam's top, letting my pelvis sway with his, telling myself the message could wait. Liam drew me closer, fondling one breast while continuing to peck and lick at my fixed-open mouth. I couldn't help but feel turned on by those half-kisses, how they gently taunted me, mocking the predicament in which the harness placed me. But also, despite myself, I couldn't stop thinking about the text awaiting me in my bag. Old habits die hard.

I withdrew from Liam, gesturing apologetically to signal I wanted the harness removed. Liam unhooked one brass claw from my cheek while I removed the other, our knuckles knocking as I fumbled to free myself. 'You OK?' asked Liam, concerned.

I dabbed at my damp lips and swallowed. 'Yes, fine,' I said with a laugh. 'I'm horny. Does your client need more photos of me wearing this?'

'No. It's practically finished. He's picking it up this week then I get the rest of the payment. Why, what are you thinking?'

'That we should go back to mine and do this properly?'

Liam grinned. 'Cool,' he said. He pushed at his ginger curls in a cute, bashful manner. 'But do you mind if we leave the harness here? It's really great and everything. But it just feels wrong to, you know, give it a test run when I'm making it for someone else. Shouldn't really be messing about like this when you're wearing it.'

I smiled, relieved we weren't going to explore this uncertain dynamic developing between us. The prospect made me anxious, afraid it might prove awkward, embarrassing or dissatisfying.

'No problem,' I said. 'You're so principled, you know?'

Liam unbuckled the straps and lifted the soft cage from my head. 'I know. Sometimes wish I wasn't.'

I shook my hair out and, trying not to appear over hasty, retrieved my phone from my bag.

The text was from a number rather than a name. It read: '*I have made mistakes. I have treated you badly. Can we meet Tuesday? Will try to explain. Make amends. Sonny's Bar at eight? Desperate to see you.*'

I laughed aloud, elated. So, I thought, he finally admits he wants me! He's going to quit playing games and atone. Well, well, well, this was a turn-up for the books. He hadn't been fobbing me off when he said he'd be in touch. The impact of my surprise appearance at the conference was clearly more significant than I'd realised. This was definitely going to be interesting.

'Shall we grab some beers on the way?' said Liam.

'Excellent plan,' I said. 'Sorry, just got to reply to this then I'm good.'

I thumbed in my response, deliberately clipped: '*Much appreciated. Let's talk Tues. See you at eight.*'

He replied: '*Love you xx*'

Sonny's Bar had a rooftop terrace overlooking the sloping, lamp-lit sprawl of Saltbourne. In summer it was a joy, in early-November, less so, but being high above the town made me feel I could breathe. In the dark evening, the town glittered like fallen constellations, the sea shone like coal, and street lights beading the coastal road snaked into the distance. Occasional fireworks burst overhead, their jewelled colours falling over tiled roofs, and pink and gold domes.

I was early and nervous, wrapped in a fake fur jacket and

determined not to appear too eager. I would listen to what Den had to say to justify his cruel disappearance after our kidnap game. I'd give him the benefit of the doubt and tell him he didn't need to pretend he loved me to get me on side. Sweet of him to try but I wasn't that gullible and, besides, I didn't want his love. Our relationship wasn't about that. Sex was our motivation and, given how well we clicked, that could carry us a long way.

I'd also mention the need for us to make a habit of negotiating scenes. Even though I fantasised about being forced, it didn't mean I wanted to be genuinely forced, nor was I prepared to give my blanket consent to anything Den might want to do. As he got to know me better and as I learned to trust him more, then, sure, we could make the rules less rigid. But for now, let's tread carefully, eh?

I hoped I wasn't expecting too much of our meeting. But if things went well and we were to resume our relationship, I also hoped we'd be able to seal the deal tonight with more than a kiss. I wasn't planning on mentioning it to Den but, with sex in mind, I'd booked the following day off work in case we ended up at my place, fucking until dawn.

The roof terrace was a humble affair, a small stucco-walled square, bare foliage stems threaded through trellis, a few potted palms and strings of tiny lanterns. I switched on a tall patio heater and sat at a wooden table beneath the lamp's amber warmth, my breath clouding when it met the night. I envied the only other people there, a couple huddled close and smoking in silence. They looked so relaxed and comfortable, poles apart from anxious, jittery me.

My phone beeped. I checked my messages. Den: *'Sorry, running ten mins late. Xx'*

I replied: *'No worries. Am on rooftop.'*

I lay my phone on the table and sipped my Rioja, pleased at this new, more communicative Den. Ten minutes to gather my thoughts. That was good. My phone beeped again, the screen glowing in the half-light. An unknown number rather than a name popped up. The message was a photo that threw me until I realised it was of me modelling Liam's leather bridle, my features and hair distorted with whatever editing software he'd used. The accompanying text said: '*Your head looks great in a cage.*'

I laughed. Was Liam drunkenly sexting me? As I'd suspected, the contraption seemed to be stirring something in his loins. I wondered if he'd be interested in making another one for us to use. I replied: '*Easy tiger! Am at Sonny's Bar. Got a hot date! Can't reply much.*'

Liam answered: '*Slut.*'

I laughed again and set down my phone, thinking how lucky I was to know Liam and share such an easy, friends-with-benefits set-up. If he met someone else and needed to change our arrangement, I'd miss him. But hopefully, if that happened, we'd be able to remain friends.

I checked the time, my nerves returning. I glanced at the doorway where narrow steps led down to the pub below. Having a civilised drink with Den would be a peculiar experience but if we were to continue this relationship, a conversation about our expectations was vital. I began to question the wisdom of taking the following day off work and making it as easy as possible for us to have crazy, late-night sex. More sensible, surely, to make it inconvenient then we could demonstrate our commitment to this relationship with a discussion unaffected by twitchy fingers and an urge to tear each other's clothes off.

The two smokers left, returning downstairs. The patio

heater by my table timed out so I tugged on its string. The lamp's fierce warmth filtered my view of Saltbourne through a smudged, orange lens, the town's shimmering streets suspended in pale fire, white surf on the distant black sea licking at its edges. A firework screeched and shattered, the reflection of its cascading beads fluttering in the corner of my phone screen. I sensed change, a movement in my life. This was one of those golden nights I would look back on in years to come. Whatever conclusions Den and I reached would tell me something about myself.

Impossible to know how badly you want something until you're tested. And the test here wasn't simply of how badly I wanted him or the dark sex he could offer, but how much I needed to stay true to myself. Years ago, I'd vowed to take my sexuality into my own hands. The goal, my Northern Lights, was to become a fully-realised woman, comfortable with her sexuality. Was I there yet or was I about to screw up?

Easy enough to promise yourself you won't compromise your self-respect in pursuit of a valued end. But when your kink entails someone pretending to strip you of your dignity and worth, then distinguishing damaging compromises from actions pursued for kicks can be tricky. It wasn't as simple as marking out a metaphorical bedroom territory; as giving the thumbs up for whatever happened there and thumbs down for bad behaviour beyond that. Reality wasn't so clearly demarcated. With experience, I'd get better at this, I was sure.

The trouble was, I'd embarked on a sexual relationship with a man who liked blurring the boundaries between reality and fantasy. Unfortunately, I liked that too. I might insist on a need to negotiate and be clear about where a scene stopped and started but, deep down, I knew the thrill for me lay in walking the margins, in testing the imprecision of 'safe' with edgeplay.

I got off on being taken to the limit in games of force and non-consent, yes. I loved the murky borders of danger, especially when the lure of uncertainty could help stave off heartache. And I liked feeling used, cheap, worthless, sure I did.

However, the trouble with Den, I began to realise, was he left me feeling valueless afterwards. Being rendered whorishly disposable as a fantasy and sexual practice worked for fucking because it meant I got a lot of cock, a thing I'm rather fond of. The nice-guy Grants of the world who were super attentive and unremittingly selfless in the sack failed to move me. I wanted to see a man's unchecked lust and passion; wanted to see him with a big, determined boner, a man driven half-insane with a need that returned and returned, and every time I benefited.

But I had no taste for the reality of feeling bereft, humiliated and cockless because a man I'd fucked had then proceeded to ignore me. I didn't enjoy him acting as if I didn't matter because I was merely a single transaction and he'd somehow pretend-paid me. Worthless in the game, worthless out of it. No thanks.

I hoped Den and I could thrash some of this out tonight. He'd sounded contrite in his text but, given how erratic his behaviour had been to date, it was probably wise not to set too much store by that. And if we couldn't agree on a way forward, well, I would renew my search for a sexually dominant guy who played well with others.

Heavy footsteps in the stairwell snagged my attention. Was that him? If so, good timing, Dr Jackson. It would be useful if we had the roof terrace to ourselves so we could skirt the need to keep our voices low. The footsteps ascended. My heart beat faster than it ought. I tried to appear casual, not overly keen to greet him. Much as I wanted to gawp at the entrance to the stairwell like an eager puppy awaiting its master's return, I gazed out across town, playing it cool.

From the corner of my eye I saw a man. A bigger, bulkier man than Den. I turned as he approached, a burly figure in a suit, collar askew, his dark, wavy hair flopping over his forehead. He set his pint down on an empty table and strode towards me, arms held open, a faint, regretful smile on his lips.

The bottom dropped out of my stomach. Somewhere far away, a firework exploded.

'Hen,' he said. 'My God. It's been too fucking long.'

Seventeen

There was a hotel, once. He was on call in another town, mid-week, standing in for a sick colleague. The night was likely to be quiet, till the pubs shut at least. Would I join him?

Hell, yes. I'd swipe the little toiletries and enjoy not having to tidy up in the morning. Shortly before midnight, Baxter got called out to the police station. He was needed to give solicitor's advice to someone who'd been brought in 'for being a pisshead', as Baxter put it. In the past, I'd heard him on the phone advising regular clients, the ones constantly getting banged up for the night. 'Just hush your fucking mouth, Jonesy! "No comment", remember?' He'd once described his job as being a 'friend to the great unwashed', adding 'because some fucker's got to be'.

We were still awake, talking on the bed, naked and post-coital. I was drinking wine but Baxter was sober since, technically, he was working. He needed to shower before heading out so we continued our conversation in the poky hotel bathroom, even though he'd told the station he'd be there in ten. Baxter had a tendency to overpromise.

Still naked, I sat on the lid of the toilet, glass of red in hand, while next to me, Baxter showered in a corner cubicle with two Perspex walls. Steam fogged the sides, condensation and droplets of water cutting a track through the mists. Behind the screens, Baxter soaped himself, rubbing vigorously under his pits and between his legs. Steam veiled him, suds and water sliding down his powerful, hairy body. His voice billowed out of the top of the unit, rising above the hum of the extractor fan and pattering water.

He was talking animatedly about a film he'd seen some years previously, while expounding a theory romance was dying. 'People don't want to know who you are,' he said. 'They want to ken what you do for a living. As if that'll tell you a fucking thing. Where's the spark, the risk? Where's the chemistry?' As he spoke, he periodically rubbed the fog from the side of the shower cubicle so he could see me, making brief, eager eye contact while he babbled away. 'And relationships? Love? Gone too quick. Reduced to the need for a mortgage, a family, a fortnight in the sun. Your freedom's fucked, people, fucked. You fold into each other till you can hardly tell yourself from herself and the magic's dead as stone.' His fingers rubbed at the misted Perspex. Baxter's face emerged, peering through the frame of a dripping cloud, hair plastered to his head. Back to the soap, talking in the shower as if he were singing with no one to hear him. 'Then you start to hate, and you don't know if what you hate is something in her, in yourself, or in the monster the two of you have fashioned. Anyway, in this film I saw . . .'

I couldn't follow him. His words seemed to be more a stringing together of half-formed thoughts than a coherent argument. I remember I was watching rather than listening. I found the sight of him amusing. He looked as if he were trapped in a glass cage, waving at me from afar.

Later, after we split, I revisited that moment so many times. In my mind, the scene became a metaphor of the distance between us, a barrier I hadn't noticed.

He *was* trapped, or so he thought. And, as the poem goes, not waving but drowning.

When Baxter walked across Sonny's rooftop terrace, his breath condensing in the dark, I was undone, demolished by his tender smile and craggy, shambolic beauty.

He'd lost a little weight but other than that, everything about him was shockingly familiar. Too familiar. He must be a replicant or a dead man reanimated because this couldn't be him. Baxter Logan was a memory, not an actual living person. I couldn't believe he was real. Not here, now, on a roof terrace in November. Yet he was so solid, so immediately vital. His face hadn't changed a jot, ruggedly handsome in a desk-job kind of way, nose a little pudgy, brown eyes gleaming under dark, shaggy brows. He moved with the same hefty grace he'd always done; a robust mass of a man, comfortable in his own skin.

Our past flooded my present. As he strode towards me, I was half-expecting him to whip off his tie, shuck off his jacket and tell me his dick was hurting to get inside me.

He neared my table, slowing and raising his hands in a gesture of surrender. He tried to smile fully but his pain was evident. 'So we're no doing hugs, then?' he said. 'OK, I can go with that.'

I stood, wanting to bar him from my space and prevent him from joining me at my table. 'What the fuck are you doing here?' I glanced anxiously past his shoulder to the stairwell, praying Den wouldn't turn up yet.

Baxter frowned, opening his mouth but saying nothing.

Behind him, the icy white glow of fairy lanterns bled into the night.

'You have to leave,' I hissed. 'Or I do. This is seriously not a good time.' I stooped to grab my bag.

Baxter stepped forward and snatched my wrists. He pinned my arms against the air, trapping me with a light clasp, an old, familiar move of ours. I smelled his skin, a catch on the night I wouldn't have noticed unless I'd recognised it. Him. The oils of his skin blended with a hint of faded aftershave; memories of a place where over and over I'd yielded. My bag slid to the crook of my elbow, swinging clumsily between us.

He gazed down with something akin to angry disbelief, a reflection of how I must have been looking at him.

'But you agreed.' His grip squeezed harder on my wrists.

I stared at him. I agreed? How so? The blood left my head as the penny dropped. The text. The unknown number. My assumption the message had come from Den. I'd even added the name to my contacts list. I felt queasy, all my expectations going haywire. I recalled his sign off text: '*Love you xx*'

As if Den would send anything like that. As if. Jeez, I was an idiot.

'You were expecting someone else, weren't you?' The fingers around my wrists loosened a fraction.

I nodded, lightheaded.

'Someone who loves you.' Baxter's voice rose to a crack.

The patio light clicked off, darkening our surroundings and causing an instant chill. Our breath misted in the space between us, mingling like spectral kisses.

I swallowed hard, trying to read those brown eyes, now glimmering with hard tears. 'No,' I said, quiet but firm. 'There's no love.'

We became self-conscious in the same moment, glancing

sheepishly at our stance. Baxter released his hold on my wrists as I withdrew. He dusted his cheek, raked back his hair, his movements fast and brittle. I hooked my bag onto my shoulder and rubbed my wrists as if to erase his fingerprints. We stood inches apart, saying nothing. I reached back and tugged the cord on the patio heater.

At length, in a hoarse voice, Baxter said, 'I've missed you. Missed you so badly, heh –' He couldn't manage the final word, 'hen'. He glanced aside, pressing his lips together as if fighting back tears.

I shrugged, hitching my bag higher on my shoulder. 'Missed you too.' I attempted breeziness but managed only to sound petulant and defensive.

'Can we talk?' he asked. 'Will you stay?' He reached out to brush my fingertips.

I shrugged again, not knowing what to do.

'I know I acted like a cunt,' Baxter went on, 'and you don't owe me a thing. And I'm not here to ask anything of you. But I'd like us to talk. If you'll give me that.'

I said nothing, mulling over his request, still wildly confused. I wasn't prepared for this. I was psyched up for a different conversation with a very different person.

Baxter stayed silent, awaiting my answer. I drew a deep breath, about to speak. But Baxter's rotten at waiting and he cut in, saying, 'I still want to fuck the lights out of you, you know?'

I laughed, despite myself.

Baxter stepped close and seized my upper arms. 'And you ken why?' he said. His eyes were wild, his frown pitching his thick brows together. He gave my body a tiny shake. 'Because I know I never will. I know I can't.' He spoke through clenched teeth, saliva slicking his lips, and oh God, the smell of him, the smell of him where I used to kiss his neck, the smell of skin and a worn, laundered collar, so familiar I almost felt the rasp of stubble on my lips, tasted the peat-rich Scotch on his breath. His face was close, blocking out everything, his expression angry, his hair awry. 'You have a light, Nats,' he said. 'You don't see it but you have a light. Soon as I met you, I saw it. Something in you. Something bright and burning.'

I shook my head. 'No,' I said. 'That's not me.' I made a feeble effort to step back. 'If you saw something, it's only because you lit it.'

His hold tightened on my arms, fingers pinching through the fur of my jacket.

'Every day since we split,' he began. 'My – ' His voice splintered and he drew a long composing breath. I heard the air shiver as he inhaled. He tried again, enunciating his words. 'My every waking moment . . . has been haunted by the terrible and beautiful things I want to do to you.'

He looked at me, searching. He was so close. I could see the individual lashes on his lids, the blood vessels in his eyes. I thought I'd never see that again, never see individual pieces of him, having instead just a fading memory of his face and a few fossilising photographs.

'I want to wreak havoc on your body,' he whispered. 'I want you to let me, Nats. Oh God, I want you to let me.'

Now it was my turn to press my lips together. I blinked rapidly, shaking my head. I couldn't speak. I wanted to tell him he shouldn't have confessed to such thoughts. But I couldn't say the words.

We gazed at each other, on the brink of knowing a new thing, of being changed one way or the other. I wondered about the dividing line between safety and danger, between happiness and pain. Was there a line or did one thing merge into another? Here, now, the risks were enormous and the stakes were my heart. What to do?

Impossible lines; invisible until you've crossed them. Impossible decisions.

I released a breath I didn't know I'd been holding. My body sagged. Then, impossibly, my wine glass was on its side, rolling towards the table edge. Rioja poured like spilled blood through the wooden slats of the table, splashing onto stone. Glass shattered. And I was flat on my back, blinking at a star-spangled sky, at hair and skin as Baxter pinned me to the table, his hand surging between my thighs, his lips hot and wet as he tried his darkest to kiss my lights out.

During our relationship, Baxter's Blackberry was practically an extension of his body. He couldn't take a bath without placing the device on the side. He rarely clocked off, maintaining he needed to keep on top of emails or he'd face a deluge on returning to work. I used to joke I was a Blackberry widow. Sometimes, I openly wished we had more quality time together. I didn't complain too much though since he claimed to wish for the same.

And he did important work. He wasn't slogging his guts out to earn shedloads of money. If status and wealth were his motivations, I'd have been less sympathetic. But I cut him some slack because he had a strong moral code. He believed in the right of those without money to have access to legal representation so everyone, whoever they were, was innocent until proven guilty.

Baxter was one of the good guys. He had principles. And he'd exploited those principles to mask his deceit, forcing me to re-evaluate who he was. He used to make out he was permanently busy, the unpredictable pressures of work limiting his free time. But, as I discovered, it wasn't simply the job making demands on him; it was the responsibility of having a hidden wife. Or hidden to me, at least. My very own Mr Rochester. Except Mrs Logan, as far as I knew, wasn't barking mad, although being wed to Baxter, you could understand if she were hopping mad.

Debra Logan. Baxter had not only betrayed her and me but himself and what he claimed to represent.

I'd stumbled upon his secret when he'd left mine one morning without his Nokia, the piece of technology that ranked a close second to his work Blackberry. I wasn't aware of his phone until it blared with a text message. I was in bed, still dozing. In my sleep-addled state, I understood Baxter had left his phone behind and the message was to inform me of that. Don't ask why but that made sense at the time. So I'd lazily picked up the phone and checked the screen. The message was from Debra.

Debra, the ex-wife who'd returned to Scotland; the woman he didn't like to talk about much. Odd for her to be texting so early in the day. He'd told me they had little to do with each other now, just occasional practicalities.

I opened the text, too perplexed to consider the rightness of doing so. The message said, *'The boiler is broken and u r never here.'*

Was she visiting? He'd never said. Maybe she was in town for a few days, seeing friends and staying at her old home. He hadn't mentioned it because her visit wasn't significant. She was sleeping in the spare room. Or, no, she was in Scotland and she meant her life was domestically difficult now they'd separated. She didn't expect him to be there; it was just a strangely phrased wish he were around to help.

No, she'd intended to text her new partner and had got

the numbers muddled up. No, no, no! Don't be silly, Nats. The text was meant for the unpunctual plumber whose number was next to Baxter's on her phone and she'd been heavy-thumbed when selecting the recipient.

Sheets of blackness rose and fell in my mind. I felt nauseous. My skin was white and sticky like pastry dough. I could feel the whiteness of my flesh, so cold and heavy. The bed I lay on receded while the room around me blurred and pulsed. Was I on the slab in a morgue, a tag around my toe?

I had never felt so alone. Never so lost. In that instant, the world changed for the worse. I trusted nothing I knew. Was the colour blue actually blue? Was I human? Alive? Dreaming?

I stared at the text. *The boiler is broken and u r never here.*

No, Debra, he's never there because he's always here. We've both been betrayed.

I deleted the text, my response instinctive. The words were too much. Get rid. A few hours later, I wondered if I'd imagined them. But when Baxter popped by to pick up his phone, I said, 'Debra called.'

He knew that I knew. I watched his face die.

As far as I was concerned, we were finished. It was all over, bar the shouting.

Talking across the table on Sonny's chilly rooftop, I remembered how I used to think Baxter wasn't the marrying kind. In part, that's how he'd got away with the lie for so long. He had a defiant loner quality to him which, combined with his restlessness, made him seem more suited to the single life and a string of unwise relationships. I used to wonder if I would end up belonging to the latter.

So he told me, after we'd dusted ourselves down from our frenzied, table-top kissing on the roof, he and Debra had split and he was living in a wee flat a couple of miles outside Saltbourne. His quick, lilting accent bubbled like a river as he went over old ground. He claimed they'd been considering splitting when he and I were together but making the final leap had evaded them. Emotionally, he'd checked out of the marriage a long time ago and so had she. But they'd drifted along, thinking it might get better. And it never did because it never fucking does. Their relationship had been in tatters, he said. In fucking shreds. How else could he have spent so much time with me? He figured Debra knew the truth but she'd stopped caring and who could blame her?

To be fair, he'd told me some of this when we'd split but back then, the magnitude or otherwise of his lie wasn't my concern. It was the fact he'd lied. I didn't care if he'd lied because he thought it was for the best or because he'd feared he might lose me. I didn't care if he'd wanted to tell me but thought he was too far down the line to be forgiven. I didn't care if he had a plan to maintain the act until eventually they'd separate and I'd be none the wiser. I didn't care about his excuses. His words were hollow because ultimately, whatever he said, he would go back to her and their shared suburban house with its broken boiler and cold, empty mornings. He had lied and I never wanted to see him again. He was not the man I'd thought he was.

I stuck to that because I'm stubborn, or in Baxter's words, 'a thrawn auld bugger'.

But now I did care. I wanted to know why he'd lied and what I'd meant to him. I also wanted to know why he'd got in touch again.

'I've been getting my act together,' he said. 'Been on my tod near eighteen month. Been drinking less too. Even been to the gym a couple of times.'

I laughed at the unlikelihood of Baxter on a treadmill.

'I could have got in touch with you ages ago,' he went on. 'But I wanted to be in a better place, wanted to feel like myself again. Didn't want to have a hint of rebound. You know, to be sniffing around you for comfort or be blocking out the hurt.' He began speaking in a hurry. 'Not that I'm expecting anything to happen. No, no. I just wanted to see you, catch up, you know? I guess you've got your own life now, eh?' He tried to sound jovial, as if his were making a conversational enquiry, but his eyes betrayed him.

'I've always had my own life, Bax.'

As if to taunt me, my phone beeped with a text message. My thoughts jumped to Den. He seemed irrelevant and exasperating. Baxter was sitting opposite me, hefty, beautiful, fucked up and hopeful. While he'd lied to me with devastating repercussions, his open-hearted passion was a far cry from Den's inconsistent behaviour and over-constructed performances.

I put him from my thoughts as Baxter and I talked but when Bax went inside to get more drinks, I was quick to check my phone.

The message was from Liam. Did I fancy a pint? He was in The Regency with Marsha, Phil and Glen.

But I'd already told him I was on a date.

Confused, I replied. '*Am with Baxter at Sonny's*'

Liam took a while to reply. Then: '*Baxter?! The ex?*'

I thumbed back: '*Don't ask. Did you send photo to me from another phone?*'

Liam: '*No photo, sorry. Have fun! Take care. X*'

Huh? I didn't understand. Someone who had my number also had one of Liam's photographs. They knew I was the model for his bridle even though my features had been blurred out. Was I recognisable? Had Liam messed up and sent the pictures to his customer, forgetting to disguise my face in one of the shots? And the customer knew me? Or had Liam sent a pic to someone else, showing off his work? But either way, to whom? Someone I worked with? A mutual friend?

A phrase from long ago swam into my mind: Closer than you know.

I replied: '*Who did you send photo to of me in bridle?*'

Liam: '*I didn't send you a photo*'

Me: '*Before. The photos you took of me. Who has them?*'

Liam: '*Just customer*'

Me: '*Who is customer?*'

Liam: '*Den something. Bit smug. Why?*'

I felt the colour drain from my face. My ability to process information grew faint. Goosebumps lifted on my skin, and my heart rate soared. I clutched at fragments. Den was Liam's customer. He knew I was the model. Oh Hell. Somehow, he knew Liam was my friend, knew about his business at Community Crafts. Had he known all along or a lucky coincidence? What madness was he planning now?

Baxter returned with a pint and a glass of red. 'You all right, hen?' he asked, setting down the drinks. 'You're suddenly looking a bit peely wally.'

Eighteen

Baxter, Liam, Den.

A year ago, I couldn't get a man for love nor money and now, potentially, I had three in my life. If I'd had anyone to confide in, I might have made a quip about them being like buses: you wait for ages and so on. But I'd told no one about Den. To my shame, I hadn't even mentioned to Liam I was seeing someone else. Although 'seeing' was probably too strong a word to describe the chaotic trajectory of my relationship with Den.

Had I been at a bar with someone other than Baxter, I might have left or gone mute on my companion to try and unravel the mystifying texts. But this was Baxter, springing up out of the blue. I couldn't tear myself away. I kept getting flashbacks to how it had been, to Baxter clutching my hair and feeding me his cock; Baxter tying me up or hitting me; Baxter muttering obscenities in my ear as he pounded with his fingers; Baxter fixing my legs apart, lapping at my cunt but not letting me come until he was good and ready; Baxter fucking me as if the world were about to end and we were all going to die.

I wanted to reach out to him, to stop all the talk, and say, 'Do you remember that too, Bax?'

Hard to believe the skin inside my clothes and the skin inside his had touched countless times; that we'd made physical impressions on each other, the smeared kisses and soft caresses as much as the bites, scratches and hurts. We still had the same bodies. I wanted to ask him: Does skin have memory, do you think?

I wanted him. Still wanted him to turn me inside out as only he could. The more we talked, warmed by the glow of the patio heater, the more I felt myself on the verge of tumbling into something unwise. He'd screwed up, he was repentant, we could find a way forward and repair the trust, he said. If my groin had been in charge, we'd have sorted everything out by going back to mine and fucking with our usual relish for debasement and excess. No, sex would have been crazier than that, given we hadn't held each other close for over two years. But I knew I needed to keep my legs crossed and think beyond the short-term. Could I trust him again or would I always be wondering if he was playing the field, turning me into the new Debra?

I had too many questions that needed to stay unasked, especially since other questions about Liam and Den demanded my attention. In all the confusion, my single, clearest thought was that I mustn't rush into anything tonight. I had to weigh up the pros and cons of getting back with Baxter. Had he caused too much heartache for us to be happy again? Did he deserve me? Did that even matter?

'I need to go,' I said when Baxter offered to get another round in. 'We do need to talk some more. But not tonight. This is too fast. And I have so much other stuff going on in my life. Everything – everything's in a mess. Everything's nuts. I need to go home. Sorry. My head's spinning with too many thoughts.'

Baxter nodded, respecting my decision although it was plain he wanted me to stay. But he had the advantage of having expected to meet me. I was still shocked to see him, still stunned by his revelations and the changes he'd made in his life.

Plus, I had some phone calls to make.

'You staying?' I asked.

'Aye,' he said, rubbing at his arms. 'I need a wee dram to warm me up.'

We stood, putting on smiles to indicate we were friends although neither of us wanted to smile much. There was still too much sadness. After a pause, Baxter pulled me to him, clasping me in a bear hug that was reassuring rather than sexual. The wall of his strong, solid chest tugged at my craving for comfort in his arms. So I let him hold me, realising that, for the first time in a long time, I wanted to feel safe. And I thought, maybe lately I'd been resisting safe because in the past with Baxter, safe had let me down. Safe had turned out to be emotionally dangerous, painful and false.

Safer, then, to stick with danger.

'Next time we talk,' said Baxter, holding my fingertips, 'will you tell me about the guy you thought you were meeting tonight?'

'If you want.' I shrugged. 'But he's not important. I just fancy him. It's a kinky sex thing, that's all.'

Baxter nodded and swallowed. He clamped his lips together, his eyes growing pink and filmy, then he croakily asked, 'So . . . does he, you know. Does he hurt you?'

I shook my head, hot tears stabbing. My throat tightened.

'Not as much as you do,' I said. Then I hitched my bag onto my shoulder and left.

I walked along the desolate seafront road, hoping the night air would clear my head. The fairy lights, strung between the coastal lampposts and pocked with dead bulbs, seemed tragic now we were out of season.

I had half a dozen texts from Liam: *'Are you OK? I think something's wrong here. What's your middle name? Where are you? Call me.'*

Above the inky water, the sky was sequinned with hard little stars, their light and the moon's throwing silver ripples on low, frothing waves. The soft murmur of the sea beat steadily below the sporadic roar of cars, while the tang of brine mingled with the acrid edge of spent fireworks. My breath misted in cloudlets, my cheeks cold.

In the distance, a screech soared high before a dull boom thudded against the night. A fountain of green and purple poured to earth. Bonfire night was still a day away and letting off fireworks in advance was generally frowned upon. I had a vague recollection late-night fireworks were technically illegal. But Saltbourne thrived on petty lawlessness and cheap kicks.

My phone beeped. Another text from Liam: *'You still in Sonny's?'*

I paused by the wooden kiosk of the swan-pedalo lake, the water flat and black, stars hanging in its depths. The big plastic birds were secured in a huge wire pen, huddled under tarpaulin until spring. I wanted to join them. Forget it all. Emerge when everything's bright and fixed.

I replied: *'Am fine. Not sure what's going on. Middle name India. Embarrassing! Speak soon. X'*

I put my phone away and walked on. Crazy, crazy times. Baxter wanted me back. Den was still trying to fuck with my head. Liam was entangled in something he hadn't asked for. This was all going wrong and it was my fault. I'd played with fire. And now the fire was spreading fast, out of my control.

If I were the only one to get burnt, well, maybe I deserved that. But putting Liam at risk was unforgivable. What to do? If I told Den to leave me alone, would he? Did I want that? Supposing I got back with Baxter and Den tried to ruin things for us? Who was Dr Dennis Jackson? What was his history? What was he capable of? Why did he intrigue me so much?

Come on. Think straight, Nats, think straight. Don't panic. Deep breaths.

My boot heels clicked along the promenade. The space of the seafront created space in my head, allowing recent events to unfold.

OK. Here was the score. Den knew who Liam was. Den had therefore commissioned some leather gear from Liam. Or had the commission come before he'd known my connection to Liam? No, this was deliberate. A couple of months ago he'd broken into my house, so not too much of a stretch to imagine him watching my life more then he'd previously admitted. Conceivable that he'd trailed Liam, too. So the request for photographs from Liam of the work in progress, with me as model, were presumably part of Den's game. Whatever that game was. Had he specified I was the model? No, impossible. He'd taken a chance, guessing Liam would ask me, knowing I'd agree.

But why? And what had happened between Liam and Den? How much did Den know about me? Why couldn't he do ordinary relationships? We'd played kidnap and we'd had a threesome. Fine. Wasn't it time to move on and communicate like adults? I prided myself on being someone who didn't do game playing and yet, somehow, I'd found myself embroiled in this cat and mouse madness. At the conference, Den had said he'd call. And surprise, surprise, he hadn't until now, although sending me a photo of myself in bondage hardly constituted a phone call. But presumably this meant he was still interested in continuing what we'd started and, typically, he was expressing his desire in a rather sinister, stalkerish manner.

A new thought chilled: Could Den be spying on me now as I walked along the deserted prom?

In that instant, I knew I was in trouble. He'd texted me with the photo. 'Your head looks great in a cage.' A new number. I'd thought it was Liam. He was always losing phones. I'd told him I was in Sonny's Bar. 'Slut,' he'd replied. On reflection, that didn't sound like Liam.

I'd told Den where I was.

I quickened my pace, my breath pumping hard. I should be at home, doors and windows locked. I should have Baxter with me. I should get a taxi. I should start running. Fuck, I should really start running.

My phone beeped. I fished around in my bag, moving at a trot as I passed the crazy golf course. I retrieved the phone.

Fast, soft-soled footsteps approached from my left. I spun around, phone in hand. A figure ran at me, leaping over a tiny picket fence, face taut with anxiety, light glinting on the shaved dome of his head. His body slammed into mine, knocking the breath from me. He clamped a hand to my mouth, stifling my scream, and hooked an arm around my waist. My phone clattered to the ground, rasping along the tarmac.

By my ear, his voice said, 'Good to see you, Natalie. Didn't I promise I'd call?'

Frantically, I scanned left and right, my heart banging against my ribcage. The promenade and the black, endless sea spread above the blur of Den's hand. I wriggled in his grip. Cars passed, headlights zipping through the dark. To the drivers, we'd be nothing but shadowy movement beyond the dinky windmill and plastic castle of the golf course.

'Keep calm,' said Den, 'I'm not going to hurt you. I just want us to talk and have a little fun together. OK?'

I nodded, my breath hot and humid in his cupped hand. We stood as still as statues, getting accustomed to each other in this ludicrous situation. My idiotic weakness for him pulled inside me, a physical sensation as if I were melting into long, indolent throbs.

Den removed his hand and I gulped crisp air, tasting gunpowder and salt. For a tentative moment he was motionless, as if wondering whether I'd scream or skedaddle. But I had no urge to do either. I was startled and angry but now he was beside me, my fear was abating. I turned to him. Streetlight cast an amber tint on the oblique slopes of his scar-stippled face. I'd seen that face on stage as he'd delivered a dry, academic paper. He wasn't dangerous. Silly even to think that. Besides, he knew I liked to flirt with scenes of dubious consent. If kidnap-play and fake force hadn't been part of our relationship, I'd have yelled for help, but this wasn't as serious as it might appear to people passing by. Not that anyone *was* passing by.

I nodded, not knowing what I was agreeing to, but wanting to get to the bottom of him and his behaviour.

'OK, this way,' he said, trying to guide me.

'Wait, I dropped my phone,' I said.

'Grab it.'

The back had come off and the battery had fallen out, something that never happens when I actually want it to. My hands were shaking as I bent to retrieve the phone's three parts, fumbling to slot them back together.

'Here, do that later. Come on, let's get warm.' Den took the broken phone from me and popped the pieces in my bag. He wrapped his arm around my waist as if we were lovers out for a stroll, except his hold on me was possessive, an attempt to propel me in his direction.

I shouldered him away. 'I'll walk beside you, it's fine,' I said. 'Where are we going?' I wanted to bombard him with questions but I knew enough about Den to know I wouldn't get straight answers. Pacing myself seemed strategic. Slowly, slowly, catchee monkey.

'Back to the theatre,' he said, setting off again.

'Doesn't sound too warm to me,' I scoffed. 'A derelict building in November?'

'Trust me,' he said. 'I've got something up my sleeve.'

'I'd class those two statements as contradictory.'

'Hey, don't worry,' he said. 'Just come with me. We have unfinished business, don't you think? The last couple of times were great but we haven't really got to know each other yet. Not properly.'

We reached the pedestrian crossing and I jabbed the button even though the road was quiet.

'I'm no longer sure I want to know you properly,' I said as we crossed. 'Your behaviour's been pretty shitty lately. It's one thing to try and play mind games with me but when you involve other people, that's bang out of order. Liam hasn't consented to any of this. I have.' My breath streamed in fast, silvery mists. 'And another thing, you're making massive assumptions about me and what I'm prepared to go along with. When I got involved with you, that didn't give you the right to decide how and when we play together. By agreeing to one thing, it doesn't mean I'm agreeing to everything. Do you understand that?'

Behind us, the green man beeped in the silence. So much for me pacing myself.

'Well, just say if you want out,' Den said calmly.

I didn't reply save for an exasperated huff. Damn, he was infuriating. I wished I could make a snap decision and have done with it. I did and I didn't want out, but too many strands of my choice were contingent on what might happen with Baxter. Without Baxter, Den might still be worth another chance. I'd be prepared to put the effort in to see if we could make this work. With Baxter, I had no need of him; had no need to risk getting genuinely hurt or humiliated.

We walked past a boarded-up amusement arcade and a lairy pub where music thumped. In a narrow side street was a parked police car with only one headlight working. Jeez, what kind of night was this?

'I just want us to have a straightforward conversation about what we're doing,' I said. 'We talked a lot in the beginning. Well, we emailed. But it's different now. I think we're due a reassessment. We need a clearer idea of limits. We should negotiate and agree on how we play. And you need to stay away from my friends and butt out of my life. It was kinda flattering to start with but now – '

Den cut me off, jostling me into the dark, scruffy doorway of a sweet shop. I squealed as he pushed me against the wall, leaning into me with his weight.

'But you don't like having a clear idea, do you?' His voice was amused and confident. 'That's the buzz for you.' He ground his crotch against my hip, his thigh lodged between my legs. 'That's how you get off.' He tried to kiss me. I turned aside, staring at peeling paint on the shop's pink door. I didn't protest when he stuck his hand between my thighs and groped me through my jeans, his fingers hard and punishing.

'The novelty's wearing thin,' I said but even as I spoke I was aware of my blood rushing faster, of tiny beats of need flickering in my groin.

'Yeah?' he said. 'How thin?' He reached under the hem of my fur jacket, his hand latching on to one breast. As if testing me, he fondled with a strong, measured touch. A small groan of desire left my lips. I cursed to myself, wishing I could retract the sound. I looked past Den, my gaze fixed on the side of the shop window with its protective grille and garish display of confectionary. I wanted to feel nothing, but all the while I let him touch me I was liking it.

Den withdrew, giving me a cocky grin. 'Come on,' he said. 'Let's get comfy and sort you out.'

I didn't move. Den stood, smirking. 'Oh, give it a rest, Natalie. It's me! You don't need to act reluctant and respectable. I know you want it so quit with the act. I'm not going to judge you for wanting to get fucked like a whore. We're in this together. We're the same, you and I. We understand each other. We understand the pull. You have to cherish connections like this. They don't come along too often in life.'

He held out his hand, a gallant gesture as if I were about to step off a boat.

'I have one condition,' I said.

Den raised his brows in exaggerated curiosity. 'Do tell.'

'You promise to stay away from other people in my life. From Liam and anyone else. If I want to take another chance on you, that's my choice. I'll handle the fallout. But stay clear of my friends or we're through.'

'OK, deal,' he said lightly. 'I've finished with Lee anyway.'

'Liam.'

'And he got a few hundred quid from me so I doubt he'll complain. Great harness he made. I had him initial it. N.I.L. Natalie India Lovell.'

'How do you know my middle name?'

Den grinned. 'I'm an academic. Good at research. Do you like it? N.I.L. Nil, zero, nothing. And nil by mouth when you're all trussed up in the bridle, your lips stretched wide, that cruel gag hooked inside your cheeks.' He pressed my shoulders to the wall, catching lengths of hair in his fists so my scalp pinched when I moved my head. He continued to speak, punctuating his words with small, teasing kisses.

'Nothing but cock and come. That's your food. Ah, God, I'm getting hard just thinking about it. Your head criss-crossed in leather, you on your knees, gazing up at me, ready to serve.'

He released my shoulders and forced his fingers into my mouth, two at either side. He stretched my lips wide, his fingers rough and dry. I pressed back against the wall, rocking my head to escape him and making awkward noises of complaint.

He laughed and removed his fingers.

I coughed and wiped my hand across my mouth. 'What are you all about?' I said. 'Why do you have to make such a song and dance about everything?'

He looked down at me, shadows falling across his slanting face. His eyelashes were so short. I'd never noticed that before. 'Don't you like song and dance?' he said, chirpily sarcastic. 'The theatrics of fucking?'

Noises approached and I tensed. Three skimpily dressed young women tottered by, arms linked, laughing and yelling conversation at each other. They didn't notice us. Right then, I hated Den, hated his gloating, arrogant coolness and inability to engage. '"One chance, one meeting,"' I said. 'What was that all about? What's the grand plan?'

His confidence slipped from his face, his smile emptying. 'My paper?' he said. 'Are you seriously asking me about my research?'

'The thing you said to me when . . . at The Hippodrome. At the end. You said, "One chance, one meeting." What did you mean?'

He shook his head, genuinely baffled. 'I said that to you?'

'Yes. And then you fucked off.'

'I don't remember. Does it bother you? I was probably working on my paper and the phrase was on my mind. Don't read anything into it. Come on.'

'That's it?'

He shrugged. 'What were you expecting?'

I shook my head, wishing it would clear. Even though I was learning more about him, he still made no sense.

'Any more questions?' he asked airily.

I sighed, frustrated by his evasiveness.

'Come on, let's give the bridle a whirl.' He held out a chivalrous hand again. 'I've been itching to see how it looks on you. And now I'm gagging – ha, forgive the pun – I'm gagging to clasp your head and ram my cock into your throat. I want to see the tears pouring down your face. Want to see how much you're prepared to suffer in order to satisfy me.'

I was silent for a short moment. At my core, I was wet, red and pliant. I felt such shame for still wanting him, for allowing lust to make an idiot of me. My cunt drummed with need but my motivation surpassed mere arousal. Drawing me to him was the longing to submit and surrender, to abase myself before his cruel, mean dominance.

So with mock-ladylike delicacy, I placed my fingertips in his outstretched hand. 'You know how to twist a girl's arm,' I said.

Nineteen

I'd vowed never to go near The Hippodrome again after my encounter with the security guard. But when I'd made that decision, I hadn't anticipated being invited back by Den and entering the building via legitimate, albeit slightly dodgy, means.

I enjoyed picking my way along dilapidated, torch-lit corridors, believing this time that Den and I were on a more equal footing. I had a sense of what lay ahead: some kinky sex involving a gorgeous piece of bondage gear made according to Den's specifications. I'd take that for now. Maybe afterwards we could talk, if the mood was right. Perhaps I could start by mentioning my need for him to offer aftercare as he had done the time I'd unmasked him.

I told myself Liam wouldn't mind us using the harness if I didn't. Yes, Den had conned him into making the object to fit me but now the piece existed, a waste to reject it simply because the process of creation had been comprised by deception. Desire drove me as did a longing to fly away from the drama of Baxter's reappearance. Too many thoughts clogged my mind, too many emotions swelled my heart. I craved escape.

The prospect of dark, dangerous sex with Den had the irresistible lure of drugs and alcohol. For a couple of hours, I could forget everything. I could put on hold all the problems that needed fixing. I would be like those swan pedalos under their tarpaulin, taking some time out. I'd put aside questions and fears, indulging instead in sensations of the flesh and temporary obliteration as Den ran the show, making me do things I longed to do. Tomorrow I would think.

Besides, tomorrow would be better. Whatever happened with Den tonight would help clarify my feelings for him.

When we re-entered The Hippodrome's auditorium, I caught my breath – the crepuscular ruins igniting vivid memories of the strange, sexy time we'd shared. The mere sight of the theatre was enough to send a send a slow, swollen pulse to my groin. As we walked forward, a small feather fluttered down from the glass chandelier. The concrete floor was bigger than I recalled, a brutal contrast to the chipped gilt curlicues, fallen velvet and sweep of balconies in crimson, gold and green.

But the details were peripheral, my attention grabbed by the sight of a fire burning merrily within a ragged ring of red brick and masonry chunks. Its existence was so preposterous I laughed. Yellow-amber flames leaped and spat, shadows trembling on surrounding surfaces. Was that sensible? Then again, health and safety regs wouldn't count for much here. The long-forgotten theatre was virtually outdoors, birds, buddleia and ivy encroaching on its interior; broken windows and rotten woodwork welcoming in the night's crisp chill. I shivered with excitement, inhaling deeply. The place was so cold you could practically taste the starlight, and I swear, on my tongue the taste was of pewter and diamonds.

'It's beautiful,' I said.

Den led me towards the fire. Heat rose from the flames, warping the air above and making the balcony shimmer like a mirage. Still there from last time, several yards from the fire, stood the cluster of furniture representing a surreal, kinky half-home. The pine dining table was pushed aside and the birthing stool gleamed darkly, its polished oak seat cupping the fire's glow, the rings for hands and head shining like heavy halos. The mattress, now stripped of bed linen, looked thin and dank on its platform of pallets. I could hardly believe I'd once contemplated spending the night on that thing.

'Told you we'd be warm,' said Den. 'A cosy night in together. What do you reckon?'

The flames' heat intensified as we neared, wood crackling in the fire's belly, smoke pluming towards the cavernous domed ceiling. Once again, Den was ahead of me, his out-landish scenario surpassing all my expectations. But something wasn't right. Stupid to leave a fire unattended. If Den were part of a community venture to restore the old building, he wouldn't risk the theatre going up in flames while he lurked outdoors, tracking me, would he?

'Are we alone?' I asked.

'Yes,' he replied.

'Properly alone? We're not being watched or anything?'

'No,' he said 'Just me and you.'

I struggled to believe him, perhaps because those rows of empty velvet seats forever suggested an audience.

'Are you going to tell me what to expect?' I asked.

'Where's the fun in that?' he said. 'Just trust me. Here, let me take your coat. Will you be warm enough?'

I handed him my jacket and bag, knowing I ought to take this opportunity to insist we discuss scenes beforehand. But I didn't tackle the issue, reluctant to spoil the mood, and I thought instead I'd take one last chance on trusting him.

Carefully, he laid my belongings on the pine table. The opportunity to try and wheedle more out of him while he was in this unusually solicitous mood was too good to pass by.

'I liked Ty,' I ventured. 'Your academic colleague.'

'Yeah, we're a good team, me and Ty. Go back many years. He's one of the few people in my professional life I'm out to.'

I recalled the two men high-fiving each other above my body when I'd climaxed. 'So do you do that kind of thing a lot?' I asked. 'The two of you and other women?'

Den rested his buttocks on the table's edge, head tipped towards one shoulder. He seemed momentarily absorbed in assessing me, his smile small and calculating. At my side, the fire was a bank of heat. I turned, toasting my hands in front of the flames. Far away stood the decaying stage framed by cracked, big-bottomed cherubs, its collapsed canopy at an angle, the fallen green curtains spreading across the boards like pond moss.

'We've had our share, yes,' said Den. 'Ty's my partner in crime at sex parties.'

I rubbed my hands together, arms still outstretched. I was so innocent and square. 'You go to sex parties?'

Den smiled, crossing to me. Gently, he drew my body to his, clutching my buttocks as he ground his hips, his groin rocking against mine. 'Sometimes, yes. You want to come to the next one?'

Oh, he was inviting me to a sex party, as if we might have a future beyond tonight. I smiled up at him, uncertain. Firelight flickered across his face, throwing gold on the broad sweep of his pitted cheekbones and the temples of his stubble-dark head. His narrow eyes were shadowed, chips of blue winking from the depths like forbidden treasure.

He had the keys to a world I knew nothing about. How might that fit with me and Baxter starting over? Could Baxter come along too? No, of course not. Did I even want to get back with Baxter. Stop it, Nats. Think about the tricky stuff tomorrow. Savour the moment for what it is.

I cupped Den's buttocks, mirroring his stance, the two of us swaying in a crotch-centric smooch. 'What, like an orgy?' I said. 'Maybe. Although I'm not sure. I like the fantasy. In reality, I dunno. I think two men at once might be my limit.'

Den chuckled. 'But you liked two men?'

'Yes,' I said, smiling, remembering. 'Loved it. It was amazing. I loved it when Ty was fucking my mouth and you made me come.'

Den nudged my hair from my neck, pushing the curls over my shoulder. 'So you liked being forced to take a big, black cock in your mouth.'

I frowned, thinking it was a peculiar thing to say. 'I just liked the cock,' I said. 'Colour wasn't relevant. But yeah, I'd be happy to have two men again. More than happy.'

His erection pressed against me through the bulge of his fly. 'That's good to know. Very good.'

I wondered if he were being kind to me to make amends for having behaved badly. Or did he think, after I'd expressed reservations, I needed to be won over with a conventional seduction? Well, not that conventional, admittedly.

'I'm not ashamed of anything we've done,' I said.

'No?' He feigned surprise. 'Then I'll have to try harder.'

I grinned.

'So.' He slid his hands higher, caressing my back through my layers of clothes. 'How might I do that? How might I shame you?' One hand stole higher and he wound a fist in my hair. Slowly, he forced back my head, exposing my neck and making my spine arch. My pulse thumped and I clung to him, gazing up at the vast chandelier.

'By stripping you naked and making you beg for my cock?' he said. 'By spreading you over that table and fucking your arse? Or would you like that too much? Maybe I need to whip and spank you till you're red raw and screaming. An incoherent wreck who's too broken to beg for mercy.' He gave a little tug of my hair. I was motionless, suspended in his embrace, balanced on his forearm. 'Would that shame you?' he asked. 'Or do I need to take you to a place you profess to dislike? Say, to a sex party or a gangbang?'

I whimpered, my desire surging and shrinking at the prospect of being forced to do something I might hate and regret.

Den laughed. 'See? I reckon you'd enjoy it. Imagine the scenario. I take you to a party and invite all my friends to fuck you.' He released my hair. With steady, unrushed fingers, he unfastened the top button of my jeans. He eased down the zip. In the silence, the fire crackled and popped. Slowly, he raised my top and ran his hand over my bared belly, edging higher to fondle my breasts. I was still bowed backwards in his arm, holding on to his neck, dissolving, my bones turning to nothing, my cunt expanding to hot, tender thickness.

I wished I could resist him. He nudged my bra up, underwire and lace frothing above the swell of my naked, pink-tipped flesh. His cool, controlled hands cupped and massaged. My breasts were all sinew and sensation, shifting and rippling in response to his knowing fingers. Again and again, I moaned. My sounds seemed far off, as if they weren't made by me at all.

'Yeah, I think you'd like having a dozen or so men queuing up to fuck you.' His voice was low and intimate, rough like gravel and old records. 'And I'd stand guard, watching, making sure you treated them well and didn't complain. Would that make you ashamed, Natalie?' He thumbed circles around one nipple then squeezed its crinkled point, eyes fixed on my face. My throat made another noise that didn't belong to me. I couldn't look at him. I was bombed out on pleasure, drifting away with his words. 'Would it, Natalie? All those strangers using you like a whore? Let's see, shall we?'

Whore. He pronounced the word so elegantly. With excruciating slowness, his fingers slid past my open jeans and into my knickers, down past my pubes. He found my wetness and I groaned heavily, unable to stop the sound. He glided through my folds and I was as wet as a hundred rivers. I closed my eyes. I was fleshless, juices pouring over him. I cried out again as his fingers slipped effortlessly inside me, plugging the damn.

'I think that's my answer,' whispered Den. 'You're sodden.' He stirred his fingers. My fluids clicked, a small, sloppy sound like a faint echo of the spitting fire. His thumb brushed my clit and moved across the bud, ticking left, right, left like a metronome. 'All those men,' he murmured, and though my eyes were closed and I was floating away, I knew he was scrutinising every flicker on my face.

'Now stand up properly.' Briskly, he withdrew his hand and nudged me upright. Someone had filleted me. My bones were gone. I could barely stand. With a couple of hard tugs, Den shoved my jeans and underwear down to my ankles where they rucked inelegantly around my boots. I swayed, dizzy, shackled by denim, my smeared arousal cooling on my inner thighs.

'Get undressed,' said Den, his tone now brusque and stern.

The instruction seemed too complicated, its execution requiring a stamina I feared I lacked. Undress? Where to begin? I wobbled on one leg then the other as I removed my boots. Slowly, I stripped. With a feeble throw, I aimed my clothes at the skanky mattress, removing everything except my socks, sporty-looking grey and blue knee-highs, because the floor was rough and cold. As I undressed, Den rummaged in the holdall I recognised from last time. Equipment clinked inside the bag. All those exciting possessions reminded me of his experience. He selected a bunch of black leather cuffs, again familiar to me, and heaped them on the pine table.

I edged closer to the fire, trembling and rubbing at my bare arms.

'Cute socks.' Den rested his butt on the table's edge, folding his arms. 'Now I want you in the stool, legs spread. Move it nearer the fire if you're cold.'

I was cold, yes. It was November and I was naked in a derelict building. But the prospect of sitting in the birthing stool, presumably cuffed and powerless, sent a charge of heat through my limbs. With wry aloofness, Den observed as I repositioned the stool. My body was useless for anything except sex, making the stool heavy and unwieldy. A remnant of practical thinking told me the fire's heat needed to catch me at the front rather than down one side. Flames shimmered in the antique's varnished depths as I dragged the object into place. Obeying instructions, I perched on the narrow seat, glad to take the weight off my wobbly legs. The wood's cracks and crevices imprinted hard ripples on my flesh while the slender strip of the back-rest pressed against my spine.

'Good girl,' said Den, his tender approval getting me right in the groin. 'Now then, you can see how this functions.' He took the bundle of black cuffs and strode towards me. 'I fasten your ankles to the chair legs, your wrists to the hand-holds and I collar your neck to the head-rest. OK?'

I nodded, my arousal swelling as he began cuffing me with brisk efficiency, using chains and clips to link the leather manacles to the stool's legs and hoops. The ornate balcony curving around the arena gleamed to my right, patches of orange firelight shimmering on the supporting columns. Dark shadows hid in distant corners, light sources I couldn't identify glowing softly here and there. I felt submerged but the waters around me were rose, amber and gold.

'You OK?' asked Den. 'Warm enough?'

'I'm good, yes.' My tongue was thick, my throat dry.

He walked away, out of sight, then returned, Liam's bridle hanging from his fingers, a brown leather net tangled with brass. The pulse between my thighs beat harder. 'Did you enjoy being the model for this?'

'Yes.' My voice was husky. 'Till I found out I was doing it for you.'

He smiled. 'But wearing it turned you on?'

'Yes.'

'I like that,' he said. 'Devising ways to turn you on, even when I'm not there.'

I said nothing. This was neither the time nor the place to discuss the past. Besides, I wasn't sure I had the mental capacity to conduct a conversation.

'Now, let's check this out.' Den lowered the strappy cage over my face, the dark, earthy scent of leather filling my nostrils. 'The advantage is, we know it's a perfect fit.'

I couldn't argue with that. I stayed silent as Den fiddled

with straps and buckles, adjusting the webbed half-hood. When he was done, leather bands lay against my forehead and framed my eyes, trammels running either side of my nose when I glanced down. The two straps of the claw gag dangled from the bridle's bit-rings on each cheek. No need to alter their length.

Den stretched my mouth, deftly popping one brass claw around the corner of my lips. He did the same on the other side. My mouth was fixed wide, the metal hooks cold on my inner cheeks and my face, the gag's rounded tips knocking against my teeth with every movement. Immediately, the harness felt right on me, all the necessary tensions aligning to encase my head while pulling my lips into an ugly, embarrassing rictus. The horribleness of the device made my blood rush and my senses swim. It was such a cunning, contradictory piece of kit, gagging me by forcing my mouth open – more of a non-gag than a gag.

Den stepped back to admire his design. 'Delightful. Absolutely exquisite.' His eyes ran up and down my body, taking in my leather-cocooned face, my bound limbs, spread thighs and faux hockey socks.

'Look at her,' he said as if to himself. 'A sweet submissive and she's all mine.' He ran a hand down my neck, over the bump of the leather collar, then down between the valley of my breasts. He tapped the underswell of one breast then, with a sharp, sideways cuff, swiped my flesh. I groaned, pressing my head back against the ringed head-rest of the stool.

'You can't help loving it, can you?' he murmured. His hand trailed further down my body and his fingers toyed with my pubes. I was so wet I was leaking onto the concrete floor. Den crouched in the vee of my thighs and peeled my puffy lips apart. He reached forward and lapped at my slit.

Just that single stroke of his tongue had me moaning deeply, the sound rushing from my pinned-open mouth.

He looked up at me, grinning. My need was torture. I stared back, trying to beg for more with my eyes. He kept on smiling until, after an apparent eternity, he slid a couple of fingers inside me. I groaned, arousal sinking to my groin. Den's eyes never left my face. 'What I really want,' he said, his elbow driving slowly back and forth, 'is some help here. You have a lot of appetite, Ms Lovell. I'm not sure one man is enough to satisfy you.'

My heart raced, his words spiking the fog of my lust with alarm. Did he have someone in mind? Was Ty around? I wished now we'd had that conversation about the need for him to stop springing surprises on me. This was absolutely the last time I'd invest so much trust in him. His actions in our last two encounters had been seriously borderline. The abduction, the balcony fucking, the pain. And then summoning Ty without my agreement. But being on those limits thrilled me and he hadn't breached them, not quite. He seemed to know how far he could push me. But nudging was a game of chance. Supposing this turned out to be third time unlucky?

Then I reminded myself I could kick or jerk three times if I wanted us to stop. He would respect that. Everything would be fine, no need to panic. Trust him, just surrender to it and trust him.

Den withdrew his fingers and stood. He moved behind my chair. Ahead of me, the fire roared and spat, the theatre beyond the flames hazy with heat. Then the balconies lurched and so did my stomach. Colours streaked past me. I fell back. I was half upside down. I gasped for breath, trying to work out what had happened. I glanced around, dizzied.

Den had the circular head-rest in his hands, the stool angled back on its hind legs like some freaky wheelbarrow. I was left with my socks in the air, gazing up at the red and gold ceiling and at dulled pendants dripping from the tiers of the glass chandelier.

Den peered spookily over my face, shadows leaping across his low features. 'What I need,' he said, 'is for someone to hold you like this, see? Then I can stand astride your shoulders and fuck that wide-open hole of a mouth. How'd you like that?'

He righted the chair and moved a couple of feet away. My heart pounded. What the Hell was he planning?

'So you liked it with Ty?' he asked.

I stared at him and a trickle of saliva spilled from my lips. I longed to wipe it away. Though I knew it was pointless, I jerked my hands against the cuffs. The reminder of the restriction troubled and aroused me. I turned my head aside, the leather collar gliding loosely against my neck.

Den knelt in front of me. 'Don't be shy.' He turned me back to face him, his finger gentle on my cheek. 'Did you?'

I nodded. Ty was here, I felt sure of it.

'Meaning you're not, in theory, averse to a third party?' asked Den.

I was motionless, eyes fixed ahead. How many chances would I give him? Was this really the last?

'I have a proposition,' he continued. 'I have someone I could call on who'd be here within minutes.' My heart boomed and a rush of sweat rolled across my skin. I was right. Ty was here. Den paused, allowing me to digest his words. 'It's not someone you've met before. He would – '

I thrashed in the chair, fighting against the cuffs, shaking my head in refusal.

'Hush, hush,' said Den. 'Listen, let me explain.' He waited until I'd calmed and I glared at him as he continued. 'He would walk in here, the three of us would have some fun, then he'd walk right out. A complete stranger. You've never seen him before and you'll never see him again. How does that sound?'

Again, I shook my head.

He smiled, waiting a while before he spoke. 'Come on, Natalie. You know you'll love it. Two horny men, and they're all for you. We're going to work in tandem to give you all the pleasure you can take.' He lay a hand on each of my thighs, his thumbs massaging close to my wetness, driving me half-mad. He tipped forward to softly suck on one nipple, his tongue swirling. My thoughts grew woolly as my arousal brimmed. 'Come on,' he said. 'Surrender to what you want. Trust me to choose a man whose style you'll like. Someone who'll team with me to dominate you in the ways you crave.'

He traced a finger over the lips of my swollen split, his touch light as a feather, his eyes locked on mine. I groaned heavily.

'Well?' he asked tenderly. 'What do you think? Tempted?'

I stayed silent, my reply too complicated to be articulated through a claw gag. Internally, I was anything but silent. Den's proposal sounded so hot and easy. Me, Den, and presumably some sex-party friend of his who did this all the time. A man whose style I'd like. Double domination. Oh God, how could I resist? Such a rare opportunity. And I'd loved our session with Ty. From my point of view, the main drawback to our threesome was that it had been too short – a snatched, spontaneous moment in a classroom during lunch break. Tonight, in the lost opulence of this lonely theatre, we would have much more time to indulge, not to mention lots of kit to play with. What had Den said earlier? You have to cherish a connection like ours. He was right. Grab it while you can, Nats.

Den touched me under the chin. 'See how considerate I'm being,' he murmured. 'I'm not going to spring any more surprises on you. Small surprises, maybe. Nothing drastic. I think we've had enough of that, don't you?' He let a single finger roam over my body, swirling patterns over my tits and my belly. 'What do you say? Do you want to meet my friend?'

I was stuck for a reply. The fire spluttered as my silence lengthened.

'OK, let me rephrase that,' said Den. 'Do you most definitely *not* want to meet my friend?'

His finger drifted down to the trim thatch of my pubes. Again I made no noise, made no signal with my head. He stirred my body's soft hairs, awaiting my answer. I wanted another man, oh God, did I ever. But I was loath to appear such a pushover.

Den laughed. 'So is that a yes?'

I nodded, desire sliding through my veins like a narcotic. One chance, one meeting. What did I have to lose? And this wasn't about our relationship, it was about sex.

'Excellent.' He stood, took his phone from his pocket, and thumbed in a contact.

'You set?' he said into the phone. 'Cool. Because she's good to go.'

I winced at his words, the lust flooding my body and the anxiety surrounding the choice I'd made at odds with his casual, confident manner. I told myself it didn't matter who this other guy was or what impression he might gain of me. We were just three people playing together for mutual kicks. What I kinked for was as valid as what Den and his friend kinked for. No one was forcing me to do this. If anything, I was the lucky one, getting my needs catered for without having had to put much effort in.

Moments later, as if he'd been waiting in the wings, a figure emerged from the shadows. He strode towards our peculiar cluster of firelit furniture, a small, stocky man in a bulky jacket. He had the regulation shorn head and swagger of an average security guard in an average town. But even before I saw his face, I knew he wasn't average. This was the bruiser who'd caught me sucking Liam's cock in the grounds of the theatre.

I writhed against my bondage, protesting noisily through stretched lips. The straps on my ankles and wrists slammed at my flesh, the collar threatened my breath, the claw gag clattered against my teeth.

'I thought you'd like him,' said Den, grinning.

Blood roared in my ears. I tried to get a grip but couldn't think of anything except the hateful way this man had humiliated me and Liam, making us perform for his warped pleasure. I thought of how I'd whacked him in the nuts with the crowbar, leaving him howling on the ground after Liam had decked him. Oh, holy fuck. He was going to be pleased to see me, wasn't he?

The domed ceiling swooped before my eyes. My centre of gravity got knocked for six, feet in the air again, neck stretching from the weight of my head. Den had the chair tipped back. 'I want you to hold her like this,' he said.

'No worries, boss,' replied the thug.

Den set the chair upright again. I felt sea-sick. I glanced sideways at the thug who looked down at me, ostentatiously flexing his fingers. He hadn't recognised me, oh thank God for that. Perhaps I could get away with this. But did I want to? For one night only? I was delirious with lust, filled with a craving to enter that dark place of self-abandonment. This man was nobody to me, just some grunt I'd never see again. He had a cock, presumably getting hard right now. And I could use him for that, much as he might appear to be using me.

The thug smiled down at me, his gaze dropping in quick assessment of my naked, open body. I squirmed under his inspection, hating and loving it, trying to clear the past from my mind and position him as some randy, anonymous brute.

Then he looked at my encased head for too long. A shadow crossed his face, a frown puckering. Slowly, his smile broadened, his eyes lighting up. He'd recognised me. He'd seen beyond the straps. My fear spiked, blood running cold. The man cast a sly glance towards Den who was kicking off his jeans, tugging his hoodie over his head. Returning his attention to me, the thug leaned in and quietly said, 'Such a pretty cockhole.' He inserted two fingers into my gaping mouth and stroked along my tongue. 'A shame I never got to try it out.'

I squealed, thrashing against my bonds. The man jerked his hand away and clamped his fingers to my shoulder, his grip fierce. He leaned towards my ear again, his voice fast. 'Does Dennis know you were creeping around here the other week?'

I quietened, heaving for breath. That Den might discover the lengths I'd gone to in my pursuit of him appalled and embarrassed me.

'Our little secret, eh?' said the man. Shielding me from Den with his body, he grazed one taut nipple, making it harden further. 'So long as you behave and let me have a ride in your fuckholes, then mum's the word. I'm told I've not to touch you unless you're up for it.' He squeezed my nipple. 'But you'll be up for it. Won't you?'

He stood, stepped behind me and grabbed the chair's head-rest. He tipped me back, dramatically fast. The domed ceiling flashed past, the chandelier a blur. I tried to scream, the fixed grimace of my mouth distorting my noise of terror.

'That's it. Lift her up a bit,' said Den. The chair bobbed higher. I slotted my eyes sideways to see Den striding towards us, naked and erect, firelight dancing over his athletic contours and the black tattoo on his muscular upper arm. Den, yes please. The thug, no thanks. Because ultimately, his attempt at blackmail was weak. How much did it matter if Den knew I'd been stalking him? I'd turned up at his conference so he was aware I hadn't exactly been home alone, pining and wishing he'd call.

I was about to kick the chair leg hard, one, two, three times. Would Den remember that was our signal to stop if I couldn't safeword? He'd specified an agreed gesture the first time we were here. Did it still count?

I didn't have time to find out because my eye caught a movement. High in the distance, rippling above the fire's heat and its pluming blue-gray smoke, the royal box wavered in the air. And in the gaudy box, framed by scallops and swirls, stood Liam, gazing out like an apparition of a slender, copper-haired prince.

I was hallucinating. I had to be. He looked as if he ought to be surrounded by foliage, a unicorn nuzzling up to him. I blinked, and then Baxter was by his shoulder, a quick blur of a burly, dark-haired, furious king. Where was his crown and his ermine cape?

I blinked again and they were gone. The royal box

quivered with ghostly imprints. Did I imagine it? Was I
tripping? How much had I drunk? Two glasses of red, and
not even large ones.

Den stood by my shoulder. I was so shocked my mind
went blank, a total, idiotic blank. When I rolled my eyes
backwards, I could see the thug, his bulky jacket a parody
of body-builder muscle. At my side was Den, cock jutting
up from his clipped black bush, fingers curled around his
shaft, his hand moving with slow threat. I peered forward to
the royal box. Empty. What had I seen? Was my sense that
ghosts watched me manifesting itself as visions of my lovers?
Or were they here as flesh and blood?

No, impossible. Baxter and Liam didn't even know each
other, had never met. And why would they be here? My
thoughts ground to a halt, my ability to act now paralysed.
I had a vague sense I'd been on the brink of safewording
but I no longer knew what I was doing. Trying to enjoy this.
Trying to escape. Trying to make sense of an evening steeped
in impossibility.

Gently, Den touched me between my spread legs.
Safeword. I had to safeword. That was it. Take control. He'd
gone too far although I doubted he knew why. Or was he
aware of what had gone on between me, Liam and the thug?
What the Hell.

I kicked the chair leg three times. Not the wild kicks of
a struggle but three distinct beats. I grunted three times as
back-up. I wanted to be free. Den took no notice. Oh God,
he wasn't paying attention, wasn't expecting me to bail so
shortly after agreeing to this. He slid a finger along my crease
and dipped down into the warm well of my wetness. 'That's
what I like to find.' He curled his fingers forward, pressing
and pumping. 'Enthusiasm.'

The thug gave a grunting half-laugh. 'Me and all. Slut's well up for it, no question.'

I writhed violently, making loud noises of protest. They would think I was roleplaying the shamed victim they were coercing into submission. How could I communicate?

Den strummed my clit with his thumb. 'You see, Natalie, my friend and I – '

He snatched his fingers from me as if burnt.

'What the – '

His body swung away. Somebody roared. I was pitched forward so hard the chair rocked dangerously. My feet hit the ground. Hurtling towards us from the shadows came Baxter, face red with rage, his tie flapping, his suit shifting clumsily. Liam was with him, brandishing his crowbar. Firelight glinted on the hooked, metal rod. Liam, lithe and rangy, rushed at us like a savage bearing a flaming torch.

My eyes skittered in all directions. The fastening on my cuffs clanked against the wooden stool as I jerked and squealed. Den was already on the other side of the table, naked, alert, his fingertips on the surface, opting for defence rather than attack. As the thug hurried to remove his jacket, Liam leaped at him, emitting a terrifyingly wild, guttural cry. The noise chilled to the bone. In one swift movement, Liam drove the thug backwards, crowbar across his thick, dumb neck. He slammed the guy against a supporting column with such violence I feared he might bring the dress circle crashing down.

Then Baxter was by my side on his knees, eyes darting as he fiddled impatiently with my chains, trying to fathom how I was secured. His breath pumped, a sheen of sweat glossing his face. I was beyond relieved and yet at the same time, Baxter's assumption I was a damsel in distress irked me already. Was this jealousy masquerading as a rescue? Was this an attempt to win me back? Had he followed me here? Jeez, I was getting quite the collection of stalkers.

'For fuck's sake, Nats,' said Baxter. 'What are you like?' He kept glancing across to Den, his dark chaotic hair flicking on his forehead, fire reflected in his gleaming sweat.

I grunted, nodding and shaking. Baxter got the message and stood. With big, gentle fingers, he unhooked the claw gag from my cheeks. I slurped back a mouthful of moisture. 'What are you doing here?' I gasped. 'What on earth – ?' I licked along my gums and waggled my aching jaw.

'What's it fucking look like?' he said. 'I'm rescuing this stupid, wee bitch I'm in love with.'

He unbuckled the bridle and slipped it from my head. Den watched from a cautious distance. Liam kept the thug against the column, chin angled high, crowbar across his neck. The thug grunted and huffed, making no attempt to fight back.

'I chose to be here, Bax,' I hissed. 'You of all people should know this might not be what it seems. I like getting tied up. Remember? I might not have needed the Sir Galahad act.'

Baxter unfastened the collar from the chair's hoop and unbuckled it from my neck. 'I saw you safeword,' he snapped, flinging the collar to the ground. 'The signal was fucking obvious. You need rescuing from yourself, that's your trouble.'

'In your dreams,' I scoffed.

Baxter gave an incredulous laugh. 'No! No, not in my fucking dreams.' He freed my hands and I rotated my stiff, creaky shoulders. 'You're dangerous, you know that, hen? A fucking liability. You don't know when to stop. And neither does your chappie over there.'

He shot a scathing glance in Den's direction. From

behind the table, Den watched us warily, fingers steepled on the pine surface. His face was slack with shock, its composure and cleverness gone.

Baxter knelt by my feet, briskly unbuckling my ankle cuffs. 'And for fuck's sake, Nats,' he said, 'why the Hell are you hanging out with that . . .' He glanced at Den, struggling for words. 'That *yoga* teacher?'

Den's eyes shifted from Baxter to Liam and back. I could tell he wasn't thinking about anything except himself and his own welfare. Probably wondering if Baxter was going to lamp him.

Baxter was right. Den didn't know when to stop and it was stupid of me to get involved with someone like him. Not all thrills are worth having. I hardly dared think what might have happened if Baxter and Liam hadn't stepped in. Well, charged in, to be exact.

Baxter tapped my calf. 'Stand up.'

I stood, free of all shackles. Baxter rose with me. Shaking his head, he shucked off his jacket and draped it over my shoulders, urging me to put my arms in properly. He tugged the lapels together as if he were about to send me off to school. I felt doll-sized, my hands lost in the sleeves, the jacket's broad shoulders sloping from mine. The silky lining soothed where it slid against my skin.

I smiled at him, full of gratitude and dazed by his presence. 'I love it when you're all bossy and protective.'

He grinned back. 'Aye,' he said, his tone softer. 'And that's another reason I'm here. Now come on. Say goodbye to your nice, wee chums. I'm taking you home. I think you've had enough excitement for one evening.'

I hugged his jacket around me. 'Bax,' I said. 'I don't think I have. Not quite.'

Twenty

You know what they say: two's company and three will knock your socks off.

Well, maybe they don't but I was saying it to myself later that night, along with the qualifier that it had to be the right three. Foolish of me to have trusted Den to introduce a man he thought I might like. He'd got away with it once when he'd invited Ty to join our games and had almost repeated the success with the security guard as our third player. But when the thug had hinted he might blackmail me into consenting to more than I was comfortable with, the precariousness of my situation became stark. I could see now I'd lost control in a way that was very real. I should have seen the warning signs earlier and not escalated the dangers by taking more and more risks for the sake of my sexual highs.

Lucky I'd had Baxter and Liam looking out for me, ironically because Den had pushed it too far by sending me the photo. His clever games had finally caught up with him and he'd snagged himself in a net of his own making. I couldn't criticise him for the times he'd toyed with the clarity of mutual consent. After all I'd been complicit in that.

I understood now I'd expected too much when I'd taken all those chances on trusting him to not push me too far. He wasn't telepathic. But his attempts to manipulate me with psychological games were out of order. How can you refuse to join in something if you're not aware it's happening? And involving Liam was beyond the pale.

After the drama of my rescue, the three of us wanted to decompress and pick over recent events. Baxter suggested the pub. I suggested bed.

'Done,' said Baxter. 'Let's grab a bottle of whisky en route.'

'Um, hang on. I'm not sure about this,' said Liam.

With a little more discussion, Liam came round to the idea, won over, I think, by Baxter's no-nonsense attitude, filthy tongue and gargantuan sexual appetite. Hard to stay anxious when confronted by such enthusiasm.

Back at mine, Baxter treated my house with his former familiarity, bounding down to the kitchen while Liam and I were still removing our coats. I notched up the central heating and Liam crouched to tickle Rory's small, sooty ears. She was tense; green eyes wide in her white-splashed face. The fireworks would have unsettled her, as would our arrival, in particular, Baxter's. She used to scarper whenever he was around. He was too big, loud and quick. He made her nervous. I sympathised, except I liked the faint threat he presented and had no urge to hide.

Baxter returned, three glass tumblers in his hand. He headed for the next flight of stairs, marching up to the bedroom. Rory slunk off, belly to the ground.

'Come on!' snapped Baxter. 'This dick isnae gonna suck itself.'

We were magical together, lost in creating a world of lust, exploration and pleasure. My bedroom isn't overlooked so I left the curtains open, fireworks cascading down, making the room shiver with bursts of colour. A futon, we discovered, is ideal for a threesome, allowing bodies to move beyond the mattress without disrupting the flow. Baxter played nice, relatively speaking, keeping the full extent of his dominance in check, presumably to accommodate Liam. He didn't want to intimidate or turn off my other lover. Nor did he want to go too far when he and I were still emotionally fragile.

We fucked, sucked, licked, kissed and came, sporadic rainbows falling on our entangled, sweat-shiny limbs. The noises outside worsened, sounds so alarmingly loud they had to come from illegal imports. Explosions rocked the town.

'Strewth, it's like a war zone out there,' said Baxter when we were taking a breather. 'Even more so than usual.'

He sat naked on the futon, a debauched emperor propped against a heap of pillows. His glass of single malt glowed with honeyed light. I couldn't stop looking at him, could barely keep my hands from pawing and petting. Dark hair cloaked his torso, swirling around his dusky, flat nipples and thinning over his padded girth. A broad streak ran from his navel to his bushy pubes and his colossal thighs were densely covered. Oh, those thighs, as powerful as a rugby player's, as thick as tree trunks.

I saw him as if through a lens that had just been brought into focus. I'd forgotten the precise shape of him, the position of stray hairs and moles, the lump of his Adam's apple, the variations across his skin, the network of veins and faint silvery stretch marks in the small of his back. I'd forgotten his beautifully flawed ordinariness. Inevitably, I would lose the tiny details when he left my house but the sight of Baxter, restored to my bed, had a trippy clarity.

I stretched across the futon, setting my tumbler on

the floor. The fairy lights around my mirror cast pools of coloured lights on the polished bare boards. I rested my head on Baxter's thigh, eyeing the pretty curve of his soft, damp cock and the pouch of his balls, fuzzed with wiry hair. Liam was on his back, gazing at the ceiling. He had his knees hooked over mine, the end of a joint pinched between thumb and forefinger.

The racket and flashes of bangers and fireworks took me back to the stormy night when Den had broken in. I recalled his note: CLOSER THAN YOU KNOW.

Well, not any more. I wanted to know how close someone was to me. I didn't want to play bewildering games where I was toyed with for another person's kicks. My taste for submission was here to stay, but I wanted my darkness encircled with honesty and light. I had no desire to see Den again. The shutters had crashed down on my lust and fascination, cutting him off.

With the distance brought about by Baxter and Liam's fury, I realised I'd become so drawn in by Den's cultivated mystique, not to mention his cruel manner and gym-honed physique, I'd lost perspective. I'd taken too many risks, had justified my behaviour with too many excuses. I could find no reason why he'd asked Liam to make the harness and photograph me, except he was intending to prove how much secret control he could exert over my life.

Enough was enough. I wasn't going to contact him, not even to give him a piece of my mind. I didn't imagine either he'd be keen to take on the formidable duo of Baxter and Liam.

Liam rolled over to extinguish the joint. 'Oh man,' he said, laughing. 'That guy's face when we stormed in.'

'Wish I could have seen it from your point of view.'

I giggled from the hash I'd smoked, wishing I could have seen many things from their point of view. I was particularly charmed by the story of Liam, worried, heading over to Sonny's Bar when I'd failed to answer my phone. He'd hoped to find me but, instead, had stumbled upon a hefty, mop-haired guy in a suit, tie undone, nursing a whisky.

'Never met him before in my life,' Liam had recounted. 'But he may as well have been sat under a sign saying "Here be Baxter Logan".'

'And I'm thinking to myself,' Baxter added, 'ach, here we go again. Here's some wee bastard I don't recognise, about to kick off 'cause he blames me for his stint in the nick.'

In a garbled rush, Liam had explained to Baxter who he was and what he knew, expressing his fear I might be in danger. They'd left Sonny's and hung around outside the theatre, thanks to Liam's suspicion the derelict building might be involved. Initially, he hadn't clocked that Den, his client, had been mentioned in the article he'd sent to me about The Hippodrome, but after checking the webpage on his phone, he realised they were one and the same. When I'd texted to tell him my middle name was India, he knew the harness was intended for me.

They'd seen me enter the theatre with Den and then had broken in, aiming only to ensure I was safe and wanted to be there. But Liam's anger had rocketed on recognising the security guard, and his objective had changed. Baxter, irrational, possessive and protective, wanted to thump any-body who encroached on territory he regarded as his. The final straw, he said, was seeing me kick the safesign against the chair leg.

'Although to be fair,' he added, 'if I hadn't seen that, I don't think I could have walked away and left you there.

Wrong of me, I know, I know! Your choice. It's what you're into. But I cannae bear the thought of someone hurting you. Well, not unless it's me.'

He had no qualms about sharing me with Liam. I fancied his broad-minded willingness stemmed from knowing Liam didn't want to top me. He wasn't competition.

Baxter drained his whisky and set his glass on the floor. 'So are you two going to show me this wee squirting trick again?' he asked. 'Because I don't think there's been anywhere near enough obscenity tonight.'

'Speak for yourself,' I replied.

Baxter sprang up from his sprawl, dislodging me from his thigh. He grabbed me under the arms, hitching me up against his torso as he scrambled to his knees. He hooked a playful arm around my neck, bending me backwards so my tits were thrust out. 'You,' he said, amused, 'have got it coming to you, you cheeky wee bitch.'

I laughed as Liam rolled onto his elbow, grinning. Lazily, he reached up to trace a hand over my belly, his touch sliding towards my pubes.

'Show me,' said Baxter. 'Show me how you make her squirt.'

Liam sat up, his glazed eyes sharpening as he focused on my exposed, sloping body. 'You cool with this?' he asked.

Before I could reply, Baxter clamped his hand to my mouth. 'Just fucking do it to her,' he said.

I squealed against Baxter's hand then tugged him away, laughing. Baxter and I knew each other well enough to play rough but it was unfair to expect Liam to join in.

'I'm good, Liam,' I reassured. 'Go for it.'

So he did, giving Baxter a broken commentary as he demonstrated his technique. 'I like to start off slow, make sure she's turned on.' His hand roved over my flesh and he bent to print kisses on my body.

'Aye, well, I think I can help you out there,' said Baxter. He fondled one breast, his big hand encompassing me, massaging heavily so I grew slack and lustful. As Liam kissed along my inner thighs, Baxter muttered filth into my ear. His low words drifted into my desire-addled consciousness. 'You're all mine, you know that? You're a slutty wee bitch, Nats. And no one loves that as much as I do.' His lips tickled my ear. 'No one understands you the way I do.'

Liam's fingers slithered through my folds, splitting my lips. He sprawled on his front, his long legs sticking out from the futon, his toes resting on the dark, wooden floor. With a wide, wet tongue, he lapped at my crease, tickling my entrance and sloshing wetness over my clit.

'And no one's ever seen me as you do,' continued Baxter. He kept caressing my breasts, his hand warm and gentle. 'No one.' He took the lobe of my ear between his teeth and pressed. I whimpered as the pain spread, reading his bite as a secret reminder of our connection and a warning of worse pain to come. He released my lobe, briefly covering the soreness with a nibbling kiss. He dropped his voice further, his broad thumb circling one nipple. 'I cannot wait till we're alone,' he breathed.

A bolt of lust hit my groin. I groaned, my cunt turning to molten throbs. 'Aye, you and all,' Baxter murmured. 'I can see it in you.'

He spanned thumb and forefinger below my chin, tilting my head against his stomach, holding me tight as if offering me to Liam. Liam stopped licking, replacing tongue with fingers. He latched on to my swollen clit, sliding the little hood over the tender nub beneath. I gasped, sensation rippling along my thighs as he worked me. But he didn't stay there. Instead he knelt and eased his longest two fingers inside me, curling them high and hard on to my plumped-up sweet spot.

Before long I was dissolving in Baxter's arms, Liam's strong fingers hooked inside me. Baxter's cock bumped against my buttocks, while in front of me Liam's jutted up from his chestnut-red pubes. Hands and kisses moved on my body. I hardly knew which caresses belonged to Baxter and which to Liam. I hardly cared either, preferring to switch off my concentration as I gave up to the bliss of being indulged.

'You've got to really work it.' Liam slammed his middle fingers into the pad of my G, his elbow shunting as if he were trying to tug something from me. 'It can look quite violent.'

'Ach, I dinnae mind that,' said Baxter.

I wailed as the pressure swelled within me. All too soon, my walls loosened and I was slushy around Liam's pounding fingers. I slumped in Baxter's supporting arms, crying out as liquid rushed from me in a hot, unstoppable fountain.

'There,' breathed Liam, pleased. He withdrew from me, his wrist and hand glistening.

'Fucking beautiful,' said Baxter. 'I reckon I'll have that mastered in no time. Now shall I show you what else she likes?'

Without giving me chance to catch my breath, Baxter tipped me forwards, manhandling me with firm hands and a chivvying slap on my buttocks. Even something as simple as that, as the way we changed position, was perfect. I felt as if I'd been wearing someone else's clothes for the last two years; clothes that almost fit, but not quite.

When I was on all fours, Baxter pushed my head to the

mattress so my butt was in the air. I heard the squelch of lube. My heart thumped. I knew what was coming.

'She likes it up her arse,' he snarled. 'Don't you, you nasty little slapper?'

I whimpered, embarrassed and immeasurably horny. Evidently, Baxter had reached his limit for toning down his dirty-talking dom-self. He whacked a generous splodge of lube into the split of my buttocks and rubbed, efficient and brisk. Liam and I had never done this. Arse-play was too crude and intense for the dynamic we had. To know he watched as Baxter initiated the act made me awkward and shy. And yet I loved the implication I had no choice but to suffer because Baxter was lord and master.

Baxter nudged at my crinkled pit with one finger, locating my opening rather than penetrating me.

'Ah, ah,' I bleated, instinctively tensing.

'Here we go,' he said in a breezy sing-song. 'Straight in there.' He eased two fingers inside me, combating my resistance with greasy, inexorable pressure. With a begrudging pinch, my slippery band of muscle dilated to take him. He drove in knuckle-deep, his other hand keeping my head to the mattress. I wailed as he began gliding in and out, his rhythm quickly rising until he was pumping with voracious strokes.

Above me, he panted as he pounded, growling out ragged fragments of filth. 'That's what she likes . . . hard in the arse . . . forced to take it . . . don't you, huh?'

My awareness of Liam's non-involvement intensified both my shame and arousal. What was he thinking? Flashes of wishing he were elsewhere battled against my love of being made to endure humiliation at Baxter's hands. Heat flooded my face. I couldn't look up from the futon, my cheek squashed against the bed sheet, Liam's pale, bony knees visible in my peripheral vision. Shimmering beads of light accompanied a series of hard explosions outside. My narrow hole became pliant and greedy around Baxter's fingers. More, I wanted so much more. I wanted to devour and be devoured.

Baxter pulled out of me. I offered no objection as he jerked me into a kneeling position. Desire dizzied me, the swollen openings between my legs a blur of sensation. Leaning across the futon, Baxter flipped the lid off the floral hat box where I keep my toys. Liam knelt at a distance, his cock in his fist, while Baxter rummaged in the box.

I recognised his mood. He was firing on all cylinders, ready to get rough and nasty. Sure enough, he tossed onto the futon a handful of wooden clothes pegs and a frayed, slender length of hemp. The rope we'd used before; the pegs I'd bought after our split, having read about DIY bondage tips online. No one had used them on me yet. How typical of Baxter to choose cheap basics rather than anything I'd spent my hard-earned cash on.

'And here's another thing she likes,' he said. 'Hurting.'

He knelt before me, his cock ramrod stiff, its tip marbled with a livid, blood-blue flush. I stroked his length then clasped his thick waist, caught between wanting to be done to and wanting to touch and take. Baxter held one of my nipples and, without ceremony, fastened a peg onto my tip. I hissed at the first bite of pain, then again as he fixed a second peg to my other nipple. He glanced at my face as he worked, methodically adding more pegs to my breasts. Nips of pain merged into each other, channels of sensation forking and connecting. Soon, my breasts were transformed into strange, spiky flowers.

'You good?' asked Baxter.

I nodded, trying to go with the pain not against it.

Baxter dropped to his belly, as if he were wriggling into a pothole, then examined me between my legs. I swayed, molten with need. He split me, clipping a peg to my labia. He pressed open another peg. I held my breath, my inflamed tissues throbbing as a second pair of jaws took hold. I gasped, resting a hand on Baxter's head, wanting an anchor. Another nip then another. Woozy with lust, I gazed down at the slab of Baxter's back, at the track of faint stretch marks in the hollow, and at his high, rounded buttocks, furred with dark hair. He was so beautiful to me, so perfect.

When he'd finished, he knelt up. 'Now keep still,' he said. He doubled the length of hemp then doubled it again to make a hoop of two coarse strands. Lightly, he flicked the rope at my belly, his touch a warning or a test. He repeated the gesture a couple of times, striping my skin with soft swishes. Then he drew his arm across his body as if launching a backhand stroke. With a jerk of his wrist, he cracked the rope at my waist. I yelped. The pain detonated, worse than I'd expected.

Baxter chuckled, turning to address Liam. 'See, she loves it. Didn't I tell you?'

Again, he struck me, swiping my thighs and belly. He moved behind me, making the mattress bounce, and began swatting my buttocks. Heat burst on my skin, my cheeks becoming tender as he thrashed, catching the edge of my flesh with fierce, evil stings. I tried to keep in position, kneeling up and absorbing the blows, but the task grew too difficult. My body became raw with sensitivity. I cursed, cowered and flinched as he whipped me. Occasionally, I was reminded of the pegs fixed to my breasts and labia but for the most part, unless movement knocked them, I was oblivious to their grip.

'How about this?' said Baxter. 'You ready?' He paused then lashed the backs of my knees. I swear, I nearly hit the roof. Tears stung my eyes and it was all I could do to stop myself from thumping him in retaliation.

Liam spat on his palm and began working himself faster, his freckled biceps flexing. A firework exploded, briefly pouring pink light onto his slender, milk-white muscularity. Baxter glanced at him. 'I might need some room, laddie. Could you?'

Liam edged back, still pumping his cock, while I braced myself for whatever sweet cruelty Baxter had in store. Baxter smirked, twirling the doubled hoop of rope onto his open hand.

'This is gonna hurt,' he said. 'But if you want to get fucked, you've got to take it.' He continued tapping his hand with the rope. 'Do you want to get fucked?'

I held his gaze, wanting to fall into the depths of his long-lashed, black-brown eyes. I nodded.

'Do you want to make me proud?' he continued. 'You want to show me what a brave lassie you are?'

Again, I nodded. I'd never thought of it that way before. But yes, in that moment, I wanted to prove I would take the pain for Baxter because I adored him. In return, I wanted the glow of his adoration even though I already knew he adored me. If he hadn't done, he wouldn't have asked me to take pain for him in the first place.

A wicked smile spread across Baxter's face. He raised the doubled loop of rope and brought it slicing down on my peg-clipped breasts. The pincers clattered against each other, some snapping off, others tugging at my flesh. I howled as returning blood surged into the numbed patches, one freed nipple throbbing with searing hot pain.

In that instant, I decided I sodding well hated Baxter, and all who sailed in him.

Baxter looked at me, gauging my response. I glared at him, tears brimming. Seconds later, with even greater ferocity, he brought the hemp loop crashing down on my tits. I yelled again, the rope catching the bared, tender patches of skin, more pegs pinging off.

'You fucking, fucking bastard,' I cried.

'Damn right I am,' said Baxter, grinning with pride.

He reached between my legs and waggled the dangling pegs, making pain ripple. A tear spilled down my cheek. I didn't know if this were one of the terrible and beautiful things he'd imagined doing to me, or if, ever resourceful, he'd invented this method of torture when his fingers had found rope and pegs. Either way, it was a far cry from Den's elaborate stage sets and protracted headfuck.

'You ready?' asked Baxter but he didn't wait for my reply. With a series of tugs, he snatched the pegs from my swollen lower lips, one, two, three, four.

I gasped, panting to stay calm, the pain less than I'd feared.

'Look at her,' said Baxter to Liam. 'Taking it all because she's gagging for a piece of dick. So, have we got some dick for her? Let's see, shall we? Bend over, you little beauty. Show us your arse.'

I did as told, the remaining pegs on my tits making my flesh hang and sway like bizarre udders. Baxter sheathed his cock and moved behind me. 'Oh, the nights I've dreamed of plugging this greedy arsehole again.'

He parted my buttocks, slathered more lube along my crease then skewered a couple of fingers into my passage, opening me with the cool, slick gel. I whimpered until he withdrew.

'Hold yourself wide for me,' he said, his voice groggy and low.

I tipped forward, turning to rest on my head and one shoulder, then I reached back with both hands to pull my buttocks apart. From the corner of my eye, I saw Baxter lubing up his cock. Further back, Liam knelt, still slowly wanking. I winced to think of Liam watching as I shamelessly offered up my arsehole, the pouched little dent no doubt glinting lasciviously in the oiled crack of my cheeks.

Baxter edged closer. His hard, fat end nosed at my entrance. Oh God, I could hardly believe this was happening, that I had him again. I groaned as he pressed into my narrowness, my body tightening with the impulse to lock him out. I willed myself to relax, knowing it would hurt less if I did. Baxter grunted with effortful pleasure, his cries deepening as the ring of my hole widened to take him. I wailed as he pushed, his progress eased by the lube until he was lodged deep. He paused.

'Oh, fuck, yes,' he whispered. 'I'm home. I am home.'

In my rear, he was solid and dense, my stretched passage nipping around him. Slowly, he withdrew. My body clung to him, my muscles still tight. He knocked my hands away from my cheeks and plunged back. Gripping my hips, he began hammering at me, the two of us grunting and huffing. With every stroke, my arse grew softer until we were fused in a hot, slippery mess at the juncture of our darkly intimate fuck.

Behind us, Liam watched, still jerking his cock but clearly uncertain of his role. I reached out, beckoning him closer, calling for him between gasps of pleasure. On his knees, he shuffled forward. I took him in my fist, clumsily working him as Baxter's relentless thrusts buffeted me.

'Stick your dick in her mouth,' rasped Baxter.

'Yes,' I gasped, and I opened wide.

Liam didn't waste a second. He drove into me, making me cough and splutter as he knocked deep. With uncharacteristic roughness, he bunched my hair in his fists and began drawing my head down his shaft, exploiting the jolts from Baxter's pounding to establish a rhythm where I was see-sawing between the two men. When Baxter hooked his arm beneath me to find my clit, my nearness coiled.

My cries of pleasure were distorted, cock-muffled wails. Baxter shaped his fingers into a vee, rubbing my clit on either side before fretting the taut, tender bud with a fast, focused touch. I came hard, clawing the duvet and pleading for respite. No one took a blind bit of notice.

'Here.' Baxter tossed a condom onto the mattress. 'You OK about fucking her cunt while I keep doing her arse?'

Liam withdrew from my mouth and grabbed the wrapper. 'Oh man, yes!' He bit off a strip of foil while Baxter slowed. Carefully, Baxter moved us into a new position, doing his best to keep inside me. But we were too slippery and his cock fell out of me. 'OK. Again. Backwards,' he said.

He lay back on the bed and I reverse-straddled his hips, thigh muscles pulling in my struggle to span the breadth of his body. The feel of his bulk beneath me was almost too much to believe. I'd never dared dream this might happen. I was convinced he'd gone for good, leaving me with memories, emptiness and a fissure in my heart that could never fully mend. Now, in contrast to that, he was in my bed, so brutally, beautifully physical, so present and alive.

I lowered myself onto his jutting cock, sinking to the root of him and re-filling my arse with his girth. Baxter held me steady, easing me towards his chest while Liam positioned himself between Baxter's knees, shuffling closer. He aimed his tip at my entrance, fumbling briefly for access before sliding into my wetness.

'Oh man,' said Liam. 'She's so tight.'

I wailed, the barrier between both my orifices seeming to melt. I hooked an arm around Liam's neck, clinging to him for balance. Baxter's hands were on my shoulder blades, supporting and guiding me. After a rocky start, I was rising and falling on their double penetration, my holes fuller than they'd ever been. I was so crammed with sensation, I didn't think I had the capacity for more. But when Liam knocked a peg off my nipple, agony and ecstasy chased around my body. I cried out, lost.

'Sorry,' gasped Liam.

'More,' I said. 'All of them.'

After a nervous pause, Liam unclipped the remaining pegs. The fire in my breasts merged with the heat consuming the lower half of my body. Someone touched my clit and I came again, gasping, incoherent, wrecked.

'Oh man, I'm gonna come,' said Liam.

'Yes,' said Baxter with an exultant growl.

I slammed down harder and Liam came, stuttering out a twisted roar. He withdrew quickly, leaving Baxter in the driving seat, so to speak. Moments later, Baxter snatched himself free. He snapped off his rubber, moving with frenzied urgency.

'On your knees,' he barked. 'I'm gonna explode all over your face.'

I scrambled to obey as Baxter stood on the futon, rising above me, tall and magnificent, wanking furiously. I opened my mouth, aching to taste his come after so long without. He uttered grunts of desperate need then, with roar that sounded like the darkness made audible, like tar and coalmines and

black, bitter secrets, he came, scattering pearls on my face
and splashing salt on my tongue.

He stood, legs apart, panting for breath. The hairs on his
upper thighs were damp with sweat. I smeared his stickiness
into my mouth, wanting to consume him. With a dramatic
grunt, Baxter fell to his knees, his weight slamming into
the mattress. He laughed, shaking his head in disbelief, and
dragged me close. He kissed me hard, tasting himself on my
tongue before he flung himself onto the bed, laughing again.
'Ah, hen,' he said. 'I'm a broken man. What have you done
to me?'

Liam laughed as well. 'I can't feel my knees,' he said.

'I can't feel my anything,' I added.

The three of us lay in a tangle of sticky, sweaty recupera-
tion, the fireworks outside banging like mortar bombs and
dripping colour into the room.

'I think Saltbourne's being shelled,' said Baxter. 'About
fucking time and all.'

After a while, he poured us a round of whiskies and Liam
skinned up. We talked with lazy companionability, the noises
fading outside as the hour grew late. Rory came to join us,
seeking comfort after the fireworks. On cautious white paws,
she crept into the room, tail swaying warily. On the floor lay
the brown leather bridle, its rich lustre and brass attachments
gleaming in the colour-smudged dimness. Curious, Rory
nuzzled at the tangle of straps, flinching from each tiny touch.

'Look,' said Baxter. 'Even the fucking cat's a pervert.'

We laughed, beyond happy. I wasn't sure about the
harness. I'd need to disassociate the object from Den to be
comfortable wearing it. Liam said he'd help. I was surprised
he'd taken the bridle from the theatre. Later, he'd said he
couldn't bear the thought of his work being sold to such a

tosser. Ever principled, Liam said he'd refund Den the money. Better still, he was going to remove the strap embossed with NIL and replace with a plain piece of leather, help make the piece mine again. After all, it was designed for me. A shame to let that go to waste.

Outside, a late, lonely firework exploded. Liam sat up with a stoned version of decisiveness. 'I'm going to head off,' he said. 'I think you two have a lot of catching up to do.'

'Aye, we certainly have.' Baxter beamed at me, brushing a wisp of hair from my face.

Rory wandered off as Liam dressed. 'You mind if I leave my crowbar here?' he said. 'Don't fancy walking home with that.'

'Sure,' I said. 'And will you lock the door when you leave? My keys are on top of the telly.'

'No worries,' Liam replied, and I knew that he, like me, was remembering the night of the storm. I hadn't yet told him it was Den who'd broken in but I would do soon, although I suspected he knew already.

When he was dressed, Liam knelt on the futon to print a goodbye peck on my lips. He gave Baxter a stiff smile, holding out a polite hand.

Baxter, unfazed by the contrast of his own nudity against Liam's propriety, dragged his new friend into a manly hug, clapping him on the shoulder. 'Excellent night,' said Baxter. 'Excellent to have met you, laddie.'

We listened to Liam's footsteps on the stairs, heard the lock click then my keys clatter on the doormat as Liam posted them through the letterbox.

I said, 'I'm not giving him up for you.'

'I'm no asking you to,' Baxter replied. 'Although the other fella can take a hike.'

'Yeah, I think he'll have got that message.'

For a moment or two, we let the silence of the house settle around us as it had done on so many nights in the past. Nothing stirred outside, the sky beyond the window black and peaceful. Baxter and I were the only people in the world.

I swirled a hand over his torso, fingers drifting through his crisp, dark chest hair. 'Now what?' I asked.

Baxter rolled onto his side, propping himself on his elbow. He gazed at me, tracing a finger across my lips, smiling.

'Now,' he said, 'I'm going to fuck the lights out of you.'

A heartbeat passed, a gentle pause, then he sprang up. I squealed as he straddled my hips, pinning me beneath his glorious thighs. He raised my wrists, gripping tight, and shoved my arms against the pillows. His hair tumbled over his forehead, his grin triumphant.

I squirmed beneath him, laughing hard. 'Try,' I said.

And he did and he does, over and over. And I burn more brightly than ever.

Acknowledgements

Enormous thanks to Gillian Green, my editor, for encouraging me to explore more deeply and involving me in decisions about my supremely handsome book cover. To Emily Yau for speed and efficiency. And to all at Black Lace for reviving the imprint with such enthusiasm and style.

To Alison Tyler because it's high time I thanked you for constant support and for being an ever-present reminder of the importance of integrity.

To my friends, especially Alice, Anne and Lorelei, for understanding when I can't come out to play. To Jackie for accompanying me on my first trip to Hastings, and to Mike for my second trip. Who knew I would corrupt the town so? And to Anna because last time, I never got to thank you for being my village bike.

To Peter for, um, technical assistance (and the pig).

To Mum and Matt in France for not minding that I turned up as a holiday guest then wrote each day until it was time to start drinking wine (which, admittedly, is quite early in France). And to Mum, especially, for being proud of what I do.

And to Ewan, light of my life, for reading version one on train station platforms, for inspiration, being awesome, and for all the love, across the years.

Introduction to S. M. Taylor's 'Forbidden'

the winning entry from the Y*OU magazine/Black Lace*
erotic short story competition

In 2012, Black Lace and *The Daily Mail's YOU* magazine ran a short story competition, the prize being publication by *Black Lace*. I was privileged to be on the judging panel along with bestselling Black Lace author, Portia Da Costa, and our editor, Gillian Green.

We received over two hundred and fifty submissions. Many entrants told us they were inspired to put pen to paper for the first time, or dig out stories previously abandoned. The enthusiasm for the competition, not to mention the high standard of stories we received, makes me genuinely excited about the future of erotica. As judges, ours was a difficult task but, after whittling the entries down to a shortlist of thirteen, we chose 'Forbidden' by S. M. Taylor as our winner.

When I first read 'Forbidden', I got goosebumps. S. M. Taylor's voice immediately felt fresh, her exploration of conflicts in British-Asian culture giving the story an extra heft. I'm looking at my hard copy of the piece as I write this introduction. Scrawled in the margins are my pencilled notes and at the end, a simple, enthusiastic, 'Yes!'. As Portia said, 'Forbidden' has the 'it factor', that indefinable something which makes a story glow.

'Forbidden' tells of a young Muslim woman, Sofina, and

her secret love affair with a tattooed, Cockney boxer, Patrick. Sofina and Patrick have a sizzlingly hot encounter in a derelict yard in Brick Lane, the heart of London's Bangladeshi community, and an area long-famed for its bustling markets. The scenario is as far away from aspirational erotica featuring long-fingered billionaires as you could possibly get!

Followers of my work will know I'm partial to mean-looking men, urban decay, and sex scenes that play with danger and dubious consent. These themes feature in my second novel, *Asking for Trouble*, in many of my short stories, and once again in *Thrill Seeker*. S. M. Taylor's story includes these elements and so, inevitably, it pushed a lot of my buttons. However, my judging criteria weren't based solely on what a story could do for me!

In 'Forbidden', the sex is raw and brutal while the story-telling is anything but. S. M. Taylor demonstrates a sophisticated use of theme-building, perspective shifts, erotic tension and pacing. Sofina and Patrick are well-defined, realistic, likeable characters. Their dialogue is top-notch: witty, tender, passionate, sexy and natural, drawing the reader into their intimacy and bringing their connection alive to us. We're made to care about this couple, meaning, as readers, we're emotionally involved in the unfolding of their clandestine lust in that tatty, East End yard. And when the heart's involved, the groin is seldom far behind.

And there's the bigger story. Sofina and Patrick are in love, but Sofina's family would disapprove of the relationship. The stakes are high and so is the tension. S. M. Taylor neatly encapsulates how the couple's feelings and the difficulties they face are embodied in the sex: 'Somehow, the ferocity of the way he fucked her made their love stronger. It was tangible. It was real. It hurt.'

In good erotic fiction, the sex has to matter. A story which describes two people merrily making out, with no consequences to their interaction, isn't enough. Here, the sex matters because this young couple's love matters, both on a personal and on a wider, cultural level. Patrick is a fighter in the ring. With Sofina, he must face a different fight if their love is to survive. This is a story about Sofina and Patrick; it is Romeo and Juliet with the battle lines drawn on contemporary ground. It's a story about the changing landscape in multicultural Britain and, crucially for our genre, it's also beautifully, boldly erotic.

I can't wait to read more of S. M. Taylor's work. I hope you enjoy 'Forbidden' as much as I did. If you want to know more about S. M. Taylor, please stop by the Black Lace website www.blacklace.co.uk to read my interview with this exciting, talented, new writer.

Kristina Lloyd, May 2013

Forbidden

by S. M. Taylor

The silver kitten-heel sandals lifted away from her bare feet and clicked back again like finger cymbals against the pavement. She adjusted the red silk dupatta covering her hennaed hair, which was freshly oiled and jasmine-scented, and plaited down to her waist. The scarf cascaded over the matching shalwar kameez, and Sofina smiled at her flowing reflection in the shop window.

The outfit was handmade in Pakistan by a renowned tailor, a gift to herself for all her hard work, and bought with the first pay cheque that she had earned in her new job. Her mother would say that the silk was too clingy and the heels were too high and she would get a reputation as being 'that sort of girl', and who would marry her then?

But this outfit was not for her family, nor in readiness for some stranger who was 'a nice boy'. It was for her, Sofina.

She stopped at a market stall piled high with ethnic fruit and vegetables. She stood still for a while, regarding the array of produce and, then here and there, Sofina reached out her French-manicured hands to touch and squeeze the offerings. After a brief exchange with the trader in a patois of Urdu and

English, she purchased a lush bunch of coriander, a handful each of red and green chilli peppers and a couple of very ripe brown figs.

As Sofina paid for the contents of the brown paper parcel, her mobile phone rang.

She moved away from the busy stall and, trapping the phone between her ear and her shoulder, she juggled it with trying to manage the contents of her overflowing shoulder bag.

'Fatima!' she said excitedly. 'Listen. You are now talking to Sofina Khan, ACA. A very proud and very relieved, newly qualified chartered accountant!'

Across the street, leaning against a wall papered with tattered posters and painted with graffiti tags, a tall, muscular man watched the young woman weave in and out of the crowd, smiling and laughing as she talked on the phone. He sported a black eye and a buzz cut and wore a grey hooded sweatshirt rolled up to the elbows to reveal sleeves of black tattoos.

From a distance, he watched how the delicate silk outfit caressed the contours of her shapely figure – outlining the fulsome bust, bottom and thighs. As she got closer, he saw how the black kohl eyeliner enhanced her chocolate-brown eyes and the ruby-red lipstick her full lips. She passed him and he noticed the way the shiny thick plait swung at her bottom like a pendulum as she walked. He also heard the chinking of the rows of heavy Indian gold bracelets adorning her wrists.

'And why is it that the first word is "congratulations" and the second is "husband"?' Sofina laughed. 'Fatima, I'm twenty-three years of age, hardly a spinster.'

The man shadowed her from across the street, hands dug deep into his jeans pockets, gradually moving through the crowd and looking about, to the left and right and behind, as he followed her.

He loved the way she moved. She sashayed. With every step, her large bust bouncing, the broad hips swaying and each ample buttock rising and falling. He felt his cock stiffen. This woman was fucking perfection, he thought.

Sofina continued with her conversation, unaware of the eyes upon her or the sexual attention that she elicited.

'No, sorry, Fatima, I can't now. I've – err – I've got a dental appointment. I'll call you later. OK? Bye.'

She ended the conversation quickly and dropped the phone into her bag, which she swung by her side as now she almost skipped along the path.

Sofina made her way out of Brick Lane market, leaving the spiced air of the Bangladeshi restaurants and the buzz of the crowd behind her. She turned left into a road lined with old warehouse buildings and then, after about a hundred yards, she turned right into a backstreet marked 'Private'.

Suddenly she felt a sharp tug at the back of her head and a feeling of being reeled in backwards. Her plait was being coiled around the man's fist and in seconds the back of her head was cradled in his arms.

Her voice was caught in her throat.

He held her in a firm embrace and swiftly drew her towards a rickety wooden door, which he kicked open to reveal a cobbled backyard. Sofina's body stiffened as she was propelled against the brick wall. She lost one of her shoes and her handbag was flung to the floor.

The man pulled off his sweatshirt and threw it across the yard. His expansive chest was adorned with a tattooed Celtic cross. He pinned her to the wall with just the strength of his groin forced into her pelvis.

Staring down at her, held fast before him, he methodically took each of her arms by the wrist and held her hands above her head, grazing them against the rough brick. She could feel the hard muscular contours of his athletic frame cutting into the soft flesh of her body and she knew immediately that physically she was helpless to resist this man's brute strength.

He was a foot taller than her and she had to crane her neck to look up at his face. In an instant, she took in the bruising around his left eye and the old silver scar on his right cheek. And then she connected with his piercing blue gaze that bore into her wide brown eyes and held her there transfixed.

In contrast to this man's solid, cocksure presence, Sofina betrayed her desperate state with her breathlessness and trembling limbs.

He leaned in to her, bringing his face down to a level with hers and slowly traced his nose over her soft dusky skin, from her nose, across her cheek, to her earlobe. His sweet-sour breath left a warm moist trail across her face.

'Now what's a nice girl like you doing in a place like this?' he whispered in her ear. His Cockney accent was rough but his tone was playful. 'Are you looking for someone, darlin'?'

She unconsciously bit into her bottom lip. The scent of him, of his sweat blended with that aftershave, Trussardi Uomo, intoxicated her mind, her heart, her sex.

'Come on. You can tell me. Tell me what you want, love.'

He licked her gold-droplet earring into his mouth and sucked on it, tugging at her fleshy lobe.

She felt faint and nauseous. She had to shake her head to bring herself to. She caught her breath.

Sofina stuttered, her words almost unintelligible, 'I . . . I want you.'

'Again. Say it again,' he demanded.

Now he bit into her earlobe and held it between his teeth. She whimpered, 'I want you.'

'Who?'

'You, Patrick. I want you.'

He released the marked, swollen flesh. 'Do you?' he whispered.

'Yes. Patrick, please...'

'And do you feel how much I want you, Sofina?'

She could feel his stiff cock bulging against the metal buttons of his jeans and digging into her belly, forcing her bottom against the wall. His powerful sex trapped her there in the alley.

But she had enticed him, she thought, and smiled to herself.

Patrick bit into her earlobe again and whispered between bites, 'Do you know I can only get hard when I smell jasmine or sandalwood?' He laughed. 'You're my drug. I'm addicted to you, Sofina. You're opium.'

He brought his face to hers, seeming to kiss her then pulling away at the last moment, again and again. This man was toying with her, testing her. Then he lunged at her mouth, forcing his over hers, scratching her harshly with his facial stubble and bruising her lips. His tongue penetrated her mouth, thrusting deeper and deeper and licking her inside-out; overwhelming her with his carnal passion.

He pushed his knee between her legs, roughly spreading them.

'I'm the only man who's ever had you. And I'll always be the only one. The *only* one. Do you understand, Sofina?'

'Yes,' she nodded.

'You're mine, Sofina. Since the first time I saw you. I've only wanted you.'

He stretched one hand around her slim wrists and with his other he hoisted her silk tunic over her breasts to her neck and then pulled at the cord to loosen the paijama, which dropped to her feet.

She was left naked, exposed in that derelict yard off Brick Lane. No bra and no panties to cover her most intimate parts. The parts of a woman that only her husband should see, her mother had warned her. And especially that part between her legs that would be opened up by her husband on the wedding night.

She was torn between the instincts of fight or flight – but the fight in her with this man was more primitive than that. The energy was caught between her legs.

Patrick looked her up and down, from her eyes to her mouth, her breasts to her sex, and slowly back up again. God, he loved her. But he was caught up in this place between love and lust and madness. He wanted her. He ached for her night and day. And he wished he had never set eyes on her.

He traced his wet tongue over her parted lips, under her tilted chin, down her arched neck and over her full breast to the large, berry-brown nipple. Sofina gasped as gently he took the sensitive flesh in his mouth and grazed it with his teeth. He teased it with his tongue while he watched her beautiful face react to his touch, to the pleasure and pain of oral foreplay. He sucked hard on the erect nipple between his teeth and she moaned long and loud.

While his mouth worked at her breast, his hand worked its way between her legs. His fingers stroked the soft delicate skin at the inside of her thighs, following the curve, and reaching the wetness of the mons. She was shaven according to her cultural habit, and the smooth plump folds were open to him like the succulent flesh of an exotic fruit.

Its musky scent and nectar drew him in. Was he hunter or was he prey, he wondered.

'Is this for me?' he asked.

Sofina nodded and smiled, biting her lip again.

'Beg for it, Sofina.'

'Please –'

Before she could finish, he thrust two fingers deep inside her.

She responded with a sharp intake of breath and her whole body tensed.

'You're really wet. I like that. Excites me.'

He felt her pelvis gyrate her sex against his cupped hand.

'You want it, don't you? You want my cock inside you.'

Sofina swallowed hard and mutely indicated her desire with the longing in her dark eyes. He made her want him so badly. She would say or do anything for him. It felt like she had lost her mind to him. She hated losing control of herself yet she craved the release.

'I'm going to fuck you now, really hard and fast. Just the way you like it, Sofina.'

Patrick withdrew his fingers from her wetness and unbuckled the belt of his jeans.

Sofina loved to watch his hands at his belt buckle. It was so sexy knowing that he was about to unleash his manhood. And his hands were so elegant even though he was a fighter. The leather belt was soon hanging open and he fingered the top button of his jeans. Sofina was aching to see his cock and feel it deep inside her.

In her most private moments, when she would think of Patrick, it would most often be with the image of him with his big, hard cock in his hand, smiling down at her with those sea-blue eyes, somehow both intense and playful at the same time.

All the while, he watched her – her head back, her eyes closing, her mouth opening, breathless as she anticipated him entering her.

So rare was the time they had together, Patrick had willed himself to commit her every feature, every expression, every movement to memory. In these snatched meetings, he studied her face and body like a work of art in a gallery. The areas of light and shadow on her dusky skin, the fine dark line from naval to pubis, the large dark rounds of her areolae, the auburn and chestnut tones of her black hair.

In one swift move, he took his erection and slammed it up into her tight, wet hole. Still holding her hands fast against the wall with one hand, he cupped her buttocks with the other, lifting her away from the wall and impaling her on his thick cock.

Patrick was an athlete and a martial artist. His body was testimony to a punishing training regime for strength, speed and stamina. This physical prowess thrilled Sofina. She loved how he could so effortlessly overpower her. She marvelled at how he could hold her down simply with his body weight and that he had the energy to fuck for hours.

Patrick made her feel so intensely alive.

'Look at me, Sofina!' he instructed. 'Watch me fuck you.'

She opened her eyes to his smile.

He thrust all the way into her and pulled out almost immediately and then rammed his cock back inside her again and began to pound into her sex. She cried out as Patrick fucked her painfully hard, just as he knew she liked it. She could barely breathe; he slammed into her so hard and fast with no time for her to recover between strokes. His cock filled her and stretched her, time and time again, in a frenzied fucking action. She took his entire length and savoured every inch of the divine penetration.

Suddenly he withdrew his sex from her and stopped in his tracks, his erection poised at her now empty, gaping hole. The shock of his withdrawal brought Sofina back from the ecstatic brink. She opened her eyes to his face staring down at her. His eyes were blazing.

'I love you, Sofina,' he panted. 'I fucking love you.'

He pressed his mouth over hers, catching the skin of her lips with his teeth. She could taste the blood in her mouth as he kissed her, violently, possessing her. He kissed her like his life depended on it. And she kissed him back with a passion that fuelled his desire.

He released her hands and she held on to his neck and gripped his hips with her thighs as if she were riding a stallion. His sheer strength bounced her entire body up and down on his throbbing erection. Her breasts were pummelled against his chest and her legs ached with the tension of being fucked in that contorted position. Sofina's sex was impaled on his shaft, bruising the delicate flesh, but the pain made it all the more pleasurable for her. Somehow, the ferocity of the way he fucked her made their bond stronger. It was tangible. It was real. It hurt.

'I want all of you!' he told her through gritted teeth as he increased the tempo of his thrusts.

The yard echoed with the slapping sound of his cock and balls slamming into her soaking wet pussy.

'I'm coming!' Sofina cried out.

He covered her mouth with his hand as her cries grew in volume.

He felt the bite into his finger and then he felt her vagina contract around his cock, gripping and releasing him, pumping his cock to orgasm as she experienced the waves of her climax flooding through her body.

'Come for me, Sofina,' he demanded.

He could feel her juices running down his shaft and he was unable to hold back any longer. Patrick arched his back and spasms surged through him as he gave up control and spurted his hot come deep inside her. His fingers dug into the plump flesh of her arse cheeks as he pumped the final drops of semen into her pulsating sex.

In the afterglow of coitus, catching their breath together, he held her there suspended in mid-air.

He bent to gently kiss her forehead and then her lips. She had gone limp in his hands.

'I love you,' he whispered against her damp hair.

Sofina moaned softly.

Patrick gradually set her down again to stand on her own two feet. Her sex was soaked with their come and she felt it trickle down her legs. She slowly pulled up her trousers and retied the cord. Sofina did not want to wipe away the memory of their brief time together. It prolonged the pleasure to so intimately carry him about with her. She held on to anything of him that she could. These were stolen meetings.

He helped pull her top down over her bust.

Holding her close, he told her, 'Sofina, I want more than just this.' He kissed her hair. 'I want to be with you. I want to wake up with you. I want to come home to you,' he said quietly.

Sofina's heart ached. Tears filled her eyes.

She shook her head. 'Patrick, I need more time. You don't know what it's like for me. I could lose everything.'

She reached up and held his face in her hands as she kissed him tenderly. 'Please, Patrick.'

He nodded and stepped back.

'How could they say no to the chessboxing champion of the world?' He grinned as he buttoned his jeans.

Sofina surveyed the black eye and tattoos and imagined her father's look of horror.

'A chess-playing doctor or lawyer would be infinitely better,' she replied. 'With brown skin and circumcised,' she added.

'I could do the snip, at a push.'

Patrick shadowboxed around her, unleashing a flurry of jabs and uppercuts in her direction. He jabbed at her face and she shielded with her forearm and kicked out with her foot at his shin.

'Nice try but in the real world aim the kick to the balls or use the heel of your shoe as a weapon,' he said.

'Very romantic, Patrick!'

'And don't forget to go for the eyes.'

'You're mad, bad and dangerous to know, Mr Riley!' She laughed.

'And you love it, Ms Khan.'

He moved in again and his fist connected with her cheek but deftly turned from a punch to a caress on impact.

'Of course, you know, in the game of chess the queen has all the power,' he told her.

'Not in its original form, *shatranj*. She was the weakest piece. My lot invented the game, remember.'

'But this is twenty-first-century Britain, Ms Khan.'

She sighed. 'I have to go now, Mr Riley.'

'And what about my tax return?' he asked.

'That's funny, Patrick. I didn't know you paid tax!'

He winked with the good eye.

Patrick took hold of her hand. He brought it to his lips and imprinted it with a kiss. 'Always my queen?' he said.

'Forever my king?' she responded, smiling.

They paused for a moment, eyes locked, silent.

Then she spoke, thinking aloud, 'How is it that love can hurt so much?'

He let go of her hand and walked away quickly to the gate. She knew that he had tears in his eyes and that he did not want to share them with her. Big boys don't cry, he once told her; they get drunk and start a fight and then cry.

Sofina blinked back her tears and went to pick up her shoe and bag from the floor where she had dropped them just a short time ago. She smoothed down her hair and threw over the dupatta.

Patrick opened the gate and poked his head out to look left and right down the alley. It was clear.

'Go on,' he told her. 'And take this,' he added, pushing a crumpled brown envelope into her hand. 'I did it for you.'

Sofina squeezed past him. She took a few steps out then stopped and hurried back to the gate.

'What's wrong?' he demanded.

She threw a fig at him. He raised his hand and caught it.

'A gift for my champion,' she said. 'Forbidden fruit.'

Patrick immediately put the fig to his mouth and bit into its velvet-brown flesh. The ruby-red innards released their secret juices to his tongue and he noisily licked his lips of the honey-sweet stickiness. In only two bites it was gone – as was she, out of the gate and out of sight.

In minutes Sofina was safely concealed within the hustle and bustle of the lively Brick Lane crowd and heading for home. She wound the dupatta more fully around her head so that just a part of her face was on show. The spiced air was chilly now and she wrapped her arms tightly around herself as she walked, with her head down and her eyes to the ground.

The paper gift was tightly balled in her clenched fist. It was a flyer from the recent chessboxing world championship fight between Alex 'The Invincible' Ivanov and Patrick 'Hunter' Riley dated a week ago.

On the back of the flyer, in a familiar black spidery scrawl, Sofina had read the following words.

> *Sonnet for Sofina Khan*
> *Imagine my lips touching yours through this*
> *Suffocating fears with breath of a kiss.*
> *Our hearts entwined now no harm may befall*
> *My lady, my light, my love with you all.*
> *Whispering words across worlds far and wide*
> *To stifle your fears with faith deep inside.*
> *No cell can confine truth, no court outlaw*
> *The heart and mind ever cling to love's shore.*
> *This supernal spirit true love doth make*
> *Will fiery dragon lay tamed in its wake.*
> *My angel, my honour in you I bide*
> *Needed not until with you I reside.*
> *Trust in and await your lover so nigh*
> *I will against your beating heart soon lie.*

Sofina smiled through the tears as she held on to the precious words of the poet, the boxer, her lover. She crushed them in her fist to draw the strength from him that she needed to fight this battle. She was on her way home, to her mother and father, to ask to be allowed to be free to marry the man who had won her heart with his strength and vulnerability.

The only man for Sofina was a fighter who had handed her his heart to keep and was begging her not to break it.

And he just happened to be mind-blowing sex on very strong legs and to have eyes so blue that looking into them was like floating in the deep, blue sea.